P9-CEC-183

WHISTLE

BY JAMES JONES

—There was an almost standard remark the night medic on duty would make to the newly arrived patients at the hospital. He said, "If you want anything, just whistle for it."

(*Memoirs* 1918)—R.J. Blessing

JAMES JONES

WHISTLE

DELACORTE PRESS/NEW YORK

Published by
Delacorte Press
1 Dag Hammarskjold Plaza
New York, New York 10017

Copyright © 1978 by Gloria Jones as executrix for the estate of James Jones

All rights reserved. No part of this book may be reproduced
in any form or by any means without the
prior written permission of the publisher,
excepting brief quotes used in connection with
reviews written specifically for
inclusion in a magazine or newspaper.

Manufactured in the United States of America
A limited edition of this work has been privately printed.
First Delacorte Press edition

Designed by Ann Spinelli

Library of Congress Cataloging in Publication Data
Jones, James, 1921–1977.
Whistle.

I. Title.
PZ4.J77Wh [PS3560.049]   813'.5'4   77–11980

ISBN 0-440-09548-4

This book is dedicated to every man
who served in the US Armed Forces in
World War II—whether he survived
or not; whether he made a fortune
serving, or not; whether he fought
or not; whether he did time or not;
whether he went crazy, or didn't.

Bounce, and dance; bounce, and dance;
Jiggle on your strings.
Whistle toward the graveyard.
Nobody knows who or what moves your batten.
You'll not find out.

—Ancient French Jingle
Trans. from the French by
the author

CONTENTS

Introductory Note
by Willie Morris

James Jones died in the hospital in Southampton, Long Island, New York, on May 9, 1977, of congestive heart failure. He was fifty-five.

Whistle was to have had thirty-four chapters. Jones had completed somewhat more than half of Chapter 31 when he again became seriously ill. However, he had already plotted in considerable, and indeed almost finished detail his remaining material.

I was his friend and neighbor, and in tape recordings and conversations with me over several months prior to his death, he left no doubt of his intentions for the concluding three chapters. As late as two days before he died, he was speaking into a tape recorder in the hospital.

He planned for these last chapters to be relatively short. The ending of *Whistle* was firmly in his mind. All he lacked was time. Had he lived another month, I believe he would have written these chapters to his satisfaction. But he leaves what is essentially, by any judgment, a finished work.

In his note about this book (see page xix), Jones has described his intentions on the scope of this work. This is the third novel in his war trilogy: *From Here to Eternity* (1951) being the first, then *The Thin Red Line* (1962), and now *Whistle*.

He was obsessed by *Whistle*. He worked on it off and on for a very long time. He kept coming back to it, and it kept "turning on its spit in my head for nearly thirty years." After his first attack in 1970, he had two recurrences of his serious heart ailment, and I sensed he had a premonition that he was fighting against time to complete this book. For the last two years, in the attic of his farmhouse in Sagaponack, Long Island, he worked twelve to fourteen hours a day on it. He survived another attack in January 1977, and between then and his death he went back to writing several hours a day. As a precaution he also made the tape recordings and the notes.

Jones wished to have a few introductory words about why the name of his city in *Whistle* is Luxor, rather than Memphis, Tennessee. In his notes and in an earlier essay, he wrote:

> Luxor in fact does not exist. There is no town of Luxor, Tennessee. There is no Luxor in the United States.
>
> Luxor is really Memphis. I spent eight months there in 1943 in the Kennedy General Army Hospital. I was 22.
>
> But Luxor is also Nashville. When I was sent back to duty from Kennedy General, I went to Camp Campbell, Kentucky, which was close to Nashville. Nashville supplanted Memphis as our liberty town. Luxor has recognizable traces of both. In my book I did not want to break off with the characters, love affairs, habitudes, hangouts, familiarities, and personal relationships of Memphis. For these reasons I was obliged to turn the real Camp Campbell into my Camp O'Bruyerre, and place it near Memphis.
>
> So I have called my city Luxor and used the Memphis that I remembered. Or imagined I remembered. People who know Memphis will find my city disturbingly familiar. And then suddenly and even more disturbingly, not familiar at all. They should not think of it as Memphis, but as Luxor. Sole owner and Prop., Jas. Jones, who must also take full responsibility.

A brief explanation about the Epilogue:

On page 447, there is a set of asterisks. This is the point that Jones reached in Chapter 31. As reconstructed from his own thoughts and language, and at his request, I have put down in considerable detail his intentions for the concluding three and a half chapters. Nothing has been included that he did not expressly wish for these chapters. The last, indented section of the Epilogue is the author's own words, from a recording made only a few days before he died.

Bridgehampton, Long Island
May 28, 1977

A NOTE BY THE AUTHOR

I first began actual work on *Whistle* in 1968, but the book goes back a much longer time than that. It was conceived as far back as 1947, when I was still first writing to Maxwell Perkins about my characters Warden and Prewitt, and the book I wanted to write about World War II. When I was beginning *From Here to Eternity*, then still untitled, I meant for that book to carry its people from the peacetime Army on through Guadalcanal and New Georgia, to the return of the wounded to the United States. A time span corresponding to my own experience. But long before I reached the middle of it I realized such an ambitious scope of such dimension wasn't practicable. Neither the dramatic necessities of the novel itself, nor the amount of sheer space required, would allow such a plan.

The idea of a trilogy occurred to me then. *Whistle*, still untitled and—as a novel—unconceived, was a part of it. So when I began *The Thin Red Line* (some eleven years later) the plan for a trilogy was already there. And *Whistle*, as a concept, would be the third part of it.

Which of course it should be. It was always my intention with this trilogy that each novel should stand by itself as a work alone. In a way that, for example, John Dos Passos' three novels in his fine *USA* trilogy do not. *The 42nd Parallel, 1919,* and *The Big Money* will not stand alone as novels. *USA* is one large novel, not a trilogy.

I intended to write the third volume immediately after I finished *The Thin Red Line.* Other things, other novels, got in the way. Each time I put it aside it seemed to further refine itself. So that each time I took it up again I had to begin all over. My own personal experiments with style and viewpoint affected the actual writing itself.

One of the problems I came up against, with the trilogy as a whole, appeared as soon as I began *The Thin Red Line* in 1959. In the original conception, first as a single novel, and then as a trilogy, the major characters such as 1st/Sgt Warden, Pvt Prewitt and Mess/Sgt Stark were meant to continue throughout the entire work. Unfortunately the dramatic structure—I might even say, the spiritual content—of the first book demanded that Prewitt be killed in the end of it. The import of the book would have been emasculated if Prewitt did not die.

When the smoke cleared, and I wrote End to *From Here to Eternity,* the only end it seemed to me it could have had, there I stood with no Prewitt character.

It may seem like a silly problem now. It wasn't then. Prewitt was meant from the beginning to carry an important role in the second book, and in the third. I could not just resurrect him. And have him there again, in the flesh, wearing the same name.

I solved the problem by changing the names. All of the names. But I changed them in such a way that a cryptic key, a marked similarity, continued to exist, as a reference point, with the old set of names. It seems like an easy solution now, but it was not at the time.

So in *The Thin Red Line* 1st/Sgt Warden became 1st/Sgt Welsh, Pvt Prewitt became Pvt Witt, Mess/Sgt Stark became Mess/Sgt Storm. While remaining the same people as before. In *Whistle* Welsh becomes Mart Winch, Witt becomes Bobby Prell, Storm becomes John Strange.

After publication of *The Thin Red Line,* a few astute readers noted the similarity of names, and wrote to ask me if the similarity was intentional. When they did, I wrote back saying that it was, and explaining why. So far as I know, no critic and no book reviewer ever noticed the name similarity.

There is not much else to add. Except to say that when *Whistle* is completed, it will surely be the end of something. At least for me. The publication of *Whistle* will mark the end of a long job of work for me. Conceived in 1946, and begun in the spring of 1947, it will have taken me nearly thirty years to complete. It will say just about everything I have ever had to say, or will ever have to say, on the human condition of war and what it means to us, as against what we claim it means to us.

Paris, 15 November 1973

BOOK ONE

THE SHIP

CHAPTER 1

We got the word that the four of them were coming a month before they arrived. Scattered all across the country in the different hospitals as we were, it was amazing how fast word of any change in the company got back to us. When it did, we passed it back and forth among ourselves by letter or post card. We had our own private network of communications flung all across the map of the nation.

There were only the four of them this time. But what an important four. Winch. Strange. Prell. And Landers. About the four most important men the company had had.

We did not know then, when the first word of them came, that all four would be coming back to the exact same place. That is, to us, in Luxor.

Usually, it was us in the Luxor hospital who heard news soonest. That was because we were the largest individual group. At one point there were twelve of us there. It made us the main nerve center of the network. We accepted this responsibility without complaint, and dutifully wrote the letters and post cards that would keep the others informed.

News of the company still out there in those jungles was the most important thing to us. It was more important, more real than anything we saw, or anything that happened to us ourselves.

Winch had been our 1st/sgt out there. John Strange had been the mess/sgt. Landers had been company clerk. Bobby Prell, though busted twice from sgt and only a cpl, had been the company's toughest and foolhardiest sparkplug.

It was strange how closely we returnees clung together. We were like a family of orphaned children, split by an epidemic and sent to different care centers. That feeling of an epidemic disease persisted. The people treated us nicely, and cared for us tenderly, and then hurried to wash their hands after touching us. We were somehow unclean. We were tainted. And we ourselves accepted this. We felt it too ourselves. We understood why the civilian people preferred not to look at our injuries.

We hospitalized knew we did not belong there in the clean, healthy areas. We belonged back out in the raging, infected disaster areas; where we could succumb, die, disappear, vanish forever along with what seemed to us now the only family we had ever had. That was what being wounded was. We were like a group of useless unmanned eunuchs, after our swinging pendants had been removed, eating sweetmeats from the contemptuous fingers of the females in the garden, and waiting for news from the seneschals in the field.

There was arrogance in us, though. We came from the disaster areas, where these others had never been. We did not let anyone forget it. We came from the infected zones, had been exposed to the disease, and carried the disease in us to prove it. Carrying it was our pride.

For our own kind, an insane loyalty flamed in us. We were ready to fight all comers and sometimes, drunk and out in the town, did fight them. We would fight anybody who had not been out there with us. We wore our Combat Infantryman badges to distinguish us, and nothing else. Campaign ribbons and decorations were considered contemptible display. All that was propaganda for the nice, soft people.

And the company had been our family, our only home. Real parents, wives, fiancées did not really exist for us. Not before the fanatical devotion of that loyalty. Crippled, raging, enfeebled, unmanned in a very real sense and hating, hating both sides of our own coin and of every coin, we clung to each other no matter where or how far the hospital, and waited for the smallest morsel of news of the others to filter back to us, and faithfully wrote and mailed the messages that would carry it on to the other brothers.

Into this weird half-world of ours the first news we had of the four of them came on a grimy, mud-smeared post card from some lucky-unlucky man still out there.

The card said the four of them had been shipped out to the same evacuation hospital, almost at the same time. That was all it said. The next news we got was that all four had been shipped back home on the same hospital ship. This came from the base hospital, in a short letter from some unlucky, or lucky, man who had been wounded but had not made the boat. Later, we received a letter from the company's tech/sgt, giving more details.

Winch was being shipped back for some kind of unspecified ailment that nobody seemed to know much about. Winch himself would not talk about it. He had bitten through one thermometer and broken another, chased a hospital corpsman out of the compound, and gone back to his orderly tent where he was found slumped over his Morning Report book in a dead faint on his makeshift desk.

John Strange had been struck in the hand by a piece of mortar fragment which had not exited. The hand had healed badly, the wound becoming progressively more crippling. He was being sent back for delicate bone and ligament surgery and removal of the fragment.

Landers the clerk had had his right ankle smashed by a heavy-mortar fragment and needed orthopedic surgery. Bobby Prell had taken a burst of heavy-machinegun fire across both thighs in a firefight, sustaining multiple compound fractures, and heavy tissue damage.

This was the kind of personal news we ached to hear. Could it be that we were secretly pleased? That we were glad to see others join us in our half-unmanned state? We certainly would have denied it, would have attacked and fought anyone who suggested it. Especially about the four of them.

There were quite a few of us sitting in the shiny, spotless, ugly hospital snack bar, having coffee after morning rounds, when Corello came running in waving the letter. Corello was an excitable Italian from McMinnville, Tennessee. No one knew why he had not been sent to the hospital in Nashville, instead of to Luxor, just as no one knew how his Italian forebears happened to wind up in McMinnville, where they ran a restaurant.

Corello had been home once since his arrival in Luxor, and had stayed less than a day. Couldn't stand it, he said. Now he pushed his way through to us among the hospital-white tables, holding the letter high.

There was a momentary hush in the room. Then the conversations went right on. The old hands had seen this scene too many times. The two cracker waitresses looked up from their chores, alarmed until they saw the letter, then went back to their coffee-drawing.

Rays of Southern sun were streaming through the tall plate glass from high up, down into all that white. In sunny corners lone men sat at tables writing letters, preferring the clatter and people here to the quiet of the library. There were five of us from the company at one table and Corello stopped there.

At once, men of ours sitting at other tables got up and came over. In seconds all of us in the snack bar had clustered around. We were already passing the letter back and forth. The patients from other outfits looked back down at their coffee and conversation and left us alone.

"Read it out loud," someone said.

"Yeah, read it. Read it out loud," several others said.

The man who had it looked up and blushed. Shaking his head about reading out loud, he passed the letter to someone else.

The man who took it smoothed it out, then cleared his throat. He looked it over, then began to read in the stilted voice of a student in a declamation class.

As he read the news, a couple of men whistled softly.

When he finished, he put it down among the coffee mugs. Then he saw it might get stained, and picked it up and handed it to Corello.

"All four of them at the same time," a man who was standing behind him said hollowly.

"Yeah. The same day practically," another said.

We all knew none of us would ever go back to the old company. Not now, not once we had been sent back to the United States, we wouldn't. Once you came back to the States, you were reassigned. But all of us needed to believe the company would continue on as we knew it, go right on through and come out the other end, intact.

"It's as if— It's almost like—"

Whichever one of us it was who spoke did not go on, but we all knew what he meant.

A kind of superstitious fear had descended over us. In our profession, we pretty much lived by superstition. We had to. When all of knowledge and of past experience had been utilized, the outcome of a firefight, or a defense or an attack, depended largely on luck. Awe of and reverence for the inexplicable, that heart of the dedicated gambler's obsession, was the only religion that fit our case. We followed a God which coldly incorporated luck within Itself, as one of Its major tools. For a commander, give us the commander who had luck. Let the others have the educated, prepared commanders.

We were like the dim early human who watched his mud hut destroyed by lightning and created God to explain it. Our God could be likened to a Great Roulette Wheel, more than anything.

We had thought the God looked warmly on us, or at least our company. Now it seemed the Wheel was rolling the other way.

There was nothing to do about it. As superstitious men, we understood that. That was part of the rules.

We could only not step on the crack, not walk under the ladder, try not to let the black cat cross our line of advance in front.

But it was difficult to accept, without fear. That the old company could change so completely. Become the home, the family, the company of some other group. It was about the last thing we had left.

"Well—" one of us said, and cleared his throat massively. It sounded like a shotgun fired in a barrel. We all knew what this man meant, too. He did not want to pursue it. Otherwise, might not some of the bad luck rub off?

"But all four of them at once," someone said.

"Do you think one of them might get shipped here?" someone else said.

"If we could get Winch here," one said.

"Yeah, it would be like old times," another said.

"Anyway, we could get some inside scoop firsthand," someone said. "Instead of letters."

"Speaking of letters," another said, and got up. "Speaking of letters, I guess we might as well get on with our chores. Huh?"

At once, two or three men got up with him and moved away toward a couple of clean tables. Almost at once, two other men followed and joined them. Paper, pens, and pencils appeared, and post cards, envelopes, and stamps.

In the sweet, reassuring, late-summer slant of Southern sun which exploded in a dazzle below against all that white, they began to write the letters that would pass the news on to the other hospitals across the country. Some wrote with their tongues sticking out of their mouth corners.

The rest of us went on sitting. There was curiously little talk for a while. Then there was a sudden wave of signals for more coffee. Then we went on sitting. Most of us stared at the white walls or the white ceiling.

We were all thinking about the four of them. The four of them could legitimately be said to be almost the heart of the old company. Now those four were making the same strange trip home. We had all of us made it. It was a weird, strange, unreal voyage. We had made it either on the big fast planes, or on the slow white ships with the huge red crosses on their sides, as these four were doing.

We sat there in our demiworld of white, thinking about the four men making it as we ourselves had done. We wondered if those four were feeling the same peculiar sense of dislocation, the same sense of total disassociation and nonparticipation we ourselves had had.

CHAPTER 2

Winch was loafing in his cabin when the word passed that Stateside landfall had been made. Some breathless hysterical trooper stuck his head in, bawled out the news, and rushed away.

At once it seemed the whole ship was galvanized. Winch listened to steps running back and forth across the transverse corridor outside. His four cabinmates put down their cards, and began tightening their bathrobes to go on deck.

They were all staff/sgts or above in the crowded cabin. Morning rounds, about which the day was strictly centered in Army hospitals, and which on this Godforsaken meat wagon were only a grotesque formality anyway, were over. They were free to do anything they wanted for the rest of the day. Winch watched them, and did not move. He arbitrarily had decided he was not going to take part. Nor talk about it.

"Aint you coming, Winch?" one of them asked.

"No."

"Oh, for Christ's sake, come on," one growled. "It's home."

"No!"

Winch swiveled his head toward them. He did not really

know which one had spoken. They were all strangers anyhow. He flashed a freakish kind of cannibal's flesh-hungry grin at them. "I've seen it."

"Not like this time," one said, and gestured at his other arm encased in plaster, "not like this time." The plaster went up to and around the shoulder and held the arm out at right angles above an aluminum frame. The uncovered hand looked purple.

"Oh, leave him be," one said. "You know how he is. You know what he's like. He's a goofy."

They traipsed out, dragging themselves, two of them leg-wounded and hobbling, all four of them moving slowly with the caution of damaged men. A goofy. It was the kind of reputation he had tried to establish with them. It was the kind of reputation he had tried for years to establish everywhere.

Them gone, he stretched out in his berth and, alone, stared up at the smooth underside of the berth above. He had no desire to go on deck and look at the American coastline.

Home. Home, they'd said. It did not mean anything to him. Could it really mean something to them?

We all of us feel the same way at some point, he told himself. All of us who knew anything. Home could get to be very unreal. Besides, it didn't seem fair, to us. All of us being so lucky. Getting to lose a leg or an arm or an eye and come back home out of the fire to all the bars and pussy. While the others, the healthy ones, had to stay out there and try to live and breathe in the smoke.

Winch felt for his worn musette bag and unfastened the catches and pulled out a bottle of Scotch and brought it up to him. He told himself not to drink from it. He told himself he was not allowed. Then he uncapped it, and took a long, hot double swallow.

Well, so long out there, you! Toast, you fuckers!

He dipped the neck of the bottle in salute of his toast. If booze was a poison, a particular poison for him now, it was sure one hell of a marvelous poison.

This thing of reputations. It was peculiar. People were always talking about command presence. They said, either someone had command presence, or he did not have it. They said, if you did not have command presence, you could not learn it. A lot of bullshit.

A new word for it, which was really a very old word for it,

was beginning to be popular again after five hundred years. An old Church word out of the Middle Ages, charisma. You either had charisma or you didn't, and if you had it you could do anything you wanted, demand anything, and people would follow you and obey you.

What people did not understand about command presence was that it did not come from the inside but was imposed upon some object person, from the outside, by the followers themselves. They wanted something to look up to. They wanted someone to tell them what to do. Command presence was created by the eyes of the commanded. A kind of massive human conspiracy. Maybe it also existed in the eyes of foolish commanders. But no smart commander believed it. He merely utilized it. Hadn't he been doing it himself for years?

Winch sighed and put one hand behind his head. Winch had been one of the charisma people, one of the "stars" of his Division for years. So much so that he was known in other Divisions, across the Army. What he had learned from it was that all celebrities were alike. They were a secret club of thieves. They recognized each other on sight, and they never attacked each other in any depth. The club's secret password was a look of shrewdness in the eyes with you, a look of complicity. They never talked about charisma. What Winch had learned from charisma people, from being one, was that charisma people were a race, a den, a nest of Super-liars.

When you learned that, it took away everything. It took away the satisfaction and it took away whatever had given you the drive in the first place. It made it all worthless. And ludicrous. It put you right back down there in the barnyard, looking like —and smelling like—the rest of the livestock. The livestock you had wanted to avoid being one of.

And he was supposed to be his own company's hero. Damn them, damn them, Winch thought suddenly and savagely, God damn them. They weren't worth the turds to put in a sock and thump them over the head with. Why should he give a damn about them?

The bottle was still sitting on his chest. He let the hand holding it slide away down over the berth edge and put it away.

God damn their souls, cannon fodder was what they were. He couldn't be expected to keep them all alive forever, could he?

Winch raised up on his elbow and stared through the open

door, across the passageway. Across the passageway was what had once been the ship's main lounge. There was your cannon fodder.

There were easily several hundred of them. All the chairs and tea tables had been removed and replaced with hospital beds. In ranked rows. Here in the one huge room were the serious cases which needed constant attention. White-jacketed figures moved among them under the high ceiling. Here and there a medic squatted, supervising the giving of glucose or plasma from a glass jug hanging on a white stand. The room had not been repainted, and all its gay gilt and vermilion and mirrors stared down on all the slow quiet pain.

Only four of Winch's company were on board this trip, four including himself. And only one of them was in there in the lounge.

His first look at the main lounge had made him weak in the stomach. We all of us feel that way when we first see it, he thought. It made such a clear, concise picture of the cost for you. The only ones of us who didn't notice the lounge were those who traveled in it, and only those who traveled in it failed to notice the smell it gave off.

Apparently the news of landfall had passed that way, too, because a murmur was fluttering weakly across the lounge. Many of the reclining figures had raised up in their bandages. It was an eerie picture. Some of them had their entire heads bandaged, as they peered about. Winch went on staring at them, rapt. The smell from it was almost insupportable.

Man-stink. How used to it he had gotten over the years. And all its various flavors. What was that word? Effluvia. Sweaty male armpits and smelly male feet. Socks and underwear. Fetid breath. Uninhibited belches and farts. Ranked open toilet bowls and urinals in the early morning. It mingled with the smell of toothpaste and shaving soap from the row of washbasins all down the other side.

And now he could add a new one. Suppuration. Suppuration and granulation. The sweet foul smell of injured flesh trying slowly, painfully to heal itself down there under the lymph-stained bandages. It diffused itself throughout every part of the big lounge, and overflowed its doors. It would stay in his nose with the others the rest of his life.

Which in the case of Mart Winch might not be too fucking

long. If he didn't take care of himself. He wasn't supposed to drink. He wasn't supposed to smoke, either. Defiantly, he reached down for the musette and pulled the bottle up and had another, and lit a cigarette.

Neither gesture helped. He was still standing at the same junction as before. A night junction. Trailer trucks whammed by. Nobody stopped. How unmanly could you get, here at the end of the string? Where there wasn't any audience. An aging, pitiless, tough, old infantry 1st/sgt, looking desperately everywhere for a shot of pity. It was laughable.

Hell, he wasn't even wounded. He was only sick. An unaccustomed hollowness opened up in him at the word. Shit, he had never been sick a day in his life. Under the hollowness, the booze seeped through him its insidious, seductive, golden-honey, poisonous message of sunshine and good will.

He looked over again at the lounge. He only had one of his people in there this trip, thank God. That fucking Bobby Prell.

He wanted another drink. But this time he drank water, from a loose uncoupled canteen in its canvas cover that was lying under the berth.

"You'll get over the dengue fever," Col Harris had told him. Col Harris was the Division Surgeon. He had come out into his jungle tent hospital personally to see Winch. "Everybody does. Though it's painful."

"Thanks a lot, Doc," Winch had growled.

It was the dengue that had brought him down. Like a green-ass recruit, he had fainted dead away across his makeshift desk.

"And you'll get over the falciparum malaria," Doc Harris said. "That'll take longer. It's the worst kind. You should have reported it, Mart."

Winch had managed to keep his malaria secret for over two months. Lying in the hospital field cot with his bright red, swollen palms and the rash of dengue all over him, he had been through the first bone-breaking fever, the twenty-four-hour euphoria, and the second fever period. He felt terrible.

"Okay, Doc, okay. What the hell? What the hell? So?"

Doc Harris had begun to tap his prominent front teeth with the eraser of a fresh long yellow pencil. Fresh long yellow pencils were a thing of his.

"I'm afraid there's more, Mart," he said. "You've got high blood pressure."

Winch for once had no answer. Finally, he laughed. "High blood pressure? Are you kidding?"

"And I would guess a pretty serious case of it. Usually, fever makes it go down. They'll check it out down the line after we ship you out. But I'm pretty sure. If I'm any judge, they'll find you're suffering from what we call primary hypertension."

"What's that?"

"High blood pressure," Doc Harris said. "Just what I said."

He came back in a couple of days and they talked about it more. Winch could move around a little bit by then. But Winch was feeling peculiarly unmanned, lying there in his cot. Why did intelligent men feel the need to measure everything by physical vitality? But they all did.

"You've had it with the Infantry, Mart. You're going to have to watch your diet. Must not drink. Must not smoke. Don't drink coffee or tea. Don't get overexcited. If I could, I'd put you on a salt-free diet right now. I certainly can't send you back up."

"Christ, that sounds great," Winch said. "Like some old lady's school for girls. Coffee and tea."

"I sure can't send you back to any line outfit," Doc Harris said.

"I'm a lucky man, huh?" Winch said.

"How old are you, Mart?"

"Forty-two. Why?"

"A little young for hypertension."

"So?" He certainly did not feel lucky. Only half of you wanted to go. The rest wanted to stay, and felt a failure. Ashamed, and guilty, for leaving. No matter how badly you were sick or shot up. All of us, Winch thought. "Just what is this disease, Doc?"

Hypertension? They did not know everything about the disease, that was the truth. It was one of those usually bland diseases whose course could not be measured easily. You could have a heart attack or stroke tomorrow or you could go on living till you were eighty. In Winch's case it was Doc Harris' opinion that a constant very high intake of alcohol could be a lot of the cause. That, and smoking. But there had been some interesting research on effects of alcohol recently.

"What a fucking joke," Winch said bitterly.

This was not to accuse him of being an alcoholic. No alcoholic could hold down his job. But his alcoholic capacity was a legend. How much did he drink a day?

"Yeah. Some legend," Winch said.

How much? Half a bottle? A bottle?

"Easy," Winch said staunchly.

"A bottle and a half?"

"Oh, sure," Winch lied. "If I can get it." The truth was he didn't really know.

How much did he smoke? Two packs a day? Three? In any case, Doc Harris predicted that once he had recuperated, and gotten rid of these fever ailments, they were going to find his blood pressure shooting way up.

Winch only nodded. For the first time he could feel somewhere in himself a beginning to give up. It was like hanging onto a high window ledge by your fingertips and feeling your fingers begin to straighten. In one way, a vast relief. Every cripple feels that, finally, all of us, he thought.

"You really mean I'm really through."

"I'm afraid so. In the Infantry."

That was how it had turned out. Winch had known Doc Harris for over six years. Harris pretty well knew his stuff. He predicted it exactly. The high blood pressure had mounted. The stranger doctors down the line were more secretive and circumspect about it with him. But that was the upshot of it.

Apparently their theory was, Do not tell them anything you do not have to and you will not frighten them. Winch had very little use for the bulk of the medical profession.

That was why, shrewdly, he asked Doc Harris about it all one time more before he left.

Death usually occurred from congestive heart failure in the fifties. That was assuming it was fairly well contained and there was no heart attack or stroke. On the other hand, long survival was not at all a rarity. Congestive heart failure was a gradual failure of the heart. It became enlarged and feebler, and the pulse got faster. Finally this caused a congestion of fluids in the body called edema. In the final stages the lungs themselves filled up with fluids. It accounted for death in about 50 percent of the cases. It wasn't so much a disease as a condition. And in that sense, it was incurable. But still there was a vast extreme of difference in life expectancy running from a few years to several decades. "I'm trying to tell you that very likely you can still live a long time if you take care of yourself," Doc Harris said.

Winch had listened intently. We all of us did that, when it was our own personal diagnosis, and our own prognosis, he thought briefly. It was at that point that you felt distinctly peculiar. Like the man in the movie standing up before the judge. While the solemn judge, after an excellent breakfast, pronounced word by slow word some horrible sentence on you, for having done some damned thing or other.

"There is a lot to be said for clean living," Doc Harris said.

"Clean living!" Winch exploded. "Sure. Okay, Doc, look. You've explained it all to me. I understand all about it now. Why don't we just forget this talk we've had? And why don't you just mark me fit for duty and send me back up there to my company? Huh?"

"You know I can't do that," Doc Harris said angrily. "I swear I don't understand you, Mart. Most of the people around here are bucking their heads off to get shipped back home to the States, and can't."

"Well," Winch said, "you know."

"You've got a wife and kids back home, haven't you?"

"Oh, well, sure. Somewhere."

"You don't even know where?"

"Well, sure. They're in St. Louis. I guess."

"I simply don't understand you," Doc Harris said.

"Oh, it's easy enough." Winch stood up. "To understand me. Then that's your absolute final last word?"

"I'm afraid it is."

For some reason, Winch felt like saluting. He aboutfaced. That was the last he saw of Doc Harris. They had flown him out the next day, with some others, to the New Hebrides.

Despite the excitement, the ship's motors had not altered their steady hammering. But Winch could still hear the unaccustomed scurrying caused by the American landfall. Here he was, on this stinking, suppurating, stockyard-smelling scow of a hospital cattle boat, headed home. He continued to lie on his elbow, staring across the passageway at the shattered figures in the main lounge.

He wondered why Doc Harris had looked so shocked? Hadn't he ever heard of men giving up on and quitting their wife and kids? He did not know what kind of man Doc was around the house. But Winch was sure Mrs Harris at least tried to get along with her husband the colonel. A picture of his own sloppy, fat-assed wife and two tow-headed brats tried to flash onto the screen of Winch's mind. He thrust it violently aside. Thoughts of them only caused a sort of irascibility to take him over. His wife and her two blond, cow-eyed kids that looked just like her were no great thing to come home to. She was certainly not hurting any there in St. Louis without him. Not with all the outside fucking she had managed on posts where they did live together. That was what you got for marrying some drunken master/sgt's daughter on some flea-bitten post out in the boondocks. She liked to speak of herself as statuesque. They looked so much like her it was impossible to tell who their father was. There wasn't even any way to tell if the boys were his. He was pretty sure they were. But it didn't matter. Winch didn't care if he ever saw any of them again.

In front of him the top half of a human head stuck itself around the door jamb, disrupting his demon's vision of the lounge, the faceless eyes peering at him like a sniper.

Quickly, Winch changed gears in his head, adopting the bantering snarl his long association with his former mess/sgt had fixed into a ritual. "Johnny Stranger," Winch said. "Go away. Go on away! Go up on deck and play with the big kids."

The head, tilted till the thick brows were perpendicular, parallel to the jamb they peered around, righted itself and a body appeared below it and came on in in a slow saunter, its face making the briefest of grins. John Strange was deliberate and slow about everything. He was oddly built, Strange, his legs just a little too short for the rest of him. And his right hand hung down now against his thigh, a maladroit claw whose fingers looked misplaced.

"I mean it," Winch said. "I got nothing to talk to you about, Strange. Except your asshole reminiscences. And that bores my ass."

Strange nodded appreciatively. "I figured *you* wouldn't be up on deck."

"To see what?" Winch growled.

"I went," Strange said, looking a little ashamed, "for a little. It's mighty pretty." He moved his head. "They all whooping and hollering."

Strange grinned again, in his tough, broad face, a strange scornful-sorrowful rictus of malevolent appreciation. In the unusual broadness of his face there was a kind of peasant's long-standing patience with the universe, and a sadness. And yet the thick line of brow hair, which formed one single hairy bar of dark brown across the upper third of his head, carried an unbelievably angry, furious look about it.

You had to know the man before you recognized the expression as a smile instead of a sneer. They had all of them learned, learned very early on, that Strange was a man who liked to bark, and that his bite was a whole hell of a lot worse than his bark.

"How's the old health there, First Sarn't?" Strange said now.

"Better than yours," Winch said. He had told nobody about his ailment, and he was absolutely sure Strange had no idea what was wrong with him. "And don't call me First Sergeant. I'm not one any more. I'm a casual in transit, just like you."

"You still carry the rank and draw the pay."

"Asshole!"

"Sure," Strange said. "Why not? My sentiments exactly."

"Then we understand each other."

"I also thought I'd stop over the lounge see Bobby Prell awhile," Strange said more softly.

Winch would not answer this.

"You want to come along?"

"No."

Strange moved his head. "Go by myself then."

"Stupid son of a bitch. He wouldn't be over there if he hadn't been trying to play hero."

Strange moved his head again. "Some guys got to play hero. Anyway, he must be feeling pretty down, right now. Today. The scoop the doctors putting out say he won't never walk again. Say he may still lose one of his legs."

"Whatever happens to him, it's his own damn fault," Winch said promptly.

"He's still one of the old outfit," Strange said.

"That shit's all over, too," Winch said. "And you better believe it, Johnny Stranger. You better get it through your thick Texas head."

Strange made his brief grin. "I don't think so. Not quite yet, for a while, it aint. You sure you won't come?"

"No."

"Suit yourself. You're a hard man, aint you? I was just telling somebody today what a hard man you are." He wrinkled his lip. "I was going to offer you a congratulatory drink. On the land-fall, and all. But I seem to forgot my booze."

Winch peered at him a moment. Then reached down for his musette and sailed it across to Strange, overhanded all in one motion, as one might sail a manilla envelope of papers. Strange caught it effortlessly, edge-on, between the thumb and extended fingers of his good hand, his left.

"Why, thank you, First Sarn't." In high, grand style he dipped the neck of the bottle at Winch before he drank. He held the bottle in his clawlike right hand, whose fingers did not seem to open and close except very slowly.

He inspected the bottle, then handed it back. "Getting low. You want anything, First Sarn't, you come see the old Stranger."

"Me want booze?" Winch shook the bottle. "You kidding me? This tub has more sources than a fountain."

"Might want something else."

"You mean like an old buddy? Haw. Fuck yourself. At my age?"

"Never can tell." The mess/sgt half-saluted. A dry joke, with his crippled claw hand. He went out and across the passage into the big lounge.

Winch stared after him. He stretched back out. In a way, Strange was Winch's hero. If he could be said to have such a thing. The thing Winch admired about Strange was that he really did not give a damn about anything. The others, like Winch, pretended they did not but, really, they cared. Strange really didn't. About anything. The Army, the outfit, his job, people, women, life or success or humanity. Strange pretended to care but really didn't. He was completely alone inside himself and content with that. And for that Winch admired him.

He reached down and tickled the cool neck of his bottle under the berth with a finger, through the flap of the musette. It was funny how they went together, whiskey and sex. Especially when the whiskey was forbidden. Secret, illicit drinking was as exciting, and in exactly the same way, as going down on some woman. Well, tomorrow. Tomorrow he would drink nothing.

Damned dumb fucking morons, all of them! his mind flashed

at him suddenly. Would his field tech/sgt be able to handle them now at all?

Dreamily, in a kind of despondency that was like a drug effect almost, and which ate bone deep but no longer hurt more than a chronic low-level toothache, Winch thought about all those fools up there on deck goggling away at the landfall they idiotically believed to represent some haven.

CHAPTER 3

Without exception, each shipload had felt moved and disturbed and somehow stricken by the home continent landfall. And the voyage of Winch and Strange and the rest was not much different from the voyage the others made.

Hardly a handful of them actually believed it would really be there, really appear. But exactly on schedule it came up over the horizon. The long blue landfall appeared in the east, exactly as they had been told it would.

On the empty vastness of the slowly pulsing ocean the single steamer trailing its black plume was the only visible sign of life. The white ship with its big red crosses moved slowly along through the flat sea, which heaved and breathed beneath it like a separate existence. The ship plowed on. The sea continued to sparkle and show just the slightest froth of white now and then in the breeze and bright sun.

On the eastern horizon the long blue cloud, only slightly darker than the sky, appeared and disappeared like a mirage at first. Home. The word sped whispering through the ship like a prickle over the skin. The ship steamed slowly on and imperceptibly the blue cloud fixed itself above the waterline until it could

be stared at without disappearing. Most of the cases on board
had been serving overseas for at least a year. Home. The way
they said it to each other, it was more a word of anxiety and deep
unexorcised fear, of despair even, than of relief, love or anticipa-
tion. What would it be like, now? What would they themselves
be like?

It was the same with everything. The bulletin boards and
newssheets had told them they were going home. But after so
long a time away, they no longer trusted bulletins and communiqués. Bulletins and communiqués in general were more
concerned with morale and with their beliefs than with realities.
They all knew their beliefs were okay. God forbid anyone's
beliefs among them should be bad. But it was difficult to know
if a bulletin or report had been created to affect morale, or to
pass on specific information about the long blue cloud.

They could not see it from everywhere. It was visible only
from the forward part of the upper decks. Of these, the only one
not off-limits to them was the deck once called the Promenade
Deck. Here as many of them as were able, wanted to, and could
squeeze themselves into the available space, came to have a look
at it.

They were a sorry-looking bunch. In the gray pajamas and
maroon bathrobes, wearing the heelless duck slippers that
would never stay on their feet, they pushed out through the
doors onto the open forward deck and squeezed against the rail,
or against those already squeezed against the rail. Shaky, skinny,
stringy, yellow of eyeball and of skin, bandaged and suppurating or wearing plaster, they crippled their way up from below,
some tottering, some helping each other along, a number limping along on leg casts. They were the lucky ones out of all the
casualties. They had been judged sufficiently damaged to send
all the way back home.

A few cried. Some laughed and clapped their hands, or
slapped each other on the back. All gazed around them and at
each other with anxiety. Anxiety at being so immensely lucky.
A screened, secreted terror in their eyes suggested that they felt
they had no right to be here.

Down below them, out on the more roomy space of what in
normal times was the ship's crew's working deck, was crowded
a mob of blueclad sailors, and whiteclad medical personnel. All
of them were hired, paid, ranked, and organized, solely to service this steadily accumulating jetsam of a modern war. And the

jetsam on their one small deck, indecent as a herd of turkeys, gobbled and craned and jostled and elbowed to get their look at the homeland they were all so vividly and happily aware none of them had yet died for.

Deep down in the ship in one of the cabins Marion Landers had tried to stay in his berth and found he couldn't. Finally he rolled out and got laboriously to his feet in the small place. This was no easy operation since his right leg was in a cast to the knee. But it was impossible not to get caught up and carried along in the excited hubbub.

As a company clerk Landers was only a buck sergeant. He did not rate any airy stateroom with a porthole, like Winch and Strange. He had grown used to living mostly below decks in the half-gloom of bare electric bulbs. He felt under his pillow for his cheap sunglasses.

Involuntarily, he groaned a little. The pain was not due to his wound so much. That had stopped hurting. This was due to the stiffness caused by trying to live with the heavy plaster cast. It was impossible to sit, stand or lie comfortably in it.

On the other side of the tiny, six-man cabin there was a rustle. The kid Air Force tailgunner, who had been crying again, this time over the landfall, raised his head.

"Are you going to leave me, too?"

"I guess I'll go up. Have a look, yeah," Landers said. He tried not to sound irritated. He got his crutches from the clothes hook.

"Please, don't leave me."

Landers paused in the doorway, and turned deftly on his crutches. You did get used to the damn things, finally. He peered at the boy.

All of us were burdened with the same thing, at one point, Landers thought. In every cabin there was the one weak sister. The cabins always sifted themselves down into a pecking order, with the weak sister at the bottom. There was always a moral problem with him. Everybody had a responsibility to him. It was part of the code. None of us liked it much, but if you wanted to be one of us you had to go by the code. And the weak sister could use it against you. Had the moral right to do so. That was part of the advantage he gained by giving up, and accepting to be the weakest.

Landers and his kid gunner had not said a word in the half hour since the others had left to go up on deck. Landers had not felt like talking, himself. He had simply lain and stared at the ceiling shadows. Then the Air Force kid had started to cry again. It was partly what had driven Landers to his feet.

"Aw, come on, kid," he said.

"You're like all the others," the thin voice piped from the depths of the berth. "I thought you were different. You're the only decent one here. You know how I can't stand to be alone."

"I'll call the ward boy for you. He'll sit with you." Landers paused. "He's probably bored to death with all of us," he added.

"I'm sure he is. Him and that damned prescription pad of his. Doodling and drawing cocks and pussies, all the time."

Landers felt he had to get out of there or die. Explode, blow apart. It wasn't only the boy. Something was eating at him terribly. Had been since the news came. Anyway, what a thing to be saddled with. It was not bad enough to be cooped up in here, six miserable bastards in a space meant for four healthy men. They had had to draw him. A skinny kid tailgunner with eyes as big as dinner plates in his emaciated face and dry gangrene in both legs.

He had been a hero, for his one brief day. In flight an improperly mounted .50 cal had bounded loose from its mounting and falling to the deck had locked itself on Fire and begun spraying the inside of the plane. Like a loose fire hose. The kid had dived forward and collared it and unlocked it, but he had taken four .50 cal slugs in his shins. By the time they got him back in the ripped-open refrigerated plane he had his dry gangrene. He had been given the DFC and the Silver Star and been put on this hospital boat home, and he was a crybaby. The smell was bad enough, a deep acrid bronzegreen odor that bit deep at the back of your throat like copper pennies in your mouth. His poor bare feet were the same verdigris color, and shriveled like a mummy's. He complained all the time, and cried half the time, and he had been a college sophomore. Landers didn't know why, by what incredible administrative mixup, he had been put on this boat. Especially since he was Air Force. They should have flown him home.

"I know it smells," he said now. "But please stay with me."

"I'll call you the ward boy," Landers said.

"Thanks. You selfish prick. I only hope someday you get in my shape."

"Thanks," Landers said. "Look. At the risk of sounding fatuous, I will say to you that we have all of us got to live alone. You've got to learn to live with it. I can't help you. Nobody can."

"I don't *want* to live with it." He began to blubber. "I want my mother."

Landers ran his tongue over his teeth. "Look, they're flying you to Walter Reed from San Diego. They've got the best men in the world there. If anybody can save your legs, they will. And they promised you your mother would be there to meet you."

"Do you believe that? Anyway, the doctor told me yesterday there wasn't any hope," the boy said in a tiny voice.

This was an out and out lie, and Landers knew it. "I was here," he said. "I didn't hear him say that." Usually when they changed his dressings, everybody stampeded like a herd of cattle out the narrow door. But at least once in a while Landers felt morally bound to stay and pretend he did not have an olfactory nerve.

"Well, he did."

"No, he didn't either, God damn it! I was here!"

"Yes, he did. You just didn't hear him. Look. You're the only college man in here. The only college man in this whole deck, probly."

"I heard every word he said. Anyway, my three and a half years of college didn't do me much good. Not for this. No good at all. I'll send the ward boy to you," Landers said, and swung around and fled.

He could not flee quite fast enough, on crutches. The boy's cursing followed him. Then it changed to crying again. Landers felt anyone would agree the kid was going beyond all code rights.

He signaled the Army medic ward boy, who shrugged irritably but put down his comic book. Landers commenced laboriously to struggle up the steep, iron, ship's stairs. Climbing them could be seriously dangerous, to a man on crutches.

He came out on the long glassed-in Main Deck. It had no open deck forward like the Promenade, and was deserted of troops now. Usually it had half a dozen poker games going on the deck, down its long perspective. Landers swung himself over to an opened glass and stuck his head out into the sea breeze.

For a while the sea air was enough. It took a little while for even a sea breeze to blow that awful smell out of the back of your throat. For a moment he wrestled with himself whether he had been cruel with the Air Force boy. Where did responsibility end? To your fellow human being?

But it was not the kid that had driven him up on deck. Something else had done that. When the news passed that home was sighted, a terrible reaction had seized him. An evil, awful depression. The worst thing was that he did not know what it represented, or what caused it. Also, it was totally unanticipated. Yesterday he would have bet all his unpaid back pay, which was considerable, that home landfall would have delighted him.

Now he stared at it, the faint, blue coast. From the ship's side he could only see dimly a very short length of it. Then it faded swiftly into invisibility to the south. And such a violence of not caring raged through him that he wanted to yell out loud. It was such a mammoth, massive country. He was realizing that fact for the first time, with the shock of seeing clearly something known vaguely before but never defined. It was so big that how could you care? And all his life Landers had been taught that to care was important, that caring was the most important thing of all, whatever it was you were involved in.

There was certainly no place for a twenty-one-year-old Landers there, in it. Not Landers, staring at it from a hole in the huge side of this big ship. This ship that was now carrying toward it such a load of human meat. It frightened him, frightened him down to an unreadable depth. And at the same time, like some deep contrabass figure repeated over and over, was the thought that he did not deserve it, this return to safety.

Two men passed by behind him. They had come down from the Promenade Deck. One of them clumped along in leg plaster, his walking iron ringing on the metal deck. Their presence broke Landers' concentration.

"Hey, Landers," one of them said. "Thinking about all that homegrown pussy we'll all be shafting?"

Landers only waved. He did not trust himself to speak. He saw that the second man had plaster on his arm and body, the bent arm held out rigidly and horizontal from the shoulder in the case. There seemed to be so many arm and shoulder cases like that on board. Perhaps they were just more conspicuous.

The men went on.

Over the sea the coast did not appear to be getting any nearer. Not to the naked eye. But that was an optical illusion. In the slight swell the ship hardly rolled at all on the easy sea. College man! Jesus!

Something had happened to Landers with his wounding in the New Georgia islands. But it was hard to say exactly what it was. It had been an easy enough wounding. Commonplace, even. A big-sized mortar round had landed close by him and blown him up and knocked him out. It must have happened to thousands. That part had not been bad at all. There was no pain, nothing hurt him, there was no time to be afraid. The noise-fire blossomed so swiftly to engulf him that he had hardly heard it. Then swift comforting blackness, buzzing up. If anything at all, there was only a half-beginning of a surprised thought: Why, this isn't so bad—

He assumed, later, he meant dying. The thought seemed to include the idea that he would never come to. Then he did come to, his nose bleeding, his head heavy and unable to think. His head was bleeding and his helmet had disappeared. Contrary to all the rules of first aid, somebody was rolling him around and slapping his face. There was the usual comic moment of panic when he felt all over his crotch to make sure he had everything. Then he walked out. At the aid station the medical lieutenant had told him he had a mild concussion and said he would send him back to rest a couple of days. It was not till then, when he tried to get back on his feet, that they discovered his smashed ankle. He had walked out on it.

It was during the time he was waiting to be jeeped out that the peculiar thing, the something, happened to him. They had cut off his shoe, which turned out to be full of blood, and had bandaged his ankle. Four men had placed him on a stretcher and carried him over and put him down where there were others waiting. He sat on the stretcher on the crest of the ridge and with some of the other wounded placidly, contentedly almost, watched the battle in progress below them.

At this point Landers' job designation was Battalion Communications Sergeant. Wandering around with his company, where as company clerk he was not even supposed to be, he had been picked up four days before by the lt colonel commanding the battalion and impressed as his communications sergeant, to replace the original who had been killed. He had been up forward to deliver a message from the colonel to one of the platoon commanders when the mortar round knocked him off.

Being a replacement as well as a clerk, this was only Landers'
second time up in fighting country. The first time he had
roamed around with his outfit a few days, been part of a small
firefight, watched several men wounded, then been uncondi-
tionally ordered back to the regimental rear area to his job by
the company commander, at Top/Sgt Winch's instigation. The
second time, he had armed himself with three three-day passes
from the head of G-1 who thought his request marvelous.
Charming, if not actually quixotic. Landers himself thought it
bizarre, a good story to tell some day, how he had to get a pass
to go *toward* the fighting. But under that was the nagging feeling
which always gnawed at him, that he was back in the relative
safety while they were up there in the smoke and fire. But after
one day with them he had been caught and shanghaied by the
battalion's colonel. The truth was, he at once became the pet
enlisted aide of the colonel, who had looked up his dossier and
found he had a twenty-one-year-old with three and a half years
of college. All of this had infuriated Winch, whose clerk he'd
been. But the result was he spent most of his time intellectualiz-
ing the war with the battalion officers and doing organizational
things fairly far back. And probably, if he had not been
wounded, he would have been transferred to the colonel, with
a raise in grade. But at least he could have said he was doing his
share.

But on the ridge all that changed. At some unspecified point.
Landers watched as below him in the shallow bowl men roared
and shouted and hollered and yelled, ran forward carrying
things, ran back carrying things (as often as not other men), fired
guns, threw things, struggled and fought. Landers thought only
one thought. They were all silly idiots. What did they think they
were doing? They were ridiculous. He did not know then that
most of them felt the same way when they were wounded.

On his ridge Landers watched with perfect equanimity as
they bopped and banged and shot and exploded and stabbed
each other. Good. Good for them. They deserved it. They deserved whatever happened to them. He felt completely acquies-
cent. But he was outside of it. But being outside went further
than just being on the ridge. It extended to his special pet colonel, to his old outfit, to the whole Army, to his entire nation, to
the enemy nation—to the whole human race, finally. He was not
part of it.

He realized this did not particularly affect anything. They

could still give him orders. They could put him in jail. And he would go to jail. He could be bayoneted and he would scream. They could even give him a medal and he would salute and say Thank you. Or they could kill him, and he would die. But that was all. Because all the rest was bullshit. Just plain bullshit.

It was not because they were insane. He had suspected that before, from the beginning. It was not that modern war itself was insane. He had known that, too. It was not even that in ten years these same men battling down there, those who survived, would be making trade agreements with each other, signing mutual business deals for mutual profit, while the dumb luckless dead ones moldered in some hole. Landers had been cynically aware of all that, long before. It was that, seeing it, it was all so foolish, so abysmally stupid and ridiculous and savage, he could not consider himself a part of it.

Suddenly, sitting there on the hillside, he began to weep.

Crying was no catharsis for it. When he stopped, he did not feel any better. Perhaps he felt worse. His tears had washed two striking, clean streaks down his dust-caked, gaunted cheeks. Around him other men were weeping, too. They displayed the same two striking, white streaks down their faces. This did not impress him.

All his life Landers had prided himself on being an outsider. Now he really was outside. It was not at all a pleasant feeling. They were a quarrelsome, violent race. Worse than baboons. A race of beasts. They came from a long line of beasts. Whatever they pretended. Straight back to *Australopithecus*. He did not want to be a part of them.

In the hours, then days, then weeks, that followed, the "outside" feeling never left Landers, nor did it change or loosen up or soften. At times the sense of it there in him made him frantic to get rid of it. But nothing could do that. The frenzy drove him to do some wild, extravagant things occasionally. But always it settled back into that strange acquiescence, without having touched the feeling.

In a couple of days he was flown out, first to Guadalcanal, then to the New Hebrides. In the Naval base hospital there the doctors looked into his eyes and ears, tested him here and there, and after a few days said his concussion was cured. They were ready to operate on his ankle.

The surgeon was a young man, a major, with a boyish handsome face which showed clearly that nothing bad had ever happened to him in his life. The same handsome sense of handsome invulnerability showed in the way he went about things.

"There's no problem about the metal fragments. They can be removed easy enough. The problem is, there are two ways to repair your ankle," the major smiled. "It comes down to my way against the Army way. The Army way is to patch you up and get you back to duty. The Army way, you'll have a nearly adequate ankle out of it. But it won't be perfectly repaired. It will almost certainly bother you the rest of your life, particularly as you get older. But you'll be out of the hospital and back to your outfit in five weeks.

"If I fix it my way, the way I would fix it for a patient back home, you'll be in a cast at least two months. There'll be no choice but to send you back to the States. You're the patient. The choice is up to you."

Landers suddenly wanted to yell at him, curse him. Landers could remember back when his life had been like the major's, when nothing bad had happened to him, either. That was back before his misshapen sense of honor got him to enlist in the infantry as a private.

"I suppose getting shipped back to the States would be the best thing," he said, instead. "Wouldn't it?"

The major had thought the answer a foregone conclusion, and Landers had rattled him. "Are you trying to tell me you prefer *not* to go back to the States?"

"No, sir."

"Well, what *are* you trying to tell me, Sergeant, uh"—he looked down at the papers—"Landers?"

Landers felt wacky. His extravagances again. Suddenly he lowered his head and peered up at the youthful doctor through his eyebrows, and leered. Not even knowing his name seemed the last, ultimate joke. "Well, *I* think they're going to get me," he said, leering, "*one* way or the other. If you want to know the truth. That's what *I* think. *I* haven't got a chance."

The young major was brought up short, for a moment. "Who's they?"

"Them. You know," Landers said. "Whoever. The same ones you're trying to fight, isn't it?"

"I see . . . Yes. Well." The major scratched his nose. "I don't think you understand. I'm not fighting any 'them.' I'm fighting a government policy. I'm doing my work the way it ought to be done, the way I was taught to do it."

"Oh, I understand all right," Landers said. But he really wanted, again, to shout at the major, simply fill his lungs with air and bellow it back out. How could he be so fucking sure of himself about everything? How could he be so safe?

"Look. Tell me something. Do you *want* to go back up there?" the major asked.

Landers thought this over seriously. "No, sir," he said finally. "I don't want to go back."

"All right." The major slapped his hands down on his knees. He stood up. "I'll have you prepared for tomorrow."

"But I don't think it'll make any difference," Landers said.

As if he had not heard, the major said, "After all, my job is seeing that you men are fixed up as well as possible for your later life."

"Yes, sir," Landers said sourly. "Thank you, sir."

"Also, it's a job of work I'd like to have a shot at. It's got interesting problems."

Landers stared at him. "Sir."

"Of course, it'll make a difference!" the major said suddenly. "Why wouldn't it make a difference?" Still standing, the major put his hands on the desk and looked at Landers. "I don't think you're acting very rational. Well. It's probably perfectly normal." He sighed. "I'll have you gotten ready for tomorrow." But he looked hurt. As if somehow Landers had let him down. If he had been the type to get angry, he would probably have gotten angry.

Landers was certainly angry. But he was confused. And then he began to feel guilty. By the time he was rolled back to his ward, he began to worry. He worried all that night about their misunderstanding, about how he had treated the major. But in the morning when they rolled him in half-woozy from the shot and put him on the table, the surgeon smiled at him. Then they put the anesthetic to him.

Lying comfortably in the hospital bed after the operation, he slept a lot.

But they kept him full of dope for several days, and something kept coming back in his mind.

Going up with the message from the colonel he had carried

a full canteen. The heat was terrible, and soaked with sweat he had conscientiously conserved his water. But after getting hit, he had drawn the canteen and allowed himself his first, luxurious drink. Nothing had ever tasted better in his life than the warm, gritty canteen water.

Standing among the prone members of the taut-faced, sick-faced advance platoon—as if being wounded once, already, made him invulnerable to being hit again—he thought of leaving the rest of the canteen with them. They were not even one of his own platoons. But they had been without water since midmorning. He had only to wait to drink until he was back at the aid station.

Wacky from the concussion and from shock and fear, half-laughing and half-blubbering, standing on the wounded ankle he was still too much in medical shock even to know was hurt, the issue hung in the air in balance for a long moment. Then he took another drink, letting the water run out of the corners of his mouth luxuriously, and put the canteen away, back in its cover.

A number of them were looking at him, but there was no envy of his water on their faces. Perhaps there was a small envy of his wounding. Mainly there was a general look of sympathetic distaste. They wanted him to go away. He had been wounded, lucky bastard, he should leave. And quickly. They didn't want to look at him. They didn't want to be reminded.

Back on the hilltop he had sipped at the canteen until jeeped out, as most of the wounded around him were doing, while down below in the hot valley the waterless platoons bungled ahead.

This was the scene that kept presenting itself to Landers in the hospital bed. His mind seemed not to include the walk out, or the medical officer's examination, or the discovery of his mangled ankle. Only the canteen part. He would wake in the night under the dope and babble about it to the night medic on duty. Because, in his dream, the men of the platoon wanted his water, looking at him silently with beseeching eyes, and he, Landers, would not give it to them. The night medic could never understand what he was trying to say and would always bring him water, which he always refused to drink. When they stopped the dope, it went away and he had not thought about it again.

Not until just now, that is, Landers thought. In his berth. On this reeking hospital meat boat, with the news that they had sighted home. He sighed suddenly.

The two emplastered men had passed on along the Main Deck promenade going forward. Landers had pulled his head back in out of the breeze.

From inside, framed by the edges of the big, square port, the piece of dim blue coast was like a living painting. It seemed some kind of terrifying panacea to Landers, capable of remedying all your problems, but at a terrifying cost that would leave you permanently crippled.

The air inside was tranquil, quiet. Just outside the wind caused by the ship's passage still blew, and if he stuck out his arm his bathrobe sleeve would flap wildly. But Landers did not want to stick his arm out. The air of the long, deserted corridor gave a sense of security that washed against the feelings which fluttered wingless flutterings inside him.

He was just thinking of going to look up goddamned Mart Winch, just for someone to talk to, when a hallucination took him. Fixed him, the way a man is frozen by some kind of seizure.

Vision, illusion, waking daydream, dementia, whatever, Landers suddenly found himself outside the ship and moving up and away from it in the air.

He could look down and see the big red crosses on its white flank. There was no breeze now; the air was still. It was just as if a big helicopter was hook-lifting him away from the ship. Except there was no noise. Everything was silence. And he was hanging free and moving upward—until from a great height he looked down upon both the immensely diminished ship and a far distant shore.

Below him, slowly, the white ship moved soundlessly—and, curiously, with no smoke plume smudging the air—on toward its distant goal across the gently heaving blue expanse, whose swells ran on and on before the ship to crash in white, silent breakers against the far-off coast. The staring Landers knew that neither ship nor shore was inhabited, just as he knew the ship would never reach its coastal destination. The coast would gently recede, cunningly adjusting its movement to the ship's own speed, so that the distance between the two would remain the same forever in the bright warm cheerful sun—a sun that, strangely, did not move in the heavens and at the same time cast no shadows.

That the empty ship would never reach the empty continent did not matter. Indeed, Landers knew from somewhere that it was the ship's express purpose not to reach that shore. The ship itself was not even a ship any more but something else. And the unpeopled mysterious blue continent was—what? Landers did not know. But it was the most beautiful and serene and peaceful, and *right*, sight he had ever seen, and looking at it filled him with the greatest composure and sense of pleasure he had ever known.

Down below somewhere, he knew, another man called Marion Landers stood gazing with eyes widened in a trance. Landers knew that if that other man blinked the vision, dream, revelation, whatever it was, would disappear. But this could not scratch or dent his pleasure. That was part of it, too.

And far off, the white breakers clashed gently on the unpeopled sands of that long blue coast, where forests of great green-leafed trees and green supple grasses remained the only living things. That continent which, uninhabited, enigmatic, unfathomable and vast, loomed beckoning. And upon which no ship would ever make its landing.

Landers did not blink. He refused to. He would not let himself. But it didn't matter. Slowly he felt himself coming back into himself, anyway. He felt a part of him pouring back in slowly in a thick solid untrickling stream like liquid chocolate poured from a bowl. Then he did blink.

What was happening to him? A jerky panic ran all through him like a jolt of electricity. Slowly he turned away, and limped off to look for Winch. Somebody, anybody, to talk to.

But before he reached the top of the flight of ship's stairs to Promenade Deck, he had changed his mind. Winch was Landers' hero. And had been, since Landers was first assigned to the old Regular Army outfit, and because of his clerical knowledge been dragooned to work for Winch as clerk. But Winch would be no help to him in the things Landers was wrestling with now. And maybe no help to him ever. That was another new revelation.

So at the top of the stairs, he veered off and headed for the main lounge. Where Bobby Prell would certainly still be. Prell, all trussed up in traction like a chicken going to market, was not about to go on deck.

As he approached the door, Landers began preparing himself

for the soft sick smell that would engulf him. The only thing to do was to breathe it in, and not try to avoid it. As he opened the door, it hit him in the face with a warm, wet, slippery splash like glissading sewer water.

Then, as he stood still inside the door a moment, to get used to it, he saw the old company's former mess/sgt Johnny Stranger was leaning over the end of Prell's bunk halfway down the big room, laughing and talking.

After standing indecisively a moment, Landers opened the door and went back outside. He did not want to talk to Strange. He had not really wanted to talk to Prell. Rather hopelessly, but cautiously, he started back down the steep ship's stairs on his crutches.

Going down the steep, slippery iron stairs was even more dangerous than climbing them, to a man on crutches.

CHAPTER 4

They docked late that night, in San Diego. No one felt like sleeping, but it would have been impossible anyway. Dago was where the Navy and Marine Corps wounded were being taken off.

The little ship, dwarfed now by the Navy fighting ships nearby, blazed with lights. Shore-based stretcher-bearers and the whiteclad shipboard medics moved down the aisles and passageways, calling to each other in loud voices. Berth after berth in the staterooms and bed after bed in the main lounge were emptied, and the occupants carted away. Some of them were coming from as far away as the edge of the Indian Ocean, from Australia, from New Zealand. From New Guinea, the Solomons, the Coral Sea.

On shore under the dockside floodlights there was a great bustle, as ambulance after ambulance drove up, was loaded, and pulled off into the darkness. In the big harbor packed with wartime shipping, lights shone everywhere, on ships, in shore installations, from cars and buses and trucks.

And above the harbor the lights of the city blazed as if for a festive occasion, or as if welcoming the wounded home. To the men on board, used to blackouts and brownouts, the sight was breathtaking. Some began to weep again.

When the unloading was over, and the lights on board began to dim down again, a third of the berths and beds were empty. The rest, the Army personnel, would have to wait for San Francisco. Frisco was another two days run up the coast. Those last two days, in the partially empty ship, were going to seem the longest, and the worst. And everybody knew it.

John Strange certainly knew it. When things settled down, Strange made his way back to Bobby Prell's bed in the diminished-seeming main lounge. Strange leaned over Prell's bed foot again and tried hard one more time to think of something funny to say. He had hoped once again, because of the greatness of the occasion, to get Winch to come with him to visit Prell. If he had, it would be the first time. The first in fact since Winch had suddenly appeared at the Naval base hospital in the New Hebrides, on his way out apparently, but not looking wounded and not even looking particularly sick. Even back there, Winch had flatly refused to visit Prell or have anything to do with him.

Because of Prell, Strange had spent a lot of time in the ship's main lounge. They hadn't called him Mother Strange for nothing, back in the old company. But he had never gotten used to the lounge, or gotten so he did not feel uncomfortable in it.

Long afterward, Strange noted, they all of them still spoke about how during the voyage the main lounge was never far from anyone's thoughts. No matter where they went, or what Stateside hospital the post cards and letters came back from. They all of them said or wrote the same thing about the lounge. All of us, Strange thought. It was as if all of them, hunting, casting around, were trying to find the common factors that would hold the whole experience together for them. And the voyage was the final act of the play, the dividing line. Like the International Date Line, when they crossed it.

Among themselves, they had calculated that 13 percent were damaged bad enough to have to travel in the lounge. The statistics of being wounded fascinated Strange as much as they did the rest of them. And on board, it was their biggest game. Next to card playing. Blackjack. And poker.

Of the 13 percent of them in the lounge, one-fifth, or 2.6 per cent of the total, had to go into the extra-care unit. The 2.6 per cent were almost all lung wounds. Only about a sixth of them were abdominals or head wounds. Because the head wounds almost always died before they got on board, and the abdominals either died or recovered sufficiently to travel out in the open lounge with the others. Among the infantry, us infantry, Strange thought with a chief cook's smile, it was an interesting note that 75 percent of the lung wounds were caused by rifle or machinegun bullets, but only 50 percent of the abdominals were bullet wounds. They did not know why, and they did not know whether these figures also applied to other types of outfits.

Strange found it a well-run, put-together place, the main lounge. Once your nose got over its outrage at the smell. And once the dark part of your mind got over its supernatural, witches-and-broomstick feeling about it. The feeling that right here, traveling with you, was the true hell of your Christian grandmother. It even looked like it. Pincers, and needles, and tubes and scissors. With its working imps, and gory damned ones. All of them paying out or receiving the punishment for human sins. It could seem the repository, the collection-place and bank, of all human evil. It often gave Strange that feeling.

Strange was not a religious man. Or at least, not a very religious man. Better to say, a poorly religious man. Who wasn't much good at living up to it. But Strange believed in God. And believed he would pay someday for his lapses. And it was not too big a jump of the imagination for him to see the main lounge as the hell where he might someday be paying.

Like so many others, he carried a big reluctance to enter it or breathe its air, or even to touching the door handles that opened its doors. Out of a superstitious fear of contamination. But once you got past all that, it was remarkable how well it did and ran the things it was supposed to do and run. As no doubt hell did, too, Strange thought.

The extra-care unit was in one corner. It was cordoned off from the rest by curtain screens. Generally silence prevailed there. But all sorts of gruesome medical noises kept issuing from it. Enhanced perhaps by the silence. Liquid gurglings. Soft hissings of air. Louder air blasts. Peculiar tickings. Heavy breathing. No visitors were allowed in it.

If you wanted to carry the hell idea further, you could think of the extra-care unit as the seventh level of your grandma's Christian hell, Strange often thought. The lowest. The worst of all.

If it had not been for Prell, Strange might never have gotten to know the lounge as well as he did. He spent a good part of

every day in there with Prell, talking and laughing and trying
to cheer him up. He doubted if he would have done as much for
another man. Not in that lousy place. He hadn't even bothered
to look up Landers, Winch's clerk, during the voyage. But Landers was a wartime volunteer. And Prell—like Winch—was from
the old outfit.

Strange with his bad hand had preceded Winch by a week to
the Naval base hospital at Efate in the New Hebrides. And
when he left the company up in New Georgia, Winch to all
appearances had been healthy and in good shape. Bobby Prell
of course had preceded both of them by several weeks, when the
New Georgia campaign was getting up to its peak of fighting.

Strange would not have put it past Winch to simply decide he
had had enough combat, and simply have himself shipped out
back to America. Winch was perfectly capable of it, and Strange
was convinced he had enough pull to do it. If that was what he
decided he wanted to do.

Gossip around the New Hebrides base hospital said that
Winch had something wrong with his heart. Just as gossip in the
hospital had it that Prell was going to lose one or both of his legs.
But Winch did not look or act like a man who had had a heart
attack, any more than Bobby Prell looked or acted like a man
who was going to let them take off one or both of his legs.

Gossip around the hospital also had it that Prell was being
recommended for the Congressional Medal of Honor by the
Division's commander. But when Strange told this to Winch,
Winch only snorted with outraged disgust. If anybody knew
anything definite about Prell's potential recommendation, it
would be his own 1st/sgt, Winch. But Winch refused to admit
he had heard about it. Prell himself had heard nothing about it,
apparently. And Strange had felt that if he could get Winch to
back up the fact of the recommendation, it might do Prell a
world of good.

It was not that Prell was depressed, or defeated, or suicidal.
Or anything bad like that. That wasn't Prell's style, any more
than it was Winch's. Prell was just as mean and ornery as he'd
ever been. He'd always been a stubborn, proud West Virginia
hardhead, which was part of why Winch had never liked him.
It was why Strange liked him.

But underneath Prell's toughness about being wounded,
Strange was acute enough to sense a canker. A sort of well-
encrusted, walled-off cyst of despair. Which had hardened, and

been sealed off. But which might flare up. Or burst, and pour
out its morbid fluid. And if that happened, Prell would be in
trouble. Some news, even unconfirmed, about a Congressional
Medal would be damn good medicine for that.

But Winch was not about to come through with it, even if he
had it.

Strange had learned to live with Winch. It wasn't so hard. You
just had to understand that he was a little crazy, and make
allowances for it. In fact, just about everything good that had
happened to Strange in the past three years Winch had been
responsible for. Strange couldn't forget that.

Back in early 1940, when the old peacetime Division was
stationed inland at Schofield Barracks on Wahoo, long before
the sneak attack, Strange had been a second cook in the Coast
Artillery at Fort Kamemeha, with a 4th cl specialist's rating
and no prospect of advancement. Winch, who as a staff/sgt had
been in the same outfit with him at Fort Riley, Kansas five years
before, had come down to see him and invite him to transfer into
his infantry outfit at Schofield. It was a crazy thing to ask. Fort
Kam was close to Honolulu, and had its own swimming beaches,
and Strange was drawing down a spec 4's pay. But Winch had
promised him that within three months he would be mess/sgt
of his company. Winch had a mess/sgt he wanted to get rid of.
This was back in the days when mess/sgts and 1st/cooks reen-
listed in place, just to keep their jobs. Strange had accepted. And
Winch had come through. Exactly as he'd said.

The move had changed Strange's life. After his big jump in
pay, he had sent home to Texas for his girlfriend and brought
her out and married her. This was something Strange had not
expected to be able to do for another three years. But with the
grade of staff/sgt he could get married NCOs' allowances, and
quarters on the post. He had stopped his wild living, and spending his pay on booze and the whores and running around, and
had settled down. With Linda Sue with him it was easy. She had
even started them saving some money. By the end of 1941, when
the sneak attack came and the war, they had saved two thousand
dollars.

All of this had been directly due to Winch. Strange figured he
owed him more than he could ever hope to make up to him. And
if Winch wanted to be a nut and an eccentric, and do his crazy,
bitchy things every now and then, Strange was not going to
intervene and try to put him straight. Anyway intervening with

Winch was like trying to intervene with a force of nature like a line squall. You couldn't do it.

Between them (with a little help from some NCOs they had gotten made), they had turned Winch's company into one of the best the Division had had. Maybe the best the Division had ever had. Strange for one at least would never forget it the rest of his whole life. Now the war was ruining it. Mangling it, tearing it to shreds. But that was what it had been designed and put together for. It couldn't go on forever. And when he had left it, and then Winch left it, Strange was sure it had virtually ceased to exist. Their old outfit. But Strange would not forget it.

Whatever else, we were pros, Strange thought with grim satisfaction for the five-hundredth time. Whatever else they could say about us, we were professionals. He was unaware, again, that he had used the past tense.

And whatever the company was, it was crazy Mart Winch who had made it. Winch might be unorthodox, and cheat, and even be downright dishonest on occasion, in his methods. But the results he got were phenomenal, and amounted to a kind of crazy genius. Strange had to love him for that.

But if he was willing to back up Winch and make allowances for Winch, Strange also had a very special feeling about Bobby Prell.

There had been a couple of moments right after the war began in Wahoo when Strange had looked at his wife and regretted being married. Prell made him feel a little bit like that.

Strange had wanted to kick himself in the ass, for feeling that way about Linda. He had not even seen all that much of her, after the sneak attack. The company had moved out right away to defense positions. Soon after, all the wives and dependents had been sent back to the States. Twice before her ship left, he got an overnight pass from Winch to meet her in town in a hotel. Both times, with the war all around them, he had a sense of regret at having hurried into his marriage. It would have been so nice and easy and relaxed, if it had just been some hooker. Instead of all this weeping and carrying on about being parted. She had not understood why he wanted to stay, or why he felt the way he did about the company.

And Strange realized, that if he had only known this war was coming, he would not have married her in such a hurry.

It tore his heart for her to sail off home, but half of him was

relieved to see her go. He felt it would be different and like the
old days again, with her out of the way. But it wasn't. The one
time he had gone to the whores in town with a bunch of the
guys, after things loosened up in Wahoo, he had been both bored
and guilty. He no longer liked to go out on pass and get drunk
with the guys. And when the outfit arrived in Guadalcanal to
relieve the Marines, Strange found a new caution and new
thoughtfulness in him had replaced the old desire to take risks.
And he missed his wife terribly.

Not Prell, though. There had always been a streak of the
heroics-lover about Prell. With his unbending West Virginia
pride. Prell wasn't a gay carefree laughing-boy type. He was
dead responsible, and steady, cool, calculating. But he was vain
to a fault. He took bigger risks than the motorcycle-jockey,
wild-ass kind. He had done unbelievable things on the Canal.
Like walking all night through the jungle alone out beyond the
lines, to get back to the company which was cut off somewhere
a mile up ahead. And had never blinked an eye about it afterward. Strange envied him, even before the outfit left the Canal
for New Georgia.

Small, slight, with long hollows under his high cheekbones
and narrow eyes, Prell now was emaciated. There were huge
purple circles under the coalblack eyes. He had been broken
from sergeant twice in the past two years, the last time after the
Canal campaign ended. But before New Georgia, he had worked
his way back up to corporal. And to acting squad leader, in
addition. He was too good a soldier, and everybody knew it.
Then, to get all torn up in a crappy little campaign like New
Georgia. Back home in the States nobody had ever heard of New
Georgia, apparently.

Oddly enough, Prell was cheerful about being hit so bad,
more than Strange had ever seen him be about anything. As if
he felt it was required of him. He had raised his head up off the
pillow and grinned, behind the terrible fragile hollows under
his eyes, as Strange came up to the bed.

"Won't be long now, hunh?"

Strange made himself grin. "Two days they say. Two days,
and then the old Golden Gate, and the Bridge, and the old
Presidio." He looked around the lounge. "Looks pretty empty
in here."

"It was a big scene in here," Prell said. "People sniffling. And
crying."

"I bet. But not you."

"No, not me. I been around the Horn before."

"You been out and back. You're no cherry. And you wouldn't show it if you were."

"No. I wouldn't."

Strange squatted, a countryman's squat, his haunches on his heels. There were no chairs. There wasn't any room for chairs. Prell had, with a medic's help, rigged up a rearview mirror for himself out of a shaving mirror and some coat-hanger wire, so that he could see the part of the lounge that was behind him. Now he looked in his mirror, and shifted himself slightly with his elbows, before he spoke again. With his legs both hanging from the pulleys, he could only move himself a few inches.

"Goddamn bedsores are starting to kill me," he said. He paused, but only for a second. "How's Winch?"

"He's all right as far as I know. I don't see much of him."

"That son of a bitch will always be all right. As long as there's anything to steal. He hasn't been in here to see me once."

"Hasn't he?" Strange said. "I thought he said he was coming in to see you."

Prell's obsidian eyes looked up into his rearview mirror a moment, scanning the hall behind him. "Landers has been in to see me six times."

"He has? I haven't even seen Landers since we got on board. I ought to look him up."

Prell ignored that. "You've been in to see me seventeen times."

"I have? What are you, keeping some kind of a scoreboard or something?"

"I sure am. Sure, I am. I aint got anything much else to do," Prell said authoritatively.

"How's your crossword book coming?"

"I finished it."

"I'll have to rummage around, see if I can't find you another one."

Prell pressed his elbows into the bed, and moved himself an infinitesimal inch. "I'd appreciate it. It sounds kind of empty in here, doesn't it?"

"Yes," Strange said. "It does. I was just going to say the same thing." He raised himself up and looked around the lounge, again. There weren't all that many empty beds.

"They took out a little less than one-third. But it makes an awful difference with the acoustics," Prell said, watching him look. His voice got more casual, a little hollower. "Where do you think they're going to send us?"

"Got no idea," Strange said, squatting again, then sitting down. On the bare floor. "And nobody seems to know. Doesn't seem to be any system to it. They say they're supposed to send you to the hospital nearest your home. In principle. But that's only if you can get the medical service you need, there. If you can't, they send you where you can get the medical attention."

"That means they'll be splitting us all up," Prell said.

"Yeah. I suppose so."

"I don't like that. You'd think they'd know enough to send all the guys from one outfit someplace where they're together. At least until we all get used to it."

"I guess they aint got time to be worrying about shit like that," Strange said lightly.

"It's funny, you know," Prell said after a moment. "We never really knew what happens to them, after they get hit and leave the outfit. And now we're doing it ourselves. They get hit and they walk off the field, or get carried off, and that's just sort of the last we ever see of them. Some go to Efate, some to New Zealand, some to New Caledonia. And then they get flown or shipped back to the States and they—just sort of disappear into thin air. And we never know. And now it's happening to us."

"Some of the guys got a couple of post cards," Strange said.

"I know. Yeah. I ran into so-and-so at such-and-such. And such-and-so lost his arm. But we never knew what it was really like."

"Well, now we'll know, I guess."

"You'll probably go somewhere in Texas," Prell said. "I don't know where I'll go. Where will I go? I'm from down on the Big Sandy on the Kentucky border. But I aint been back there in twelve years. Wheeling? Washington? Baltimore? I don't even know where all the general hospitals are."

"You and me might wind up together after all," Strange grinned. "I won't go to Texas, I don't think. My wife's family all moved back to Kentucky, to work in the defense plants in Cincinnati. And she moved with them. I aint got any family left in Texas."

"I haven't any either in West Virginia," Prell said.

"You and me may wind up in Cincinnati."

"Where's Winch from?" Prell asked.

"Somewhere in New England, I think."

"That's good, anyway," Prell said. He settled himself in the bed with his elbows. "I think they're about to turn the lights out."

"Yes," Strange said. "I think so. I better get to going. It feels to me like maybe we're under way again. I'll stop in tomorrow."

"Don't do it if you don't feel like it," Prell said, stiffly.

Strange gave him a grin. "Okay. I won't. If I don't." He was already back on his feet. Down the way some of the medical personnel were stripping some of the emptied beds. The sight gave him a sudden lonely feeling. He waved his hand and walked away. At the big double swing doors he stopped and looked back.

A little over halfway down, Prell was watching him in his rearview mirror, and stuck his arm up in the air. Strange realized that if he had not looked back, Prell would probably have held that against him. He raised his arm in a wave and went outside onto the deck's promenade. As he walked, he clenched and unclenched his crippled hand, although it hurt to do it.

Something about Prell had the ability to make Strange feel guilty whenever he was around him. It certainly wasn't anything Prell did. But he always came away from Prell's bedside with an elevated sense of his own inadequacy. It was a rare feeling for Strange.

It was very similar to the feeling he had had when he looked at Linda back in Wahoo, after the war had started.

The glass windows of the deck's promenade were lined two deep with men watching the American shoreline in the night light. Strange stopped and watched them a long moment, still clenching and unclenching his bad hand, then walked on down the passageway.

Of all the woundings Strange knew about, Prell's was the best and the most enviable. The most warrior-like. The most soldierly, in any serious, valuable way. Leading his squad on a long jungle patrol he had *not* volunteered them for (Prell never volunteered his men for anything), and still a half a mile inside Jap territory on the way back, Prell had stumbled onto a troop concentration in a valley. The Japanese were in the middle of preparing an unsuspected attack, and with them was General Sasaki.

Sasaki was the Jap New Georgia commander, and his picture

had been circulated around the Division with a bounty placed on him. So Prell had sent his squad back along the trail and crawled in to try and get a shot at him. He hadn't. They had been discovered, and in the firefight and the run out he had been hit, and had lost two of his men killed and two others wounded. Bleeding badly and unable to walk at all, he nevertheless had organized the escape from the Jap search parties and the walk back, and had brought all fourteen men out including the two dead. He had delivered the intelligence report about the attack himself, before passing out.

It was for this patrol that the Division commander was reputedly recommending him for the Congressional Medal. And it was this patrol that Winch was down on him for.

Compared to that, Strange felt his own wounding had been little more than a dirty cosmic joke.

His had happened back on Guadalcanal. Way back. In January. It was just at the time when the company had successfully terminated its first big combat and first big attack against the Japs. Strange and a couple of his cook force had walked up with a resupply to visit the company. They were bivouacked on top of a hill they had taken two days before. Some staff colonel had named it the Sea Horse. They sat around on the slope talking, the guys filling Strange and his cooks in on all that had happened, and Strange had noticed how they were all somehow changed. He did not know exactly how they were changed. They just were different. Then suddenly there was the soft, almost soundless shu-shu-shu of mortars coming in, and someone squawked, and everyone hit the dirt. Strange threw himself flat. There was a yell from somewhere, during the explosions. When he sat back up, he noticed the palm of his hand was burning hot. A sharp, hot, toothy little piece of fragment half the size of your little fingernail had hit him in his palm between the knuckles of his middle fingers but hadn't come out the other side. There it was, sticking in his palm, just above the center. While the wounded man who had yelled was being taken care of, Strange started showing his hand around. He had been briefly terrified, his heart somewhere up between his ears, but when he found himself to be all right, and the man who was wounded was found to be okay, neither maimed nor killed, he began to laugh. And soon they were all laughing. It was a great joke, his hand. Mother Strange had come up to visit the company and had got himself a Purple Heart. There was no blood on his hand. The hot metal apparently had itself cauterized the wound. Carefully they pulled the piece of fragment out, and Strange put it in his pocket. No blood followed it out. There was only this longitudinal little blue slit. Like a miniature pussy, someone said. They took him around to the command post, everybody laughing, and showed it to the company commander to make sure of the Purple Heart and then a medic put a Band-Aid on it. A little later, still laughing, he and his two cooks left and walked back with another, returning resupply.

Later on, though, he hadn't laughed. When he thought about it, it was with a sense of irritated anger. What he remembered was the sense of fear, and the momentary feeling of total help-lessness. He hadn't liked either worth a damn.

Along the ship's promenade, Strange spotted a window that was empty and went over and stood and watched the American coastline himself for a while.

It was summer here back home, mid-August, and the glass was open. He pulled up the sleeves of his bathrobe and leaned on the glass and let the light breeze of passage along the glass riffle the hairs on his forearms.

It was enough to bring the fear back to him, just for him to think that if it had been a little harder, it would have gone right on through his hand; and if it had hit hard enough to do that, and had hit him in the head, he would be dead. And none of it meant a damn thing. Not to anyone but Johnny Stranger. It just hadn't happened to hit him in a vital spot, and that was all it meant. It was at that point that the irritated anger always rose up on him.

Each time he clenched and unclenched the hand it hurt him and inside his head he could hear it grate. The doc had said there was still a tiny piece of metal in it. And that a tendon was rolling over the piece of metal, or over a bone growth. But getting the metal out was the least of it. The trauma and continued use had caused a degenerative arthritis to set in in the hand, in the six months since he got it.

Studying the black, hilly shore, Strange drew a deep breath of the sea air, and then blew it back out into the sea airspace, through which the ship was again moving steadily now, across the flat uninhabited wastes of moving salt water. Strange was not at all averse to being home.

In the clear, calm, moonless night the shore and the sea seemed to be illumined by a lemon-pink night light that did not come from anywhere. Behind both the mountains made a black presence, visible only in silhouette, by the stars they blocked. Once, the lights of a city made a dull glow on the shore. And Strange thought of all the blackouts he had seen, as far south as New Caledonia.

After six months, he had let one of his cooks talk him into going on sick call with his hand. They had immediately clapped him in the hospital for evacuation, and had flown him out. In Efate they had said they would not even attempt to operate on it there. So they would have to send him home. The doc there said there were only a few men in the States who could do the operations. He would need more than one. It would be a long painful process, but he ought to have an 80 to 90 percent recovery, when it was finished. The whole thing was the result of his not having come in with it when it first occurred. He should have reported it when it happened. The doc went on to say that, fortunately, the Army would still do all this for him. And the government would pay for it all. But if he had been an industrial worker, his negligence would have cost him the insurance. Strange could not tell him he had been ashamed to report it, embarrassed to go to the hospital, where so many badly mangled men were lying stretched out moaning and would see him. He had only nodded, repeatedly, and said nothing.

Nor could he claim to anybody, even to himself, that he was miserable and unhappy when he heard all this terrible news about his hand.

Way back on the Canal, in the very beginning, Strange had decided early that he was not going to get his ass shot off unless it was absolutely necessary.

When the company went up into its first combat on Guadalcanal's Hill 52, everybody who could had grabbed his rifle and wanted to go along. Cooks and bakers, supplyroom men, drivers, clerks, and Strange and his kitchen force. Everybody wanted to be in combat. Two days of it was enough for Strange. Nobody but a nut would get himself shot at when he didn't have to. And when Strange left and went back down, most of his cooks and the supplyroom men went with him. The rest came down the next day. They were under no orders to stay up there. Their orders were to stay back in the rear and guard the company baggage and try to get hot food up to the men, and Strange saw to it that they did just that. They didn't have much luck with the hot food part. But they did keep the company's "A" and "B" bags from being rifled by a new outfit who had just arrived. And when the battalion moved up to New Georgia for the invasion, Strange had held himself to the same principle. He would follow his orders, and follow them to the letter. But no more. And he would see that everybody under him did the same. If their orders required them to go on up on the line in the New Georgia jungle, they would go. But not unless.

You could always get yourself knocked off in one of the air raids that came over every day. Without going up on the line to the company. But the percentages were minuscule, compared to what could happen to you up there with the company.

And Strange, like most intelligent men trained in the various logistics disciplines, had realized right away that the wins and losses of this war were going to be governed by industrial percentages and numerical averages, not by acts of individual heroism. And that included survival.

And yet he stayed. When at any moment he could have turned himself in with his bad hand and been evacuated, he had stayed. And even now he felt terrible about leaving. Strange was perceptive enough to understand the paradox of that.

At the window, Strange straightened up from watching the night sea and the dark coastline, and looked around. Most of the men were beginning to drift away, bored as the newness wore off of watching the homeland coast. He leaned down on his elbows again.

His move with Winch from Fort Kam to Schofield back there in Wahoo, and his subsequent marriage, had changed more than Strange's life. It had changed his ambitions. Strange spit out the window into the sea's airspace, and watched the breeze grab it. Or at least it had changed Linda Sue's ambitions. As Linda liked to say, she wasn't always going to be married to an Army staff/sgt. The two thousand dollars savings they had collected was going to be stashed away until after the war and then it was going to go into a restaurant and Strange, who up until two years before had always considered himself a thirty-year man in the Army, was going to become a restaurateur.

Linda had bought a car with the first of the money and taken a job downtown in Honolulu as cashier in a big restaurant, and started taking courses in restaurant management. As much of their joint savings had come from her salary as from Strange's pay. By the end of the fall of 1941 Strange was calculating that one more three-year hitch would do it for them. They'd be able to leave the Army, and give Linda Sue her restaurant.

Then the Japs had arrived in December, with their sneak attack. But the two thousand bucks was safe at home with Linda. And Linda was working and adding to it. She was also getting the biggest pay allotment Strange was allowed to send her, to add to the rest.

Strange had never told anybody in the company about the restaurant. Something about leaving the Army, and particularly about leaving the company, made him too uncomfortable. A couple of times he almost had told Winch. But Winch's reaction to the earlier news that he was getting married stopped him. Winch had hooted and howled and pranced around the orderly room, and roared with laughter and sneered at him with insulting contempt. It was the nearest he ever came to an open falling out with Winch.

He knew of course that Winch was married and had a wife somewhere. Or was divorced. Although apparently nobody else knew it. But back at Fort Riley Strange had seen the tall, long-necked, broad-hipped woman, Winch's wife, walking around the post. And the fact that Winch had not brought her to Wahoo with him indicated that something had happened to them. So once again he had given Winch the benefit of the doubt and made allowances for him.

Strange was aware that his reluctance to mention the restaurant was unusual. That the idea of quitting the Army for good embarrassed him and left him feeling uncomfortable. Sighing, he stood up straight again from the open window-port, his hand hurting. Most of the coast watchers were gone now. The ship was moving farther out from shore, and soon even the high mountains behind the coast would be unnoticeable.

The constant clenching and unclenching of his hand had caused a dull, deep ache in his palm, which had spread all across the hand, then up into his wrist and on up through the wrist into his forearm. He would have to ask the medic for a pill to sleep tonight.

In six months he could be out of the Army, if he played his cards right. This war was going to last a lot longer than that. Six months in the hospital, an operation or two, wasn't so very long. With his mustering-out pay, plus all his back pay and allowances, plus all the money Linda had been making working in the defense plants around Cincinnati, they could open the restaurant right there as soon as he got discharged. And get in on the wartime boom with it.

But the thought depressed him. At the same time that it made him both happy and glad, it depressed him.

And it hurt him physically, in his gut, to see Prell all trussed up that way. Prell was one of the people who should never be laid up like that. And yet Prell was one of the ones who would always get hurt the worst, and the most often, in his life. He was too young to know that, yet. Or maybe he was just learning it, now.

How old was Prell? Twenty-three or -four. Strange was twenty-seven.

Getting hit wasn't so bad. As long as you didn't get killed. It only took a second, and you didn't really feel anything. It was all that time afterward, that it took you to get over it, that really did you in.

After a last look out the window-port, Strange turned away and headed toward the iron stairs, thinking he ought to get to sleep, if he wanted to get up early and go see if there was anything he could do for Prell.

CHAPTER 5

They came in just at six o'clock. Behind them the sun was lowering in the west. It turned everything in front of them a reddish gold. The great red bridge with its great bellying bight of cable and flimsy-looking roadbed suspended under it, visible from miles away out at sea, was golden in the sun. So were the hills at both ends of it. It was indeed a golden gateway into America, its twin supports towering up. Time seemed to hang as the ship slid along, homing to it. Facing it, tough grizzled old troopers with years of service broke down. Restrictions limiting the open upper decks to officers had been removed and everyone who could hobble or crawl was up there on them. In the channel, the great stately bridge moved slowly, majestically toward them. As the ship passed under it, hooting its arrival blasts on the ship's horn, the heads of the men craned back to look straight up at it and a ragged cheer went up. Inside the bridge was home ground, and they had finally reached it. Inside the channel, first Alcatraz and then beyond it Angel Island and Fort McDowell, the place where most of them had started their Pacific voyaging, separated themselves from the bay coast behind. Along the starboard the Embarcadero glittered. The ship curved, then turned in slowly toward it. Behind the docks Telegraph Hill and Nob Hill made rising curves. Hungry eyes studied every detail. This scene was about all of San Francisco and the bay area that any of them, almost without exception, would get to see. If the owners of the eyes had known that, they would have studied each detail even more closely. At the docks Army and civilian ambulances were waiting for them, and continued to roll in in a long line. As the ship nosed in, ship's medical personnel began to move through the crowds of bathrobed men on the open upper decks, telling them to get below.

The main impression they got was one of enormous growth. Urban, industrial, maritime, civic. Even men who had only been gone six months, like Landers, thought they could see a difference. Whole new forests of smokestacks seemed to have sprouted. Industrial smoke seemed to have doubled. Shipping had tripled. Truck traffic had at least doubled. There were many more installations, and many more people, everywhere. To men who had been away one year, or two, or more, like Strange, it did not even seem the same city. Then they were whisked below, bundled ashore and hustled into the ambulances. From which they could see next to nothing. They were being moved around with all the ceremony of a stockyard delivery. Then, in a long string, aided by policemen and stopped traffic lights which halted all cross traffic, the ambulances headed for the Army's Letterman General. They traveled in convoys of twenty and thirty, with sufficient distance between to let the backed-up cross traffic through. Some of them made four and five trips. A few of the men, seated by the ambulance rear windows, caught glimpses of a city.

Forty-eight hours later the vast majority of them were on their way east, or south, the bulk of them by train, a few, like the Air Force boy with dry gangrene, by plane.

One of the men the reprocessing was hardest on was Bobby Prell. Although he said next to nothing about it, Prell was in constant pain from his legs. The pull of the traction he was in assured that. In addition, the slightest movement of the ship transmitted itself through the weights on his feet up his legs to his shattered thighs. During the voyage, he had lived in mortal terror of a storm at sea. Fortunately, the weather had stayed fine.

From the moment the ship nosed into the dock, Prell feeling each particular bump in a series of shocks through his broken bones, to the moment he was laid out in a hospital car berth on the train east, Prell and his legs were taken out of traction twice, carted ashore, jounced across Frisco in a seemingly springless damned ambulance, moved twice in a rolling bed to different wards, rattled to the train station in another springless ambulance, hoisted through a hospital car window to his berth. Only sheer stubbornness had kept him from crying out a dozen times. But he had made up his mind he was not going to let anybody see him blubbering.

He had seen nothing of San Francisco, and he had had no desire to.

From the time he had been wounded and had got his squad back inside the lines, he had been carded, tagged and stamped, indexed and inspected, numbered and catalogued increasingly the closer he got to home and any kind of civilization. In certain of his worst moments, it seemed to him it was more important to them that they keep track of him and not lose him than that they keep him alive. It seemed to Prell there ought to be a better way to treat men who had given their life and limb for their country, but there didn't seem to be any better way of handling it. If there was, nobody had figured it out. He had come almost to feel that he was actually a piece of that "living meat" the casualties on the ship jokingly so liked to refer to themselves as. But so far he had managed to keep his mouth shut about it.

He had already gone through two major operations, and been wired and screwed back together. And would apparently have to go through another, to get the wires and screws out of him. When the first group of doctors at Letterman examined him, one of the younger surgeons studied his file and whistled, then smiled with admiring disbelief the way a man might over a piece of brass sculpture hammered out by another. It gave Prell a certain thrill of pride.

Because Prell wasn't fighting only to save his legs; he was fighting to save his life. He had already made up his mind that if they took off his legs, he was going to kill himself. He would shoot himself in the head. Or perhaps in the heart. He hadn't decided which yet. But he certainly wasn't going to go on living around the clock in a Veterans' Hospital without any legs. Even if they took off only one of his legs, it would not be enough. He wouldn't live with one leg, either. He didn't have to do it, and he wasn't going to. So the way Prell figured it, he wasn't saving only just his legs. He was saving his whole life. And he wasn't particularly ready to die yet.

So at Letterman the young surgeon's reaction was a shot in the arm. It meant at the very least that there was still some hope. There was an indifferent impersonality in the admiring smile but that didn't matter to Prell since he knew the surgeon was looking at him as a job of work. He had no way of knowing how hard Prell had fought, and how many times, to keep them from amputating. Prell did not tell him. He compressed his lips and kept his mouth shut again. Nor did he mention all the incredible, unbelievable pain all the moving around had caused him. Prell was playing his cards, the bad hand he had been dealt, as tight and as close to his shirt as he could, and was taking no chances. The enormity of the pain might be a point in favor of amputation. The surgeon, however, seemed to know. All Prell had in front of him now, he said, was the three-day train trip, and then soon they would begin to be able to tell. Only three days on the train, then he could rest. The reason they were sending him so far, to Luxor, Tennessee, was because not only did they have one of the best orthopedics leg surgery teams there, they also had about the best postoperative team in the country.

"I can do it standing on my head, sir," Prell said cheerfully. But he was already sweating from the pushing and probing.

The doctor gave him back a funny, arrogant smile. "Let us hope you don't have to," he said, in a snobby superior way. Apparently he didn't like brash confidence in potential amputees. Prell didn't care, or even get angry, since this one wasn't going to be making any of the crucial decisions. Through the sweat on his upper lip and forehead, he made himself grin.

It was, however, a lot easier to talk about the train trip than to do it. High physical pain that did not cease could over a long enough period be supremely tiring. To both the body and the spirit. It could drain the will away like an open sewer vent. The two days of movement from the ship to Letterman to the train had taken an enormous toll from him, more than he had guessed, and by the time he was finally deposited, weak and sweating, in his berth in the hospital car at the station, Prell could only look ahead with a kind of stunned unbelief to the idea of three whole days in a jouncing, swaying train.

When you were very sick or very bad hurt, your very consciousness seemed to withdraw into the deep inside of you, until you were no longer aware, except vaguely, of any life outside of you. Bit by bit you were pushed further back into yourself by pain until your will was reduced to one simpleminded, sin-gleminded, dedicated thought, which in Prell's case was that he would not cry out. He would not make a sound. He knew if he did, he would begin to holler "Mama!" Or start begging them to take him off before the train started, back to Letterman and amputate the goddamned legs. It was like those slugs in the jungle that pulled in their eyestalks and shrank when you stepped near them or touched them with a cigarette. Prell had not had a mama since he was eleven. And he did not intend to give up the only pair of legs he'd ever had.

Then, finally, even that thought left him. He simply lay, si-lent, waiting for them to start, driven back to his uttermost, most basic, bedrock consciousness of existence.

It was almost like a—a religious experience. That was the only word Prell could think of to use. He might as easily have said mystical, but mystical was not a word Prell used except in crossword puzzles. So instead he used religious, lamely. It was as though the pain alone by itself had made him drunk. As though the pain, by slowly but effectively sealing him off from other awareness, had turned him inward in a total, uninterrupti-ble concentration as if he had passed through the outer yellow flame of a candle into its center, which was not hot but purple and cool. And in there with him in that cool center was an awareness of another presence. Somebody or some thing was in there with him. It, or she, or he (it was not a personality) did not do anything. It was not an added strength. It was not an aid. Nor was it a detriment. It was just there. Prell realized that what he missed most was Strange. Strange, or somebody from the com-pany. And it made him angry. Angry that they were not with him, and angry that he needed them to be.

The medics had filled him with as much dope as they safely could before bringing him down, and Prell lay in a kind of delirious euphoria, more pain-induced than dope-induced, wait-ing for the jolt in his legs of the train starting, and thought about the company. And about his squad. And about their last patrol.

There were many ramifications. The patrol itself was the patrol. But everything after it had been added on to compound and complexify it. Prell imagined, in his rapturous state, that he could see through it all clearly now.

The patrol was the least part. Prell had no scruples or misgiv-ings about the patrol. He had handled everything the best way he could. And no matter what anybody said, he had made no mistakes. The retreat with the dead and the wounded after they had been hit he had handled superbly. Just getting the dead out was a feat. Not many could have done it. And he had made fucking damn sure he got the intelligence message back accurately. He had given it himself. It had saved the Division a lot of men two days later.

The squad he felt less good about. But any qualms he had were not qualms of conscience. Nobody liked to see their buddies they had lived with get killed and shot up in front of them. Nobody liked to command, then. But in a firefight men got wounded, and they got killed. It was enough testimony and evidence about his squad, to see how they had all made a special trip to come down and say good-by to him before he was flown out. He had got out of it with two dead and two wounded out of fourteen men, not including himself. Not many noncoms could have done as well.

All the rest of it had started afterward. With Winch. Or if not with Winch, with somebody else and Winch had picked up on it. Simple jealousy. As far as Prell was concerned that was what it was, jealousy. Although how anybody could be jealous of a poor son of a bitch about to lose both legs, Prell could not figure.

It had really started with the battalion colonel. He too had made a special trip down to see him before he was flown out. And it was squatting beside Prell's cot in the big tent, with his aide and a couple of other men standing there to listen, that he had said he wanted Prell to know that he was going to recommend him for something. He didn't know what yet, but something. Prell had been in too much pain and too worried about whether he was going to lose his legs to give it much attention. He had said he didn't want any medal. But it had given him a certain thrill. He had thought, then, maybe a "V" Bronze Star, or maybe even a Silver Star.

Then it had been the regimental commander, at the New Hebrides Base Hospital. The Jap attack his patrol had forewarned them of, and the resulting battle, had brought enough casualties in the regiment that the regimental commander had decided to make a quick flying trip down to the New Hebrides to visit them. Beside Prell's bed in the big ward he had said his own office was recommending Prell for the Distinguished Service Cross. He would, he said, have liked to have a celebration, but since that was impossible with Prell in bed he had brought along an Australian imperial quart of Scotch whiskey as a present. Since Prell couldn't drink it, the American Naval nurse had taken it and kept it for him until after his second operation, when he could drink it. Or at least a part of it. After that he had become the prize pet pig of the hospital staff, the nurses, the ward boys, the doctors. And it was after that that the rumors went around the hospital that the Division was recommending him for the Congressional Medal. One of the nurses had told Prell. It could well have been that the regimental commander's visit, and the Distinguished Service Cross recommendation, had helped him a lot with the doctors in his fight to keep his legs. Prell had certainly used his new notoriety to aid him when he could.

A DSC was not something to snort at. Prell did not honestly think he deserved a DSC. He had told the regimental commander he didn't think he deserved it. Still, it would, as the regimental commander said, jokingly, look good up there on his chest alongside his two Purple Hearts. And Prell knew a Regular Army thirty-year soldier with a DSC could pretty much write his own ticket in any outfit he went to, after the war. As for the Congressional Medal, that was something in an entirely different category, and he simply put the rumor out of his mind. Prell was a conservative about decorations, and believed with the old-timers that if you were alive and there to receive it, you did not deserve any Medal of Honor. If he did not deserve a DSC, he certainly did not deserve any Medal of Honor. Besides, he was much too busy fighting with the doctors, and everybody, about his legs. The whole thing had faded away, and had been forgotten. Until Winch appeared.

Prell had already heard that Winch was calling him a glory-hunter. Somebody had brought it down from New Georgia. Then Winch had appeared in Efate, not wounded, not even looking especially sick. And had started saying the same thing there. People were always quick to bring you that kind of news; they loved it. Winch was saying Prell had lost two of his squad killed, and two others badly wounded, because he was trying to earn himself a medal for killing General Sasaki. Fortunately, Johnny Stranger had arrived a week before Winch.

There was little Prell could do. About anything. Lying there trussed up like a chicken, in his plaster casts and ropes and weights. He certainly couldn't get around much. Winch had come in to see him, once, just after he arrived. Winch almost had to. It was almost a necessity, if he didn't want to create a serious scandal. They had just looked at each other. Then Winch had given his sneering smile, and sort of contemptuously offered his hand. Prell had had to decide whether to take it. All his instincts told him to say, "Go fuck yourself." But he had to decide whether it would look better to take it, or look worse. If he did not take it, he was afraid it would look as if Winch's gossip and accusations were upsetting him. In the end he had taken it, shaken it once, and let go of it. After a just barely decent interval, and one question about his legs, Winch had left. Later, Prell wished he hadn't taken the hand.

If there was anybody around anywhere who knew whether the Division was recommending Prell for the Congressional Medal, it would be Prell's company commander up in New Georgia, and if the company commander knew, his 1st/sgt would certainly know, too. Prell literally would rather have died than ask Winch. Prell would not even mention it to Strange. Winch, if he knew, was not mentioning it to anyone in the Efate hospital.

Strange's arrival at the hospital a week before Winch was a big lucky break for Prell. Prell could tell, just from the way Strange treated him, that back up in the company in New Georgia, at least, nobody was thinking badly of him. No matter what Winch was saying. Strange thought Prell was some kind of a dumb hero, or something. Strange was a big help.

But all of that was just extra stuff added on the top. The patrol itself was still the patrol.

Whenever Prell thought of his squad and the patrol, a kind of fluttering qualm of apprehension rose in his stomach. It was not a qualm of conscience. It was a spasm of responsibility, dread and helplessness—a simple reflex to cry out No! no! It verged on panic. He always wanted to cry No! no!—and always, crying No! no! did not help or was too late. Their individual portraits flashed across the front of his mind like in-motion close-ups on a movie screen. A head turning sideways to grin. A shoulder rising beside a smiling face in a gesture. Then the anguished but clearly focused mental pictures he had of the hurt ones, each man of them, would follow. Dead, or dying, or wounded. He would never lose those. That horrible, Godawful clank that had given them away. A canteen, it had sounded like.

They were not even Prell's own squad. Prell had been moved

to them when the original squad leader was shipped home sick. But he found little to improve on or change. They worked well together without him.

The mission was to patrol out and seek contact. A large Jap force had moved away from the center of the line in front of Munda and couldn't be found. Specifically, they were to find out if the Japs had reoccupied a small steep valley on the right that they had previously abandoned but now, intelligence thought, might have moved back into.

It was an almost routine job. If you counted it ordinary and routine to be walking miles in enemy territory along jungle trails that might at any moment be trip-wired or foot-mined in a jungle too dense to travel off the trails. It was impossible to describe the fatigue and exhaustion of that kind of walking. The narrow foot trails slicked over with mud. The valley they were to inspect they found empty.

On the way back, on a hunch, Prell decided to take them on a little detour up a side trail, to look at a small side valley. The trail veered off to the left uphill two hundred yards through the jungle to a low ridge. And the trail had been heavily used lately. Both Prell and his point man sensed something was going on over there beyond the ridge.

Halfway to the top he halted the squad and he and his point man crawled on up to have a look. The valley was alive with Jap infantry. The opposite valley wall was a semicliff and there were some small caves and overhangs on it and Japs were crawling all over it. They obviously were preparing an attack.

Both of them recognized Sasaki immediately. It wasn't hard to recognize a Jap general. Whenever he said anything, everybody else jumped. Sasaki was a heavy-chested man, well-fed, with a thick graying British-officer-type mustache. His picture had been posted around the Division, and a reward of $1000 was being offered to the man who killed him. Prell and the others knew about him only that Imamura and Admiral Kusaka, joint commanders of the Jap Southeast Area, had sent General Noboru Sasaki to command all of New Georgia after the American invasion. It gave Prell a sudden thrill to know that he held the life of an important man in his hands, and had carte blanche to kill him. He knew how political assassins must feel. Sasaki was with a group of other men, obviously officers, and they were studying two maps. In addition, Sasaki was smoking a big, fat, very un-Oriental cigar. He walked back and forth gesticulating with the cigar as he declaimed to the others. Prell put the binoculars he had been issued for the mission on him, anyway, to be sure. It was him, all right.

A lot of things were going through Prell's mind at that moment. He was already getting down into prone position and loop sling to fire. First was the idea Sasaki might get away, walk off somewhere out of sight or into one of the caves, the way he was moving about. Second was the thought that he himself, Prell, was the best shot in the squad, in any case. Third, the New Georgia campaign and the possible effect on it if he succeeded. Only fourth, if at all, was the splintered fast flash of thought of the personal fame and that $1000 he might get by knocking off the Jap commander in New Georgia. Prell was absolutely certain about the thought sequence.

As he got into his sling, he was already whispering to his point man. To go back. Get them ready to move out. No, get them moving now. But quietly. No noise. When he heard the first shot, he should start them running.

Prell was not worried about how he himself would get out. He would get out, all right. If only to claim that reward. But it had already occurred to him it was odd that with a general like Sasaki present there were no outposts around.

Thank God the two of them had gotten off the trail into the undergrowth, before they peeked over the crest. Prell had never felt more fully and more joyously alive than at that moment.

With the point man moving, he rolled down to get his sight. He was satisfied he had done everything correctly. He had his men already moving out. Everything was proper. He had forgotten nothing. Now all he had to do was shoot. Hoo, man. He had not scored High Expert and high regimental rifle four years running for nothing. But he wished he had a 1903 Springfield for this shot, with its folding leaf sight, instead of a Garand. He should have kept the point man here with him as a witness to the kill.

Below him the general was still walking and gesticulating. He must remember to allow for shooting downhill. He moved the rifle ahead of the general, to where the officers with the maps were. The general would stop, just there, just when he came up to the map . . .

It was then that he heard the single, loud clank of American equipment somewhere on the trail behind him, and wanted to curse.

It stopped him. And he lost his sight picture. The general was moving away from the maps again. Well, he would catch him at the other end of his pacing, when he stopped to turn. Prell moved the rifle ahead of him again.

Then he heard—or sensed—the jungle plants move behind him, and a Jap soldier leaped on him screaming and firing his rifle.

It was amazing the Jap did not hit him, at that short range. It did not say much for their rifle training. Warned a fraction of a second ahead of time, Prell was already rolling, and fired three fast rounds into the man's chest as it touched his rifle barrel. Then he was on his feet ready to run. But nobody else was there. More firing and screaming was coming from back down the trail. It had the sound of catastrophe.

Prell cast one last, anguished glance behind him. There was no hope. The general was moving swiftly, into one of the caves, surrounded tightly by the bodies of the other officers, to protect him. There was nothing to do. Prell ran.

They were lucky. A big, well-prepared patrol would have killed them all, at once. Apparently the group that heard them was a small one of only five men, and had no help nearby. When he came running down, his men were just finishing killing the fifth. One of his men was slightly wounded. A nick. His own single Jap trooper apparently had been all alone.

Prell slowed long enough to yell at them to move. The ones in front were already running down the trail, and needed no urging. The others began to follow. "Move, move," he screamed at them. The Jap troops often called mortars down in on themselves, and Prell had anticipated it.

Mortar shells began to whump in around them. One man a little in front of Prell went down from a near direct hit. Prell and the man immediately in front of Prell, hardly pausing, scooped him up by the armpits and half-carried him. A man up ahead dropped back and took over Prell's half of him to free Prell. Prell paused, to make sure they were all in front of him and running, then turned around to fire rear guard, running backward. But no enemy were visible behind them on the trail. Another man went down from a mortar round but got up and ran on by himself. Then the patrol was apparently through the mortar screen. That was when the .50 caliber took them from the flank.

The Jap was firing from an obtuse angle to the line of the trail.

Fortunately, they had run nearly through his field of fire by the time he could get his gun going. Fortunately, most of them were already through. Only the men at the tail end caught the fire.

Prell, of course, was the last man. A burst caught him across the thighs, and cut him off from his legs and feeling them just as if a big scythe had swept through a field, and Prell knew he had had it, or if he hadn't, his legs certainly had. The impact seemed to fling him forward. As he started to fall, he watched the same burst, drifting higher, take the two men running downhill in front of him across the lower back and lungs, inches higher on the third man than on the second. There was no question they were killed. The third man was his point man, Crozier. Both bodies went on running several yards before they fell. Prell, his teeth clenched, by sheer force of will, helped along by the push of the heavy bullets, managed to run past them on his non-legs before he too folded up like thin cardboard and fell straight down on his face, headlong, sprawling. He had the curious impression that he was continuing still to run, horizontally, even as he struck. But as he fell his mind told him none of it really mattered anyway, because his mind told him he was finished.

He yelled and a couple of his squad ran back for him, in tandem, like a pair of matched, finely trained horses, and got him by his armpits. But in the same moment, miraculously, all firing stopped. The jungle quiet, always ominous, and never really quiet, which seemed to drip from the trees like moisture, fell on them.

They turned him over on his back. His number two crawled over. Their faces looked scared. "Well, let's see! Let's see!" Prell demanded irately. "Damn it!" He needed passionately to know. See for himself how bad it was. "Don't just sit there!" His number two and another man unbuckled his belt and began to pull his pants down. Prell, beginning to sweat as they moved him, sent two men back up the trail for the two dead. Crozier, and Sims. He was damned if he was going to leave them here, for the Japs to piss on, or eat, or whatever it was they did with their captured dead.

The legs were a mess, when they got his pants down. Like hamburger. It made his belly go cold inside, looking at them. The skin across his thighs was already turning blue from bruise. It was impossible to tell how many of the heavy .50 caliber bullets had hit him. He was bleeding badly. But there didn't seem to be any arterial bleeding. The first hopeful sign. His number two sprinkled sulfa powder on them and began tying on tight compresses. While he did, Prell briefed him, through clenched teeth, on what he had seen and on the presence of Sasaki, "In case anything should happen to me."

Prell knew he had to get them out of there. And do it swiftly. There wasn't anything he could do for Crozier and Sims, but he could still do something for the others. The other two wounded could walk, after a fashion. He himself couldn't walk, and he could feel the bones grate together in his legs. Two other men were already improvising a stretcher out of their buttoned-up fatigue blouses and two rifles. When they got him on it and hoisted him, Prell thought for a moment he would pass out. Then he got them moving and out of there.

As they moved away, mortar rounds began to drop singly around the trail junction, searching for them with tree bursts. By a matter of minutes he had anticipated them again.

As they moved along, the thought of the state of his legs made Prell's belly go cold again inside. You never considered how important your legs were to you until you didn't have them and couldn't call on them. There was no way you could move much at all, when you didn't have legs. It was then that he made up his mind that if he lost them, he wouldn't stay.

They knew they only had half a mile to go. But on the mud-slicked trail the going was difficult. For the walking wounded, the men carrying the dead and the men carrying Prell. Up to then Prell had not felt much pain, just a dull toothache in his legs that warned him the pain would be coming and he could depend on it. On the march, it came. With each step of the men carrying him he could feel the splintered ends of his femurs moving around in the already tortured flesh of his thighs like sharp instruments, further lacerating the already torn meat. He was worried one of them might cut its femoral artery, and tried to hold as still as possible. But it was impossible to be still. For Prell it was the beginning of an odyssey of movement and pain that would continue for two months and carry him halfway around the world to the Army hospital in Luxor. And the pain part wouldn't end then. He had put one of his BAR men back as rear guard and the other out front, to try to fend off any Jap patrols hunting for them. Luckily they did not meet any head-on. As they got nearer to their own lines, the trail branched out into a series of parallel trails and transverses that the Japs had built to supply their now-abandoned line. Here he could maneuver a little and give them the slip. Twice they hid, as talking Jap squads moved along nearby parallel trails looking for them. But the fatigue-blouse stretcher under Prell's legs was beginning to be soaked with his heavy bleeding. He went halfway out and came back several times. When they got within hailing distance of their own line, they decided they had better take a chance and yell for help.

A reinforced patrol with a medic in it came out to cover them while the medic worked on Prell and strung a plasma bottle on him, and then escorted them in, to everybody's vast relief and delight. At the battalion aid station the battalion surgeon looked at the legs and shook his head. Dolefully. He crudely splinted the legs to keep the femurs from working any more and had Prell strapped on a regular, real stretcher to be jeeped out. For Prell this was the end of it, and he knew it, at least with this outfit. He would probably never see this outfit again. There had been times when he had hated it, and every person in it, but now he hated to leave it. As they hung him on the body-loaded jeep, he kept his face set. He was flown out the next afternoon. The battalion commander gave the whole squad the morning off, to come down and see him. That did not sound as if anybody suspected him of misconduct.

It had not been a lucky patrol. All the same, Prell knew he had done everything right and correctly. He had done everything both according to the rules themselves, and according to the unwritten law that, unspoken, went along with the rules. The unwritten law was that you never risked your men. Unless the gain was worth it. Double worth it. In Prell's case the gain had been worth more than that. Even if it had never got realized.

At the aid station, while they splinted him up and took care of the other wounded, there was a lot of rehashing of the patrol by the healthy, and the subject of the loud clank that had given them away to the Japs came up. Prell only heard the first part of it. He made his report to the battalion commander, stressing the coming attack and how close he had come to getting Sasaki, and then, relaxing his control and aided by the shot the doc gave him, quietly passed out for a while. There was more rehashing in the Division hospital when the squad came down to say good-by to him, and the clank of equipment they had all heard came up again. None of them, nor the other wounded either, would admit to having been the cause of it.

Several men thought the point man, Crozier, had done it when he came running down to them. Perhaps one of the dead men, Crozier or Sims, had done it. If one had, both had certainly paid dearly for it. More than anyone could punish either for now. Prell could only think bitterly how that single clank had kept him from becoming famous, kept him from getting $1000, and how it might still cost him both of his legs. It probably had kept him from singlehandedly shortening the whole New Georgia campaign by a month. Because in the end, the cocky, strutty General Sasaki had put up an obstinate, gallant defense that was still going on in August, when they reached Frisco, and would go on into October. It was still winding down when Prell reached Luxor. He only heard of the end of it there. By that time he no longer really cared about New Georgia.

Prell had had a hard time of it, in the Division rear hospital, to keep from breaking down completely when the remnants of the squad—there were only nine now—filed out of the big tent after saying good-by. He had had to exercise all his considerable will power to keep tears from coming in his eyes. These nine men had saved his life. They had put together a makeshift stretcher for him without even being asked, and had carried him at least a mile along slippery trails, without being ordered to. At great risk to themselves. And without so much as one word of complaint or grumble. They had performed like princes. And they had saved him, and Prell hated to see them go away from him a last time. What they thought of him meant more to him than whether he ever got any medal, and they clearly thought well of him. For this, he loved them back.

In the railroad hospital car, the pain in his legs hurting him more than he could remember it ever had, he missed them deeply and he missed the company. At least on the ship he had had Strange and Landers to talk to once in a while. But after the shake-up at Letterman, he hadn't seen either again. He had caught one fleeting glimpse of Strange at a distance, ambling down a hospital corridor in a GI bathrobe. That was all. He did not know whether either of them was going to Luxor. In fact, both of them were on the train, in other cars up forward, but Prell had no way of knowing that. He knew that there were some members of the company at Luxor; he had heard it vaguely somewhere. He hoped he would be able to get together with them. Without the old company, Prell did not really feel he belonged anywhere. And he was beginning to suspect that that was the way it was going to be, from now on, and go on being. All that was past, and in the past, and every hour and every mile put it further and further behind them all.

As the train started, sending a painful jerk up his hurting legs to the broken thighs, Prell realized he had not even seen one building of all of San Francisco. Before, on his way through, he had picked up a girl downtown on Market Street, and spent two days with her screwing in a hotel. He wondered how she was, and what might have happened to her. As the train began to fall into its peculiar rhythm of movement and speed up, he shut his eyes.

CHAPTER 6

Winch was one of the few who did not have to go through the reprocessing. Almost before he was settled in, Winch found he had a friend in court at Letterman.

While the others were being sifted and sorted, and shunted from clerical team to clerical team, or hauled off in the ambulances down to their trains with their blue tags or green tags or yellow tags tied on their arms, Winch sat on his bed in a nearly empty ward and played solitaire or dealt himself poker hands, and waited for the three-day or five-day pass the hospital administration was sending down to him.

This was what came of knowing people in high places. Winch found it ironic. Most of the wounded from the ship would have given their eyeteeth to stay on, and get out into the town and taste again an American city. Winch had no desire to stay on, or to go on pass in the city. It was almost laughable. But Winch could not scare up enough good feelings in him to laugh. On the other hand, you didn't turn down an unexpected, gratuitous pass into San Francisco.

They had assigned him to the heart ward. For a check-out, they said. Winch had not been in it an hour, when a baby-faced

2nd/lt opened the door and stuck his head in, and asked if 1st/Sgt Winch was there. When Winch admitted he was, the boy handed him a sealed envelope. "I'll wait," the lieutenant said, "in case there's any answer, sir."

The envelope was a handsome one, with an embossed Letterman General return address on it and no stamps. "Deliver By Hand" was scrawled across the face. The letter inside it, when Winch unfolded it, was from old T.D. Hoggenbeck. Winch had known old T.D. in Fort Sam Houston six years before. Old T.D. had been a tech/sgt when Winch was serving his first tour as a newly made staff/sgt. Old T.D., nicknamed "Touchdown," naturally enough, was now a senior warrant officer, the typed signature showed, and sgt/maj of Personnel Records Section at Letterman. Winch should, "Come up and see [me] sometime," when he had nothing to do.

Sgt/maj of Personnel Records at Letterman was no mean, lousy job. God knew how many wounded passed through there. And each soldier's sacred Service Record booklet and 201 File had to go with him wherever he went, and could not be lost. The records a hospital ship carried for its wounded must have taken up almost as much room as the bodies.

"Sure, sir, any time. I'll take you up there right now if you want," the lieutenant said, when Winch asked him. "I can show you the way." Winch stared at him curiously, and only nodded. He was not used to being called "sir" by officers, however young. The lieutenant was authoritative enough with the ward boy and the nurse on the ward, though.

The corridors were jammed. Another ship was due in from New Guinea in a few days, and space had to be cleared, people had to be moved east to make room. When they got to the right building, making their way along through all the frenetically moving men in uniforms or bathrobes, the Personnel Records Section was on the top floor.

The office itself looked as big as a basketball court. There must easily have been fifty or sixty desks in it. Down at the other end, where the lieutenant led him, and where there was a plate-glass window through which old T.D. could look out over his toiling slaves, was old T.D.'s office. It was not a cubicle.

The w/o himself stood leaning his meager buttocks against his desk edge, his skinny arms folded over his thin chest. He must have seen them coming through the plate glass, but he made no move and said nothing, until the lieutenant had gone out and closed the door. Then he stood up and grinned. But he did not shake hands. Instead, he came forward with both arms out. With his two hands he took Winch by both shoulders, and shook him a little, and then embraced him, putting both arms clear around him. Watching with a cold curiosity, Winch wondered if T.D. was not actually going to get tears in his eyes.

"How are you, Mart old boy, how are you?" old T.D. said.

"Hello, T.D.," Winch said. "Looks like you got yourself a fair berth here. Even got second lieutenants to run errands for you."

"I got more than that," Hoggenbeck said, grinning, and went behind his desk, where he got out a bottle of Seagram's Seven Crown and two glasses. "See? I even remembered your brand." He did not bother to close the curtains over the plate glass. Winch was acutely aware of its openness behind them. "When I seen your name on that manifest, I sent somebody right out for a bottle." He paused to take a breath. "You fellows who are doing so much for us out there, you by God deserve every by God thing we can give you." Winch thought coldly that this time there actually were a few tears in the chicanerous old hypocrite's eyes. Probably they were even sincere. "Yes, I got a lot more than that," Hoggenbeck said, taking back up his first thread. "Second looies for office boys, and captains and majors for assistants. They're finally beginnin to realize just how valuable and important some of their old-time Regular noncoms are to this nation. There's more worthless commissions floating around, that don't know how to do nothing, than you can shake your dick at. Political commissions, that somebody bought for their kid or their cousin. They're full up to choking with them. Nobody knows what to do with 'em and men like me and you can just about write our own ticket. I got me a big house outside the Presidio, and buying another. Got a piece of the NCOs' Club. I'm in on a piece of the PX. Got a half interest in one of the gambling sheds. My wife's got a shop. I tell you the sky's just about the limit around here nowadays. The sky's not even the limit. They need us, Mart," old T.D. said, "they need us. Without us, nobody can run this damned civilian Army for them." He filled the glasses. "Here," he said, and poked one of them across the desk. "I knew your Division was out there. Relieved the 1st Marine on Guadalcanal. Then I saw your name on that boat roster, and you could of knocked me down." He drained his own glass. "Tell me, what's it like out there, Mart. Pretty rough? Hunh? Where were you hit?"

Winch thought his own mind must be deserting him, because he felt ice-cold all over. The whiskey in his glass seemed to have disappeared even before he touched the glass. Old T.D. refilled it. Winch's teeth clenched. He wanted to pick up the beautiful, precious bottle of Seven Crown and crown Hoggenbeck with it, split his skull. In full view of every eye on the other side of the plate glass.

"Pretty tough? Pretty rugged, hunh? Is it as rough as the papers say? Don't want to talk about it, eh?"

A picture of his blank-faced, fear-eyed platoons, bleeding and breathing mud for every yard of ground, passed across the inside of Winch's eyes. Through it, he studied his old drinking buddy, coldly. Icy. All of that had nothing to do with any of this, nothing at all.

"It's hell, T.D.," Winch said, straight-faced. "Real hell. They're great, tough fighters, those Japs. Rough. They're mean."

"I know they are, I know they are," T.D. said.

"And they know the jungle. But we'll lick them, T.D., we'll lick them," Winch said.

"I know we will, I know we will," old T.D. said.

Winch realized his second glass was gone. T.D. refilled it. And refilled his own. "That jungle's rough, hunh? Where did you get hit?"

"In the leg," Winch said.

"Was it bad?"

"It was pretty bad. In fact, it was terrible, T.D."

"Did you have a heart attack, too?"

"No, nothing like that. Just what they call a murmur. But the two, together. You know. And I was pretty sick, from dengue and malaria. I figured it ought to be enough to get me home, and that it was about time."

T.D. cackled, and his bushy eyebrows went up and down. "I figured, I figured," he giggled.

Winch winked, and then noted his third glass was gone. The straight, blended American whiskey, neat like that, was like the ambrosia of the gods. They could have all the Scotch in the world, if he could have one bottle of Seagram's Seven. Old T.D. pushed the bottle over to him.

"You help yourself," T.D. said. "I've got to keep my head about me. Got work to do. But you go ahead."

Winch shook his head.

"You always could drink more than me," T.D. said. "Or anybody." He grinned. Leaning back in his deluxe swivel chair, he told Winch what he wanted to do for him.

There was no need for Winch to go through the reprocessing. By evening T.D. would have a three-day or a five-day pass for him. A five-day, if he could slip it through. After that, Winch could have another five-day, and another. When he was ready to go east, Hoggenbeck would get him on an Army Transport Command plane and fly him, to any of the eastern hospitals he chose.

Winch, in his depression, had not even thought about San Francisco. Now he thought about it. "I haven't even got a uniform, T.D.," he said.

"They'll issue you a uniform!" T.D. grabbed a book of chits on his desk, and a pen.

"Oh. I know those hospital issue uniforms," Winch said. There seemed no way to escape from T.D.'s overeffusive generosity.

"Wear them outside the gate, and go to a tailor shop!" T.D. cried. "You can get an officer's tropical worsted with shoulder straps at any joint on Market Street for thirty-six bucks!" Did he have money? Otherwise, old T.D. would arrange it for him to draw a partial-pay voucher.

Winch said he had money.

"Then you're all fixed," T.D. cried. "For a fine time. I wish it was me. You won't believe this town, Mart. It's changed. It's like it must of been during the Gold Rush."

He'd be glad to invite him out to the house for dinner, T.D. added. But he was sure a quiet dinner with his old woman was not what Winch was looking for. Not after them jungles.

The petty stuff out of the way, Hoggenbeck hitched his chair closer and, grinning, said he had something else to tell him. When he had seen Winch's name on that early ship's roster, he had started doing a little exploring. He wanted to send Winch to the hospital in Luxor, Tennessee. The point was, T.D. could do just about anything he wanted to from here, with in-transit casuals. He knew Winch's wife was installed in St. Louis, and that might prove a big hitch. He had looked up Winch's records as soon as they came in. But if Winch did not mind not going to St. Louis, he thought he had something pretty good lined up for him.

"Between you and me, T.D.," Winch said, "I'd a whole lot

rather not go to St. Louis. And if my wife didn't receive any official notification about where I was sent, I wouldn't be disturbed at all."

"That can be handled, that can be handled," old T.D. said. "Notifications git lost."

The point was, Luxor, Tennessee, was also the headquarters of the Second Army Command. And Second Army Command would shortly be in need of a new sgt/maj for its Personnel G-1 office. Old Frank Maynard there was about on his last legs and they were going to retire him. Hoggenbeck was still in touch with a couple of his old commanding officers who were down there now, and had already spoken to them about Winch. The point was, when Winch came out of hospital at Luxor, if he went there, he would automatically go right into Second Army Command in any case. And from there it would be just a simple step. They could discover him. "If you're interested, Mart," old T.D. grinned, "I'll write them right away today. How about it?"

The point was, it was the kind of long-term, not very killing kind of a job—a sinecure, old T.D. said—that Winch or a man like him should have, and that Winch deserved. And it wouldn't hurt old Frank Maynard, because old Frank was going out anyway.

Winch looked up. It was one of those refined, delicate, shrewdly juggled pieces of old-Army-type manipulation, as finely balanced and calculated as any Winch had ever put together. As an old, professional manipulator himself, Winch had to admire it.

Winch had been nodding and hardly listening, but his ears and attention straightened up when he heard Luxor, Tennessee, mentioned. Luxor, he seemed to remember, was one of the places where a good-sized number of men from his old company happened to be congregated. He dimly recalled someone mentioning it. Then he pulled himself up short. It was he who had warned Johnny Stranger that all that of the company was finished and over. Still, it was a good deal old T.D. was proposing to him. It was exactly the kind of deal that, a few years back, before Guadalcanal, he used to dream of and imagine for himself. But he had imagined himself as old.

"Tell them I'd be very pleased to have it," he said.

"By God, I'll do just that," old T.D. said, and cracked his palms together. "You'll make junior warrant officer out of it within a year. That's great, boy, that's great."

Winch realized suddenly that, although it rankled, he was going to have to thank old T.D. Hoggenbeck for it.

"I'll tell you something, Mart," T.D. said. "I'm sitting pretty right now, and I know it. But I won't be for very long and I know that too, once this war gets over and we go back to anti-Army and the reaction sets in. But I aint going to stay in a full thirty years. Or twenty, if it's that. When it's over, I'm getting out. You'll be smart to do the same. I know what I am, and I know what I'm worth. And I know I'm valuable, for right now, anyway. And if there's anything I can do for any of my old buddies who've been out there and come back through here, I'm sure'n hell gonna do her. You're the first one to come back that I know of. If there's anything I can do more for you, don't you hesitate to pop up here and let me know it."

He rubbed his hands together. "Say, I'll tell you something else. Did you know you're getting the Distinguished Service Medal?"

Winch looked at him unbelievingly. "Who the hell did that?"

"Not me, not me. Don't look at me," T.D. said, enjoying his surprise. "There's some things I can't do. No. But it's all on your records. Recommended by your Division commander. With personal recommendations from your battalion commander and your company commander. And, of all people, your old Division surgeon."

Before Winch left, T.D. hauled out two flat pint bottles of the Seagram's and thrust them on him. "Stick 'em down inside your pajama belt, and hold them up with your bathrobe pockets. Go on, take 'em. No, don't thank me, Christ's sake. You fellows, you've been out there. That's all I need to know." At the door, he offered one last word of advice. "When you're set up down there, buy real estate. Buy a bar. You can't go wrong with a bar."

A little less than three hours later, not quite five hours after the ship had put her nose against the Embarcadero dock, while the others off her were finishing their warmed-over supper off compartmented tin plates, Winch was standing on the corner of Geary and Market at Lotta's Fountain with his hands in the pockets of an officer's tropical worsted with shoulder straps for thirty-six dollars, from a tailor joint on Market Street. He was already half drunk. It felt wonderful.

CHAPTER 7

The Mark Hopkins, of course, was the place to go. It was on the top of Nob Hill, and its "Top O' The Mark" was famous all over the South Pacific as the place to head for, if you ever got back home. Winch hailed a cab and headed there.

If you ever got back home. The very phrase, and all its insinuations, made the pit of Winch's stomach fall. Well, Winch was back home. Wasn't he? Fuck the rest of them. Winch sat back and looked out. In his mind was his constant admonition not to drink. Or smoke. He listened to both, constantly. Each time he took a drink or lit a cigarette he listened to them, he thought; and laughed out loud in the cab.

It was pretty hard not to drink around this place. Outside all the ritzy hotels they passed on their way up Nob Hill, parties of girls and sailors or girls and soldiers roared and hooted, or cackled out nighttime laughter, and went off up the streets playing kids' games. Everybody seemed so rich, with money to spare, and time to spend it. It was unbelievable. Winch thought suddenly of his waterless, gasping, sweating platoons. And his stomach sank down through him to somewhere in the vicinity of the soft, springy cab seat. Unbelievable. Again he had the disturbing feeling that all this had nothing to do with all that, out there. They were not connected. His momentary fine mood was gone.

The "Top O' The Mark" was a bust. Flyboys, both Naval and Air Force, dominated it. With their medals and decorations and Midway campaign ribbons. Fruit salad. And their crushed-wing officer's garrison caps. They hopped from table to table, and shouted with gay laughter, and danced jitterbugging dances, and bought bottles and bottles of champagne. And had apparently already usurped all the luxurious-looking women in the place. Winch wore no ribbons or insignia. In his pocket he had two brand-new 1st/sgt's chevrons, but at the last minute had not had them sewn on. Like an aging private, in his tailored officer's uniform he had no right to wear, he stood at a bar, had two drinks, and left and rode down to the street and went outside. He had been accosted twice, by two different but equally exquisite call girls wanting a hundred bucks a throw, and had talked for a minute to a cutely giggling upper-class college belle, who was whisked away to dance by an Air Force captain she called by the name Jim.

These were the only two types the "Top O' The Mark" had available. And Winch did not feel like buying the one, or spending the week of evenings it would cost to make out with the other. Apparently most of these people already knew each other.

Outside on the street Winch stopped a moment, then stepped back quickly to let a laughing party of girls and sailors go loping past. They went on into "The Mark." Winch turned down California Street, heading down the hill toward the honky-tonk and low bar area of North Beach. Momentarily he regretted not having taken on one of the hundred-dollar hookers. He had the money. And they were delicious. But it had happened to him too suddenly. For eleven months he had so stringently put women completely out of his mind that he was experiencing difficulty letting them back in again. It was all too fast.

With it so nearby, he decided to walk on down through Chinatown on Grant Avenue. It was a walk of about three-quarters of a mile, and it was all downhill, but by the time he got to the bottom he felt tired and worn-out.

Into North Beach, the number of bars multiplied swiftly. Servicemen were everywhere. Women were nearly everywhere. Jukebox music drifted out of the bars. It was like the last last-ditch, desperate dream of his badgered, beleaguered platoons, here, and his heart sank again. Winch figured he would have no difficulty finding himself some kind of lady friend before too long.

Winch had promised himself he would not have another drink until he got to Washington Square. But before he did, with the Square in sight up ahead, he broke the promise and stepped inside a bar. The single drink refreshed him, and put some energy back into him. It also raised his spirits. He was watching himself carefully, since those first three fast drinks in old T.D. Hoggenbeck's office. He was keeping the level of drinking up only to just that exact point where everything was painless and life was tolerable. But he did not want it to drop below that.

Back outside the music from the bar jukes drifted along the street. The Andrews Sisters rendition of "The Boogie-Woogie Bugle Boy of Company B" competed for attention momentarily with "I'm Gonna Buy a Paper Doll," sung by the Inkspots. Farther along, the Andrews Sisters faded, and Glenn Miller's "String of Pearls" came up strong from somewhere. Under it Winch heard a song he had never heard before, called "Paper Moon," sung also by the Inkspots, or perhaps the Mills Brothers. Winch drifted along with it, toward the Square.

He found her in the third bar. She was seated at a table with a girlfriend, who was with a drunken young Marine. She was obviously on the lookout for somebody, and sent Winch over an open smile of invitation where he stood at the crowded bar nursing a drink.

The two girls were around twenty-eight. Or thirty? Too old for a drunken nineteen-year-old Marine, who could not seem to get enough liquor down him. If he didn't slow it up, he was not going to be of any use to any lady. But that was her girlfriend's problem, not Arlette's, and Arlette made that quite plain. She also made it plain to Winch that everything was going to go by the proper rules of first meeting and seduction, and that she was not just some floozy.

The two women were dressed almost identically, which was to say mannishly, in slacks, and shirts open at the neck, with big kerchiefs tied around their heads, which advertised that they were workers. Like hundreds of others Winch had seen since crossing Pacific Avenue. It was almost a uniform. Winch had even read about it, in old, fifth-hand, mud-stained copies of Pacific *Yank*.

She was a welder. In some machine manufacturing plant over

in Oakland, that was classified as Defense Industry. So was her chum. She was no raving, beautiful lovely, like the two exquisite call girls at the "Top O' The Mark," but Winch did not think he could have tolerated a real lovely at this point, this first time, and she was attractive enough. She was also married. There was no ring on her finger, but there was the white mark where there had been one until very recently.

Winch's stomach sank again. A kind of suspicious fear seized him. What if she was the wife of one of his own bemired, panting, mud-marked draftees? He thought he had some from northern California. Seeing him looking, she rummaged in her purse and giving him a sad, grim little smile, slipped the ring back on.

She wanted to dance. Winch moved her stiffly around in the press on the postage-stamp-sized dance floor. Winch was normally a good ballroom dancer, but there was nowhere to move on the crowded floor, and anyway Arlette was clearly not one. It did not matter. He welcomed the chance to dance; it gave him time to get his nerve back. What did he care if her husband was some poor draftee son of a bitch? Back at the table he bought her more drinks and listened to her talk, mostly about her work. Arlette loved welding.

At one point her friend's drunken young Marine, who wore a Rifle Sharpshooter's medal, glanced up from his booze and studied Winch's Army uniform and lack of ribbons or insignia with contempt and belligerence. Winch bent on him his hard, official, on-duty 1st/sgt's stare, which seemed to touch some well-trained, still-unnumbed nerve in the boy. Because he suddenly straightened up in his chair and felt for his necktie with panic-wide eyes, before putting his face back in his glass.

At the hotel, which was right around the corner and apparently had some deal going with the bartender of the bar, after they had visited a package store for liquor and were getting undressed, Winch asked her about the husband. He felt he had to, though he already had his shirt off. The guy was out there, all right. He was not in the Solomons, though, Winch was relieved to learn. He was in New Guinea. But Jesus, New Guinea. Buna! Gona! Morobe! Hell, they were in Salamaua right now. But the guy was not in the 32nd or 41st Divisions. He was in the Signal Corps. Not the infantry. Winch felt a little better. But still it made him angry at her. "Doesn't it make you feel a little bit like a shit?" he said.

Arlette's eyes flared. "No, it doesn't make me feel like a shit! Why should it? We made an agreement before he left. What do you care?"

"I don't care."

"Well, good for you. Then shut up. Why should I feel like a shit? He's out there getting all he can get. Everything he can get his hands on, while he's out there."

"There's nothing to get," Winch said. "Except a bunch of scrofulous natives nobody wants."

"He was in Australia," Arlette said.

"Well, Australia," Winch had to admit. "Their men are all in North Africa. I hear Australia's great. But I was never there."

"Are you trying to talk yourself out of a lay?" Arlette demanded. "For some reason?"

"No," Winch said. But he had to think about that a minute.

"Because if you are, you're doing a pretty damn good job of it. You're from somewhere out there yourself, too, aren't you?" Winch nodded. "I knew you were, damn it. I knew it. I knew it the minute I saw you in that bar, without any ribbons or insignia or rank markings on your uniform. But that expensive, tailor-made uniform, it fooled me. Listen, nothing ever stopped him any before, when he was here at home, before the war," Arlette said. "Before the Army. I'll tell you something else."

It was as though Winch had opened some floodgate. Nude to her panties, she began to scold at him, exactly like a legal wife, her bare breasts jiggling violently with her vehemence. Going right on ahead and stripping off the panties, and exposing a gorgeously luxurious bush, she went right on with her tirade, about all the unfair practices women had to suffer.

Winch had heard most of them before. Most were fair enough complaints. Hers had mostly to do with work, and work habits. All her life she had never been allowed to work, to do anything, all her life she had had to sit at home, like some hothouse flower, until this damned war of theirs came along, and they all went off to play soldier. Well, they should never have let her get the taste for it. Because she loved working. They were going to have a damned hard time taking it away from her again, after their damned war was over. Winch could easily have sympathized with her. But he was angry with her, for what she was doing to her husband. And he didn't see what any of it had to do with anything. He stopped listening, and concentrated on looking at

her deliciously jouncing breasts and her gorgeously hairy, gorgeously gropable crotch as she flounced back and forth in front
of him.

Abruptly, she stopped. And looked embarrassed. As if suddenly surprised to find she was nude. "I'm acting pretty silly,
aren't I?" She smiled.

Winch just looked at her. "I don't know," he said, honestly
enough. It suddenly occurred to him that she was exactly like
old T. D. Hoggenbeck. She did not understand anything at all
about any of it. They could not get it through their thick heads
that all that out there had absolutely nothing to do with any of
this back here. Suddenly he wanted to split her head open with
the bottle, in the same way he had wanted to smash Hoggenbeck.

"Did you really just get back from out there?" she asked. She
was a thin woman, Arlette. Almost bony. But not angular. Her
well-defined breasts hung straight from her lean armpits without any fat supporting the skin. The hair-covered labia of her
crotch hung a little loosely, not tucked up tight underneath her,
like a girl's, as though they had received their full share of wear
and tear. Winch could feel all the rigorously suppressed lusts of
eleven months welling up in him.

"And you haven't had a woman since—? For how long?"

She came immediately and sat nude on his knee and ran her
hand through his hair. "Oh you poor darling." Winch did not
know whether to seize her and beat her head on the wall till he
beat some sense into her, or to fuck her cross-eyed.

A sudden light of understanding dawned on her face. "You
arrived today? Then, you were on that boat, that hospital ship,
that pulled in today!" She got off his knee and stood staring at
him. "Listen, you haven't got anything wrong with you, have
you? Is there anything wrong with you? I mean, you haven't got
an artificial leg or anything, or something like that, have you?"

Winch stood up himself, and dropped his pants and stepped
out of them. He didn't wear underpants with khakis. "I had a
girlfriend once who—" Arlette began. Winch interrupted her.
"A guy with an artificial leg has straps across the chest, for
Christ's sake." Then he noticed that in taking off his pants, the
two new 1st/sgt's chevrons had slipped out of his pocket onto
the floor. It was too late to retrieve them.

She picked them up off the hooked rug. "You're a *first* sergeant?" She smoothed them out in her palm. "Why didn't you have them sewn on?"

"I don't know," Winch said, "it didn't seem important. Because they're new, I guess," he added. They were sitting on the sheets, somewhere along the bed's edge. Arlette rolled over into it. She positioned herself firmly in the middle of it, opening wide her legs, as if ready and preparing to receive an actively violent, murderous assault. Winch accommodated her. He drove his cock, and redrove it, into her with all hate and fury and anger and rage, and outrage, that had been accumulating in him a long time. This did not disturb her a bit. It seemed only to make her happier. "Oh God, I love to fuck," she said from under him in a clear voice. Winch however did not last long. Eleven months of denial were too much for him. Then it seemed he went blind and that his eardrums blew out. Arlette, though, was not upset. She seemed to understand, and patted his shoulder. "That's all right, that's all right, we've got plenty of time," she said soothingly.

Winch simply stared at her, and lying beside her leaning on his elbow, fondled the one of her breasts nearest him, although his hand felt awkward and unfamiliar doing it. His stomach sank in him again. At being here with her like this. It was so unfair to all the others. He again suddenly wanted to punch her face. Instead, he put his hand, which seemed to have forgotten all about how to do this too, down between her legs. Winch felt exactly as if somebody had split him in twain with an ax, and he was desperately striving to pull the two parts of him back together.

After a while he sat up, and got up out of the bed and went to get himself a drink. He felt tired and worn-down and winded.

"Make me one, too." She smiled at him from the bed. "I told you the truth, about having plenty of time." She explained that her crew at the plant was just coming off night shift and going on to swing shift, so they had a full day and a half off before going back on to afternoons. "But what the hell," she said, "I don't give a damn, I'll take a couple more days off AWOL, and spend the rest of your pass with you. If you want me to. They can't fire me for it. They need people too bad. And I'm too good at my job."

Winch grinned briefly at the wall, over the shocking suddenness with which people would arbitrarily piece together and glue up an alliance between them, just out of having been to bed together once.

If it lasted a week, they called it love.

But her offer had given him an idea. If he was going to have to give up drinking definitively and finally, he ought to have himself one last fling, one last bender, to celebrate the final separation. Final separation from the booze, and final separation from the company. What better place to do it than San Francisco. What better companion to do it with than Arlette.

He brought her drink back to her in the bed, and sat down on the bed edge, and smiled at her. "All right, we'll have ourselves a time."

It was like one of those ideas that kept flirting around the edges of your mind, but needed a special event or special statement to bring it into awareness. It seemed to him now he had had it ever since he first stood in Hoggenbeck's office. On the other hand he knew he was drinking too much. But he didn't give a damn. Winch was well aware of the theorem that will power to resist booze diminished in direct proportion to the number of ounces consumed. In fact, he had made a serious life study of it. And he was aware that he had been boozing it up pretty heavy on the ship during the passage. He had had a fair number of drinks today. But what the hell, on the other hand he felt fine. The only thing wrong with him at all was a slight cold he had picked up on board the ship, and the slight, persistent cough it had left with him. He slid off the bed edge and reached over the bottle for them. Secretly, he was thinking that if he could only get her into some kind of a dress, he would take her to the "Top O' The Mark."

"Have you got any kids?" he said.

She stared at him. "Kids? Yes, I've got kids. I've got two kids. They live with their grandmother. My mother. She's got a house. We couldn't live on what I get for an allotment."

"Don't you think they need you?" Winch said.

"They see all of me they need to see," she said sullenly.

She suddenly looked angry again. Winch didn't want that to happen.

"Arlette, honey, we'll have us a ball, you and me," he smiled.

By the next afternoon he had made a public speech in Washington Square, nearly gotten picked up by the MPs for it, and his cold had developed into a serious bronchitis.

Arlette had gone out up to Chinatown to get them a Chinese

dinner to bring back to the hotel. Winch decided to go out and do a little bar-crawling on his own. It was coming back to the hotel past the Square, after three or four bars and three or four drinks, that he got the idea to make the speech.

It was all the old duffers on their soapboxes, droning out their worn-out, ancient, old-fashioned political speeches that gave him the idea. Socialism. Unionism. Communalism. And Winch thought with a snort, Why not? Although he had siphoned a huge amount of it off into Arlette, there was still a thin, ashy residue of outrage left in him. He walked over to one of the old duffers and gave him a five-dollar bill to borrow his soapbox.

The concept for it was one he had had quite a while. It had occurred to him first on Guadalcanal, last year, lying up under a mortar barrage. He had developed and expanded it later, playing with it at times when he sat alone drinking, or watched from a ridge with the company commander as their overheated, mud-breathing platoons tried to advance. He had summarized the whole concept in the slogan he worked out for it. *"Soldiers of the world, unite! You have nothing to lose but your guns!"* That was what he began to shout from the soapbox.

A crowd of amused servicemen formed fairly quickly. At first they were laughing, and cheering him on, but some began to get disturbed as he went on. "Hey, you," he singled out a private. "What are you making a month? Thirty-eight bucks, right? What do you think you'd be making if we were organized, hah? No, don't laugh. Think about it. What couldn't we do, if we were organized? Every country needs us, right? Everybody else has unions, why not us? Jap soldiers, German soldiers, English soldiers, US soldiers. Russians, French, Australians. All united. We'd corner the market. Hell, we could take the explosive charges out of the mortar shells and artillery! Put white flour in them instead! How would that be?" A couple of derogatory whistles came from the back of the crowd. "You don't like that? Why not? No more casualties!" Winch bellowed in his command voice. "You simply walk to the rear. We could have arbitration committees to decide where the battles would be held." He spread his arms. "No more jungles, right? Who'd pick a jungle?"

"What are you? A Communist?" a voice yelled from the rear. "They're our enemies."

"Me? Hell, no. Look at me. I'm a first sergeant. Look at my stripes," Winch yelled. (Arlette had wanted to sew them on, and he had let her; she was so proud of them.) "But I'm more like a Jap first sergeant or a German first sergeant than I am like these civilian sons of bitches." That brought cheers. "And you! You know what I make a month? You could be making that as a private, if we were organized."

He saw the MPs coming through the crowd, pushing their way up toward him, and drew himself up to full height. "Soldiers of the world! Unite! I'll be back. Same time tomorrow." And jumped down off the box and fled.

Whistles and good-natured cheers and a lot of handclapping followed him.

It was only fifty yards to get into the narrow streets where he could hide and sneak off, but by the time he had run it he was astonished to find he was gasping for breath and had to stop. In an alley. He simply could not go on. A violent fit of coughing seized him. Fortunately, a number of the GIs had gotten themselves in front of the MPs, and impeded their progress. In his alley Winch was coughing up strings of foamy white mucus. But after a few minutes he was able to make it around a corner and into a bar and order a drink. The drink seemed to help.

He made it back to the hotel. But then he thought he wasn't going to make it up the three flights of stairs to their third-floor room. He had to stop and gasp at every landing.

When he got to the door, Arlette was there looking horrified, and the Chinese food was in cardboard containers on the table. All piping hot and waiting.

"Good God, I could hear you all the way up the stairs. What's happened to you?"

"Nothing," Winch said hollowly, and leaned on the door and stared at her. "A little touch of bronchitis. Nothing a good Chinese dinner, a few drinks and a fine fuck won't cure. Don't worry about it."

And, indeed, after he sat in a chair and rested awhile, he felt much better. They ate the Chinese dinner, had the drinks, and accomplished the sexual assignation. Winch felt fine. The whole attack, which seemed to have been brought on by the fifty-yard run out of the Square, seemed to have disappeared. But then in the night another coughing fit seized him, and he woke up unable to breathe. No matter how hard he pulled, he could not seem to get air down into his lungs. When he coughed, he brought up the same foamy white froth. A couple of drinks were the only thing that seemed to help it. But then when he lay down to sleep, he found he could not breathe lying down. He wound up spending most of the night sleeping sitting straight up in a chair.

Arlette, when she wasn't sleeping, or drinking or screwing Winch, worried about it, and about him. But whatever it was, the bronchitis did not seem to impair his ability to screw. But then in the morning, when they went out for breakfast, he almost did not make it back up the three flights of stairs. He wouldn't have made it, if Arlette hadn't helped him. After that, he did not go out, and let Arlette go out by herself when she wanted to go out.

He stuck it out like that for two days, but in the middle of the third night he knew he had had it. He had spent most of it leaning on his elbows on two corner towel racks in the bathroom, unable to breathe, coughing up the frothy white stuff.

"I'm going to have to go back to the hospital," he told her hollowly. "There's nothing else for it. Will you help me? I hate to ask you, but I don't think I can make it by myself."

"Of course I'll help you," Arlette said, frowning at him. "You're bad sick, you know. Anyway, I have to be getting back to my job myself."

"Then go down and call a cab."

They said little in the cab. Once Arlette took hold of his hand and held it, and leaned over and kissed him. "I put my address and phone number in your shirt pocket," she said.

"Expect me when you see me," Winch said hollowly. "They're going to be shipping me out of here someplace east."

At the hospital entrance he turned back to look at her a last time and wave. Standing by the cab, she waved back, and got in and shut the door. Winch watched her white face at the dark cab window as it pulled away.

There was a look about the set of her head on her neck which said she was glad to be going, and made Winch grin.

"Well, what have we here?" the young doc on duty said, when the orderly brought him into the emergency.

"I dunno," Winch said hollowly. "Bronchitis. You better put me in bed for a day or two. But I've got to see W/O Hoggenbeck. I'm supposed to be shipping out of here for Luxor, Tennessee."

The young doctor checked his pulse and then looked up sharply.

"My orders are already cut," Winch said. "I'm going to Luxor, Tennessee."

The doctor put his stethoscope under his shirt and listened to his heart, and then to his lungs. "Bronchitis, hell," he said. "You're in acute congestive heart failure, man. You're not going anywhere."

"Heart failure?"

"Your lungs are full of fluid," the doctor said. "Water. You're drowning."

"I'm going to Tennessee," Winch said tiredly, but stubbornly. "Luxor. Hoggenbeck knows all about it."

"I'm putting you to bedrest," the doctor said. "And a diet of diuretics. Jesus, your heart must be as big as a football. You're not going anywhere for quite a while."

Winch could only shut his eyes. He was too exhausted to argue.

BOOK TWO

THE HOSPITAL

CHAPTER 8

The hospital was out in the eastern suburbs. Luxor had no
western suburbs. Founded in 1820 and built on a bluff along the
mile-wide Mississippi, its modern downtown business and
shopping district lay right against the river. The Mississippi
barred western expansion. Coming toward it across the flats in
Arkansas on the train, its blocks of downtown buildings on their
bluff looked like the forward edge of some tidal wave of ma-
sonry, pushing against the sky. On the long bridge over the
river, the sounds of the wheel thumps slowing as the train
slowed, the skyline had a metropolitan allure. Women existed
there. And bars, and hotels, and restaurants. Even the badly
hurt were aware of them. The wounded who were getting off
were especially aware.

Their train trip had lasted nearly five full days, not three.
From Reno on, every man aboard was thoroughly exhausted.
Rolling constantly, they stopped only to unload patients. At
Kansas City the entire train was split into two trains. One
headed east and north to St. Louis and Chicago. The other came
south through Fort Scott, Springfield, and finally to Luxor. And
it was going on to Atlanta.

Just the logistics studies alone, that were required on a national scale to facilitate such a move, were staggering to think of. And another train made the same trip or a variation every week.

Bobby Prell had managed to hang on mainly by gritting his teeth and never crying out, and by squeezing his eyes tight shut when he knew he was alone. He also lied to himself shamelessly. He told himself that soon he would be able to rest. Soon the torment in his tortured legs would stop. Prell himself didn't believe a word of it. This train trip more than anything had made him realize suddenly that, even if he did manage to save his legs, the pain would probably never stop anyway. It would be his constant, loving companion probably the rest of his whole life. This was something pretty dire to think about. What it really meant was that his life was over either way, in any case —at least, the active physically vigorous life he had lived before, was over. That had stopped, at that exact moment on the hill near Munda, running down that muddy trail, in the same way as if some antique grandfather's clock had stopped. Having realized it, Prell refused to think about it and suffered on in silence. Silence had become his lucky talisman. The dope the medics kept him full of helped some. But whenever he dropped off to sleep, he was afflicted with a new, recurrent nightmare. One or two or several members of one of his squads (he had had three) would appear in his dream, and with sorrowful smiles would accuse him of errors in his handling of them that he had not committed. Sometimes it was the dead or the wounded who appeared, sometimes the healthy living. Always he was unable to convince them otherwise, and would wake up full of undigested horror. Then he would lie and listen to the slap of the steel wheels, and feel the movement of the train in his weak, still-unknitted bones.

When the medic came to tell Prell they were pulling into Luxor, and that he would soon be resting in Kilrainey Army General, Prell could not honestly say whether he was glad, or sorry.

Eight cars up ahead, Marion Landers felt the train slow further as they came off the bridge. Below it, he caught a glimpse of the famous Luxor levee, an enormous expanse of tilted concrete stretching away. Then the train slid curving into the dirty yards of the main downtown station. Stretcher-bearers, ambulance men, medical officers—and this time, Red Cross women in gray uniforms—lined the quays. This time, there were Army trucks for the walking wounded. Landers was ticked off as one of them. Eighteen vehicles, ambulances and trucks, were strung out in the convoy as it moved east out of the grimy station.

In the truck Landers stood, holding on to the truck ribs. His crutches clamped under his arms, he watched the rich-looking, affluent, clean American city roll past them in the sunny summer air, and did not know if he was happy, or angry and jealous. Well-off-looking men and women in summer clothes stopped on the streets to wave at them. One well-stacked girl with shoulder-length blonde hair, walking with two girlfriends, stopped and, laughing with white white teeth, put her arms over her head and did a couple of bumps and grinds for them. Landers wanted to throttle her, but the damaged men in their maroon bathrobes in the trucks whistled and cheered.

Farther east outside the business district, huge tall shade trees, elms and maples and oaks, stood along the wide avenues and streets, and in the yards dominated the houses. They passed a couple of homemade store fronts built right against the sidewalk, outside which old men sat on upturned Coke cases in the dirt under the shade trees. They passed a large green public park with a golf course in it, where men in shirtsleeves moved on the fairways followed by Negro caddies. Then the brick buildings of the hospital appeared, and Landers turned to get a look at what his new home for the next months would be like.

It was rawly new. The two oldest buildings, administration and recreation, couldn't have been two years old yet. Around these, covering a vast amount of acreage and getting newer and rawer the farther out they stood, lay two multiple series of ward buildings. Each ward building was a separate two-story brick building. All of them were connected to each other and to the center by strings of brick-porticoed concrete walkways. The sheer magnitude of it was disheartening.

At the outer extremities two new ward buildings were in the process of construction. Here and there a few spindly young trees stood weakly on the flat levelled expanse of new dirt and scant swatches of sparse grass struggled to make themselves a lawn.

Inexorably, the convoy turned into it led by the commanding officer's jeep, between the brick columns that bore the name KILRAINEY ARMY GENERAL HOSPITAL, and Landers' heart sank. Though he did not know what he had been expecting. Some shrewd, rich citizen who knew a senator had made himself a deal for a piece of no-good land on the edge of town. Some contractor (perhaps the same rich citizen) who knew a congressman had made another enormous profit building a hospital for the government on it. Landers would live in it. Once again, Landers felt cheated.

Landers was in almost as bad a way as Prell. If he had less physical pain, he suffered a much greater depression. The outsider-ness he had been afflicted with since his wounding, the sense of being all alone, had not diminished with the disembarkation on American soil. If anything, it had been enhanced. The impersonal way they had been handled and shipped off reinforced it. On the train, because of his crutches he was not allowed to leave the car he was assigned. The constant vibration of the train's passage caused his ankle to swell in the cast. About all he could do was sit or lie in his berth and look out the window and brood. Salt Lake City. Denver. Omaha. Brood over all the beautiful and unbeautiful places in this great country of his, this great United States of America. Where he did not belong. Over the Sierra Nevada, down onto the Great Basin's deserts, on through the Rockies and their emerald valleys, on across the hot dry Kansas plains. Reflect on the fact that in all of them there was not a single living soul who gave one damn whether he was alive or dead, including his own family back in Indiana.

Landers was also well aware that if he could have found one person who did care, or pretended to care even, he would gladly have punched them as hard as he could in the face with all of his strength. This didn't make any sense, even to Landers.

That was the state—and the place—in which Johnny Stranger had found him on the morning of the second day, as the train came down into the desert of the Great Salt Lake.

Strange was far and away the best off of the three, Landers felt. Strange's legs were in good shape. His hand was giving him no especial pain. He could travel up and down the train at will, without being restricted to one car. It was Strange who had discovered Prell in one of the hospital cars at the rear, and brought back the news that Prell was in a pretty bad way. Strange said Prell's legs were giving him so much pain on the train that he was half-delirious, and did not want to see or talk to anyone, including Strange and Landers. Strange could also say with authority, since he had been everywhere on it, that 1st/Sgt Mart Winch was not even on the train at all.

Landers felt badly about Prell. But under the circumstances, with his own distress and despair, he did not have much emotion to expend on Prell. He was much more concerned about the fact that Winch was not on the train, because he had hoped to talk to Winch. Talk about himself and his problem. The four or five times he had been alone with Winch, he had not even been able to mention it. The trouble was, there was no easy handle with which to grasp it and present it. It was not as if he were physically crippled and had lost a leg, say, or like Prell, was in danger of losing a leg. Now, in lieu of Winch, he began to look at Strange as a possible receptacle.

Landers felt he had to talk to somebody, and there was about Strange the air of a man who might be receptive. But in the end there wasn't really any choice. It was either Strange, or nobody. And Landers at twenty-one still had faith that in talking about things you helped them.

He broached it to Strange the second time the mess/sgt came down through the swaying train to sit and talk awhile.

"I've got this problem," Landers said clumsily, after they had talked for a while about Prell, and about the rigors of the trip. "Maybe you could help me with it. Something happened to me when I got hit. I've got this terrible depression. Had it ever since."

Strange sat swaying on the berth, his hands hanging between his knees, and looked at him a long time without answering.

"I know it sounds stupid," Landers said, "but nothing seems to mean anything any more. It all seems so pointless, useless. It's all worthless."

"Did they give you some new bad news about your leg at Letterman?"

"No," Landers said helplessly. "It's not anything like that."

"You ought to be feeling pretty good. You got a nice easy wound that'll keep you out of things for a while. Maybe permanently. You got six months' back pay coming, and a nice town to spend it in."

"I know," Landers agreed eagerly. Then shrugged disconsolately. "I know all that."

"All that's not something to turn your nose up at," Strange offered, not unkindly.

Landers, on his side, now that he was committed, was looking at him studiously, and wondering just how far he could go. Both Winch and Strange were old-time Regular soldiers, and Landers being a replacement didn't know them all that well. Winch he had been thrown with a lot more because of working for him. But Winch had a way of reacting with a rudely passionate arrogance in a kind of paradoxical, contradictory way that could be very unsettling. Landers knew less about Strange, never having associated with him. But the mess/sgt's sad, bitter, almost smile made him feel Strange might be understanding about a problem like his, and sympathetic. On the other hand, Landers felt Strange had always avoided him. Perhaps for being a replacement. Especially since being wounded and shipped out together with him, he felt Strange avoiding him. So he was hesitant.

"I think this whole war is asinine," Landers said. "I think it's insane, and it's useless. Did you—Didn't you ever feel the whole fucking thing was just sort of ridiculous?"

"Yes-s. I have, I guess," Strange said judiciously. "But I've never found any way to see that that makes any difference with anything."

"For example, I can see how in ten years from now all these people who are fighting each other so desperately now will be back at peace and friendly. And then they'll be making business deals and treaties with each other. And everybody getting rich. Just like nothing had happened. But all those guys who are dead, young guys like me, guys like you, will still be dead."

"Yeah, it's a pretty sorry state. For them. But it's no good to think about it like that."

"I can't help it."

"I can never forget that it was them who attacked us."

"Yeah. That's true. I can't forget that, either, I guess," Landers said. But his voice was full of despair.

From the other end of the berth, swaying with the train's swing, Strange nodded at him thoughtfully.

For his part, Strange had noticed something was not right with Landers. He had noticed it when he first came through his car and stumbled onto him, when looking for Winch and Prell. Strange had never had much use for the later draftees and volunteer replacements. They all wanted to be one of the boys so bad that they couldn't be themselves and act natural. Landers particularly he found hard to talk to. And he resented Landers' education. He had disliked Landers for getting himself transferred out of the old company to become the handyman of the battalion's colonel. But seeing him in such a disarranged state, particularly after finding he couldn't get in to see Prell, had called up in Strange all his mothering instincts the old company had evoked so intensely and which now had nowhere to direct themselves. That in fact was why he had come back down the second time. That, and perhaps because he was lonely.

Strange had been looking for, anticipating, despair in Prell and instead had suddenly found it in Landers. Briefly he wished Winch were here with his wisdom. Winch with his smart head would know what to tell Landers. If he decided he wanted to.

"Just what is it that's bothering you, Landers?" Strange said.

"I guess it's because nobody anywhere seems to think the way I do. And I've got a hunch. I've come to the realization finally that I'm going to be killed in this war. It's kind of hard."

"They say lots of men, almost everybody, feels like that after they've been seriously wounded for the first time."

"Yes. I know that."

"At least you're not going to be killed right away. I mean, not today or tomorrow. You've got several months ahead of you."

"I know all that. Oh, I'll be all right. Never mind."

"Try to take it a day at a time," Strange said.

Landers looked up, and after looking at him a long minute from the other end of the berth, he took a deep breath and said, "I don't give a damn about this war any more. That's the truth. That's what bothers me. Fuck this war. Look at all those rich, well-off fuckers out there. What the fuck do they care? I think I'm becoming a pacifist." He had thought Strange would be shocked by this, at the very least outraged. But it didn't even bother Strange.

"Of course, there're a lot of people serving the country who aren't in front line rifle companies," Strange said.

Landers had his head down and did not answer that, and Strange stared at him. Johnny Stranger in fact was far and away in the best shape of them all, Strange guessed. Mentally, and physically. He had his plans all laid, and he was getting out. He was even happy—if happy was the right word for a man who, constantly, every half hour or so, found himself remembering the old outfit. Who worried and fretted over them, and the fact that they were still out there. And who found he was constantly thirsting for news of them. Strange was happy because he had telephoned his wife from San Francisco. It had meant waiting in line for over two hours outside one of the public phone booths at Letterman. But he had gotten through to her at home in

Covington across the river from Cincinnati. And she was going to meet him in Luxor in the next week or so. Being so happy made him feel guilty in front of Landers. He got up.

"Well, let me think about it. Maybe I can come up with something. I'll come back. We'll have to come up with something to get you out of this doldrums. Summer doldrums, my granddaddy used to call it." He grinned and went off.

Landers stared after him in silence, thinking he would probably never come back now. Run like a thief. Except that he had to come back past here to get back to the rear of the train to inquire about Prell.

He did come back, though. He came back later that afternoon, and he came back again that night. And after that he came back often, as often at night as in the day. That was because on the train night and day got mixed up, had no meaning. Somebody was always calling for the medics so that the lights were never turned off anyway. By a sort of unspoken common consent nobody complained or asked for them to be turned off and they were left on all the time. People slept when they could, day or night.

Strange seemed to prefer the night, to come. As a matter of fact. As though he had difficulty sleeping at night, too.

Strange was concerned, though. He seemed to be trying desperately hard to help.

"As far as being killed goes, it's true you might be killed," he said on one visit. "If you don't change your job. Sergeant of infantry. Whereas I don't know if I would. I mean, with my kind of work. Cooking, and running a mess. I've never even seen any real combat. Like you have."

"I haven't really seen any either," Landers said.

"Well, at least you've been in a couple of firefights and killed some Japs."

"Only one Jap. And that was at pretty long range. I don't know if I killed him. I know I hit him. I'm only a clerk, really."

"Yeah, company clerk, rifle company, infantry. That's what you've got to get changed."

"Can you see me getting myself transferred to the quarter-master?"

"No. I guess not."

"I wouldn't even know how to begin."

"It's that damned getting wounded. If you hadn't got wounded, you'd have been all right."

"Yes. I guess so," Landers said. "And I'd still be out there."

Strange had managed to get hold of a bottle somewhere, and passed it over. "Well, don't go feeling lonesome and blue. Shit, we don't even know what we're gonna run into when we do get to Luxor. Maybe you'll find you're permanently disabled."

"I don't think so. Not from the way that surgeon who operated on me talked."

"Well, you never can tell," Strange said.

Another time he said, "What about your family?"

"Ha, my family." Landers laughed. The suggestions were becoming more and more ridiculous each time Strange came. "I could tell you a lot about my family. If I got killed, my mother would buy herself a gold-star flag to stick in the window, that's what. And be tickled to death she had something to cry over every week at her bridge club. My sister would have something to get attention with in her sociology courses in college. And my father. My father would be able to go down to the American Legion three nights a week and brag about how his boy fought, bled and died for his country."

Strange stared back at him expressionlessly and ran his tongue slowly over his teeth. "That don't sound like much of a family."

"They're all phonies. Hypocrites. Listen, I quit college to join the infantry when the war started," Landers said. "Well, my father raised all kinds of hell. He wanted me to stay in college till I graduated and then he would help me get a commission, he said, something nice and safe like in Washington. I refused. He wouldn't even come to say good-by to me when I left."

"But now it looks like your father was right, don't it?" Strange said.

"I suppose he was. In a way. The cynical old son of a bitch."

"What's he do?"

"He's a lawyer."

"Maybe you should let your father help you get that commission now?"

"I'd rather die," Landers said. "Anyway, now he wouldn't."

"Well, maybe there are other ways to do it. You're an educated fella. You ought to be able to use it."

"I wouldn't know what to do, how to begin. And besides I'd be ashamed."

"Hell, that's nothing to be ashamed of," Strange said. "Let me think about it awhile more. I'll come back later." He stood up, swaying with the train's sway.

This time, Landers was almost laughing when he left. It had become a personal challenge to Strange, apparently, the way he shook his head and set his jaw. And the next time he came, ambling bandy-legged and picking his way back along the swaying central corridor, Landers began to laugh almost before he sat down. Strange stopped and looked at him, nonplused, and then grinned and began to laugh himself. He had brought a newer, almost full bottle with him this time. They drank it empty, getting drunk and roaring with laughter, and each trying to outdo the other in making up newer and more outlandish, more outrageous ways for Landers to save himself. And save his life.

When he left that time, Landers watched him with warm eyes.

Strange could feel pleased with himself. But if he thought his little therapy had cured the despair, he was mistaken. He came back more and more, and they drank more and more, and laughed more and more, but whenever he left, Landers still had the night window to stare out of. The moon was full over the Kansas wheat fields on that trip. It seemed right in keeping. And Landers clung to Strange more and more. When the truck convoy stopped inside the Kilrainey General central compound and started unloading, all Landers could think of, in a kind of juvenile panic, was where to find Strange. Like most people who pick a confessor to expose themselves to, he had become the slave of the therapist.

In the confused press of the unloading, in the midst of all those to be unloaded and all those who had come to see them arrive, it was impossible to find anybody. Landers let himself be helped off the truckbed, and standing on his crutches in the crowds looked frantically everywhere for Strange, until in the edge of the crowd of observers he heard somebody cry, "There's Landers!" He looked and saw five men from the old company who looked vaguely familiar, but he didn't really recognize them. They didn't look like the same men. Their faces had changed in some way. Some way that he could not read. They weren't the old companions from the company that he'd known. Before he could do more than wave, he was hurried away on his crutches with a group, toward one of the distant wards, along the brick-porticoed-covered concrete walkways.

When he finally was allowed to get outside the big doors of his ward a few days later on his own, and find his way around a bit, he found that Strange had already left on a short convalescent furlough to Cincinnati.

CHAPTER 9

The shakedown took a full six days. It was not only that there was so much to do to and for each man. It was also the amount of time required to get the simplest thing done.

Getting an X-ray was often a full day's job for a man who could walk, like Landers or Strange. It meant going to the X-ray Section (always a long way off and hard to find) and sitting and waiting in line through a full working day, and then often having to return the next day. While the ambulatory cases waited patiently, each with his signed chit in his hand, one or two or three stretcher cases might be rolled in in their surgeon's "meat wagons" and given precedence. There were always more men waiting than the staff could get to. The Chemical Medicine Section for blood tests was equally difficult.

Each man had to have a complete VD examination. Each man had to have a full dental checkout. Then there were all the physical examinations on the ward itself. His ward intern had to get acquainted with him. His surgeon had to get acquainted with him. His file had to be studied. Questions had to be asked. And asked again.

The new arrivals learned quickly that just because this was a hospital did not mean that it would not be run in the Army way. The Army way was to achieve expertise by handling en bloc larger and larger numbers of similar objects, including casualties. While saving time and enhancing efficiency in the upper levels of bloc-manipulating, this method passed all time loss and inefficiency straight down to the lowest level of individual unit —where it enhanced and multiplied time loss, waste, human error, discomfort, all inefficiency at the individual unit level. Namely, each man. In actual fact, it was not just the Army way. It was the way of all large organizations. Such as factory forces, universities, big offices, and all hospitals, Army or otherwise.

Since most average soldiers had never experienced this managerial method, they thought of it uniquely as Army, put up with it patiently, and cursed it. And soon saw they were not going to be freed of it just simply because they were hospitalized.

By the time Landers was allowed out into the hospital proper to look around and found that Johnny Stranger had already left on convalescent furlough, he had been shut up in his particular ward for more than five full days. There was a huge general messhall somewhere, he was told, but as far as his life was concerned all meals in Kilrainey General were served on the ward.

Landers was again at a loss, without Strange to talk to.

Strange, though, had quickly developed into a special case. Partly this was because of the nature of his injury, but partly it was because his wife telephoned him from Cincinnati.

Strange lost no time in learning what he could find out about the hospital internal politics. By the sheer luck of the draw he had been assigned to the younger and more tolerant of the two chief surgeons in orthopedics, both transposed civilians. By luck also, he was put in the same ward with two old members of the old company, Corello the Italian from McMinnville and a long lanky Southerner from Alabama named Drake. These two quickly filled him in on what they knew, or had heard. The young lt colonel who was his surgeon was rumored by hospital gossip to be a crackerjack poker player. This alone showed the points he had already earned with the men. When during his rounds he first examined the articulation of Strange's hand and then looked at the X-rays, sitting on Strange's bed with the hand on his knee, he shook his head and made a wry smile. It was perhaps a snap judgment, he felt, but he was afraid the hand might come out of the operation in worse shape than before. He wanted more time to study it and make further examinations.

Behind him, standing at the bed foot, the thickset sandy-haired administrative major, who wore a bristly red military mustache and had administrative control over all the orthopedics cases, harumphed his displeasure and cleared his throat and coughed. Col Curran simply turned to smile brightly at him.

Strange watched them both covertly, the exchange not lost on him. He had heard all about the major, too. Not much of it good. The major's job, in fact, was to get every man back to full duty as quick as possible. Also, the surgeon's comment on his hand immediately sensitized Strange to the possibility that he might be up for a discharge even sooner than he had anticipated. Carefully keeping his eyes lowered, careful not to show any pleasure, Strange used the opportunity to ask in a low humble voice that if such was the case, might not the colonel see his way clear to giving him a three-day pass, since his wife was coming to Luxor to see him from Cincinnati, and he had not seen her in eighteen months.

Young Col Curran raised clear, bright, amused eyes from Strange's hand to Strange's face, and laughed silently. "Actually I don't see any reason why not. Will you see to that, Major?"

The major cleared his throat again. "Well, the policy is not to allow any leaves or passes until a man has finalized his potential operative surgical status."

"As far as I'm concerned, Sergeant—uh?—Strange?—Sergeant Strange here has a finalized operative surgical status. At least for two weeks. So will you see to it, Doctor Hogan?"

"Yes, sir, Doctor. I will." Hogan's voice was stony. "But I'm sure the colonel realizes it's unorthodox. You come see me," he said to Strange, "when your wife arrives."

Strange kept his eyes down. Though he knew he had made an enemy. "Thank you, Major, sir. My wife'll appreciate it as much as me." Col Curran's eyes were still laughing.

But then Linda Sue hadn't come. She had telephoned instead.

Taking a personal phone call on a crowded ward, especially a call that carried an embarrassing message, was as frustrating as it was unpleasant. You couldn't really say anything you wanted to say. There was a small office with a phone in it on each ward, but it was kept locked and only the ward intern and the nurse had the keys. So Strange had to take the call at the ward boy's desk.

She could not get away from her job, was the upshot of Linda's call. The job was in a defense plant making precision parts for 105 howitzers and they wouldn't let her off. Yes, she'd told them it was because her husband had just returned from overseas, wounded. They still wouldn't let her off. Strange thought her voice sounded distant and sullen. And it occurred to him suddenly that she had sounded a little bit that same way, too, when he called from San Francisco. But he had been too elated to notice. Something picked stiffly at the back of his mind. Well, why didn't she just quit the damned job? he demanded. She could get another easy enough; in wartime. No she couldn't, Linda came back. The good jobs were not all that easy to get. She had taken special training for this one. If she quit, she would have to start all over at the bottom in something else. Besides, she had made friends there. She liked the job. Strange suddenly stopped talking. He was aware without looking that faces were turned toward him on the ward. Besides, quite suddenly, he could see her point, her side of it. There was no reason to suspect her of anything. Well, what if he could get himself a two-week convalescent furlough, would that please her? There was a pause. Of course it would, she'd be overjoyed, Linda said, did he think he could? "I don't know," Strange said. "But I'll try. I'll call or send a wire when I find out." She said she loved him. He said he loved her. In a low voice. Then he hung up and walked away toward his bed trying not to show any unhappiness on his face. It was then he decided to go straight to Curran. He, Strange himself, on his own.

He knew it would make an even greater enemy of Hogan, but fuck the chain of command. He waited on the surgeon outside his little office next to the big surgery theaters. There were three of them. Curran came out from somewhere, whistling to himself with some deep satisfaction, his hands and the rest of him spotlessly clean. He was still in his "cutting" apron. "Ah, yes. Sergeant Strange, isn't it?" Yes, he could arrange to let him go. But for two weeks only. And he could not give the order. He could only recommend. Everyone was theoretically entitled to a month's convalescent furlough after getting back. But much depended on the situation at the moment. Some got a month, some got none at all. If Strange took two weeks now, he would probably not get two further weeks later on. Strange said he would waive that. Curran would want one more much fuller examination, would take him down to the therapy lab where

they had machines to check the hand more thoroughly. Then he
would recommend the leave. But during the two weeks Strange
must use the hand as much as possible. Make himself use it. Pick
up glasses, light cigarettes, pull change from his pocket. Things
like that. Even if it hurt him. And it would hurt him, a lot. He
smiled at Strange merrily, and pursed his lips again for whistling.

"Look at these hands," he said suddenly, holding them up.
They spread themselves, at the ends of the slim muscled forearms, bespeaking in their shape and movement all the delicacy
and reflexes that made them. "They're worth a fortune, did you
know that." Curran grinned. "And no credit to me at all. I just
happen to be the one to have them. Did you know I can't even
go out and get drunk and get in a fight? For fear of hurting
them?" He whistled a little, silently. "We're ghouls. Parasites.
This war is a great boon to us. This war, and you people." He
gripped Strange by the arm above the elbow, and smiled merrily. "But it's tough on you. We should show our appreciation
occasionally. Strange, eh? A strange name, huh?" He laughed
happily at his own joke.

In the taxi heading into town to the Greyhound station
Strange could not decide whether he liked him or not. But at
least, anyway, he told the absolute truth. He didn't try to doll
it all up in phony propaganda about duty and service to humanity, like Hogan. Hogan had been furious, red in the face when
Curran's recommendation came down approved by the head of
Administration.

The big Greyhound station was jammed. Servicemen with or
without their families, families with or without their servicemen, were in transit toward just about every point around the
compass. Ranks of the big blue and white buses stood in eche-
lons in their stalls, under the protective roofing. A loudspeaker's
metallic voice intoned their arrivals and departures. Loading or
unloading, or just sitting silent waiting on their huge wheels,
their mass dominated everything, making the people around
them insignificant and small. Heading mostly northeast toward
Nashville, or into the Deep South for Birmingham, Atlanta,
Montgomery, and Jackson, they rolled cumbrously in and out
of the main entrance with clockwork regularity.

Both the Negro and the White waiting rooms were crowded,
and both the Colored and White drinking fountains had lines
waiting at them. The Negro waiting room was less crowded,

and lacked the preponderance of uniforms visible in the White. Tired, sweating people crouched on their suitcases or sat on the dirty floor near the overcrowded seats. A jukebox in a corner blared out "Pistol Packin' Mama," competing with the loudspeaker. Born and raised in Texas, Strange was used to the separation of waiting rooms and fountains and accepted it as natural. But having been away overseas so long, the segregation made a bizarre pictorial effect on his eye. He paid for his ticket, fumbling the money because he was conscientiously using his bad hand, and sat on the floor with his back against a wall to wait.

Strange had often daydreamed about his homecoming. He had imagined himself returning carrying one of those sharp green folding airman's valises, full of uniforms, his other arm full of packages of presents for everyone. He had bought fanciful presents in Guadalcanal, the New Hebrides, New Caledonia and Australia, but they had all been stolen or lost or broken or just thrown away until now he had nothing. He had no suitcase. He had only the clothes he stood up in. A small zipper bag carried an extra summer uniform. He didn't mind. He was content, and sat against the wall waiting happily in the crowded steaming White waiting room, among the squalling babies and exhausted young mothers coming from or going to their husbands in the service.

Strange had traveled the Greyhounds all his adult life. It never would have occurred to him to try to go by train.

Anyway, the trains were hardly better.

The ride itself was a long half-waking nightmare of heavy-smelling bodies, paper-wrapped bologna sandwiches, swollen feet, toilet stops, beers, half pints of whiskey, oncoming headlights flashing uneasily over the sleeping faces in the darkened interior. Stopovers and changes late at night in Nashville and Louisville. He made the acquaintance of a young sailor in the seat next to his who was going home on leave from the Luxor Naval Air Station, before shipping out to the West Coast for duty in the South Pacific. When he learned Strange was just back from there, he plied Strange with an endless stream of questions. But it was hard to explain to him. Nothing was like or fit in with what the boy had already imagined. In the midst of describing the fleet base in Noumea in New Caledonia to him, Strange fell fast asleep back into his nightmare of paper-wrapped bologna sandwiches and swollen feet.

He was not sure the boy believed him, anyway. As the boy pointed out, he wore no ribbons.

But if the ride itself was a not entirely unpleasant nightmare, it was as nothing to the unpleasant nightmare he found in Covington when he arrived.

He did not know if it was his fault, or Linda's fault, or neither's. Maybe it was something that happened to every dogface who came home from overseas. But he had no genuine contact with any of them. They never paid any attention much to the newspapers and the battles that were going on abroad, for example. He could think of nothing else.

When he first arrived at the house (he had had the address, but no description or apartment numbers) it was midafternoon and he had thought there was nobody home. He had knocked and gotten no answer, so he sat on the front steps for two hours, waiting for somebody to show up, until one of the three people who were asleep in the house had waked up and come outside and found him. The three were all asleep because they were all working the night shift. One was Linda's paternal uncle, who owned the house, one was Linda's older brother who was 4-F, one was Linda's maternal cousin, the son of Linda's mother's sister, who had the top floor. All the others were at work, or already out, going to work on the swing shift, and that included all the adult females. Strange had sat with them in the kitchen while the three men fixed themselves breakfast (or lunch; or dinner) and asked him in their various-sounding drawls (two Kentucky, one Texas) how it was over there. Strange said it was all right.

One of them asked him what he had done to his hand, and when he explained he had been shot in it, they all wanted to see it so he showed it to them. After examining it, the cousin drawled, "That bullet sure didn't make much of a hole." Strange explained that it was done by a mortar shell fragment. But none of them seemed much interested in mortars.

It was about the same with the women, and the other males, when they all came home. The trouble was, they never all came home at the same time. It was hard to sort them out and keep any track of them, with all the coming and going. Not once, while Strange was there, was the whole family ever all together. In the kitchen some meal or other—breakfast, or supper, or noonday dinner—was always in process of preparation or was being eaten, and quite often they overlapped. So that, while those on the swing shift were at work, those going on night shift might be eating breakfast at the same time those coming off day shift might be preparing or eating evening dinner. All told, there were eleven working adults living in the house, and four children.

The house itself was a three-story frame structure belonging to the paternal uncle, on a shady street in Covington. The uncle and his wife had the ground floor and their oldest son, who was unmarried, lived with them. Linda's father and mother had the second floor and Linda and her unmarried older brother and her younger brother, who was still in high school, lived with them. The married maternal cousin and his wife had the top floor with their two children, a boy of four and a baby of one, and with them lived also the divorced female cousin, and her girl of seven. It was crowded. But since they all worked, and the two older children went to school, it was never actually overcrowded. Of course, now it was summer vacation and the two older children weren't in school. But they were generally outdoors in the day-time playing, or running around, and never came in except at night. The kitchen took the heaviest wear and tear, and sort of served also as the living room. The living room itself was the bedroom of the oldest, unmarried cousin. The dining room had been converted to the bedroom of the uncle and his wife.

In a way it was like separate apartments. Each family's floor was its own domain. Except, of course, they all had to use the same kitchen downstairs. When Strange asked why, since they were all working, they did not sell or rent this place and all get themselves separate apartments, it was explained that they were all saving their salaries. When asked what for, Linda's father and the uncle told him they were thinking of all pooling their combined savings and buying a big nice farm out in western Kentucky. When pressed as to where, they were vague and didn't know exactly where. Nobody had time to go out there and look, they were too busy working. Linda's father explained kindly in his sober, slow way and his Texas drawl that none of them had ever seen such a boom time in their lives, and that included the 1920s, and after the Depression they had all lived through, the point was not to spend but to work and save the money, and worry about spending it later, after the war.

Linda's kid brother, who was listening, chimed in here, to say that next year when he got out of high school he was going to work too and add his salary to the pool. He was already taking some night courses in machine work at an aircraft parts plant.

Strange was welcome to come in with them, Linda's father added in his slow way, if he and Linda ever changed their minds about having a restaurant. Strange, feeling a little as if someone had punched him in the back of the neck, and stunned him, did not know what to answer.

Linda's savings, of course, were her own. Her own and Strange's. Almost the first thing she did when she first saw him, after giving him a perfunctory kiss, was to take him aside and show him their bank book. They had a total of a little over six thousand dollars. She had a separate bedroom on the Darrells' second floor next to the two brothers who had another, and that was where she kept her bank book, locked up. She offered it to Strange almost as if it were some votive gift. One made in atonement. Perhaps for all he had suffered in Wahoo and over-seas in the Pacific for so long. His allotment payments were part of it, of course. She had fixed up her bedroom with new chintz curtains and pillow covers, and a chair cover to match for the one overstuffed chair, when she knew he was coming. It was all very wifey. She had not been able to meet him at the Greyhound station, when he arrived, because she had been working the day shift. That night when they first went to bed together in the chintz-covered bed, it turned into a nearly complete fiasco. Right in midpassion, so to speak, Strange lost his hard-on and could not get it back.

Strange didn't know what was happening to him. He tried to mumble some kind of an apology. After a little while, when nothing happened, Linda Sue patted him sympathetically on the back and rolled over with her back to him and swiftly went to sleep. She had to get up early and go do the shopping for the house before going to her job at the plant.

Deeply troubled and humiliated, Strange lay awake beside her, and wondered fearfully what was happening to him. He had dreamed of this moment so long, and so many times, it seemed absolutely unbelievable that he would not be able to perform. When he thought of all the times, and of all the places —the slit trenches, the bomb hole shelters, the kitchen fly, out in the edge of the woods behind the encampment—that he had tossed himself off and dreamed of this moment, it was not possi-ble that he could have failed to perform.

There were plenty of excuses. It was true she had not helped

him any, but then she never had. He had always been the one
to start things. Which was the way it ought to be. Only once or
twice had she ever asked him to make love to her, in their whole
married life. She had never been that passionate.

It was also true that the kid brother was asleep just beyond
the thin wall in the next room. And that the parents were asleep
in the room on the other side. But that would never have bothered Strange before. Something had happened right in the middle of it, all the excitement had gone away, and he found he was
bored.

Lying in the bed red with the humiliation, he squirmed under
the covers. And thought of himself at the last of the company's
Guadalcanal bivouacs, standing just inside the edge of the jungle, peering out through the screen of leaves at the sleeping tents
in the moonlight, his throbbing cock in his hand, fantasizing
this night with Linda Sue hot and all over him, clawing his back,
shoving it up to him, groaning and gasping with her long-sup-
pressed desires. That was not the way it had ever happened with
them, but that was the way he always fantasized it. And under
the covers he felt his hard-on coming back. Looking down from
the pillow, he could see it slowly thrusting up the covers between his legs.

After a minute, Strange threw off the covers and grabbing a
towel padded down the hall to the bathroom and locked the door
and tossed himself off in the bathroom sink, fantasizing himself
out there in the fantastic night jungle. After he orgasmed he
cleaned it all up neatly, feeling weird, and disturbed. When he
climbed back into bed, he found himself almost hating his wife
for her closed-in lack of passion. He had never been able to draw
her out of it. He was furiously angry with her. And he had to
keep telling himself it wasn't her fault. But what had happened
to him in eighteen months away, out there?

The second night was a great deal better. But then he had
spent most of the day over in Cincinnati drinking beer. So he
was a lot more aggressive, and less apologetic. For that matter,
with all the men around the house, there was a great deal of beer
always there, too. He drank a lot of that also. There was very
little else for him to do, with her at work all day. Over in
Cincinnati, it was as wild and high-living and open as it apparently also was in Luxor. Servicemen with money were everywhere, and a uniform—any uniform—was a ticket into the best
hotel bars and the ritziest places. You didn't have to be an officer.

Everybody loved you. Or said they did, as they took your money.

That night when they went to bed, he was conscious of how beery his breath smelled, but he didn't give a damn. And Linda Sue did not complain. Half drunk and with more than enough aggressiveness now, he thought suddenly that his wife smelled funny. It was as if he could smell another man on her. When he sniffed her breasts, her skin, he of course couldn't. But it made him uneasy. Anyhow, he performed. After that, he tried several times to get her to go out with him in the night, at least to a movie. She was always too tired, always said she had to get up too early to get to work. Her job seemed to have become an obsession.

They did talk some about their savings. Or rather Strange did. Linda seemed strangely passive about it. She no longer seemed so passionately desirous of a restaurant. When he suggested, just to see how she would react, that they should maybe put it all in with the family pool and go in with them on the farm, she only smiled at him, sweetly, a little sadly, and said that if that was what he wanted, it would be fine with her.

In the end he left four days early. He had never told them exactly how many days he had, that he had exactly two weeks. It was easy enough to tell them he had only ten days, and Strange could not stand the house any longer, with its constant comings and goings and the smells and agitation of meals always in preparation.

The four extra days he spent in downtown Luxor. He discovered a nonstop poker game in a third floor room at the ritzy Claridge Hotel on North Main Street, where he got himself a room and picked up four hundred dollars in the game. He spent almost all of it, drinking and running around, either at the Claridge bar or at another hotel, the Peabody, on Union Street. He avoided picking up any women, although it would have been easy. But he felt he owed it to Linda not to.

On the last day, at the very last minute, he reported back to Kilrainey General to find out what Col Curran was going to decide about his hand. And whether that Major Hogan had been able to cook up some bad news for him.

He did not feel he had been home at all.

CHAPTER 10

Landers had had fourteen days in which to start getting along without his new buddy Strange. In civilian life or at college, he might have sat in his room brooding and deteriorating and forgotten. That wasn't possible in the hospital. But he remembered their hours in the train car, and the uproarious semidrunken conversations, with a kind of grinding hunger.

When he finally did run into Strange, in the corridor outside the big recreation center, Strange acted as though nothing had happened, that there was no special bond between them, and seemed preoccupied.

As so often happened in Landers' life, he appeared to take his relationships with people much more seriously than they ever did.

In the meantime, during Strange's absence Landers had had his cast removed and a new one fitted. He had explored and gotten somewhat to know the huge labyrinth that was the hospital. He had had his first pass into Luxor and gotten himself laid —still with his cast on. And he had fallen in love—or fallen halfway in love. The girl he had fallen for was the dark, superb-legged, college-student volunteer Red Cross girl who handed out the games equipment in the recreation center. But it appeared he was not alone in this.

The removal of his cast was a near trauma. By luck he too had drawn young Col Curran. Curran, after studying his X-rays, decreed the removal of the old cast so he could get a look at the ankle, and the refitting of a new one. Landers had hobbled on his crutches with an orderly along the covered walkways to the orthopedics lab with its collection of huge scissors, big rolls of gauze and buckets of plaster of Paris. Since the first cast had been put on right after the operation while Landers was still under the anesthetic, Landers had never seen the ankle. When the lab orderly cut down through the length of plaster and the elastic stocking underneath with the big shears, and then cracked it open and worked it off, the sight that met Landers' eyes was about the most horrible he had ever seen.

The smell of it and the look of it together were enough to stultify Landers. The purplish foot had whole pieces of gray skin pulling away. The skin of the calf was scabby and flaking. The muscle of the leg had just disappeared, it was nothing but a stark shin bone covered with hanging skin. Near the end of this, attached to the bony clawlike foot, the ankle was a swollen red blob of contused bone. Landers was reduced to dumb shock. This was his own leg. It felt dangerously exposed and feeble, out of the plaster. Try as he would, he could not move it, at all. In any direction. He felt fragmented.

The lab orderly had apparently seen worse. So apparently had Curran, who came in a few minutes later, whistling softly to himself some unrecognizable tune. He picked it up, moved it a little this way and that while Landers inhaled sharply, put it down and said, "Well, you've got yourself an excellent job here." His happily cheerful mood was not at all in conjunction with Landers' mood. "Who was the surgeon?" he asked. Landers told him the major's name. Curran shrugged and smiled. "Whoever he is, he's got damned good hands." Then he told the lab orderly to wrap it right back up again and then get a new set of X-rays. This time, he told Landers, they would give him a walking iron. So he could get off the crutches. Then he left.

It was a great relief to feel the new cast go back on over the fragile, feeble member. Not only did it beg for the protective cocoon but he no longer had to look at it. The poor damned battered thing. The lab orderly chewed gum and had a way of cracking his gum with his back teeth while he worked. The wet plaster of Paris heated the leg uncomfortably as it set. The orderly explained that the walking iron he had worked into the cast could not be used until the plaster had set for twenty-four hours. So Landers would have to keep the crutches at least another day.

Landers was glad. He was so unstrung by the whole cast-changing operation that the crutches seemed like trusted old friends. He was so shaken that he was not sure he could make it back to the ward by himself. The lab orderly had anticipated this. They were often like that, the first time they saw them, he said. He had already called for an orderly to go with Landers. Back on the ward Landers lay down awhile, then gathered all his resources to make himself get up and go ask the ward nurse if he could not keep the crutches even longer. When Curran came through a little later, to look at some other patients, he heard the request, looked at Landers with narrowed thoughtful eyes, and okayed it. But only for three more days, he said; then Landers would have to start using the leg. Landers immediately became another of the partisans who adored Col Curran. But the next day, when Maj Hogan came through the ward checking new developments, he looked at Landers' chart hanging on the bed foot and ordered the crutches removed. It was only when Landers protested vigorously, and was backed up by the nurse, that he relented and left the ward furious over Curran's softness.

So it was still with his crutches that Landers made his first overnight pass into town. But he, too, knew he had made an enemy.

The pass was an automatic development, once he was all through with his surgical check-out. It was signed by Curran, but was okayed by Hogan. According to Curran, all Landers had to do was wait now, for the leg to heal. There might be a month, or six weeks, in the cast. Curran thought he would have very nearly full articulation in the ankle. And if it was the least little bit stiff, it would nonetheless be absolutely solid. In the meantime Landers would not even have to be at the hospital, except to be present for morning rounds at ten. When he had an overnight pass, he did not even have to do that. After the cast came off, he would have to start the therapy that would bring the leg back to normal shape. So, Curran grinned, he had at least three months to do almost nothing but play. "And Luxor is a great town to play in," he said.

This last was certainly true. All the same, Landers was of two minds about his pass. Col Curran's happy, hopeful prognosis for his leg was the basic cause of this. Even during the worst moments, when he had first looked at the fragile battered mess of his leg, a part of Landers' mind hidden away far at the back was saying with sly cunning, *Christ! if it's this bad, they'll never be able to send me back to duty! they'll have to discharge me!* He remembered the conversation with Strange in which Strange had suggested hopefully that perhaps he would be permanently disabled. Now, Curran's sanguine prognosis seemed to preclude that. So with the pass in his pocket, he swung out the big main door on his crutches to the cab rank outside to go to town with mixed feelings about all of it. About everything. There was a kind of wild rage in him, and half of him hated himself for the way his mind calculated.

As far as Landers was concerned, there were only two places to go in Luxor. In the few days he had been loose out in the hospital proper, he had already spent enough time in the snack bar with the six or eight other members left of the old company to have learned that. One was the Claridge Hotel on North Main Street, and the other was the Hotel Peabody on Union Avenue.

In the several days he had spent around the other members of the old company, drinking coffee or milkshakes in the snack bar, or loafing in the big recreation center, Landers had discovered what it was that had made the others all look so different when he first had seen them. So much like strangers whom he did not know that he hadn't recognized them. It was that they had all lost their sense of shock. All of them who were still here had been wounded back on Guadalcanal seven or eight months ago. They had never even seen New Georgia. And the peculiar numbness of soul that combat caused in everybody (which could be multiplied a hundred or a thousand times by being seriously wounded; and which carried with it its own kind of disclaiming innocence of new experience) had departed from them in the ensuing months at home. He and Strange and Prell hadn't lost theirs yet. And that was why he hadn't recognized them. They weren't shocked any more, and they weren't innocent any more. All that had been burned off. And in being burned off had left behind a kind of ashy residue on them that carried the sour, bitter, acid smell of furnace cinders. The kind his father used to call clinkers, and which as a boy it was one of his chores to shovel out of the furnace bottom during the long Indiana winters and carry outside and dump on the trash heap. The experience of recovering from being wounded had scorched out of them whatever innocence the experience of being wounded had given them.

Those that were going to be discharged were already discharged and gone (the lucky—or unlucky—bastards). Those that were left were all going back to duty, full infantry duty or some other. And they all knew it. And it showed on their faces. They were the ones who knew where to find the most whiskey, and the cheapest. Where to find the easiest and best girls, and the least expensive. Even freebies, if you were lucky. They were the ones who, with caustic grins, told Landers to go to the Claridge or the Peabody bar—if he had money. If you had money, those were the places to be.

Landers had the money. Although he had not written to his family, he had sent home to his bank account for $600 of the allotment money he had been saving since his enlistment.

The others, of course, didn't have the money any more. They had long since collected their eight months' or their ten months' back pay, and drawn their allotment payments, and spent them, and were now back on their regular monthly pay (less the combat pay) for their spending money. And so were reduced to the cheaper, less ritzy bars and dives. But the Claridge and the Peabody were the joints to hit if you had the loot, they said with their caustic grins.

The whole town seemed to have the same acerb, caustic grin, it seemed to Landers. The cab driver who drove him in from the hospital had it. The Negro doorman in his elegant though frayed hotel uniform, who helped him and his crutches through the revolving door of the Hotel Peabody, had it. The desk clerks and the soldiers and sailors trying to get rooms all had it. The man in the lobby package store had it as he sold him the bottle in its brown paper sack that he would need in the bar. It was the only way you could buy booze. The two barmen in the bar off the lobby, and all the drinkers at the bar tables, had it. The women, sitting with or without men at the bar tables with their own paper sacks, had the look too. It was 11:15 in the morning when Landers arrived but the time of day was not bothering anybody's drinking. About nine-tenths of the men drinkers were in uniform. There were all types and grades and service branches of uniforms. It did not take Landers very long to pick up a girl.

Usually, even as far back as high school, Landers had been excessively shy about approaching women. He always wanted to fuck them, and was afraid they knew this. This time, in the Peabody bar, he simply went straight up to a blonde girl sitting alone and asked her if she would like to have a drink. She said yes. It was only after he sat down with her, and she smiled, that he thought he recognized her as the blonde who had done the bumps and grinds for the truck convoy on the way from the station to the hospital. So he asked her. "You do some bumps and grinds for a convoy of casualties going out to the hospital a few days ago? On the street?" Somehow he knew she would know what the word *casualties* meant.

"How long ago was it?" she said with a rich Southern drawl.

Landers had to count. "Ten, eleven days ago?"

She shrugged, and smiled with the same white-white teeth. "I could have. It's possible. I don't know. Why?"

"Nothing," Landers said. "I was on it."

Her name was Martha-Lee. But she preferred to be called Martha. She worked for a big insurance outfit up the street, as a claims analyst. She was unmarried, she had come up here from Montgomery, and she loved Luxor and was never going to go back. Since it was a weekday, Landers wondered if she didn't have to be at work. He didn't mind buying booze but he hated to waste the time, if she did. A little amazed at his own temerity, he asked her. She had been thinking about going in, Martha said, but now she had about decided she wouldn't. She gave him her big white smile. Her mouth, Landers noticed suddenly, was really extraordinarily sensitive and beautiful. After about five drinks, he offered to buy her lunch somewhere. Martha said she did not feel like eating anything right now. He had not done anything about getting a room yet, Landers told her, but he would go and see about getting one, if she would wait right here, and they could continue drinking up in the room.

"You'll never get one," Martha said, and gave him her smile.

"What do you mean, I'll never get one?"

"They're booked solid. They always are by eleven. Or even ten-thirty. What do you think all those unhappy-looking boys are standing out there at the desk for?"

Landers just looked at her. "Looking for a room?"

"And failin' miserably."

Some sure instinct made him cover up, and hide his disappointment. He gave her back a grin he hoped was acerb and caustic, like all the other grins around. "You haven't got an apartment we could go to and drink, have you?"

"Not one I can take anybody to," Martha said, and smiled the white smile again. "This your first time in town on pass? It is, isn't it?"

"It's my first time on pass anywhere. For almost seven months."

She put her hand over his on the table, and smiled. "Wait here a minute. I oughtn't to be very long. But if I am, you wait. Hear?"

"Okay."

It was more than a minute. It was more than ten minutes. He had time to finish his drink and pour them both another bourbon and water. And had time to drink his new one. He occupied himself with thinking about his sudden new finesse with women, wondering where it had come from. Then she was back still smiling her white smile, and handed him underneath the table a hotel room key with a big leather tab attached to it. Landers put it in his pocket and started to pay the check.

"Take your time," Martha smiled. "There's no hurry. It's not going to go away. Let's have another here, first. Have you already got a bottle?"

Landers shook his head. "Just this one," he said, and lifted the bourbon bottle in its paper sack from the floor by the table leg.

"Did you buy it at a package store just outside the bar in the corridor, at the top of the stairs down into the lobby?" Martha said.

Landers nodded.

"Can you maybe buy another? Or maybe two?" Martha smiled. "We might need it."

Landers nodded. "Get it on the way out. Where did you get the key?"

"It's a friend's. Someone I know," Martha said. "Don't worry about it. It's perfectly safe. Nobody will be there."

"Fine," Landers said.

"What did you do to your leg, soldier?" she smiled. "Fall off a ladder?"

"Yes, as a matter of fact. That's exactly what I did do," Landers said, and was suddenly reminded of a day when he had been carrying a message across the floor of the valley for his pet colonel. He had looked up to watch a platoon attacking the crest, and had seen a man turn and jump out from the side of the hill exactly like a man jumping off a ladder. A Jap hand grenade had exploded black, seconds later, at the spot where he jumped. He had watched the man get back up and start toiling back up toward the crest.

"I guess you won't be able to dance for a while, will you?" Martha smiled.

Landers shook his head. After they finished their drinks, and picked up the new bottles, they made their way down the steps to the lobby and straight across to the elevators. They rode up in an elevator packed with servicemen. Several of these, even ones who had girls, bent envious looks upon Landers.

"Hi, Martha," one of the men behind them said.

"Oh, hi, there," Martha smiled.

The room was a big, old-fashioned, high-ceilinged suite on the seventh floor. The windows were open and it was cool. In the bathroom big fresh white towels hung on the rack. In the open closet four neatly pressed Naval officer's uniforms were hung on hangers. The blues carried two-and-a-half gold stripes. Landers wasn't sure about Naval insignia but thought two-and-a-half stripes was a lieutenant commander. Pilot's wings were pinned over the pockets. Landers looked, but said nothing.

"Those are my friend's," Martha said. "He keeps this place by the week. When he's here, there are parties all the time. But he's not here very often. He teaches out at the Naval Air Station."

After pouring a drink which they did not finish, Martha wanted to autograph Landers' cast. This was not hard to do, since to get the pants on, the pantsleg had been split up the seam to above the knee. Making up her mouth afresh with her lipstick, she pressed her lip print to the cast and then signed under it. *Martha-Lee Prentiss.* Her hands strayed up his flanks to his shoulders. A few kisses made them both begin to pant a little. Martha insisted on going into the bathroom to take her clothes off. There was nothing quite as ungraceful-looking, she insisted, as a woman getting out of her clothes and all her gear. Landers did not argue. When she came back out, she had draped one of the huge towels around her. Drawing herself up straight like a model, she pulled it loose and let it fall to the floor. "There. Isn't that better?" Then she walked to the bed and threw it back and lay down.

"I'll let you fuck me—if you want—but you mustn't come in me," she whispered. "But what I really want is to suck you. I'm a cocksucker. I'm a marvelous cocksucker. Did you ever go down on a girl?"

"Sure," Landers said. And while this was the truth, it was only just barely the truth. He had experimented a few times in college with girls as equally unknowledgeable and embarrassed as himself. He was having difficulty getting undressed because of the cast and Martha came from the bed and helped him. She helped him hobble back across the floor to the bed. "Your poor leg," she said. "Can you get on top of me? Or shall I get on top of you?" After a while she took her mouth off of him and whispered, "Do it up at the top more. Talk to me. Tell me I'm a cocksucker. Tell me I'm a marvelous cocksucker." When his loins finally exploded into orgasm, making his eyes go crossed, Martha had already come four times.

The second time around he put it inside her for a while. Then she instructed him, in and about how to go down on a girl. Landers didn't mind that at all. It was valuable instruction. After the second time, they went back to their drinks for a while. Later on that evening they ordered food up from room service. But they only stopped long enough to eat about half of it. Landers did not know about Martha, but he was catching up for many months of dry season. Late that night, just about when the early summer dawn was cracking through, Landers woke up in the dark to find a nude Martha weeping beside him.

When he put his arm around her, she leaned her face against his shoulder, and wet his armpit thoroughly with her tears.

"What is it? What's the matter?"

"Nothing. It's nothing."

"But something must be the matter."

"It's nothing. Oh, it's— My fiancé was killed. In North Africa. He was shot down. Was Air Force."

Landers patted her bare back. "I'm sorry."

"Oh, it's nothing. But my daddy is dead, too."

"In the war? Too?" He was shocked.

"No. He died several years ago. But he was so dear. Don't pay any attention to me. Please. Go back to sleep."

Finally, he did, with her face still pressed against the side of his wet chest. When he woke, he was alone in the bed and she was gone.

Landers looked all around for some kind of a note, but there wasn't any. The key with the leather tab was lying on the dresser. Somehow he couldn't feel bad about it all. How could you feel bad about a lucky windfall evening like that? But he felt oppressed and lonely. Bone-cold lonely. Martha had made him lonelier, if anything. After a while, he ordered himself up a marvelous breakfast of sunnyside eggs, buttered toast, grits and bacon and lots of coffee, and sat in the sunshine by the open window and ate it. Scrupulously, he paid the room service waiter cash for it.

While he was smoking a cigarette with the last of the coffee, with one of the huge towels wrapped around his waist, the outside door opened with another key, and the young Naval lieutenant commander came in. He hardly even seemed surprised.

"Oh, hi there. How you doing?" He shucked out of his khaki jacket with the shoulder boards, and flashed Landers a grin. "Do I know you? Guess not. You must have met Marty, huh? Well, make yourself at home. I'll only be a minute. Wash up." He stripped off his shirt and pants and went into the bathroom in his skivvies.

Some cold thing in Landers made him stay seated by the window and enjoy a second cigarette. He listened to the sound of the shower. When it stopped, the young lieutenant commander came to the bathroom door nude, toweling himself vigorously.

He looked at Landers' cast and smiled. "Where you from? South Pacific?"

Landers got up slowly on his one leg, resting the other on the walking iron. "Yes. Guadalcanal and New Georgia. How did you know?"

"You've got that sallow look. The malaria look. I was in Guadal awhile myself." He went back in and put on his skivvies and came out and began to dress. "Well, make yourself at home. I've got to run, huh? When you leave, just leave the key with the bell captain, will you? Give him your name, and if you ever want it again he'll give it to you. This place is like Grand Central Station. By the way, what is your name?"

Landers told him. "Uh—I paid the waiter cash for the breakfast. But I don't know about the dinner."

"Oh, that's all right. Don't worry about it. Several of us share this place. Marty often brings friends up here. We've all of us sort of adopted Marty. She has a sad story. Sometimes her friends are the wrong sort. But if they are, they soon drift off.

You, I can see, are not. Any man who will have himself a sumptuous breakfast in the sunshine by the window alone, has got to be the right sort." He looked at Landers' shirt, hung neatly over the back of a chair. Landers had just had chevrons sewn on it, the day before. "So come back whenever you want, Buck Sergeant Landers. And don't forget to give the bell captain your name. So he can put you on the list. If you ever want to contribute a few bottles of booze, leave them with the bell captain. We never leave booze in the room. If we do, it all gets drunk. There's a damn party here about every night. Bunch of drunks. But good-looking chickens." He was shouldering back into the khaki jacket with the Navy shoulder boards. He buttoned it neatly and then picked up the khaki black-billed cap, and waved at Landers with it. "See you. Got to run, huh? If you see Marty, say hello for me. Oh. Name's Mitchell. Jan Mitchell. Jan is short for Janus. Terrible name. Saddled with it." He waved with the cap again and went out the door.

Landers made himself a drink. A long half-empty bourbon bottle was standing on the dresser, and he stood with the drink in front of the dresser mirror. Right sort. Right sort. Landers didn't know whether to take that as a compliment or not. He supposed he should. He decided he would leave the bottle for whoever the next occupant might be. This time, he noted the four or five uniforms in the open closet were of several different sizes.

It was ten o'clock and he had an hour and a half to kill before he should start back to the hospital. He couldn't think of anyplace better to spend it than to spend it here, thinking over last night. He double-locked the door with the chain, and went in the bathroom and had a shower and shaved with the lieutenant commander's wet razor. He was sure the lieutenant commander wouldn't mind. Then he came back out and made another bourbon and water.

But after a while alone in the room, the bone-white loneliness was stronger than ever. And with it came the sense of guilt, and the wild rage. He felt he had not earned all this. But at the same time, he did not want to go back. He dressed and left and went down to the bar to drink. But before he did, he went to the state package store off the lobby and bought three bottles of bourbon and left them and the key with the Negro bell captain. He gave the bell captain his name.

When he showed up at the hospital snack bar in his official

uniform of bathrobe and pajamas, after reporting back in, he found that several of the guys from the old company—as well as a number of others—already knew about Martha—Marty. The autographed cast was impossible to hide. The leg of the pajamas had had to be split too, and the red of the lipstick showed up brightly. She had done the same thing to Corello's cast, when he first arrived.

"She's a great blow job." Corello, the Wop from McMinnville, grinned. "Did she try to get you to eat her pussy?" A couple of the others who knew her laughed.

"Any broad'd ask me that I'd break her goddamn jaw," Alvin Drake the tall boy from Alabama growled.

Landers looked at all their faces, and lied. "No. She didn't. Why?"

Corello hooted, and then laughed. "She asks everybody. Or nearly everybody. But nobody admits they did. *I* certainly didn't."

"Well, she didn't ask me," Landers said. All of the others laughed.

"You're the only one," Corello grinned. "She's a great blow job, all the same."

They knew everything about her. It was true that she came from Montgomery. It was not true that her fiancé had been shot down in Africa. She didn't have a fiancé. And never had had. One of the men who was not from the company was from Montgomery, and knew her and her family. It was an excellent family, apparently. Apparently she never went with the same man twice. And she apparently picked her men carefully. She had never tried to pick up Drake, for example.

"And she better never," Drake snarled with an evil grin. "I can't stand cunts like that. She's a fucking pervert."

When he could get away from them, Landers went into the big recreation center and flung himself down on an overstuffed couch to think about it. He had already noted that his night with Marty had made him even lonelier than before. All this other added on top of it made it even worse. Their coarseness made him sick.

The recreation center had been built as a basketball court and gym, with a theater stage at one end. When there were no basketball games, the demountable bleachers were taken down and furniture was strewn all around. Every night the folding chairs were put up on the court for a movie. After a while

Landers got up from the couch and went over to talk to the pretty Red Cross girl in her cubbyhole with the Ping-Pong paddles and athletic equipment. Maybe it was at just that moment that he fell in love with her—or fell halfway in love with her.

Her name was Carol Ann Firebaugh. She was a Luxor girl, and was going to Western Reserve in Cleveland, where she was studying acting. In the summer she was a volunteer Gray Lady for Red Cross. And she had one eye, her right, which every now and then did not track quite straight. This coupled with her long, clean-lined legs gave her a sexual attractiveness that was almost insupportable. A great many of the other patients had noted her, too, but she liked Landers because he had gone three and a half years to Indiana at Bloomington.

Landers had been talking to her ever since he was let out into the hospital proper off his ward. Now he began to importune her steadily and stubbornly for several days until finally—on the same day when he first saw Strange after his return from furlough—she agreed to have a date with him outside.

Strange, when Landers saw him, was on his way to visit Prell.

CHAPTER 11

For the first four days after his arrival Prell had done very little but sleep. Flat on his back and all trussed up again, there wasn't that much he could do. And he was totally exhausted, physically and morally. In his little shaving mirror, the fragile, purple skin under his eyes seemed to have shrunk even farther back into his head. Occasionally he would wake up and drink some water or some soup. Kilrainey was well equipped for that kind of around-the-clock care. And fortunately, Prell had a night ward boy who worried about his charges. Also—somehow or other—the gossip that he was a potential Medal of Honor winner had preceded him, or at least come right along with him, and everybody on his ward including the nurse took a special interest in him.

Unfortunately Prell had not had such good luck in drawing a surgeon. Instead of the much-liked Curran, he had drawn the other chief surgeon, Colonel Baker. Prell's troubles and his problems started there. And they started right away. As soon as Prell began to come around and be interested in things, he became aware of it. There was a sort of vibrant whisper about him everywhere around him on the ward that he could never quite come face to face with. Wherever he turned his head the whisper would cease there, and seem to begin somewhere else behind him.

Col Baker was a tall spare older man, with gray-white grizzled hair, piercing eyes, and a seamed pouchy face that bespoke an irascible temper. It was reputed that he had been one of the two or three best orthopedic surgeons in America, just before the war. Baker looked like one of those men whose short temper was due to the shortness of time, and who could not be bothered to fool around with your sentiments and emotions if he was going to get your bones patched up, put back together and healed. In policy, he was much closer to the attitude of the administrator, Maj Hogan, which was to stick them back together and get them the hell out, willy-nilly—either back to duty if possible, or if not, then discharged and back to the farm—but get them out and open up the beds and make room for all the myriad others who, inevitably, would be coming along now with each new attack, each new offensive as the U.S. began to move. Apparently, even at the first surgical conference on Prell, he had decided that the only thing to do with Prell was to amputate his right leg, which was not healing, and get him out of there and open up another bed.

Prell, who had been knocked out and only semiconscious at his first surgical conference, became aware of all this at the second conference, which was on his ninth day on the ward. Then he realized what the whisper about him on the ward was all about. But he had half suspected it already. He lay in the bed and watched and listened as the three officer doctors, Baker, Curran and Hogan, hovered over by the nurse, ward intern and enlisted ward boy, discussed his right leg as if it were some abstract problem in a chess game.

"I won't give permission," Prell said wearily when Baker put it up to him. It seemed to him he had been saying that same line all his life.

"We can do it anyway," Baker said. "Without. If we decide it is to save your life, or is in your best interest."

"Then I'll sue the Army," Prell said weakly. "I'll sue the government. For every cent I can squeeze them for. And I'll name you. For malfeasance."

"A guardhouse lawyer," Baker growled.

Prell nodded. "Yes, sir. When it's my leg." He had listened to them discussing it. He understood the mechanics. Because the splintered bone was at midthigh, it would mean sawing it off right up at the hip, so that there would be enough flesh left to make the protective flap to fold over. It made his spine go chilly.

"I don't think you understand," Baker said.

"I understand," Prell said. "It's my leg."

Baker bulled right on. "The problem is your right leg is not healing. There is no infection—no serious infection—up to now. But we are keeping you pumped full of sulfa. To avoid that. But you can't go on taking sulfa forever. In the meantime, you are getting weaker and weaker, slowly. If you do infect, you're probably going to be dead. Do you understand that, soldier?"

Hogan was bobbing his head and grumbling his assent. Curran was looking off in the distance and doing and saying nothing. The nurse and intern and ward boy were all watching, their three sets of eyes like six vacuum cleaner nozzles sucking everything in.

Prell nodded. "I understand. The answer's still no. Better dead than no leg."

Baker's eyebrows arched and his eyes narrowed. "I already told you we can do it without consent," he said sharply. "It will take me a little longer that way, that's all. I'll have to send in a report and get clearance." He peered at Prell. "Do you realize you are taking up attention and time and space that might save some other soldier's life?"

"I don't honestly give a shit about some other soldier's life, sir," Prell said. What a question to ask some man about to lose his leg. He noticed Curran had made a little movement, twisted his torso as if in protest.

The long-limbed Baker slapped both his big hands down on his knees. "Well, it is my professional opinion that we are going to have to take off that right leg of yours." He got up. He looked at the other two doctors. "Unless there is some dissenting opinion with my colleagues here." Hogan, already standing, shook his head vigorously no, and scowled. Curran, still seated, with an almost imperceptible movement, shook his head no, also.

Prell, looking at the three of them, could feel his heart beating in him with a slow, heavy ominous beat that was both exciting and doom-filled. It was exactly the way he had used to feel sometimes before an attack. And for a split moment he almost gave up and agreed. He had been fighting and fighting it until he had nothing left to fight with. Instead, he just looked at them and kept his mouth shut as, slowly, Curran got up too and they left. The worst thing was this awful feeling of being completely in their hands and totally helpless. There was absolutely nothing more he could do. Except maybe scream. He tried to get a hold on himself. But he was still so worn out, from the trip and all the rest of it, that after a few minutes, although his heart was still beating heavily, he turned his head to one side and went to sleep.

Hell, maybe the fucking doctors were right.

His last waking thought was that he must get hold of Johnny Stranger, or some of the others from the company, and tell them. Maybe—just maybe—there was something they could do. Then as he dropped off he remembered that Corello had told him Strange was on convalescent furlough, and that was why he hadn't been by to see him.

That was the way it hung for another week. Col Baker—or more often, Maj Hogan—would come by and read his charts and glower and shake his head. The right leg was not healing. Even the left was slow. On one of these visits Baker told him he had sent in the report and made the request to amputate. It didn't seem to upset Baker much. Prell wanted to spit at him, or curse him, but he had neither the heart nor the will, nor the energy.

For one second Prell thought of telling him of his intention to shoot himself and knock himself off if he lost a leg, but then he didn't. To do that would only bring a psychiatrist into it. And maybe get him put away in a lockup ward.

After a week of this anguish—on the same day, in fact, that Strange got back and came to see him—Prell had a surprise visit from the chief hospital administrator himself, a full bird colonel. The two surgeons were light colonels.

It was the first time within the memory of anyone on the ward that the chief administrator had visited a patient. In fact, it was the first time anyone, including the nurse and intern, had seen the chief administrator. Col Stevens was an elderly man and a West Pointer, with white hair, handsome features and a quiet manner. Prell knew when he saw him that screaming and threatening were not going to be any good, and that he'd have to try for something else. Rumor had it that Stevens was on the next promotions list to make brigadier. He sat by Prell's bed for half an hour and talked to him in a kindly way. The upshot of his conversation was whether Prell was still adamant about refusing permission to amputate. Prell said that he was. Col Stevens said this posed a serious problem, not only for the hospital administration but for Prell himself. Prell was in danger. Col Baker had sent in a report that it was necessary to amputate Prell's right leg in order to save his life. None of the other doctors had dissented. This was going to force a very difficult decision on the hospital administration, which in effect was himself. Col Stevens. Prell said again that he did not want to live without his legs, without *one* leg.

"Sir, it's not as if this didn't happen before," he said. Prell was not at all above using his hollow, harrowed eyes on somebody, if he thought it might help him. "Back up the line they wanted to take off *both* my legs. But I talked them out of it, and I'm still here, and so are the legs. I'm sure that they'll heal up, sir."

"That doesn't appear to be the case," Stevens said.

"All it needs is a little time, sir."

"Col Baker doesn't seem to think so," Stevens said, and drew a breath and let it out in a sigh. "You're an old-timer, an old Regular, aren't you?"

"Yes, sir. I was just winding up my third hitch when the war started," Prell said.

"Tell me, what would you do with your life?" Stevens said abruptly. "If you had your choice, that is."

"I'd stay in the Army," Prell said without hesitation. "Be a thirty-year man."

"You would?" Stevens rubbed his handsome chin. "Anyway, it's twenty years, nowadays. Not thirty."

"I'd stay in thirty, anyway," Prell said. "If they'd let me."

"Well, there's not much chance of that. Not the shape you're in."

"No, sir. I guess not. But it's my dream."

"You know, it's written into your dossier that your Division commander recommended you for the Medal of Honor. Did you know that?"

"It's the first I've heard of it, sir. I'd rather have the leg than the medal."

"Yes," Stevens said. He smiled.

"What are you going to decide about the leg, sir?" Prell asked. He couldn't help it. As he spoke, he was remembering back to when not so long ago, even just on the boat, what Stevens had just told him about the Congressional Medal would have been the biggest thrill of his life. Not any more.

Stevens shook his head, and then got up. "I don't know," he said. "I don't know because I don't know, myself."

"I had the impression, myself," Prell said, "that maybe Col Curran didn't feel quite as strongly about it as Col Baker."

Stevens' eyes sharpened, then showed disapproval. "No. That's not possible. Col Curran didn't file any dissenting opinion."

"But I'm not his patient. Am I? And doesn't Col Baker outrank Col Curran?"

"That wouldn't make any difference," Stevens said. "Not in something this important."

"It might make a little difference," Prell said. "What they call professional ethics?"

"No, no," Stevens said. "No, no." He turned as if to go, then stopped.

"You know, sir, I'm not at all sure I deserve that Medal of Honor," Prell said to his back, taking advantage of the pause. "In fact, I don't think I do. Not really. But I deserve the leg."

Stevens turned to look at him, and then after a moment nodded once, crisply. He left without saying more.

It was only an hour or so after Stevens' visit that Johnny Stranger came in to see Prell. He'd heard the news from Corello.

Prell felt he had done pretty well with Stevens. But feeling so did not make him very happy. He did not feel he had established any basic change in the chief administrator. What did the lawyers call it? Establish a reasonable doubt. That cunt Baker had called him a "guardhouse lawyer." He told the whole tale to Strange, pausing to rest between paragraphs when he was tired.

Strange, as he listened, felt a terrible guilt. Here he was, running around on a furlough he didn't even need, trying to get back in with a wife and family he didn't even seem to know any more, or understand. Loafing for four lousy days downtown in Luxor playing poker. And all the time Prell needed him, lying here trying to save his damned leg from those goddamned civilian doctors. Gone when, for once, somebody really needed him.

At least this Col Stevens was one of their own. A West Pointer and an old Army man. But you couldn't even count on that any more, nowadays. And anyway when did being a West Pointer make a man dependable? Some were, some weren't.

Strange was not at all sure that the doctors weren't right. Prell looked terrible. His eyes were sunk so far back in his head, and the skin drawn so tight over his cheekbones, that he looked like a skull. A dead man. But at least the fuckers could let him die decently, the way he wanted.

On the other hand what was there that Strange could do for him? Him, a low-life s/sgt of a mess/sgt? What colonels were going to listen to him? He told Prell that.

"I thought maybe if you went and talked to Curran," Prell said. His purplish eyes were almost desperate. "Curran didn't seem to be so strong for amputating it as the others."

"I'll certainly talk to him," Strange said desperately. "But you know how much he's going to pay any attention to me."

"Maybe if you got all the guys together," Prell said. "Get up a petition. Get them all to sign it."

"A petition?" Strange said. "In the Army?"

"Well, times are changing. And those guys aren't soldiers. They're civilians," Prell insisted. "Maybe a petition would impress them."

"I can try it," Strange said. "I can try it." He paused a minute, then said, "But listen. Wait a minute. You've given me an idea."

"What's that?"

"I'll get Landers to go and talk to Curran."

"Why Landers?"

"Well, you know. He's a college man and all that. He speaks their language. If he was to talk to them, I think it'd carry more weight than if I went."

"That's a good idea," Prell said, his sunken eyes widening to grasp at any hope. "Try that."

"I will. I will," Strange said.

He did not waste time on any formal good-bys. He found Landers in the big recreation center, talking to the pretty girl with the walleye, she nervous and behind her athletic equipment counter as if it were some protective wall between them. Strange would have laughed, normally.

"But why me?" Landers said, after they had gotten off by themselves on one of the couches on the basketball floor. "I don't know Curran any better than you do."

Landers was having difficulty concentrating. Carol Firebaugh had just accepted his invitation, about his twentieth invitation, to have a date with him outside. But instead of being elated, he suddenly found himself full of the old despair again. Inexplicably, he found himself seeing again the picture that had been emblazoned on his retinas that day on the ridge when he sat with the wounded and stared at the clean, white streaks down all the dirty faces from weeping. The two things were so far apart that there was no way of reconnecting them at all. Grown men. All of them. Himself included. She had been so circumscribed in her acceptance that it was almost a refusal. And the picture kept coming back, to oppress him. Something somewhere had stopped for Landers there that day. How could you explain that to someone who hadn't been there? How could you say it to her? It made that kind of wild rage come back up in him. Reckless. He had been just on the point of withdrawing the invitation when Strange arrived.

"Well, you're a college man. And all that," Strange said. "You talk their language."

"I thought you were mad at me," Landers said.

Strange stared at him. "What?" He couldn't connect Landers' comment with anything. "Mad at you? What do you mean, mad at you?"

"Well, you hardly even said hello, when I saw you in the corridor earlier," Landers said. "You just sort of went right off. As if you were cutting me."

"Oh." Strange felt as if he had come up against some kind of unanticipated brick wall in the dark. Here was a whole new field, new outlook opening up that he had neither the time nor the inclination to poke into. "Well, I was worried about Prell, don't you see? Will you do it? Will you go to Curran?"

"Of course I will. I'll do anything for any of the guys from the company. Especially Prell."

Landers had heard the bad news about Prell. All of the guys had heard it, from Corello. At the time Landers had shrugged inwardly, and counted it as one more inevitable loss to the jungle campaigns, the jungle war, one more casualty to New Georgia. A leg. It had never occurred to him there might be anything anybody could do about it. Now a kind of wild flame of loyalty licked up in him searing his trachea and heart. He would do any damn thing he could do, for any of them.

They would understand, if he told them about the men on the hilltop. They might laugh about it. Now. But they would understand.

"But I don't think Curran'll listen to me any more than he would you," he said. "Less, probably."

"But will you try? And tell him all of us guys from the old company are ready to get up a petition and sign it, if he wants?"

"Sure I'll try."

"Prell seems to feel Curran wasn't as strongly for the amputation as the other two."

"I'll go right now. You want me to go now?"

"Fine. And tell him about the petition?"

Landers was off his crutches by now, and was using a cane and the walking iron. He was still nervous with them, and unsure of himself on them. It took him a long time to get from the recreation center to the area of the surgery theaters. He had to work hard and move carefully going up and down the various ramps designed for rolling surgery beds and wheelchairs. When he got to Curran's tiny office, his knees felt shaky. Fortunately, Curran was in.

Curran's head was down, over some papers. Landers paused to rest, and to pull himself all together. He was going to have to remember to be tactful and polite. He didn't feel much like either.

"May I speak to you a few minutes alone, Col Curran, sir? Off the record?"

Curran looked up, his eyes immediately growing remote. He nodded. "Sure. I guess so. Come in."

"It's not about me," Landers said. "It's about a friend of mine. Named Prell."

"What about him?"

"There are seven of us here from his old company. The guys decided to sort of appoint me their spokesman. We've heard that his right leg may have to be amputated."

Curran seemed to stare, Landers thought. But not quite. Abstractedly, with another part of his mind, Landers wondered where he was getting the nerve to do what he was doing. But that was easy enough to answer. All he had to do was think of those men he had sat with on the hill. None of these people knew the first thing of what it was like to be like that. And didn't want to. Any more than we did, he thought.

"It's a possibility," Curran said. "A very likely possibility."

"Well, he's one of the best men our outfit ever had. I guess you know, he saved his whole patrol after he got shot up. He's been recommended for a medal for it. And, well, we think it will probably kill him if he loses that leg. The guys wanted me to ask you if there wasn't something you could do to save his leg."

Curran's eyes seemed to get larger, and deeper. "What the hell do you think I could do?"

"We thought something that might give him a chance. A fighting chance."

"Like what? Anyway, he's not my patient." Curran looked down and moved the papers on his desk.

"He said he felt you weren't as much in favor of the amputation as the others."

Curran's head snapped up. "He told you that?"

Landers nodded. "Well, he told one of us. Not me. He said it was a hunch he had."

"The man is in a very bad way," Curran said. "His one leg won't heal. The other is not doing all that well. There's something wrong with his system. With his chemistry. He's getting weaker and weaker, and he just won't heal."

"Couldn't you give him something?"

"We're giving him everything we can. Sulfa. Plasma. Glucose. Besides, you seem to forget that he's not my patient."

"Well, what if you stopped giving him something? If it's his body chemistry?"

Curran stared at him, his eyes narrowed. He looked down at the desk, then looked back up. "I don't think you understand. That's not the way it works. I can't disagree with Col Baker's statement. I think Col Baker is right. And he's Col Baker's patient."

Landers nodded politely. It struck him suddenly that there was the possibility that Curran might be hedging on the truth the least little bit. That he wouldn't admit that Prell was right in thinking Curran was less in favor of the amputation than the other two. He said nothing.

"It's possible that Col Baker is pushing it a little," Curran said. "But that's not important, really. Col Stevens is not going to decide to amputate immediately, when it's without Prell's permission. Which Prell won't give. Col Baker is just trying to be prepared for it. Ahead of time. As for stopping something that he's getting, there's very little that he's getting that isn't absolutely necessary. Don't get the idea that some of us are ogres here, hoping for a chance to do a leg amputation."

Landers had been nodding politely again. But somewhere inside his chest, or right behind his eyes, something seemed to be changing in him. Another personality that he did not know seemed to be taking over his muscles and his voice. It was almost like that day on the ship when he seemed to go out of himself. That kind of wild rage against everything, against life itself, seemed to flow all over him. "Nobody thinks that, Colonel.

Anyway, the guys told me to tell you that we would all be willing to sign a petition amongst ourselves against the amputation and present it to you," the new voice said. Harshly. "If you would want us to."

Curran's head snapped up again. He looked astonished. He said the same thing to Landers that Strange had said to Prell. "A petition? In the Army? Are you men out of your minds?" Then he stared at Landers a long moment. "You men think a lot of him, don't you?"

"I guess we all admire him," Landers' new, harsh personality said. Landers was suddenly seeing his hilltop ridge and all the faces with their perpendicular white streaks running down them, beyond and through the clean sympathetic face of Curran. "But that's not what it is. I don't think you understand *us*. I don't guess we any of us give much of a shit about anything, except each other. It's not so much that we think a lot of Prell. It's like we were investors. And each of us invested his tiny bit of capital in all the others. When we lose one of us, we all of us lose a little of our capital. And we none of us ever really had that much to invest, you see."

" 'Do not ask for whom the bell tolls,' " Curran quoted.

"John Donne, sure," Landers grinned wolfishly. "But that's shit. And that's not what it is with us. That's abstract. And it's poetry. That's all of humanity. We're not all of humanity. And we don't give a shit about all of humanity. We probably don't give much of a shit about each other, really. It's just that that's all the capital we have.

"So," he said finally, "we're perfectly willing to get up a petition and all of us sign it, and turn it over to whoever you say turn it over to, and to hell with the consequences. If it means going to the stockade, we'd all sign it cheerfully anyhow. If by doing it, it would help at all to save Prell's leg."

Curran's face was white. And he got to his feet, stiffly. But he didn't look angry. Landers wondered if he had gone too far somewhere, and forgotten to be tactful and polite.

"Do you realize it may very well kill him?" Curran said. "It's getting that close. Do you want him dead?"

"I guess all of us would say let the poor son of a bitch die that way, if that's the way he wants to die. Let him die the way he wants it. It's about all he's got left. Besides, he's been nearly dead before. All of us have."

"I can't promise anything, Sgt Landers," Curran said mildly. "But I can tell you that he'll get every chance we can give him. Nobody here wants to take his leg off. But we may have to."

"Then you don't want us to get up the petition?"

"Get it up and sign it, if you want to. If it makes you feel any better. But I think it would serve absolutely no use with Col Stevens."

Outside, Landers leaned against the wall of the corridor along the surgeries to collect his wits. The other personality was gone. For a while he had actively been another person in the little office. That had never happened to him before. He did not know whether what he had done was helpful or detrimental. Or whether it had no effect. After a while, he started hobbling back.

Back in the rec center he told Strange the whole story, with Curran's responses. He left out only his metaphor of the investors, which now sounded high-toned and dumb to him, and he didn't mention that feeling of another personality. Between them, he and Strange were unable to deduce whether the visit had helped at all.

"Maybe it'll make him think about it a little," Strange said sourly.

Across the basketball floor in the corner, the girl Carol Firebaugh motioned to Landers to come over, that she wanted to talk to him. Grimly Landers stared at her and slowly shook his head and turned away back to Strange.

"I just wish to hell Winch was here," Strange said sorrowfully. "If only fucking Winch was here."

"I thought Winch hated Prell," Landers said.

"He does. I mean, he doesn't like him," Strange said. "But that wouldn't matter."

When Strange asked him to come, Landers left and went with him to the snack bar to see the others from the company. Strange had decided they would make up the petition and sign it, anyway. Landers did not bother to say good-by to Carol Firebaugh, or even wave at her.

When the two of them went to report to Prell about the interview with Curran, Prell listened in silence until they were finished. Their inconclusive ending. Then still without a word he turned his head to the side and two tears squeezed out from under his closed lids. After a minute they decided to sneak away.

"I'm sorry, buddies," Prell called after them in a frog's croak. "I'm not quite myself. This thing's got me all worn down."

"Winch would know what to do," Strange said softly as he closed the ward door.

CHAPTER 12

Strange and Landers could not know it, but Winch already knew about Prell. And was already pushing forward his departure from Letterman to Luxor, because of him. Even as Strange was closing the big plywood swinging door of Prell's ward, and wishing his 1st/sgt were there.

Winch did not know what he could do about Prell, but if there was anything he could do, he wanted to be there. Not that the prick deserved it.

Winch had heard about Prell from old T.D. Hoggenbeck. After the hospital had let him out of bed, and he was finally back on his feet again and able to move around a little, he had had dinner with old T.D. and Lily. Lily was T.D.'s rawboned, long-jawed, acquisitive battle-ax of a Missus. They invited him to their three-story brick house outside the Presidio.

Winch was on the wagon so he figured he might as well go. He was unable to drink at all. It was one of the worst evenings he had ever spent. The worst nights he had spent on Guadalcanal were not as bad. All T.D. and old Lily could talk about were their recent acquisitions of property. Neither of them was what you could call a light drinker. When they had their string of whiskeys before dinner, the anguish and rage Winch suffered watching them were the worst he could remember. But he had learned about Prell from T.D.

"You remember old Jack Alexander?" T.D. said after they had put down their three huge strip-sirloins—Winch's cooked without salt. "From Wahoo? Old Alexander the Great?"

Winch remembered him. Alexander had been heavyweight champion of the Hawaiian Department during Winch's first hitch out there. "Alexander the Great" and "The Emperor," they had called him. He had held the title five straight years.

T.D. nodded. "Well, I just had a letter from old Jack. He holds down my same job in Luxor at Kilrainey General. He writes me they're going to take a leg off of one of your boys down there. Only this kid won't give his permission, and is throwing the whole place into a tizzy."

"Prell?"

"That's his name."

Winch listened, while T.D. unfolded the entire tale. It certainly sounded like Prell.

"Who's right?" he said when T.D. finished.

"Hard to say. The kid's pretty sick, I gather. None of the other doctors want to go up against the opinion of this civilian big shot, Col Baker." T.D. grinned. "It's causing old Col Stevens a lot of worry. He's the chief of administration down there. You remember him?"

Winch shook his head.

"Sure you do." T.D. unwound his long shanks and reached for the whiskey bottle. "He was at Riley with you. Had a company. Well, the kid's refusal is putting all the responsibility in his lap. And he's up for brigadier on the next promotions list. You must remember him?"

Winch shook his head again. Col Stevens was the least of his concerns. But Prell was not. Like a poker player covering a filled flush, he said, "T.D., by the way. I've been meaning to ask you. What're the chances of getting my orders cut to go on down there to Luxor? If I'm going to see about that job in 2nd Army, I had better be getting down there."

"Why, sure. Any time you say. Just as long as the doctors give you the medical clearance." T.D. looked as though he did not expect this could happen soon. An almost boyish concern flashed across his leathery hard-wrinkled face. "But you want to take care of yourself, you know. You're not in any perfect shape. You gave us quite a scare."

Winch shook his head. "I'm okay. As long as I don't do any boozing."

"Yeah. That must be hard."

"No," Winch said. "Not at all."

"I sure wouldn't like it," T.D. said, and reached for the bottle.

Winch watched him drink, without expression. Then watched him pour for Lily, and watched them both drink.

As soon as he could, he got out of there.

The next day he started working on the doctors who were handling his case. In actual fact, he found it nice to have some goal in life again. But that it should be Bobby Prell outraged him.

"You must have a lot of friends in high places," the chief heart man smiled, as he put away his stethoscope. "Normally we would discharge a man with what you've got."

"They need my experience," Winch said.

"I see no reason why you can't go," the doctor said. "As long as you remember all you're supposed to do. The diet. No heavy exercise. But what's your hurry? One hospital is the same as another."

"I've got to see about a job, that's supposed to be waiting for me down there," Winch said.

"Well, I wouldn't hold you back. You know that we're not sure as to just what the actual chemical causes are. But we're pretty sure it's tied in with all the alcohol you've put in you. You're just going to have to get used to the idea that you can never take one drink again the rest of your life."

"I'm used to it," Winch said.

But he wasn't. When he thought about it, it was enough to have him almost biting the walls. It was astonishing, when you got down in and noticed it, how much almost everything in America had to do with drinking. Every dinner. Every meal. Almost every social occasion. If you were chasing some girl. And at night, when everybody was philosophizing about life and the war and death, or dancing and trying to make out with some broad, if you did not drink you were outside everything. And bored to death by all of it.

Winch had gone back into town for one evening, after he had

been out of bed a week, but the whole place was totally impossible if you did not drink.

"Will you get a report up to W/O Hoggenbeck?" Winch asked. Another thing the attack had done was to entirely take away his sex drive. Or else, it was the medication they had been giving him.

"First thing tomorrow," the heart doctor said.

"Could you do it today?"

The doc nodded. "Sure, I guess."

After two hours of it in town Winch had come back to the hospital and had not left it since.

But the rest of it had not been really so bad. If you really wanted to die, it was probably as good a way as any, congestive heart failure. Winch wasn't sure if he wanted to. Obviously, he did not want to or he wouldn't be off drinking. But it was comforting to know about. If he ever did want to die, all he had to do was start drinking again.

They had slapped him in a bed in the heart ward and kept him there. And put him on a high dosage of diuretics and digitalis and kept an exact measurement of how much fluid he took in and how much he pissed out. Apparently, total bed rest was an excellent diuretic by itself. After twenty-four hours he was pissing out three times what he took in. And after the first night he was able to breathe easily again. They had kept him in the bed for five days.

Acute edema was what they called it. The retention of fluids. When the edema got into the lungs themselves was when it went into the congestive heart failure phase, and you began to cough up the foamy stuff. When it went into your lungs, your lungs began to fill up. This caused a further strain on the heart, which caused more edema. A vicious circle. Finally, you slowly drowned.

Once, at one point during that first night, he had nearly passed out. Everything had sort of faded away, and while he never actually lost consciousness, he seemed not to be inside himself any more. All the enormous fatigue, the exhaustion from coughing, the awful discomfort: a feeling of not being able to get enough air into his chest, no longer seemed to be coming from within himself. There never had been any actual physical pain. And now all the discomforts seemed to be somewhere else. All he wanted to do was to go sound asleep; and stay here, where all the discomforts weren't. The doctors and medics only ir-

ritated him. He could remember thinking that maybe this was
the beginning of death. From the start he had never been afraid,
all through the thing. From the beginning. And he wasn't afraid
then. As a matter of fact, it wasn't bad at all. It was pretty damn
good. At the same time, it was not as if he were *actually* outside
himself, and could "see" himself from some other place. In other
words, he could in fact "see" nothing. And yet there was this
persistent sense of another him.

Later he wasn't afraid either. It wasn't at all a bad way to go:
To shuffle off. To Buffalo. He remembered at one point he had
wanted to tell them the epitaph he had chosen for himself. It was
to be: *Do not pass Go. Do not collect two hundred dollars.* They were
to carve it in large letters on the stone, and forget about his
name. Leave the name off.

Later, one of the docs said to him, "I thought we were losing
you there for a minute." Winch only grinned at him.

But apparently his heart was not nearly as enlarged as the
excited young intern had thought, that night he reported in. He
was salvageable, as one of the docs put it. But he had come out
of it with a weakened heart. When after the five days they got
him back on his feet, he was ordered to start moving around.
They were very insistent on that.

On his feet, he was shaky on his pins. For a formerly strong
man it was an embarrassing experience. He felt too thin, too
fragile. But there was some bitterness in him that appreciated,
even relished, what had happened to him.

In the bed, it had been astonishing to watch the excess flesh
drain off his body. Apparently, or so they said, fat was held in
suspension in the fluid in the cells. And when you pissed off
water, you were also pissing off fat. He had been carrying the
beginnings of a paunch for a couple of years. This disappeared
and he had a flat belly again. He developed handsome new
hollows under his cheekbones. His feet and ankles had been
puffy and thick. Almost as he watched, this disappeared and he
could see the bones in his feet and hands again.

At least, they were willing to let him move on to Luxor. As
long as he obeyed all his dietary rules and did no heavy exercise,
and followed the injunction not to drink. Or smoke. Fine.

The next day he went up to see Hoggenbeck to make him
push the papers through. Old T.D. was getting him on an Air
Transport Command flight for Luxor. He was more than ready
to go. Prell or no Prell.

The Army car from the Luxor Army Air Base deposited him in front of the big front doors of the hospital. There were no welcoming committees, no groups of patients looking to see if they could spot somebody they knew. Winch arrived alone. For a little he stood on the expanse of concrete in the summer sun and looked up at the entrance. He was thinking about that stupid dumb fuck, Prell. Then he picked up the green airman's B-4 bag and carried it up the six low concrete steps to the big doors and inside.

He could feel it immediately in his faster breathing, and in his heart action. It was always a surprise and a shock, to have it happen to him like this. In one way it gave Winch sort of a kick. It was a little like walking around with a loaded time bomb inside your chest. One that might blow at any moment. At least, it made everything—life . . . every moment . . . every breath— an exciting event. It was a little like being back in combat.

When the orderly who picked him up at the desk read the tag on his shirt front, he looked alarmed and scolded him seriously for carrying the bag. Winch simply grinned at him. "You guys," the orderly said glumly. "You're all of you crazy."

The first thing Winch did in his new ward was telephone Jack Alexander, the old ex-pug, and arrange to meet him. Alexander had been expecting him.

But before he could keep his date with Alexander, he was visited by a deputation for the nine-man contingent from his old company, in the persons of Strange and Landers.

Somehow, by the never-quiet hospital grapevine, the word had already gotten around to them that he was here. The others, Strange said, were waiting in the snack bar to meet him. Strange had told them to wait there, instead of all coming to the ward.

Strange coughed. Both men had sort of stopped short and stared, when they first came in and saw Winch. Winch was aware how thin and frail he looked. Now the two of them eyed each other guiltily. Winch decided to beat them to the punch and said in a frigid voice, "Well, what the hell are you staring at?"

"You've lost a little weight," Strange said.

"So? I'm on a diet."

"Yeah," Strange said. "Well, good. Have you been sick, too?"

"I've been a little sick. But I'm over it now," Winch said. "Now, what's all this about fucking Prell?"

They both started in to talk at once. Then Landers shut up,

and Strange went on alone. But Winch held up a hand and stopped him. He already knew all the background, he told them. The last he'd heard, this Col Baker had requested authority to take off the leg. Col Stevens had not yet given the okay. The other doctors all seemed to agree with Baker.

"That's correct," Strange said. It felt good to have the old First Sarn't holding the reins again. Strange didn't want the job. "But it's more a question of degree. Of approach. Than of absolute agreement. There's this other doctor, name of Curran. Prell seems to feel Curran's not as hot to amputate it right away, and would give it more time. But Baker outranks Curran. If Curran disagrees, he's not saying so."

"Then we probably can't count on him for much," Winch said. "The main question is, are the doctors right? Is Baker right?"

"Who knows? How can we judge that? All we know is Prell wants to keep the leg. And we're trying to help him." Strange shrugged, happy to pass along the buck of decision-making. "Landers here talked to this Curran. Tell him about it, Landers."

Slowly Landers began to tell about his interview with Curran, and its inconclusive result. He wanted to get it exactly right for Winch. Landers was finding he was much less in awe of Winch than before. Whether it was Winch's new physical fragility, or the new wild something that kept happening to himself lately, he did not know. But he had always had this desire to be as absolutely honest with Winch as possible. Something in Winch demanded it. That hadn't changed. When he finished, Winch went on staring at him, piercingly.

"What do you think, yourself?" Winch said. "What's your opinion of it?"

"I'm inclined to think that Prell is probably right," Landers said. "I think Col Curran would probably wait, if Prell was his patient. But Prell isn't. And if he isn't, Curran isn't going to intervene."

"And that brings it back to Col Stevens."

"I guess so," Strange said.

"And what influence do you think you've got with Col Stevens?" Winch leered. "If any."

Strange shrugged. "None." Then, looking a little shamefaced, he told him about the petition. They had gotten it together, and all signed it, and Strange was keeping it in the drawer of his bedside table, about the only place patients had to keep anything personal.

"A petition? In the Army?" Winch said. "And whose idea was this?" He swung on Landers. "Yours?"

"No," Landers said. "It was Prell's own idea, I guess." He moved his head. "He gave it to Johnny Stranger."

It was the first time Winch had ever heard his former clerk use Strange's personal nickname out in the open like that, and he stared at the younger wartime-only soldier. Well, we were all changing. And fast. It was only to be expected. When the situation changes, the juxtapositions and orbits of the relative bodies within the situation change. All except Prell.

"I should have guessed it," he said in a low, iron-edged voice. "That stupid, dumbass son of a bitch. The hero-chaser. If there was any way for him to mess some damn thing up, and damage himself in the process, that hero-chaser would find the way to do it. And they'd give him a medal for it. We don't even know whether the doctors are wrong or not, do we?"

"No," Strange said, "we don't. But if it's going to kill him, and he wants to take the chance. *I* think they ought to let him do it."

"Does anybody know why it isn't healing?"

"No, they don't," Strange said. "Tell me something, Top. Did you come all this way down here just because of Prell?"

Winch swung his head to glare at Strange. "Are you out of your skull? You think I'd come here? I go where I'm sent, like all the rest of you meat-wagon candidates. Now, you men clear out of this and let me get myself shaped up. I've got a medical appointment."

"Do you think there's anything you can do to help?" Strange said.

"Me? What?" Winch said. "I don't carry any more weight here than you do. This aint the old regiment."

"We'd like to ask you to do what you can," Landers said suddenly, and loudly.

Winch did not answer him. He simply stared at them expressionlessly. As they left, he turned back to his bed. After a moment, he began to straighten his bathrobe.

Jack Alexander was a different proposition from old T.D. Hoggenbeck. His office was equally impressive, and he was careful to take as good care of his creature comforts, but there the resemblance ended. And Winch knew it.

And Winch had never served with Alexander and didn't

know him, as he did old T.D. Alexander the Great—"The Emperor"—was just finishing his reign and shipping home with his loot he'd collected as number-one fighter in the Department, when Winch was just first arriving in Wahoo as a lowly corporal. Alexander had been a legend in the Army, even then.

Now he was old. And he looked it. In fact, he resembled nothing so much as a huge, ancient, bait-wise old sea turtle. With his totally bald head and thick-wrinkled face, his only slightly flattened beak and big jaw and lipless mouth like a razor blade, bleak as the edge of an ice floe. With his faded, pale, flat, blue eyes which had seen just about everything the earth had to offer, and neither liked nor hated it all that much. An old turtle who had swum the oceans of his planet for two centuries, avoiding the traps laid by men and wearing the scars to prove it, until now he was so huge there wasn't anything for him to fear any more. And Alexander was huge. He had always been a big man, even back in the old days, but then he had been relatively lean. Now he carried a huge hard paunch that stuck out in front of him two feet, and meat packed the skin of his head and neck to bursting. And it wasn't fat. It was meat. How or why he had chosen to wind up his days here at Kilrainey General in Luxor was anybody's guess.

Winch, with his new experience, couldn't help wondering fleetingly what Alexander's blood pressure must be.

With his thick fingers he pulled out a bottle of bourbon and sat it upon the desk and gestured. Winch nodded and grinned. He wasn't supposed to, he said; but he could smell it. Alexander poured two shots and sat down and motioned to the chair across from him. So far he hadn't said a single word.

Winch wet his lips only, with the whiskey, and collected his thoughts.

"So far I can't figure out, or find out, whether this man Prell of mine ought to have his leg off or not," he said.

Alexander nodded.

"You understand, I just happen to be here."

The huge Alexander nodded again.

"If it ought to come off, it ought to come off," Winch said. "Naturally, I'd like to see him save it. But he seems to feel that at least one of these damned civilian doctors would give him more time if he had the authority."

"That's Curran," Alexander said. His voice was a deep rasp from down in the middle of his paunch, which flowed past a voice box covered with the scar tissue of many years of punches.

"Curran," Winch said.

"It's got Col Stevens upset," Alexander said. "He's up for brigadier the next promotions list. A scandal could scotch him."

It was Winch's turn to nod.

"Even getting noticed could," Alexander said.

"What's this Baker like?"

"He's a hardhead. He's in love with himself. He's good," Alexander said.

"And Curran?"

"The same," Alexander said. "Younger."

"So there's no choice. What's wrong with stalling it?" Winch said.

"Nothing," Alexander said. "But Prell could die."

"Don't other men die here?"

Alexander's huge shoulders moved ever so slightly in the expensive swivel chair. "Sure."

"So?" Winch said. He was playing it all by ear now, a response at a time.

"There's been so much notoriety," Alexander said. "Publicity. He might have relatives." He moved in the chair, an enormous bulk. "I'm telling you how the Old Man, how Col Stevens is thinking."

"He hasn't got any relatives," Winch said.

"He's got a lot of friends," Alexander said. "Apparently."

"I can promise the friends won't say anything. About anything," Winch said. "They all want the surgeons to wait."

"I guess the Old Man—if I was the Old Man, that is—would sure like to be sure of that," Alexander said.

Winch paused, as an idea hit him. "As a matter of fact," he said finally, "I've got a—" his throat choked itself off at the word *petition*, "a paper," he said instead, "that's signed by all the former members of his outfit here, which asks that Prell's leg not be amputated."

"I'd sure like to have a copy of that paper," Alexander said.

"Would you show it to Col Stevens?"

"No," Alexander said. "I couldn't do that."

"I can get you a copy of it," Winch said.

"Signed?"

"Sure, signed."

"I would like to have it," Alexander said.

"Then there's another thing," Winch said. "This man Prell's been recommended for a Congressional Medal by our Division commander. Did you know that? It ought to be in his 201 File, hadn't it?"

Alexander nodded his enormous head. "It is. The Old Man's seen it. There's an interesting bit on that. When the man first got here, I got a letter on him. From Washington. They wanted to know how he was getting along. I had to write back not so good. They didn't answer. Later I wrote two follow-ups on that medal. We got decorations lists here, you see. And every so often the Old Man makes some presentations. I got answers on all the others. But I didn't get an answer on that Prell medal. Now what does that sound like to you?"

"Where was the inquiry letter from?" Winch said, his mind racing around.

"From AGO."

"Where do the medal responses come from?"

"The Medals Division."

"So?" Winch asked. He answered himself, "So. It looks like they don't want a one-legged Medal of Honor winner right now. At least, not from Luxor."

The big head nodded slowly. "That was what it looked like to me."

"Wouldn't Col Stevens like to have a Medal of Honor winner here?" Winch asked. "Make the presentation?"

"Not a dead one," Alexander said. "With no relatives."

"The regiment would like to have that medal," Winch said.

"You can't speak officially for the regiment, though," Alexander said. His turtle-horn mouth cracked a mirthless grin. "And I think it's live Medal of Honor winners, with all their arms and legs, that they're looking for, right now."

"There's a very good chance that he'll live, I seem to feel," Winch said. "Better than even, I'd say. But this Col Curran hasn't any authority."

"The Old Man couldn't take a patient away from Col Baker and give him to Col Curran," Alexander croaked mildly. "But he does have an awful lot of work right now. Awful busy."

"And he could stay busy awhile," Winch said.

"I would like to have that paper," Alexander said.

"I can have it for you this afternoon."

"Naturally, I wouldn't show it to Col Stevens. It might look too much like some kind of a petition. You can imagine what that would do to Col Stevens. Like a red flag to a bull. But he might hear about the men, huh?"

"You'll have it today," Winch said.

"Much obliged," Alexander said. For the first time since they'd started, he picked up his shot glass of bourbon. He gestured a salute with it and tossed it off. He put the bottle away.

"Of course, I can't speak for Col Stevens, you understand," Alexander said with massive modesty in the flat turtle eyes.

"Of course not," Winch said.

When Winch had his hand already on the stainless steel doorknob, the chief w/o grunted behind his desk. Winch turned around.

"It's nice to do business with you, Sgt Winch," Alexander said. "Old T.D. Hoggenbeck wasn't wrong about you."

"Well, it's nice to do business with you, sir," Winch said.

"Maybe we'll do more," Alexander said from behind the desk, without even a crack of a smile.

"Maybe," Winch said. "It's possible." Old T.D. must have told him about that, too.

"I know everybody at 2nd Army," Alexander said.

Winch nodded. So old T.D. had told him. He shut the door behind him.

There was no difficulty in getting hold of the petition. Strange turned it over to him immediately. After the noon meal Winch read it, rewrote it in a less formal petition style, and took it with him to the snack bar where he was to meet with and say hello to the other men, and had them all re-sign it. Then he sat and talked with them awhile.

It was not much of a reunion. At least, not for Winch. Without knowing it about Landers, Winch had the same reaction to all of them that Landers had had. They did not seem to be the same men. Their faces were all different. He remembered them as the men they had been when they left Guadalcanal back in January or February on the big planes or the Navy ships, when their faces had been skeletal and hollow-eyed and haunted, and full of fear and terror and a boyish relief. Different men. More like his perpetually dehydrated platoons, who were still out there.

When he left them, he took the paper up to Jack Alexander's office and presented it, and had another ritual shot glass of Alexander's bourbon, which he tasted but did not drink.

Then he went back down and lay down on his bed. He was totally exhausted. He was so exhausted he could hardly place one foot in front of the other. He was so physically worn out he did not bother to get up when the evening meal was served, and missed supper.

Later, when he went to bed for the night, he couldn't sleep. As on so many other nights since his recovery, he was haunted by that impression he had had of another him, that night when he had almost passed out back at Letterman. Another him, outside there somewhere. Where could it be? What was it?

He had never had another sensation like it, not even during his wildest drunken debauch.

He lay listening to the breathing of the other sleeping men on the ward (there were only two others in the heart ward) and thought about Prell, and that he would have to meet him, go see him. Since he had to do it, he might as well do it tomorrow and not put it off.

CHAPTER 13

Winch had no idea what he was going to say to Prell. Nor did he have any idea what to expect from Prell when he saw him. He tried to brief himself before going, not only by talks with Landers and Strange, but also by talking to Corello and Drake and the others from the company. Corello and Drake and the rest were no help at all. Strange and Landers were almost no help.

Landers kept hemming and hawing, and saying Prell looked bad. "Well, naturally he looks bad," Winch said, "you dumbass clerk. That doesn't help me any."

After a lot of haranguing him, and some considerable but useless soul-searching on Landers' part, Landers finally looked up with widened eyes and said, "Well, he just looks like he's run out of gas."

"What does that mean?"

"Well, you know. No gas, no steam. Just what the hell do you want to find out, Top?" He was beginning to get angry. "I'm trying to tell you all I can."

"You're supposed to be a goddamned college boy," Winch

sneered. "Can't you express yourself any better than that? If you can't, you ought to pack it in and shoot yourself."

"I'm trying, damn you."

It was the first time Winch could ever remember Landers cursing him directly. Usually he would curse all around him, indirectly, but never head-on, face to face. Well, the little bucks grew up in the herd, and wanted to try their antlers, and take on the big bucks. "What the hell do you mean, no gas?" he bellowed. "No heart? No will?"

"No," Landers said. "No, he's got heart. And will. You wouldn't believe how much. I guess it's energy I mean. He's run out of energy."

This brought Winch up short. He had learned, lately, what it was to run out of energy. He had never used to.

"Well, why the fuck don't you say what you mean?"

"You can have all the heart in the world. And all the will," Landers said. "It doesn't help you a bit when you finally run out of energy."

Strange was not much better, though it was a calmer discussion. Strange talked about despair.

"I've been watching him for just that, you know, Top. Ever since Efate. And on the ship. He's made this same fight, what now? Twice? This is the third time. I've been afraid all along it was going to hit him. That he was going to get full of despair. I thought long before now. He's really a front-runner, you know."

"You can say that again," Winch said thinly.

"At least, it's better when he's out there in front, leading. And all that."

"So you think he's, uh, despaired, huh?" Winch said.

"Well, it's been a long time. Landers talked to this Col Curran, and Curran said it was something in his body chemistry. Well, what the hell is that? Who knows anything about that? Even the doctors don't know much about that. What makes a man's body chemistry be one way one time, and another way another time?" Strange paused, then shrugged his heavy shoulders. "I don't know," he said. "I just don't know."

So that was what he was left with, Winch thought. Energy or despair. Or, energy *and* despair. What good was that? Who knew? Who knew anything? About anything?

He even picked his time. He talked to Prell's ward boy, and

the ward boy said that most patients were at their best around midmorning, after they've gotten over the waking-up process, and before they have their noon meal, which always took energy and time to digest. And that way, Prell was normal. So Winch postponed his visit by a day, in order to be arriving at the proper time. He still didn't know what to say to him, or do. What did you say to a man whom you didn't much like and who was about to lose a leg, to make him get over his despair, and pump some energy back into him? It was all a goddamned game, anyway. Life. People played at it like football or chess or poker, even when they were dying. At the last minute he decided to take Strange with him, as a kind of smoothing-over agent.

There was certainly no question that he looked awful, Prell. He did not look even remotely like the same man Winch had last seen, in the ward on Efate. Spread-eagled on the bed, with his legs still up in the air like a goddamned woman about to have a baby, he looked already dead except for his eyes. His feet were purple, his face a pale mauve, shading into a purple that was nearly black under his sunken eyes.

In spite of all that, he seemed visibly to pull himself all together, when he saw who it was.

"Hello, Top," he said in a pale, hollow voice from the depths of the bed. "Come to pay your last respects?"

"Hello, Prell," Winch said evenly. That pulling-himself-together act made him think. "How are you?"

It was all such a goddamned game. Everything was. Bravado. Bravery. Fear. Pride, humiliation, dignity, decency, viciousness. And yet it was serious. Even panic started out as a game, before it got serious.

"Come to gloat, hunh?" Prell said faintly. "Come to say, I told you so."

Something flashed in the back of Winch's brain, like a green Go signal. Except this was a green explosion. Which engulfed everything. He had been playing it by ear, looking for something to say.

"Still looking for sympathy, huh?" he said. He heard Strange inhale sharply behind him. "Still hungerin' to be appreciated by everybody."

Something obsidian glittered somewhere down in the depths of the jet-black sunken eyes of Prell. A kind of evil. A murderous hatred. "That's me," he said faintly. "Always want to be appreciated."

Winch had debated long, as to whether he should tell Prell about the stalling game he had engineered with Alexander and Col Stevens. He had not told anybody, had not told any of the others, not even Strange. It was too ticklish. And they couldn't any of them keep their fucking mouths shut. One of them was bound to tell it. And if it got around and got back to Col Stevens and Jack Alexander, all the good that might come out of it would be broken. Stevens was noted for having a terrible temper, that was why he tried so hard never to lose it. And Winch and Strange still didn't know if Col Baker was right, about amputating. So Winch had told nobody.

But he had debated telling Prell. And had already decided not to. Now he suddenly knew he was right, not to. That wasn't what Prell needed. What Prell needed was enemies. An enemy, if he was going to fight. He wasn't complex enough to fight without an enemy there in front of him.

"You reckon they'll give me a tin cup and some GI pencils to sell, when they let me out of this?" Prell said from the bed.

"They'll do better than that," Winch said. "They'll give you a pension. And a leather leg. So you can go down to the American Legion on Saturday nights and show the boys your stump and tell them how you fought the war in the South Pacific. Just don't tell them about your squad."

"You son of a bitch," Prell said. His voice did not increase in tone or volume, but the timbre of it got taut, vibrant. "I'll kill you when I get out of this. That's a promise. I'll spend the rest of my life looking you up, if it takes the rest of my life, and kill your sharecropping ass."

"I don't think so," Winch said. "I'll probably be dead long before you're well enough to do anything." There was probably more truth in that than he realized when he said it, Winch thought, and grinned. Oh, well. He would be his enemy. Everybody needed one enemy.

"At least, you won't be going around leading any squads into any death traps," he said.

The Indian eyes of Prell glittered at him from the bed. He didn't answer.

"I think you'd better go," the ward nurse said nervously from beside Winch, "really."

"Okay. Well, take it easy, kid," he said. "Keep fighting." He turned on his heel.

Outside in the corridor he had to lean against the wall. He felt

drained and absolutely gray all over, and had to suck in energy
with his breath.

"Jesus Christ, Top," Strange protested beside him. "What did
you have to do that for?"

"Shut up," Winch hissed, "you dumbass. Get the fuck away
from me, and leave me alone."

After a minute Winch straightened up, and headed back for
his ward. Strange had only walked off ten steps away, and fell
in step beside him.

Four days later, or perhaps it was five, Prell miraculously
began to mend. It took that long to note the signs, and it took
several days longer to be sure the signs were real and weren't
just temporary manifestations. As if nothing had even been
wrong with it, except getting broken, the leg began to heal. The
bone to knit. Strange found it hard to believe. He had been
expecting a serious relapse, after Winch's visit. In any case, Prell
was mending, and the crisis they had all been waiting for for so
long was past. Certainly Strange gave no credit to Winch's visit.
Rather the reverse. Winch had lost control of himself. Strange
felt it showed how far gone the old 1st/sgt was, after whatever
it was had happened to him. Strange and Landers spent a lot of
time with Prell, and Strange noted that never once did Prell ever
mention or refer to his conversation with Winch. It struck
Strange that he would not like to be Winch, when Prell did get
up and around.

Winch himself didn't know what to think. He could not believe that what he had done had had that much effect. The
change was too precipitous, too sudden and dramatic, for him
to believe his action had caused it. Prell must already have been
beginning to heal when Winch came to see him, if it could
happen that fast. So, or so Winch felt, the whole thing had been
a waste.

Landers had a theory of his own. Strange had told him, and
sworn him to secrecy, about the scene with Winch; but Landers
didn't think that had anything to do with it one way or the
other. A few days after the good news concerning Prell had
circulated, he had run into Col Curran along one of the brick-
columned walkways and Curran had stopped him.

"You know I've been wanting to tell you this, but I haven't
had the chance," Curran said, with his weirdly merry grin
Landers had been getting to dislike. "Do you remember something you told me that day you came to see me? About if we

couldn't give him something more, why didn't we take something away?"

"No, I don't," Landers said. "I don't remember."

"Well, you did. And it set me to thinking. I spent half a night going over Prell's case all by myself, because of it. Well, I found something nobody else had noticed. You know, all of you men from the South Pacific are still taking atabrine. Because of the malaria. You're supposed to keep taking it for four months after you get back." He leaned forward with his smile, and took Landers lightly by his bathrobe sleeve. "Well, I noticed Prell was being given atabrine. Naturally enough. Since he's South Pacific, too. Well, I took him off it. On my own hook. Without telling anybody.

"It was after that that he began to heal."

"But is that possible?" Landers said. "I mean, medically?"

"No," Curran said. "Absolutely, positively not." His face suddenly got very sober. "But strange things happen. You never know with people. Weird things affect them. It's almost metaphysical. It's possible that in a borderline case like his, where everything counts, that the atabrine was tiring him and through fatigue inhibiting his ability to heal. But if I ever told anybody that, I'd be in hell's own way of proving it.

"So, it may well be, indirectly, that you are responsible for his mending.

"But I don't want you to tell anybody about this. Even Col Baker doesn't know. I didn't tell him I was doing it. You'll keep it to yourself, huh?"

"Sure," Landers said. And he had. He had not even told Strange. Certainly he had not told Winch.

Later on, on his own, he had deliberately gotten into a discussion—a "theoretical" discussion—with his own ward boy about it. The ward boy had looked up everything on atabrine. There was absolutely no reason to think that atabrine had any inhibiting power, or any effect at all, on any of the healing mechanisms. But then why would that crazy Curran have told Landers a story like that? Catch Landers telling a tale like that to Winch?

Winch would not have cared. Probably, he would not even have heard. After the energy and thought he had put out on Prell, beginning as far back as Letterman, he was totally depleted. It was all he could do to pull himself up out of bed to take his meals. His own doctors, on the heart ward, told him it was the natural result of his trip from California, plus the substantial steps he had made in his own recovery. They of course knew nothing about Prell, and told Winch what he needed was rest. Winch took them at their word. What with the diuretics he was still taking, which still so thoroughly inhibited his sex drive, he did not even think about going to town. The very thought exhausted him. But he was not too tired to go when, a week after Prell's start toward recovery, he got a summons from Sgt/Maj Alexander to come to Alexander's office.

Jack Alexander, of course, had sent in a progress report on Prell, as soon as it was established for sure that he was on the mend. Had sent it to the same AGO office designation in Washington that he had received the initial query from. Now he pushed a letter across his desk for Winch to read. It was from the Medals Division. They wanted a dossier on Prell. Everything that might be pertinent from his Service Record and 201 File to help them decide on a nominee and potential recipient of the Congressional Medal of Honor. Winch read it through and shoved it back across the desk.

"I know you can't drink," Alexander rasped with his boxer's larynx, "or smoke. But you ought to do something to celebrate. Why don't you go into town and get laid?"

Winch could only shake his head, and sit there, wanting most of all to roar with laughter.

They would have to wait on the confirmation but that was only a formality now, Alexander said. It would be the first Congressional Medal awarded at the hospital. They were building the next medals presentation around it. Col Stevens was already working on the plans and the list. It was going to be the biggest presentation Kilrainey'd ever had.

"You're on it yourself," Alexander said.

Winch could only nod, again. "That D.S.M."

"A Distinguished Service Medal won't look bad on your records after the war," the practical Alexander said.

So it was that, almost a month after Prell's first upward turn for the better, Winch along with most of the other souls at the hospital found himself standing at parade rest on the asphalt of the hospital's central compound. The compound was not a parade ground, had not been designed as one, and didn't look like one. It was too small, and it was too crowded, with all the formations that had been marched into it. Just about everybody who could move under his own locomotion, and many who could not, had been called out. The entire hospital staff, except those actually on duty, was present also, on orders of Col Stevens. Col Stevens had even had some bunting strung from the buildings around. The civilian press as well as the Army papers were well represented, with reporters and photographers from papers as far away as Chicago and Kansas City.

There was a large number and long list of men to be decorated. At the center of all this was Prell, in his bathrobe in a wheelchair, with his two legs out stiffly in front of him on the rests in plaster casts. Almost everybody, naturally—with the exception of Winch—received Purple Hearts. There were several Bronze Stars, some with the V for valor, some without, and one Silver Star. Landers to his surprise got a Bronze Star (without the V), for meritorious service. Winch was given his D.S.M., the only one given. Then Col Stevens marched out, Sgt/Maj Alexander at his heels two steps to the right, Alexander's huge bulk unbelievably light on his feet and in absolute step, carrying the flat larger-than-normal presentation box. When Stevens placed the light blue ribbon with its white stars around Prell's neck, there was a hint of tears in Prell's black Indian eyes. But when he looked at Winch, immediately beside him, the glitter came back in them.

Winch stood at attention with the others, in the uncomfortably hot early September sun, not knowing whether to laugh or spit, wanting to do both, doing neither.

Directly in front of him, behind Col Stevens, Alexander's right eyelid flicked down for a split second in a gesture of sanity.

CHAPTER 14

While Prell's crisis was developing, the group from Letterman who had come with him settled in, and became part of the hospital scene and part of the hospital scenery. Casts among them began to disappear and crutches began to be replaced by canes. Certain faces disappeared, and they would learn someone had been discharged. Amputees in wheelchairs who had been there when they arrived, and whose faces became recognizable, began to be seen struggling manfully along the corridors and brick-porticoed walkways with their artificial limbs and canes. Every time Bobby Prell saw one of them his stomach went sick. For the group that had arrived with Prell and Landers and Strange, it had all become only a matter now of waiting to heal.

But new groups were coming in behind them every ten days or couple of weeks, and going through their own shakedowns. Men from the European campaigns came in trains from the eastern ports. Others from the Pacific battles came through Letterman or the hospital in Seattle. The two groups found it interesting to compare notes on casualties and deaths and particular maimings, once they'd settled in. The German 88, for example, had no counterpart as yet in the Pacific jungle campaigns.

Wounds from burnings were much more prevalent in the European theater, due to the greater use of tanks. Illnesses on the other hand—malaria, blackwater, and the like—caused many more casualties in the Pacific than in Europe.

During the weeks after Prell's turn for the better, Johnny Stranger made another trip home to Cincinnati, on an illegal four-day pass produced by Winch through Sgt/Maj Alexander. Anything over a three-day pass should have counted as a furlough, of course. Winch and Alexander got around this by giving Strange two passes, one for three days and one for a day. Strange found it no better, not more livable in Cincinnati the second time than he had the first. If anything, Linda Sue seemed more distant and preoccupied the second time than the first.

During the same period, Marion Landers kept his fiasco of a date with Carol Firebaugh, had his cast off at the hospital, and received and took a ten-day convalescent furlough home to his hometown of Imperium, Indiana. The ten-day furlough, in actual fact, came just shortly after the big awards ceremony. So that Landers had his Bronze Star in its handsome gold-stamped blue-leather case to take home with him to show, along with his Purple Heart. Landers took them. By some sly, sure instinct Landers knew that the medals would infuriate his father. But Landers would rather have suffered the terrors of another wounding than to have worn either ribbon in Luxor.

Nobody from the Luxor hospital ever wore his decoration ribbons, or campaign ribbons. Among the infantry soldiers at Kilrainey, as if with some elite class, it was permissible to wear the blue and silver Combat Infantryman's Badge with its silver wreath. So Landers would wear that. But nothing else. It was an iron rule among the combat men at Kilrainey about the ribbons, and the punishment for breaking it was instant and total derision from all sides. Nobody seemed to know from where the rule came, or what started it. But they all obeyed it. It was as though some bitter secret of contempt or disdain passed among the combat casualties and caused the rule to leap full-blown into existence, an absolute law. We don't need your pats on the head, the attitudes seemed to say, we've been where you haven't.

Landers' date with Carol Firebaugh began well enough but ended up a strikeout. Landers had wanted to take her for dinner to the Plantation Roof on the top of the Peabody. "The Roof" was Luxor's "Top O' The Mark," which, whatever it might have been before, was now hectic and full of uniforms and making money hand over fist, and the scene of so many service-connected seductions. There was a wild, wide-open quality about it, as though everybody was thoroughly enjoying the idea that four months from now everyone present might be dead. Landers had been there once with a couple of men from the company, without girls, and had wanted to come back and bring a girl there. Vaguely, he had thought about himself being able to talk to her; about himself, and about what had happened to him.

Instead, Carol Firebaugh, who didn't like "The Roof," suggested they have dinner at a restaurant she knew called Mrs. Thompson's Tea Room.

It made a weird scene. For the first time in nearly a year and a half, except for one three-day pass back home in uniform, Landers found himself in a genuine homelike, non-Army, non-war atmosphere. Mrs. Thompson's Tea Room was run by three elderly white Southern ladies who were widows apparently, helped by one old Negro gentleman who did part of the waiting on tables, and apparently did much of the organization. White couples and white parties of four sat at tables covered with snowy tablecloths in the genteel, uncrowded, middle-class atmosphere, eating leisurely dinners of excellent Southern-style cooking, and talking quietly. Every table had its brown-paper-sacked whiskey bottle, and drinks were served, but as adjuncts to the food, instead of as means to get drunk as quick as possible. Almost none of the men were in uniform and those who were, looked as if they were at home.

Landers had not been anywhere like this since leaving the university. This was like what he thought about when he thought of home. Despite his despair over his family. It was certainly not the place to carry through any seduction. But neither was it the place to try to talk to someone, anyone, about what had happened to him back on the hill ridge in New Georgia. Landers could only just barely formulate it in words to himself. How was he going to connect it to this kind of place? They were like two different worlds. There was no way to pull the two close enough together for any spark of understanding to bridge the gap. Quite suddenly he was furiously angry, outraged at all this false security of snowy white tablecloths and doddery old ladies serving food they had lovingly prepared themselves to appreciative diners. He was being disloyal to

Winch and Strange and Prell and all the others by merely being
here. Instead of talking, he became tongue-tied.

So they talked about Carol. Or she did. About her ambitions.
About her frustrations. She had been going to Western Reserve
to study acting and would be going back at midterm this year
for her final semester. The war had kept her at home, with her
brother gone. But she didn't know whether she had the guts to
strike out on her own and go to New York afterward, which was
what you had to do. She was having parental problems. Her
folks wanted her to stay here in Luxor and marry some nice
young man with "prospects." Some young attorney, or some
smart young doctor. They would probably help her with money
if she went to New York, but how long could she fight the
system in New York? And there were all those producers you
might have to sleep with.

Landers mostly listened and nodded, and fidgeted. Carol Firebaugh had a deliciously soft, deliciously uneven, deliciously attractive mouth, and when she looked at you with that slightly
cocked eye of hers moving over your face as she kept refocusing,
she was so appealing and so vulnerable you wanted to take her
in your arms and pet her, and murmur reassurances in her ear
even as you fucked your cock into her. Landers couldn't help it.
That was exactly how she made him feel. And it was clearly why
all the other fellows at the hospital found her so attractive. But
everything she stood for, everything she was, everything she
liked, made his sense of disloyalty to his old outfit and his common experience with them mount alarmingly.

"I don't see how you men stand it," Carol said at one point
sympathetically, talking about the hospital. "And most of you
will have to go back again."

"We stand it because we don't have any choice," Landers said
with sour fatalism. "That's why." And more and more he felt
he should be out with them, the guys, getting drunk and picking
up whores.

After the dinner they walked for a while in a part of Luxor
Landers had not seen. There was no war here. Big comfortable
old houses lined the streets behind their big old trees. Not rich,
but comfortably well-off. Very comfortably well-off. When
finally they went inside the one owned by her parents, they
wound up on the sofa in her parents' parlor. It really was a
parlor. And it was the same kind of thing Landers had been
doing for years at the university, in the homes of girls in Bloom-

ington, or in the homes of girls back home in Imperium. She put on some records. She liked Ray Eberley. She had taken off her glasses, which she seldom wore, and tears came into her slightly fuzzy, slightly unfocusing eyes when "A Nightingale Sang in Berkeley Square" came on. Her eyes were violet-colored. And then they were necking—but not necking, really: love-kissing—on the sofa.

"What about your parents?" Landers said.

"Are you kidding?" Carol said with a sad smile. "They're in bed asleep half-drunk. They never wake up."

When the record player ran out of discs and shut itself off, she left it. But every time Landers tried to get his hand under her blouse onto her breasts or push his hand up along her stockings under her skirt, she pushed him away and fought him off hard. Once he managed to get two fingers far enough up her skirt to touch her panties and feel the cushion of pubic hair beneath. But that was all.

After two hours of this, sporting a powerful throbbing erection so swollen that it hurt him, wet in the crotch from all the unutilized lubrication fluid that was pouring out of him, Landers disentangled himself and got up and blew out his breath and looked at his watch. Had to be getting back to the hospital. Carol got up too, with a questioning look in her slightly unfocusing eyes. But she made no protests. At the door as she let him out, she said in a soft voice, only, "You're not very forceful." Landers was across the porch and down the steps and halfway down the walk before he realized what she had said and what it meant. But when he turned back to look and debate going back, the lights went out as he watched.

All the way back to the hospital he felt outraged, and filled with that wild, directionless rage he had been getting so often lately.

It was directionless, because there was nothing to point it at. Aim it at like a rifle. And because it was so directionless, it became wilder. For several days he avoided her by staying away from the big recreation center where she worked. It was hard on him to stay away from the rec center, because it was where everyone went to meet and where everything was going on. When he did reappear, she immediately called him over and wanted to know why she hadn't seen him. She seemed to think they would, or should, be having another date soon. But Landers did not ask her. When he looked at her and thought about his

evening with her, and about their dinner at Mrs. Thompson's
Tea Room and its safe genteel interior, the rage filled him,
making him want to rip their safe quiet genteelness all apart and
show her, show them, the understructure of blood and lopped-
off bone their genteelness was built on. Prell's bone. Corello's
blood.

Anyway, Landers did not feel like making any more dates
with her or anybody right then. Let her wait. Let them all wait.
That morning Curran had told him they were going to take his
cast off tomorrow or next day. Not only that, Curran said, they
were not going to give him back his crutches. He would have
to get along the best way he could on the uncased leg with his
cane. The mere thought of it filled Landers with a nameless,
helpless terror. What if he fell on it? Let Carol Firebaugh, and
her three widow ladies, try to empathize with that. Empathize,
she was always saying. If Carol Firebaugh and her three widow
ladies wanted a piece of his hot body, they could damn well wait.
Maybe he would see her later, and maybe not.

The awards ceremony was a week after the day they took his
cast off. Although his therapy sessions in the labs seemed to be
progressing, Landers was sure he would not be able to walk to
it, and claim the Purple Heart he was supposed to get. But he
did. Though it tired the leg terribly, going and standing up
there all that time in the sun. And when he got his Bronze Star
in addition, he was dumbfounded. He knew he did not deserve
it. There was no question of that. Lots of other men deserved
it more than he did.

When Curran offered him the ten-day furlough a couple of
days later, Landers accepted it immediately, although it was
probably too soon for his leg, because he could not stand to think
any more about the cushiony pubic hair of Carol Firebaugh.

Although Imperium had always been a hard place to reach by
train, Landers took the train. Two little branch lines served
Imperium. Going by train meant a lot of changing. But the
thought of taking the Greyhounds, where he would be unable
to move around at all for hours on end, was more than Landers
could tolerate with his leg as weak as it was and his ankle so stiff.

As it turned out, the train was no help. Almost before they
moved out of the station a wild party developed in the day coach
Landers was riding, so that he was terrified and unnerved and
unable to move around much. He did not have a sleeping car
berth. Pullman berths were reserved long in advance, and any-

way he did not want to spend the money on a sleeping car. He did not even know if there were Pullmans on this train, since he was too scared of his leg to try and negotiate the steel-plate couplings between the cars to go back to the club car. But if his own coach with its bottle-toting servicemen was any example, the club car must have been a pandemonium anyway.

Soldiers sprawled all over the seats and squatted or sat in the aisles. Pint bottles passed from hand to hand. Two groups at opposite ends began singing conflicting songs. The few women in the car laughed, but nervously.

Finally one of the Air Force sergeants who were whooping it up in the middle of the coach came over and asked him drunkenly why he wasn't joining in.

"I've got a bum leg," Landers said, showing him his cane. "I can hardly walk. That's why."

"What the hell?" the Air Force sergeant said. "We're all shipping out. We'll all be dead in a couple of months. So come on."

"Well, I'm just shipping back. And I'm not dead. So fuck off," Landers said. His new wild rage, righteous, flaming and lethal, suddenly boiled up all over him.

The Air Force man leered. "You trying to tell me you've been overseas already and wounded, Mack? Or something like that?"

"Yeah. That's right. I was wounded."

"Hey, fellows. Here's a guy claims he's been wounded," the sergeant called. "If you've been wounded, Mack, where's your Purple Heart?"

Landers carefully moved his hand on his cane to just below the curve, ready to jab or to slash with it. "Up my ass. You want to look at it?" he said. He looked up into the Air Force man's eyes.

He didn't really know what was happening to him, or care. He was as surprised as the Air Force man. He gave him a cannibalistic smile that, although Landers did not know it, was strangely like Winch's.

The Air Force sergeant's eyes widened and seemed to grow flat. "No. I guess not. Thanks." He was trying to appear hurt, and civilized. In contradistinction to Landers.

"Listen," Landers raged. His voice was low key but vibrating. "You know what this is?" He pointed to his Combat Infantryman's Badge, over his left pocket. "You know how you get one of those? You go away and get yourself one of those, and then you come and talk to me. Until then shut up and get the fuck away from me, flyboy."

Wooden-faced, the Air Force sergeant walked away. Landers was almost sorry. At the same time a small, still reasonable part of him was glad. He was almost sobbing. In two seconds he would have started to cry with rage. And if he had started to cry, he would have struck with the heavy hospital-issue cane. Right alongside the skull.

Across from him, a tired-looking young woman, worn-out from traveling and somehow clearly and obviously newly married, tried to strike up a sympathetic conversation with him.

"Listen, lady," Landers said. "Just leave me alone, will you? I didn't say anything to anybody. I didn't try to talk to you. So just leave me alone. Okay?"

After that everybody in the car ignored him as if he weren't there. This made Landers feel hurt and angered. He smoked and stared out the window. When it came time to change trains, he would not let anybody help him, and insisted on getting off by himself. Fortunately, he was carrying only a canvas hand satchel with an extra uniform in it. Later he would have to change again.

The little two-car local train, in contrast to the main line flyers, had almost no passengers. Landers sat by a window and watched the flat undulating countryside roll by. This was close to home. He knew almost every tree. He had come this way when he came home from school.

As usual, there was nobody and nothing at the little weatherbeaten green station. And Landers' problems began there, immediately. A couple of old men sat on the weatherbeaten green bench along the front of the station platform, chewing tobacco and spitting down on the gravel. Inside, the agent-dispatcher sat behind his telegraph desk, wearing black sleeve covers and a green eyeshade. Not another soul was there. Landers suddenly did not want to talk to anyone, only to slip away and sneak off home without seeing anybody at all. But the thought of the mile-long walk in to the center of town, with his heavy limp and his cane, was too much. The walk was more than he could physically handle. So he had to go inside and ask the dispatcher to call a cab for him. But before he could even open the door, one of the old men sidled over to him.

"Say, aint you Jeremy Landers' boy, Marion?" he asked. "Welcome home, son, welcome home."

Landers wanted to say *Go to hell,* but instead said only, "Thanks," and kept his eyes lowered. The dispatcher said almost the same words to him. He called the cab (there were two in Imperium) for him gladly, but could not resist telling the cab man who it was he was picking up. Landers stood and listened to the dispatcher's glowing report of the returned wounded hero, feeling abysmal.

That was the way it was going to be. Everybody was going to be treating him as the returned war hero. And suddenly he saw a vivid mental picture of the company's waterless platoons, with their fear-haunted eyes under their helmets and dirt on their faces and the stubbles of beard. It blanked out everything, the station, the dispatcher, the cab.

It would be all over town before he could even get home, Landers thought. And indeed it was. His mother was already weeping into the telephone when he walked in. Someone had called her. His father came home early from the law office. Somebody had called him, too. Both of them were upset because Landers had not written to them. The news of his return had been printed in the local paper.

Fortunately, Landers felt, his sister was already away at school. She had gone up a week early to get settled in for her last year, his mother said. But his mother was going to call her to come down. Landers told her not to bother, thinking of Carol Firebaugh and her last year.

Almost immediately he had his first run-in with his father, when he refused to wear his Bronze Star and Purple Heart ribbons. His father could not understand why. Once, just once, Landers tried to explain it to him, that it was obscene, immoral, with the rest of them still out there, still dying, but his father wouldn't agree. Landers forgot that he could easily have left the medals in Luxor, that he had brought them deliberately to bug his father, and silently wished that his father might try to understand him. "We don't any of us wear them," Landers said angrily, "at the hospital. This is the only thing we wear." His father glared at the Combat Infantryman's Badge, and wanted to know why that meant so much. He began to expostulate in his lawyer's courtroom voice. Landers' mother stood wringing her hands. Landers silenced him with an authoritative wave of his hand. His father wasn't used to that, either. Then his father broke out a bottle for a celebratory drink, and Landers began to drink.

A little later in the evening he had his first major fight with his father, when he refused to make a date to come down to the American Legion and tell the boys from World War I about his experiences. His father refused to take no for an answer. Landers flatly refused to go. By then Landers was drinking almost nonstop. So much his father complained about it. But Landers did not stop, or even slow down. Instead, he drank more.

It was easy enough to drink. Later on, when he escaped from the big house on West Main and limped the two blocks to the Elks Club, everybody there wanted to buy him a drink. Landers started by accepting half of the offers, but quickly progressed to accepting all of them. Everybody he met everywhere in town wanted to buy him a drink. It would begin early in the day, depending on when he got up, at one of the poolrooms or bars on the square, and progress through the afternoon and evening until late at night Landers would stumble home from the Elks Club or bum a ride in from the Country Club and fall into bed and sleep till noon the next day. Dimly, he slowly became aware that everyone was afraid of him, for some reason, but by then had usually progressed far enough in his drinking that he would forget or ignore it. He saw little of his family. His sister did not come home.

On one of these earlier evenings Landers was asked to make a speech at the Elks Club. It had become a local custom to give each new batch of departing draftees a free farewell dinner at the Elks Grille, and the local Chamber of Commerce secretary, who organized the dinners, on the spur of the moment had the bright idea of inviting Landers to talk to them. This was undoubtedly a mistake but the secretary, who was also the newshawk for the local paper, was noted for making gaffes. Landers, who was sitting alone in the club bar and grille, drinking quietly and minding his own business when the secretary came over and slid into his booth, thought about it awhile and then said sure he'd be glad to talk to them. They were having one of the local ministers, the secretary explained, to talk to them about religious responsibilities; and the principal of the high school to talk about social responsibilities; and the football coach to talk about patriotic responsibilities. He thought it would be nice if

Landers, who had been over there, could talk to them about a soldier's responsibilities. "Sure, that's a great idea," Landers said.

The draftees were just coming in and Landers looked over at them. There were twenty of them. Landers had been to school with some of them. All of them but one were poor boys whose fathers were farmers or plant workers and too poor to be members and, unless they had played varsity football or basketball, they had probably never seen the inside of the club, and so were suitably dazzled by their surroundings. This, too, offended Landers' social conscience. He nodded at the secretary.

While the draftees ate their farewell dinner, Landers drank more and prepared his speech on a soldier's responsibilities.

Landers was to follow the coach. The secretary introduced him, with a highly laudatory introduction, mentioning that though he did not wear them Sgt Landers had the Purple Heart and the Bronze Star. Craftily, when he stepped up on the little orchestra stand in the corner, Landers got hold of the microphone so they couldn't shut him up. Even so, he had decided he had better make it short. He began by saying he had listened to the other speeches with interest, but that he was not sure just how much all those responsibilities applied to a soldier in a war.

"You don't think much about God, or the Four Freedoms, or loving your country, when you're in a fight." He grinned at them. "It is true that a lot of fellows pray a lot. But that is not quite the same thing as thinking of your religious responsibilities. I can tell you for one thing that that man who said there are no atheists in foxholes was wrong. Mostly you think about getting your ass out of there, and about killing those other people so they won't kill you." Down below the secretary had sat up straight in his chair and was blinking his eyes behind his thick glasses. Landers grinned at him, too. "I've been asked to talk to you about a soldier's responsibilities," he said into the mike, which seemed to carry much louder and much farther than he had anticipated, "and I think I can safely assure you that the soldier's first responsibility is to stay alive." He felt he was warming up. "In the first place, a dead soldier is no good to anybody. And second place, a wounded soldier takes two or three other men away from fighting to take care of him. So, theoretically, it's better to wound a man badly than to kill him. I can't in honesty tell you that you will be fighting for freedom, and God, and your country—as all these other gentlemen have told you. In combat you don't think about any of that. But I can assure you that you will be fighting for your life. I think that's a good thing to remember. I think that's a good thing to fight for. And remember, if you have the choice—which you may not —always try to wound a man badly instead of killing him. Good luck, fellows, and God bless."

When he let go of the mike, the secretary seized it. "And now, boys, there will be drinks over at the bar, so cluster round, gather round," he said quickly.

Feeling pleasantly red around the ears, Landers stepped down and went to his booth and sat down with his drink. Let the sons of bitches ask him to make some more speeches. None of the draftees came over to thank him. Landers did not mind, and beamed at all of them indiscriminately. Naturally, he was not asked to make other speeches. And when his father heard about it, they had another fight.

It was not that he was the only wounded vet back home in town. There were several others. Two boys had been to North Africa as ambulance drivers, and had come back home. Another, whose father ran a drugstore on the square, was an Air Force sergeant and had been shot down in a bomber over Italy, and was being discharged. But in September 1943 there were not all that many, and each was a celebrity. Landers did not like it. It made him feel guilty, and as if he were masquerading under false pretenses.

He did not make out well with the girls either. They were all either with somebody who might soon be drafted, or were waiting for somebody who had already gone, or else they were scared of Landers. He was not the Marion Landers who had gone away a year and a half ago, one of them told him nervously. At the hospital, when he first arrived, Landers had received three letters—one from his folks, one from his sister, and one from an old girlfriend who wrote she had read of his return in the paper and wanted him to know that she would be glad to see him if he got home, that all the men like him coming back should be treated with admiration and understanding and if there was anything she could do for him she would. So on the fifth or sixth night he was there, Landers called her and asked her to go to the basketball game that was being played that night. Frances said she would love to go.

It was early in the year for basketball, but Imperium was especially a basketball town, and was playing this big exhibition game ahead of the regular schedule. Landers of course did not know then, when he invited her, that Frances Mackey had been writing in only a purely social way, when she wrote she would do anything for him that she could.

At the basketball game he endeared himself to everyone by refusing to stand up for "The Star-Spangled Banner," when it was played before the game. But nobody said anything. This not standing up for the national anthem had become quite a big thing with the guys at the hospital, where every night at closing it was played at the Starlight Roof of the Hotel Peabody and other bars in Luxor. The theory was that if you had a Purple Heart, you shouldn't have to stand up. And besides, everybody knew he had a bum leg.

After the game, it was raining. As he and Frances came out of the big gym, a little Dodge pulled up in front of them and stopped short, so violently it rocked a little. Inside it was a large older woman named Marilyn Tothe, who worked for one of the other law firms in town as a clerk. And who was a notorious bull dyke, though it was thought impolite to say so. Landers had known her all his life, too. She had come to pick them up, she said brusquely. Landers could only stare at her wonderingly. She was at least as broad in the shoulders as he was, and, at least at this moment anyway, considerably stronger. She could certainly beat him up if she wanted, and she seemed to know it. Frances Mackey got meekly into the front. Landers was invited to sit in the back. "Where do you want us to drop you?" Marilyn Tothe said harshly. Landers said he guessed the Elks Club would be good enough. When the car stopped in front of it, Frances turned back to wave but the car started forward almost before he was out, so that she was jerked back around to the front. Landers stood looking after them in the rain, feeling bemused and left out of everything.

Perhaps that was why he got more drunk that night than usual. If he was more drunk than usual. He could remember leaving the Elks when it closed at three. He could remember deciding to walk up town to the square for some food at the all-night restaurant. He could remember crossing the treeless courthouse lawn in the rain. And he could remember coming upon the old brass Civil War cannon in its marble pedestal on the courthouse lawn with a sense of shock and surprise, just as if it had not been there all his life since he could remember and he had not known about it there. He could remember putting his arm around the cannon and rubbing his cheek against the brass, and shedding a few drunken tears—or was it raindrops—for this other old soldier, whose reward for faithful service it was to be left to stand and molder in the rain. Every year all his life on Memorial Day the fake red poppies were thrust into the courthouse lawn, and the white crosses were driven into the grass in rows, and somebody read "In Flanders Field." Every fucking year. Who would write the poem for them? What would they call it? Who would read it?

Landers remembered standing up and looking across the square through the drizzle at the lights of the restaurant, in the middle of a great stillness, and that was the last he remembered. When he woke up, he had a terrible hangover, and the dazzling sun was pouring into his eyes through the barred window, and he was in a cell in the city jail with the cell door unlocked and open.

His cane was lying on the cot beside him, and he got it and walked outside and yelled. "Hey, where is everybody?"

"Down here, Marion," the chief of police's voice called from the anteroom. "You finally wake up? Come on out."

The chief, a big Swede named Nielson, was sitting behind his desk with an embarrassed look on his face.

"What the hell happened?" Landers said.

Several loafers were standing around grinning.

"Well, you know old Jeremy," the chief said with an embarrassed smile. "Charlie Evans, the night cop, took you home and the old man said to let you sleep it off in the jail."

"Well, did I do something terrible?" Landers asked.

"No, no. You went into the all-night restaurant and ordered some bacon and eggs and passed out cold. They couldn't wake you, so they called Charlie Evans. When Charlie couldn't wake you, he took you home. That's all. But old Jeremy told him to bring you down to the jail."

"My father did that?"

"Well, you got a good night's sleep out of it," the chief smiled. "You don't look so bad."

Landers looked down at himself. "I'm pretty messy. Well, what do I owe you, Frank?"

"Nothing. There's no fine or anything." He hesitated. "We would have left you at home. But you know old Jeremy. He wouldn't accept you. You're not going to hold it against him, are you?"

"Against my father?" Landers said. "Call me a cab, will you, Frank?"

"I know the Landers," the chief said, looking perplexed. "There's a cab right outside, Marion."

Landers shook hands all around. "Thank you for a pleasant stay." In the cab the driver kept grinning back into the rearview mirror so broadly that it was obvious he must already know the story. Landers only winked at him.

Back at home he showered and shaved and put on his other uniform. Then, with his mother pleading and moaning behind him, and trying to hold him back, he telephoned his father at his office.

"Listen, you son of a bitch," Landers shouted into the instrument, "I just want you to know—"

"Don't you hang up on me, you son of a bitch!" he raged at the phone. Then he slammed it down and turned on his mother. "All right then, you tell him. You tell him I said to forget he ever had a son named Marion. Jeremy Landers has no son named Marion. You tell him that. And I'll forget I ever had him for a father. You understand? You got that?"

"Marion," his mother wailed. "Marion. Please, Marion, please."

"Go to hell," Landers shouted and grabbed his canvas satchel.

At the station he had to wait an hour and a half for the next train. He waited on the green bench out in front, alone. Landers could hardly wait to get back to Prell and Winch and Strange and the others. He wondered how Prell's legs were doing. Also, they were going to have to do something about Strange's hand some time soon.

On the train the ride back did not seem nearly so difficult. Maybe the six days using it had helped the leg. Landers was even able to negotiate the steel plates between the cars and go to the club car for some drinks. As might be expected, it was full of drunken servicemen. He sat on the couch with his drink in his hand, thought about his family briefly, his ex-family, and could hardly wait to get back to Luxor.

When he reported back in to his ward, four days earlier than necessary, he found that Mart Winch had been taking out the girl Carol Firebaugh every single night since he had left.

BOOK THREE

THE CITY

CHAPTER 15

It was hard to make any real friends in a hospital ward. As their medical status changed, men moved from one ward to another. There was a constant shuffling process going on that kept moving men away from each other. Men who made friends with the men in the beds beside them would look up and find them gone, replaced by newer strangers.

John Strange found this had a tendency to throw men back for friendship onto other members of their old outfits, if they were lucky enough to have any around. If they didn't, they just sat around and brooded and withdrew. Just when they should be starting to forget their old emotional attachments and build new ones.

Strange had watched the beginning of Winch's romance with Carol Firebaugh at first with amusement, then with irritation, and finally with downright envy.

Like everyone else who went in and out of the big basketball-court lounge of the recreation building, Strange had lusted after the sweet youthfulness and shy grace of the Red Cross girl who handed out the Ping-Pong balls and paddles, and had wanted to fuck her. But being a properly married man just returned to his

175

wife from overseas Strange put it out of his mind. Still she was, as some forthright, bathrobe-clad Government Issue had said, eminently fuckable.

Some female thing about her every movement said so, and her shy self-awareness of her sex in front of so many male eyes underlined it. Her one kooky eye that kept looking off in a wrong direction half the time made her even sexier. For some odd screwball reason.

Strange had paid attention when she seemed interested in Landers, and thought that all right and in keeping with the fact that they were both college people. But when in Landers' absence she attached herself to Mart Winch twenty years her senior, Strange's mind balked. When he saw them together in town up at the Plantation Roof on the top of the Peabody Hotel, sitting together right in front of everybody, Strange was suddenly intensely jealous. If he had known she went for older fellows, he would gladly have offered himself. Only, he hadn't. Leave it to shrewd old Mart Winch to wheel in there, and sop up the gravy.

Up to now, Strange had studiously avoided other women in Luxor. He felt he owed that to Linda. But it was not nearly so easy to do as it sounded. It required more effort not to pick up women in town in Luxor than it did to meet them and take them out and screw them. The city was full of unattached women. Riveters. Welders. Lathe operators. All sorts of minor assembly-line workers. And all of them hellbent on picking up some in-transit serviceman for a one-night stand or one-week fling. Since their work shifts ran right on around the clock, it was just as easy to run into one at eight o'clock in the morning as in the evening. A lot of them didn't work at all, had quit it, or had never done it, and just went on and on, from one party to another, from one hotel suite to another hotel suite. It was hard work not to pick them up, or be picked up by them.

Just the same, Strange had resisted. He had been home—home?—to Cincinnati one further time after his second trip while Bobby Prell was mending. Making a total of three visits in all. He had not found anything there had much changed. Linda Sue was just as cold and indifferent to his bedroom advances as she had been the first time. Though she never turned him down when he asked. But Strange found it harder and harder to ask with any real excitement. He found it easier to just roll over and go to sleep. Or go downstairs to that never-vacant kitchen and drink more beer.

Maybe at the age of twenty-eight he was outgrowing sex excitement. The way his parents had done. He only knew that for the marriage and their dream of a restaurant to be maintained required fidelity. On both sides, his as well as hers.

So when his jealousy and envy of Winch with Carol Firebaugh came up in him so strong, it came as a shock. Obviously, he badly wanted to fuck her himself. And once he had seen the desire in him for Carol, he began to see it in him for others, in other places.

That he did not do anything about it was mostly due to his feelings about Linda and the restaurant and their savings. But it was also due to his concern and preoccupation with the final medical status of his hand wound. All through the business of Prell's legs Strange had waited for some word from Col Curran about his own disposition and first operation. But every day at morning rounds the surgeon would only look at the hand, move it a little, and ask how Strange was doing.

Strange had tried to stay with Curran's instructions about forcing himself to use the hand, even when it hurt and he did not want to. Finally he was obliged to tell Curran it hurt almost too much. Curran nodded, silently pursing up his mouth as if about to whistle, with that polite interested look on his face, and told him to stop using it.

Then about a week after the big awards ceremonies, at which Strange standing alongside Prell and Winch had received his absurdly unjustified Purple Heart, Curran had stopped by his bed at morning rounds and without even looking at the hand had told him he wanted to see him in his office beside the three big surgeries at twelve o'clock that same day.

Strange had been planning on spending the day in town after morning rounds. But there was no begging off from a summons like this one.

Curran was as immaculate as usual, with his starched doctor's smock and scrubbed hands, behind his little desk in the cubbyhole office. But his face looked tired and wan and in the corner an open GI laundry bin overflowed with what looked like bloody surgeon's aprons.

"I'm sorry about those," Curran said with his bright almost

lipless smile. "They were supposed to pick them up. But of course they haven't done it."

"Blood doesn't bother me," Strange said. "I've seen a lot of it, Doc."

"I expect you have." Curran rubbed his well-kept, manicured hands over his face for a moment.

"You've had a pretty heavy work schedule today, hunh?" Strange said.

"Yes," Curran said. "Now. About your hand."

"Yes, sir." In a ridiculous way, Strange felt responsible for not upsetting Curran. He didn't want to do anything that might tire or distress the surgeon. He listened while Curran went over it all. Every now and then as he talked Curran's hands moved the papers about on his desk aimlessly.

"I've probably given you more loose time than was good for your hand. This hand of yours is a ticklish piece of business. But I couldn't help it," he said, looking up. "We've had a heavy schedule of operations lately, and this hand of yours is a pretty delicate thing to operate. There are an awful lot of ligaments in there that can't be nicked or cut. In any case, I'm prepared to do the first job on it tomorrow."

He leaned back in his swivel chair. "We'll go in and take out the metal fragment first. And I'll see how it looks in there. I probably won't try to do anything about the bone growth this time. Unless I see that it looks easy. I have no reason to expect that it will look easy.

"I want to get at you early in the morning while I'm still fresh. So I'm going to have them give you a mild enema tonight, and a sedative. You won't get any breakfast in the morning. They'll probably wake you around six. All right?"

"Yes, sir," Strange said and grinned. He felt a necessity to make it a tough grin. Then he added, "Uh, sir. Will it be all right if I go see my buddies tonight? At the snack bar?"

Curran nodded slowly. "It will be all right. But I don't want you drinking any coffee, or eating." He leaned back again in his chair. "You know, you people amaze me. You're really as thick as a bunch of fleas, aren't you?" He placed the tips of his fingers together and stared at Strange over them.

Strange stared back at him, suddenly irritated. It wasn't any of Curran's business how thick they were. What was he picking at now? And why? Strange ran his tongue judiciously over his teeth before framing an answer.

"Well, sir. I guess we are," he said slowly. "We been through a lot of shit together. But probably more than that, you got to remember we come out of an old Regular Army outfit together. Don't forget, we spent like two to three years together. Before we ever got into this war. We know each other pretty good." He stopped, debating whether to go on and tell the surgeon more. But immediately something in him decided not to tell more to Curran. It was an intimacy Curran didn't deserve from him, big-shot surgeon who was going to cut on him tomorrow or no.

"Well, I'll see you tomorrow morning," Curran said, and swung his chair back up level. "But you probably won't notice it. They'll be giving you a light injection tomorrow, to calm you down a little. Before they roll you in."

Outside, Strange felt distinctly peculiar, as he made his way back to his ward. He felt as he used to feel when he boxed, or played football. Suddenly he felt he had to piss. Though he knew his bladder was empty. He headed back in his issue bathrobe to find Winch and Landers and Prell and tell them the news.

Winch, of course, did not show up that evening. He was out with his little girlfriend. Couldn't stay away, couldn't get enough of her, likely. When Strange went by to tell him at 12:45 he had just barely caught him, all dressed in uniform to go to town. Strange noted, but did not comment on it, that Winch was finally wearing those brand-new 1st/sgt's stripes of his. That was what a woman would do for you, he thought to himself wryly.

Landers and Prell did show up. At the snack bar. Landers limping and with his cane. Prell in his wheelchair: with new, white casts on his legs, in which now his knees had been slightly bent. "My knees are what are going to do me in," he told them. "I can't even move them. Christ, they're like a couple of rusty old, seized-up, frozen, door hinges." Prell, of course, wasn't going anyplace off hospital. So it was not such an effort for him to arrange to be at the snack bar to see Strange. It was a big event for him. Landers, though, had clearly missed a date in town, to be with his old mess sgt on the night before his operation. Strange, who had never been that close to Landers, felt a new warmth for him.

Prell, though he could not get off hospital grounds to go in town, had not been wasting his time. They found out as they talked that he had found himself a girlfriend. Right on his own ward.

"Hell, yes," he grinned at them. "She's some sweet little country girl from some little town just outside of Luxor. Her daddy's off overseas somewhere so her and her momma come into town every day to volunteer as Gray Ladies out here. I aint met her momma. But she got assigned to our ward, so every afternoon she spends the whole afternoon reading to me. She's reading me *Treasure Island,* right now."

Prell's eyes sparkled, as he laughed for them. "She thinks I'm the cat's meow. Big Medal of Honor winner. I can't do much of nothing yet. I couldn't fuck, with these legs. But I'll give anybody ten for five I'll have her blowing me out in the back of the ward before the month's out," he added smiling. "Or at least tossing me off."

But when they mentioned Winch, Prell's face got stiff and frozen. He refused even to mention Winch's name, nor would he talk about or listen to anything about him.

Landers, when Strange asked him, apparently did not mind that Mart Winch had taken over his Red Cross girl. "More power to him," he said. There were more women in town than you could beat off with a ball bat. "If he can get into her, good for him." Landers had been back to see his new acquaintance, the Naval lieutenant commander Jan Mitchell, who kept the suite at the Peabody. Apparently there was a party there every night. "Those Navy flyers," Landers said, "and Army flyers. They don't give a damn whether you're an enlisted man or not. They don't pull rank. As long as you're fun at a party." He wanted Strange, and Prell, when Prell was finally able to get around, to come up there with him.

Strange accepted tentatively. But he wasn't thinking about that as much as about the operation. He sat and talked with them until the snack bar closed. He promised Landers he would go down to the Peabody in a week or so. Before they separated outside the darkened snack bar, and went off along the dimly lighted walkways to their wards, Strange shook hands with both of them warmly. Since they both went the same way toward the leg wards, Landers hung his cane on the back of Prell's wheelchair and pushed it along leaning on it with his limp. Strange stood looking after them as they dimmed and darkened and then brightened under the series of overhead lights.

They caused his swallowing mechanism to choke up, and made a lump come in his throat.

As he turned toward his own ward his stomach flipped over and he had that sensation of needing to piss again.

In the morning that was all they gave him time to do. They did not even let him get out of bed, but passed him a glass duck to use. Then the guy was pricking his arm with the injection. In the operating room the anesthetist went right to work on him. Curran, already in a gauze mask and white cap, smiled with his eyes and winked and explained about the sodium pentothol the anesthetist was letting into his vein. Counting backward Strange got from ten to six before there was a sudden vast explosion of terrible-tasting fumes in the roof of his mouth. He tried to shake his head, but no longer had one.

Coming out of it, there was a lot of noise, and huge flashing revolving lights like artillery searchlights. They flashed on in a brilliant white glare, and then off in a darkness the eyes had no time to adjust to. But if it was an air raid, why were they blinking? Then it wasn't an air raid, but a grand court, and at the far end a huge figure shrouded all in white sat on a great white marble chair atop a huge white marble base. In the flashing lights, seeing it all in broken lines as if reflected in a splintered mirror, Strange stood and waited in front of all the crowds. Until the white figure, its face covered, slowly extended one huge arm, the index finger pointing. There was a vast sigh of "Ah!" from the crowd and Strange knew that he had lost. Whatever it was. Whatever it was that was at stake. Then he realized that someone, the anesthetist, was talking, shouting at him, in capital letters.

"THERE WE GO, THERE WE GO, HE'S ALL RIGHT. SURE. HE'S ALL RIGHT. YOU'RE ALL RIGHT. THERE, NOW." The anesthetist was smiling at him.

Strange managed to wink at him but the white figure still filled his mind, more real than any of the reality around him and it stayed with him all the groggy way back to the ward rolling along the corridors on the meat wagon and it stayed with him the next two days that they kept him partially doped up. It stayed sharply between his eyeballs and everything he looked at.

Curran was not one to be stingy with dope and painkillers when somebody was in pain. When he stopped by that first afternoon to see him, he said he did not believe with Maj Hogan and Col Baker that standing pain was the essence of a man. Strange only nodded and looked at him and smiled, seeing in front of him that great white figure and pointing arm. Curran still seemed less real.

It had had a profound effect on him, the dream. Or vision. Or whatever it was. It seemed so real it took on the quality of a revelation almost. But what was it supposed to mean? All Strange knew was that, somewhere, he had been tried and found wanting. But he did not even know what the trial was for. He had the feeling that in the vision he had not been told, either. He had simply been judged. No defense. It did not matter. The judgment was fair. In the dream he had felt a great sense of guilt, and then relief. An enormous sorrow, and relief. Relief that at last somebody knew.

Vaguely now, but sharply in the vision, he had the feeling he was being sent back somewhere he had hoped to be allowed to leave. That was what the silent finger seemed to indicate: you are sent back, and must stay. But Strange did not know sent back to where.

Even when he was back on his feet and the painkillers withdrawn, the powerful image of the white figure and pointing arm would not leave him and he could not get away from the feeling that he was being told something.

In the fact of it and because the painkillers they gave him weren't all that strong, he was not off his feet all that long. On Curran's orders, the ward attendants had him up and out of bed and moving around the ward before the afternoon of the first day was over.

Curran did not like to use plaster casts, and had had a molded plaster plate made and bandaged underneath the hand so that only the knuckle joints themselves were held immobile. Curran maintained that casts had caused more cripples than the wounds that had required their use.

"We're such a long, long way from what we *could* do in surgery and orthopedics," he said with his mild smile. "God only knows how long it's going to take. And only God knows what lovely advances will come out of this beautiful war." Curran's eyebrows hooked upward over his pale eyes.

Then, sitting on the bed edge, he turned and with a sharp twinkling grin asked Strange to come out with him sometime and have a few drinks, and to bring his buddies. Strange said that he would.

Strange did not know what had caused him to take such an interest in the four of them. Probably it was the saving of Prell's legs. "That first sergeant of yours, Winch, must be quite a guy," Curran said. "What he did for Prell and the way he arranged that medal for him are really something. I'd like to meet him." Strange said he would try to arrange it. He did not know what Curran meant by the way Winch "arranged that medal."

But he didn't really care. He already knew pretty much what Winch would say. Which was a flat No. He and Winch saw pretty much eye to eye about officers. Officers were of a different caste, and ought to stay there. But of course he and Winch were old Regulars. And this was the wartime Army. Full of civilians. Strange made up his mind privately that he would not even mention the invitation to Winch, and that he would not take it up himself, either. He liked Curran, more and more, and admired him, but he did not intend ever to become a buddy of his.

He felt exactly the same about the officers at the Hotel Peabody when Landers took him there.

Because of Col Curran's postoperative treatment he was able to go much sooner than he had expected, the third day after instead of a week. Curran told him only that he should be careful of the hand. "When you're on top of some girl," Curran grinned, "make sure you support yourself on the plaster plate on your palm. Not on your finger knuckles." Strange had only grunted.

He had no intention of picking up some woman. And yet, when he got there, he found himself in bed with one almost before he had time to get a few drinks down him. And before the afternoon and after it the evening were over he had been to bed with four different women. Of course so had Landers. But he would have expected that of Landers. He would not have expected it of himself.

But the operation seemed to have changed him in some deep-down basic way. Either the operation itself, or perhaps it was that damned vision or dream or revelation or whatever it was he had had coming out of the anesthetic.

Being strapped down and put to sleep and made helpless while some guy opened up and cut on a part of you to try and repair it could do a lot of damage to a man's self-esteem.

And Strange could not shake off the picture of the judging figure, its hand pointing. And he couldn't shake off the way it made him feel. There had been no anger or frustration or outrage at the figure. No crying of unfair. You could no more be outraged at the figure than you could be outraged at the universe. Both were there, both existed, it was the way things were.

It had to be accepted. In the dream he had felt a compassion. Compassion for himself and for everything. He had always been compassionate. Why else would the old company nick-name him "Mother Strange." But this new compassion was different and deeper and included everything in God's created universe. And yet deep underneath it in him was an indigestible despair. And way down deep under the despair was a fiery-red, sneaky little anger. Over the fact that things must be the way they were. This tiny little white-hot core made him rebellious.

His rebelliousness included Linda. If Linda didn't care much about fucking him any more, and probably never had done, Strange guessed that was her privilege. But there were plenty who would. And if some of these excited him, he didn't see why he shouldn't take advantage of it.

He had not felt like that before the operation. But if the white figure had judged against him and pointed him away, back to whatever it was he must go back to, what did he have to lose?

It was silly perhaps, but he was taking the dream quite seriously, in a grinding sort of way. And his sexual proclivities were a long way from being washed up, as he had thought two weeks ago.

None of that had anything to do with his commitment and loyalty to Linda Sue, and her crazy defense-plant family, and her dream restaurant. He would stand by that.

Thus Strange sat and figured it out for himself with a drink in his hand, in the loud, crowded, smoke-filled, booze-fumed sitting room of the Peabody hotel suite Landers had brought him to, before swiftly becoming entangled and intertwined with his first female body of the afternoon. He realized there was some question whether he had chosen it, or it had chosen him.

The place was so crowded a certain protocol had to be followed. The suite had a bedroom on either side of the sitting room. With doors that closed. The sitting room had a double bed. So the management could rent that room singly, if needed. This bed was a necking, feel-them-up way station while waiting for a bedroom, and couples were always sprawled on it. You were supposed to note how many couples were already there waiting when you got on the bed, and to keep track of your place in the lineup.

Both bedrooms had single cot beds placed against the wall in addition to their big beds, so that each bedroom could accommodate two couples when a serious party was in progress, like today. Propriety demanded neither couple should look at the other while arriving or departing or while at play themselves. Strange, when he entered a bedroom the first time, found it impossible not to stop and stare. "Hey. You're not supposed to look," the girl welder who was with him cried cheerily. "No. You're not," a muffled voice said from the cot. The girl welder added, "You're supposed to look only at me."

The third of the four women he took to bed during the afternoon and the evening wanted him to go down on her, make her come by licking her pussy. She was willing, more than willing, to go down on him, too. Her name was Frances Highsmith. She was a metal lathe operator, had dropped out of Washington University in St. Louis to do war work after her brother was killed in the Air Force over England, and made Strange think a little bit of Carol Firebaugh. Which was why he had singled her out. Years before Strange might have slapped her in the jaw and thrown her out of there. Instead now he only smiled and refused. Politely.

"What's the matter?" Frances said. "Haven't you ever eaten cunt before?"

"No," Strange said. "No, I haven't."

"You mean you think it's dirty? Filthy? Perverted? Something like that?" Frances demanded. "A perversion?"

They were on the narrow cot bed this time, lying side by side, and Strange could feel his heated erection beating with his heartbeat against her slim belly.

"I guess so," he said. "Something like that."

"Boy, have you got a lot to learn," Frances Highsmith said. "I've heard about fellows like you. But I didn't think I'd meet one up here."

Strange felt irritated. "Well. It's the same thing as being queer. Isn't it."

"Queer?" Frances Highsmith said. "Queer?" She peered at him. "You must be a real country boy. Didn't you ever watch dogs? It would be queer if I went down on a girl. Or if you went down on a boy. But it's not queer for boys and girls together.

"Well, haven't you ever even thought about it? In a fantasy?"

"No, I never have."

"Hey, listen. Are you married?"

"Yes," Strange said stiffly.

"Boy, am I sorry for your wife. How do you think women come?"

"I've never thought about it."

"Wow. You never even thought about it?" Frances said. "Well, maybe I better explain it to you. You know what a clitoris is?"

"Sure."

"Are you sure? It's a woman's penis. Women come from stimulating that. They don't come from having cocks shoved into them." She stopped. "Well, maybe a few do. But it's very rare. Physically, it's next to impossible. —You sure you don't want to try it?"

"No. No doubt in my mind," Strange said.

"Well, I think there's something seriously wrong with you."

"Listen," a muffled male voice said from the other bed. "If you two want to argue philosophy, will you kindly do it outside?"

"You shut up," Frances said.

"But don't let that stop *you,*" Strange said.

"No," Frances said. "Oh, no. No, sir. Let's just fuck. I'll find somebody else to come with later. I'm not going to blow some fellow that won't blow me."

"Well, fuck him then, honey, and shut up," a muffled female voice said from the big bed.

"I guess she's right," Frances said. "If we're going to do anything at all, we better get on with it."

"I'm ready," Strange said. "For everything but licking you."

She had already turned flat on her back, and now she made a practiced little sideways motion that seemed to slide her right under him, legs apart, like a card in a deck. Like the burn card going onto the bottom of a poker deck.

Later on, later in the evening, he saw her going off with Landers. He wondered if Landers would make her come by licking her pussy for her. Maybe Landers might, he was an educated college boy. Well, every man to his own taste.

Like many another boy, Strange had stared heatedly and hungrily at all the photographs and drawings of wide-open vaginas that were available just about everywhere across America in his youth. He had sat and watched the stag films that always, somehow or other, found their way to all the NCO clubs across the country. But all the photos of wide-open pussies had never destroyed the ultimate mystery of woman for him. Nothing had ever destroyed the mystery of women for him. Not even marriage had. Maybe that was the trouble. Sometimes he wished something had.

But grown men did not get down and lick women's cunts. That was just as much a perversion as being a fag. It was sick in the head. The truth was he had never even seen Linda Sue's pussy wide-open. Or closed for that matter. He'd seen her naked. But my God, what would Linda Sue say, if he asked her to let him see her pussy wide-open? Or asked her to let him lick it? He couldn't imagine it.

The trouble with women was when you had had them you still hadn't had them. He had had four, and hadn't had any. He was right back where he started before he came up here, only now he was lonelier than he was before.

While Landers was off with Frances Highsmith, he told somebody to tell Landers he would be back, and went off down to the setups bar off the lobby before they closed it at midnight, and sat by himself in a corner with a bottle.

The place was jammed with servicemen drinking. And of course with women. But no matter how many women there were, anywhere, there were always more servicemen, lonely, looking. The bar had them all the way from bald grizzled old Navy chief petty officers in whites with hash marks all the way up to their shoulders, to boys in the ill-fitting unworn uniforms of the newly drafted. Strange felt more at home here with them.

Once, upstairs—it was while he was lying on the way-station bed in the sitting room waiting with his fourth friend of the day —he had looked around at everybody standing and drinking and shouting and singing; and suddenly the mud-weary, eye-baggy, scared platoons of the company appeared before him in ghostly form, slogging away at the swampy jungle of New Georgia. And briefly, crazily, Strange wished he was back with them.

You had to be crazy to wish you were back in a place like that.

But as he sat in the downstairs bar and drank more and more in the midst of the uproar, that was where he wished he was. With a kind of horrified, aghast longing, he pictured their faces one by one, all of them more sharp, more detailed, more clear, than any of the faces he had seen since. Or before.

When they locked down the bar at twelve, he took his bottle and went back upstairs to collect Landers and go back out to the hospital.

He didn't collect him, of course. Landers was still making out, or flirting, with one woman after another. As the night wore on and people dwindled away, finally there was left only a tight hard-core little group of drunken male singers, with whom he and Landers sang drunkenly for a while, all the old songs. Nobody in the hotel ever complained about noise, to anyone's knowledge. At five-thirty with dawn coming up across the plains in the east they left to go back and sleep just enough to sober up before morning rounds. In the taxi Landers gabbled and gabbled about all the women he had fucked.

Two days later, from Curran, Strange had the deposition of his surgical status. The upshot of it was that Curran simply did not know what to do. It was possibly the best news Strange could have been given, if he had selected his own.

Curran switched on the little light screen and put the X-rays up for him to see.

"See where those knots are? All ligaments and tendons in there. Very ticklish. I don't honestly know if I can do it for you. So I'm not recommending the operation. You will have to decide if you want it done."

"And if I don't?"

Curran shrugged. A strange quiet smile came over his face. "Then I'll recommend you for a disability discharge. That won't set too well with Maj Hogan and Col Baker. But they can't overrule me."

"And if I do want it?"

Curran shrugged again. "I won't promise. If it works, you'll be fit for limited duty, or even full duty. If you're lucky. So I guess it all depends on whether you want to stay in the service. You're a thirty-year man, aren't you? If it doesn't work, you won't be any worse off than you are. You'll have about the same partial use of the hand. But the two middle knuckles will be partly frozen in a slightly different way than they are now. It's up to you to decide."

"Are you trying to give me some kind of an out if I want out of the service?" Strange said.

"No. Not at all. I'm presenting you with the proper medical prognosis. I know the Army wants men, all the men it can save, and preferably trained men. You're a trained man. But I can't let that override a proper medical decision."

"Can I have a few days to think it over?"

"Sure. All the time you want. It's your hand. And it's your life."

Suddenly, he held his surgeon's hands up between his face and Strange's, and flexed them. "I know a lot about hands."

"You've been pretty square with me, Colonel," Strange said. "And I want to thank you for it."

"I'm a doctor," Curran said. "I was a doctor before I was a colonel in the Army."

"Which is more than you can say for some," Strange said. "I'll get back to you soon, sir."

Somehow he felt like saluting. It wasn't much of a salute, with the plaster plate still on his hand. Then he went to find Winch and see if Winch would fix it up with his pal Jack Alexander to arrange another consecutive double three-day pass to go up to Cincinnati and talk it over with Linda.

When he saw Winch, he thought Winch looked better than he had seen him look in quite a long time. Way back, in fact. Since before they left Wahoo for the Canal. More relaxed, less acid, less hard-faced.

The little girl was apparently quite good for him.

CHAPTER 16

Johnny Stranger's request for passes was no trouble for Winch.
Some time back, Jack Alexander had given him a big stack of
blank pass forms, already signed, so that all he had to do was fill
in the name, and the dates.

"These are for you. And any your people you think deserve
them," Alexander had rasped in his scarred voice, the day after
the medals presentation. "Use them any way you want."

Winch scribbled out two of them for Strange, over Col Stevens' neat signature. Both men knew it was impossible for
Strange to get up to Cincinnati and back on any ordinary three-
day pass. Strange had told Winch about the operation. But as the
stocky mess/sgt walked away down the ward something about
the set of his shoulders said that everything was not as straight-
forward as Strange had made it sound.

Winch would not have agreed with Strange that Mart Winch
was looking happier than he had looked since the Division left
Oahu. But Winch was certainly feeling better than he had felt
since Doc Harris shipped him out of New Georgia.

There was no doubt in Winch's mind that this was due to the

appearance of Carol in his life. He could hardly believe his own luck. An old man like him.

Before he'd picked her up (or been picked up by her, he could never be sure which) he had been suffering one of the lowest points of his life. Even the long nights on the line in Guadalcanal and New Georgia had not been as bad as this hospital half-life at Kilrainey General.

And then, they had received yet another casualty into Kilrainey from the old company, and this had nearly done him in.

The medical stuff was bad enough. The heart failure attack had left him with what the docs called a left bundle branch block. They had had hopes the block would disappear with treatment. But more and more the docs at Kilrainey had come to think it was going to stay, a permanent impairment.

Weakness, shortness of breath, the inability to run, or carry weight, or do any but the lightest exercise. In the past month he had lost the initial feeling of total fragility he had had in the beginning. But Winch had always been a strong man physically, and depended on that as one source of his authority. Without it he felt helpless.

His need for diuretics was part of the same thing. The weakened heart muscle could not pump the blood through strongly. This caused a back pressure to build up behind the heart, between the heart and kidneys. The back pressure aided the heart, but caused the kidneys to function at less than full efficiency. The edema came from that, and tied Winch as tightly and securely to the hospital as if he had been tied to it with a rope. He was getting one big intramuscular injection of mercurial diuretic a day. Even if later they could lower the dosage, they could never eliminate it altogether. If he had not had a lot of pull, they would have discharged him. Then he would find himself among the living dead in some Veterans' Hospital, tied to it as he was now tied to Kilrainey, for his daily shot. A great future to look forward to.

And into all of this there was suddenly dropped onto him the new casualty. It was like some giant's hand steam iron falling from the sky, flattening Winch.

There was no reason for them not to expect newer casualties from the company. Men wounded after Winch left but before the campaign ended had continued to drift home. Even though the fighting in New Georgia had ended a month before. But Staff/Sgt Billy Stonewall Dodson Spencer was a special case.

Partly Billy was special because of the bad way he'd been wounded. Partly he was special because of what he told them about the company.

But partly Billy was special simply by the very fact he was a staff/sgt. That alone said a great deal about the state of the company. When Winch had left the company, Billy Spencer had just been promoted corporal. Winch, who had had a lot to do with his promotion, had assured himself that was as high as Billy could ever rise. Now here Billy was, not only a staff/sgt and former squad leader. He had been promoted platoon guide of the second platoon shortly before getting hit.

What Billy told them about the company bore out the amazing fact of his promotion. Letters from the company had been getting scarcer and scarcer since the end of the New Georgia campaign, and recently there had been none. Billy was the first uncensored news any of them had had since Winch himself came out. All of them hung on every word he had to say. Winch hung on each one, too. Though he hid this from the others.

The upshot of it was, there wasn't any old company any more. Only about fifty of the original hundred and eighty remained, most of them pfcs and privates. A few were higher-ranking noncoms. Winch's old tech/sgt, Zwermann, had not been chosen for the job of 1st/sgt and a new man had been shipped in over him from outside. The others, the rest, were replacements. Just green dumbass cannon-fodder draftees. Some of these, the better ones, were now running squads. All the officers had been changed. The old-timers, when they weren't fighting, were drunk all the time. Old Zwermann when he was passed over had tried to turn in his stripes and been refused. Then he had tried to get himself shipped out sick, and been refused that too. Everything was being clamped down everywhere. The only way to get out now was to get yourself shot up. Or be so sick you literally were dying. Even shot up, you had to be shot up pretty good. Minor wounds didn't count any more, you could forget it. Many of the draftees were joining the drunks. And the drunks, when they couldn't get real booze, were stealing five-gallon cans of peaches and pineapple by the dozen from the ration dumps, sometimes at pistol point, and making illegal swipe and jungle juice out of them in the jungle clearings. There simply wasn't any company esprit or morale any more. The rumor was that they were going in on Bougainville as soon as the Marines had secured a beachhead. Perhaps they were even going in with the Marines. Almost none of the original noncoms, who had held it all together, were left now. That was why Billy had been promoted. Some squad leader had been killed. Later the second platoon guide was killed. Billy had tried to refuse both promotions, but had not been allowed.

In the old days Billy had been a typical happy-go-lucky middle-class boy from Alabama. Now as he lay in his bed and talked with the rest of them clustered around it, it was easy to see his responsibilities as a noncom had completely changed his personality.

He had been wounded on a patrol. Taking the point himself, which as platoon guide he did not have to do, he stepped on a Jap land mine which had blown off his one foot halfway up the shin, shattered his other leg, and sprinkled his body with tiny pieces of casing. Its blast had also blinded him in both eyes.

"Is that you, Top?" he whispered in a new, hoarse voice, putting out one hand. When he found Winch's hand, he put his other hand over it and held on to it in both of his. "Is that really you, Top? I heard on the West Coast you might be here in Luxor, Top. But I never thought I'd get to see you."

Some of the men still went down to the hospital compound for each unloading when they knew the trucks were bringing in cases from a West Coast train and one of them had spotted Billy on his stretcher and spread the word. When they gathered around his bunk, Winch had been the last to arrive.

Winch let him keep the hand. Until Billy saw fit to let go of it himself. Then Winch drifted to the back of the crowd and stood while Billy talked about the company until the nurse came and shooed them all away.

Inwardly Winch was cursing savagely. All of them. The dumb fuckers. The dumb kid should never have made him into some kind of father. He had never wanted to be a father substitute to fucking dumb kids.

In the next days Billy sent for Winch a number of times to come and sit with him. Winch always went. Although all Billy wanted to do was talk about the old company. Which talk Winch hated, of course. As Billy'd said, there wasn't any more old company. But Billy wanted to talk about the good old days back on Guadalcanal, when there had been one, and which days Billy had survived intact. "We had us some great times there, up on the line. Didn't we, Top?" He had somehow got it fixed in his head that Guadalcanal was some kind of a golden-age happy time, compared to New Georgia. He wanted Winch to promise he would meet his father and mother when they finally could come up from Alabama to see him. Each time Winch promised that he would.

After six visits with Billy, seemingly on a whim almost, Winch took a couple of his own blank pass forms and locked the rest up with the nurse on the ward in a sealed envelope, and went up to St. Louis. St. Louis was where his wife and two brats were.

He had to get away somewhere. And when he thought about it, he thought Why *not* St. Louis? He didn't even have to see them, if he didn't want to.

It was more of a mood projection than the contemplation of an actual journey. Just to be going somewhere, anywhere. To be unknown. To be on the move. To be simply a watcher. With no loyalties and no commitments. He decided to wear one of his shirts that didn't have stripes. Go incognito. The mood was one of floating. Of being bodiless. Unattached to anything, or anybody. Unconcerned. It would be great.

Two hours after the idea hit him he was on his way. He had to check it out with his doc, requisition a hypodermic and the medication to use in it, take a ten-minute course in how to stick himself in the back of the arm or in the side of the ass, pack a satchel with his medical gear and an extra uniform. It was late afternoon when he was first penetrated by the idea and he arrived at the Luxor Greyhound station just at dusk, as the night trips were beginning.

It was not dark enough yet to turn on night lights, but was dark enough to make the eyes scratchy. Things looked indistinct in the thinner outdoor and thicker indoor glooms. People were beginning to move around restlessly, or eat sandwiches they did not really want, in the restiveness that comes with the basic change of light from day to night.

It all fit in perfectly with his mood of bodiless disinvolvement. He had no idea what he would do in St. Louis. And didn't care. And in fact, might just as well have been going to Chicago or Detroit. Anyplace where he was not known.

On the sleeping, breathing, crowded bus he did not sleep. There was a full moon out but he did not look at the night scenery. Only once on the 300-mile trip, at Cape Girardeau, did he rouse himself to look out over the big river. He was supremely content simply to be and to sit, and feel the motor vibrations and road tire-thumps under his thighs.

For the length of time the trip lasted there was nothing in the world Winch wanted.

The feeling was so similar to what he had felt in Frisco during the worst part of his heart failure attack, when he had felt another him outside himself, that it set him to brooding over this sense of another self outside. What was it? He didn't know. Was there really another him outside somewhere waiting to be rejoined to this part? He didn't know. Had it been a real sensation, or only his delirious imagination? He didn't know that. There were in fact no questions Winch could ask himself and give satisfactory answers for. He was left with only the haunting memory of the sensation. Under his feet and thighs the big tires thudded and scrambled against the roadway.

Billy Spencer had brought back the reality of the boggling, gasping, mud-swallowing platoons in a way that gave the mind a start. Somewhere there was a mistake, because Winch should have been right up there with them, right now. He was too sophisticated to think he could change what was happening to them. But he could have cushioned it and molded it so that some semblance of the old personality remained. Instead, he was here. And they were floundering. He felt a total failure.

Billy's talking had brought back the violent brutality and gushing insanity of combat in a shocking fashion. It made Winch aware of how strikingly it all had faded. He had never believed that it could fade, all that brutalizing. He had never wanted to be a father substitute for kids like Billy. Where did your responsibility end? Nowhere, apparently. Never. It never ended.

What kind of a thought was that to have to live with?

Beside him in the next seat a young soldier slept like a baby, cradling a Seagram's whiskey bottle.

In St. Louis Winch took a room in one of the hotels in the sleazy section down by the river. He had never served at Jefferson Barracks, but once he had stopped off there to see an old buddy and he knew the area. Whores and pimps and hustlers and muggers walked the crowded streets and hung out in all the low bars. Just as they'd always done. Naturally, soldiers were everywhere.

Once installed, he went straight to bed and slept for sixteen hours, all through the next day till eight o'clock at night. When he woke, he shaved and dressed and went out and bought himself a bottle of dry California wine and brought it back with him to the room. Feeling very like a man having a clandestine meeting in a cheap hotel, which in a way he was, he poured half a water-tumblerful and held it up to the light, then took the first sharp, tingling sip. Nothing happened. He did not drop dead. Then methodically, sitting at the cheap desk with his feet up on the bed, he drank the entire bottle, all six sharp, saliva-starting glasses of it. Nothing he had eaten or drunk in a long time tasted as sharp and appetizing and delicious.

When it was finished, he went out to eat. He had had no alcohol in so long the wine made him about half drunk for ten or fifteen minutes. It felt marvelous. He did not even mind having to ask the waitress for food cooked without salt. After he had eaten, he walked out into the street and did what he had known he was going to do all along. He flagged a cab and gave the driver his wife's address out in the western part of the city.

Winch had never seen the house, or the street. She had moved to St. Louis, after Winch left her for overseas, because her father the old master/sgt had retired there before he died. She had cousins there, she said. It was way out in one of those rambling residential sections of the city. The streets were in square blocks and shaded by big trees. The houses were big and square-shouldered and thick-waisted. They seemed to stand in row after row for miles, like hundreds of old rotund master/sgts in ranks on parade.

There was a tin panel with four apartment doorbell buttons let into the wood beside the door. The big old residence had been converted. Hers was the second floor left. From across the street, under the shade of an old large-leafed soft maple in the soft September night air, Winch set up his vigil and began to wait. After an hour and a half, when he had begun to think she must already be home and in bed, a taxi drove up and Winch watched her get out with a serviceman.

By his cap the man was an officer and a flyer. Wings and some fruit salad were visible above his left pocket. The round white insignia of a lt/col glinted from his shoulders in the street lamp. Both of them looked about three-fourths drunk. Giggling and laughing, they made their way up the short walk to the steps. At the door the man kissed her deeply, before she got out her key and opened the door. In a couple of minutes lights went on in the second floor left, and did not go out. The taxi had driven off.

Under his maple Winch set himself to wait another half hour. The lights did not go off. Nobody came out. He supposed the two brats were asleep in their own room. That was where they used to be. What the hell, they were ten and eleven now. Old enough to take care of themselves when mommy went out for the evening. After the half hour was up and there was no change, he started walking toward where he thought the nearest main thoroughfare ought to be.

It took quite a while. Winch walked slowly, and took his time, and did not get any shortness of breath. He thought he remembered the route the cab had taken but apparently he didn't. Finally he saw brighter lights down a street to his right, walked toward them to a traffic avenue and hailed a cab.

Back in the riverfront section he walked around to a few bars. He did not drink any alcohol. Finally he went back to the hotel and to bed around four.

For the next three days Winch made his small pilgrimage out to his wife's western residential section every night. It was the main anchor of his daily routine. He slept or loafed till late afternoon or the evening, before going out for his single big meal and then flagging a cab. Each day he went out for a bottle of wine and drank it sitting at his cheap hotel room desk, before going out to eat. Each night he arrived at her address by about twelve-thirty. Each of the first two nights she came home with the same Air Force lt/col.

But then on the third night she came home with another man. This one was also an officer. But he was shorter and fatter, pudgy, and wore the gold oak leaves of a major on his shoulders. Giggling and laughing, they walked up to the door the same way. At the door they kissed the same way. Again the lights went on. Again nobody left. As if released from some devil's bargain he had made, Winch turned on his heel and walked over to his traffic artery, caught a cab back to his hotel, packed his satchel, paid, and left. He caught another cab to the Greyhound station. The next bus south to Luxor did not leave for another hour. Winch spent it in a nearby bar, celebrating over a second bottle of wine for the day.

This time he slept most of the way. Only once did he wake with any seriousness, to stare out at the dark of the great brooding river rolling alongside the highway, on his left side now.

Staring, he thought about how the company in the midst of its anguish of change was forgetting them. Forgetting him. He could see how it could not be any other way. Consciously he thought it a good thing, and dozed again. Until suddenly something, a dream, woke him up wanting to shout a command, "Get them out! Get them out of there! Fast! Move them left! Can't you see the mortars got them bracketed!"

With the first word already a shout in his throat, he was able to cut it off so that aloud he only grunted. Winch shook his head. It had been something about the attack on Hill 27 that day on the Canal. Only the terrain had looked different and strange. New. Winch shook his head again. But after that he slept, until dawn and the coming of the Southern sunlight woke him. Really awake now, he stared out at the Arkansas flatlands without depression. He did not feel satisfied, and he didn't feel free. But he knew now that the disintegration of his company was final and complete, blown away. Ahead the city loomed over him, high up on its bluff, a presentiment. Any future he had at all was around there somewhere. There was no other way to look at it.

Back at Kilrainey, which he hated, and which looked more and more like a prison as the taxi delivered him through the brick gates to the main door, he found that during his four-day junket Billy Spencer's parents had been and gone. That was all to the good. Billy's mother had thrown a terrible scene, Billy told him.

That same day Winch's doctors gave him another full checkout examination and found that he was in better shape than they had yet seen him. They could give no reasons why. But his EKG readings were better than any they had taken of him. And if things continued like that, and kept on improving, they saw no reason why he could not be returned to duty soon. Winch only grinned bitterly, and did not tell them about the bottles of wine.

Two days later he had his first serious meeting with Carol Firebaugh in the big rec hall. She challenged him to a game of Ping-Pong.

Winch had seen her around there, to say hello to, from time to time. And actually had been introduced to her once, by Landers. But Winch had never spent much time in the rec hall, and had never had a conversation with her.

This time, he had wandered in because he had just been with Billy again and did not want to go back to the heart ward and sit and brood. But after he had taken one turn around the place, he was ready to leave it.

It was a place that had been created and engineered strictly for stupid men. Some smart guy, a Corps of Engineers officer no doubt, had designed it and laid it all out to be serviceable to what he thought of as stupid men, the enlisted classes.

If you were a fifteen-year-old high school student, it would no doubt have seemed great. Two Ping-Pong tables stood at the near end near the doors, neither in use. The basketball hoops and backboards had been drawn up on their pulleys and tied there parallel to the floor. They would only be let down when the collapsible bleachers were put up for an intramural game. The one-legged men, say, against the one-armed men, Winch thought evilly. Or when the Globetrotters came to play for the crippled. The theater stage was darkened, its red plush curtains drawn closed. It would be opened and the folding chairs put up on the basketball court when Bing Crosby or somebody came to entertain the injured troops.

For now, men sat around uncomfortably on the comfortable sofas, and stared off at the high windows screened on the inside to keep the basketballs from hitting them.

Thinking about cunt, probably. A few bathrobed men played checkers on the low tables. Two pairs of intellectuals engaged in chess games. In a far corner a volunteer worker in her sexless, motherly Gray Lady outfit conducted a listless class in basket weaving. As he was about to go out, Carol came up to him with a Ping-Pong ball and two paddles.

"How about a game with me, Sergeant?"

She was smiling. The sheer beauty of just her youth alone was an insult, like a slap in the face. In addition she was quite beautiful in herself, in a nonmovie star way. But had anybody ever been that young, ever? Winch wondered. Had he? There was a certain coquettishness in her eyes and in her attitude that was very Southern.

Winch had to hold himself tightly, not to respond with a cocky male truculence.

He heard his own voice saying, "Sure. Okay. Why not?"

There were a number of things Winch had done well in his career, as Landers ruefully found out when in a moment of misbegotten intellectual superiority he'd challenged Winch to a game of chess. In addition to football, basketball, springboard

diving, track, checkers, and chess there was Ping-Pong. At Forts
Bliss and Houston he had been one of the Army's top players
in the late nineteen thirties.

He took off his maroon issue bathrobe and duck slippers and
played her barefoot in his gray issue pajamas. He was able to
play her three games before he had to quit. His heart was pound-
ing unbelievably but the unaccustomed exercise made him feel
good. He beat her 21–12, 21–17, 21–18. She was a good player,
and obviously had slyly believed she would beat him.

"You're really a fine player," she said, laughing breathlessly.
Her pale, black-Irish complexion was flushed and rosy under
the raven black hair framing her forehead. "Don't you want to
play a few more?"

"No," Winch said. He was trying to hide his own breathlessness. "You better practice up with somebody your own class,
before you try me again."

"Oh!" But she laughed. Winch wanted mostly to sit down
someplace for a few minutes, but would not let himself. Instead,
he put back on his maroon issue bathrobe and duck slippers. He
walked over with her while she put away the paddles and the
ball.

When he asked her to have dinner with him that night, she
accepted almost before he could get the words out of his mouth.

He wanted her to meet him in the bar lounge of the Claridge
Hotel. He thought that would be better than the bar at the
Peabody. But she was hardly inside and seated before it was
plain she did not like being in the place.

"I haven't been in this place since my high school senior
prom," she said nervously.

"And is that such a long time ago?"

"Three and a half years." She paused a moment. "Actually,
it's not that long. I've been here since then. But I haven't been
here since the war, and all the servicemen descended on Luxor."

"I don't know any bar to take you where there aren't servicemen," Winch said.

"There are a few," she said. She looked around the place
again.

"You find this place too low-brow for you, now?"

"No. But on the other hand it's not the real Luxor any more,
either." She hunched her shoulders and then pulled them back
down, skittishly. "I don't like the way they look at me when

they've been drinking. Out at the hospital it's a different thing."

When they got around to discussing where to go for dinner, over their drinks from Winch's brown-sacked bottle, she suggested a place she knew: Mrs. Thompson's Tea Room. There wouldn't be servicemen there. Winch didn't know it was the same place she had suggested to Landers. But Winch vetoed it immediately, anyway.

"Let's get something straight. If I'm going to be taking you around to places, I'm not going to take you to places where you're well known. Your own local places. I'm going to take you places where you're not known. My places."

Carol smiled. "Is that an order, sir?"

"Call it that."

"You're ashamed to be seen with me? Is that it?"

"No. Certainly not. I'm thrilled and delighted," Winch said. "Let's just say I don't want people you know in Luxor to think you're robbing the cradle."

She laughed at that. "Yes. You're some cradle rider."

Winch grinned, briefly. "I might be able to show you some places in your city you didn't even know existed."

"I'll bet you could," she said. "But I'm not sure I want to see them."

For the dinner he took her to the Plantation Roof of the Peabody. She hadn't been there in a long time, either. But after a little while she seemed to like it.

"It's certainly got energy," she smiled, looking around. "I didn't know there were that many servicemen *in* Luxor."

Winch suddenly noticed she was not wearing her glasses. Her irises were dark, almost black. Her one sometimes uncontrollable eye was more prominent without them, and kept looking at him briefly and then looking guiltily away while the good eye went on smiling at him coquettishly. It was enormously sexually exciting somehow.

"Booze," he said grimly. "It's the energy of the doomed. Most of these people will be shipping out of here soon. Either east or west."

"Please. Let's don't talk about that." Her brother, her younger brother, Winch now found out, was a fighter pilot in Florida, finishing up his training before heading for Europe. That was why she was home from college this year.

She was a good ballroom dancer, it turned out, light and

supple and easy to lead. Winch paced himself carefully, sitting out as many dances as they danced so he would not get out of breath.

"Why are you in the hospital?" she asked when they were sitting out some dances. "What did they send you back to America for?"

Looking at him with that one unmanageable eye, she reached out a youth-smooth hand and placed it over his callused one on the table.

Winch had been anticipating this question, and wondering how he could handle it. He could not bring himself to tell her he had heart trouble.

"Dengue fever and malaria," he said, promptly and laconically.

"Is that enough to get sent home for?"

"It is if it's bad enough."

"And now you're getting over it?"

"Just about."

"Is that why you don't drink?" She had had two whiskeys out of the bottle on the table. "I didn't know drinking was bad for malaria."

Winch shrugged. He wanted badly to change the subject. "They told me not to," he said shortly.

"And soon you'll be going away again. Off somewhere."

"Probably," Winch lied. "Actually," he added, "I may be stationed here for a while. In Second Army."

"That would be great," Carol smiled.

"Let's dance awhile," he said.

It had been so long since any sexual desires had moved him. Not since Frisco. They said the digitalis and the diuretics caused that. Holding her against him dancing, her breasts lying heavy against the chest of his shirtfront, he felt no sexual stirrings. That didn't bother him. It wasn't sex he was after with her. It was that incredible, unbelievable youth. It stung him, like some furious insect.

When he took her home to her parents' house on the big, tall tree shaded avenue, he did not attempt to kiss her and told the taxi to wait as they got out.

"Let him go," she said. "Don't you want to come in for a while?"

Winch shook his head. "I'm too old to go around necking with girls on the sofas of their mamas' parlors," he said as they walked up the walk.

"Oh, there might be more to it than that," Carol smiled promptly.

"Not on any living room sofas, with papa and mama upstairs," Winch said. "Not for me. But next time I take you out I can have a place to take you. If you want."

"Is that a threat?"

"No threat," he said. "A promise."

They were at the door and instead of answering she put back her head, closed her eyes, and pushed out her lips for him to kiss her. Winch waited, deliberately, until she opened her eyes looking startled, before he leaned forward and put his lips on hers. When he did, she immediately popped her tongue into his mouth and rubbed it around hard all over the inside of his mouth in a mechanical way.

"When?" she said, when their mouths parted.

"How about tomorrow night?" Winch said, and when she nodded, added coldly, "First thing, I'm going to have to teach you how to kiss." Before she could answer that, he was on his way down the walk to the cab.

He sat quietly on the ride back. He was feeling the first sexual stirrings he had felt since the heart failure attack in Letterman and old, what was her name? Arlette. Carol pretty clearly didn't know any but the most obvious things about sex and it could be great sport to teach her. In his khakis which he never wore underwear with he could feel his cock crawling and extending itself a little, tentatively. His breathing deepened. He sat quietly in the cab and savored the sensations all the way back to the hospital, watching out the window the rich, well-off lawns and trees and avenues and then the poorer places and suburban juke joints of Luxor's Southern city landscape.

It was easy enough to arrange for a room at the Claridge. Jack Alexander kept two rooms there for players to rest or sleep or drink in, as well as the suite in which he ran the big-time, high-stakes poker game for the big winners of the Army's monthly payroll. Alexander called the Claridge for him. Jack made sure the room was on another floor from the one his game was on.

"You knew exactly how to handle me, didn't you?" Carol said with a triumphant little smile, when he took her there after another dinner at the Peabody's Plantation Roof. "I'll bet you've done that many times before, with women."

Winch sensed she wanted him to grin. So he did, briefly. "If you want to know the real truth," he smiled, "I'm just too old to fart around any more."

"You intrigued me. You said you'd teach me how to kiss. I thought I knew how."

"Well, you don't," he grinned. "The first thing to remember is never to use heavy pressure. And never be mechanical, never keep repeating the same movement. The whole art of sex is to tease just ever so slightly. That way you want more. And more. Come here. But first, let me show you how I undress you."

The covered parts of her were as deliciously, unbelievably youthful as the uncovered parts. There wasn't an excess ounce of fat on her. With that black, black hair and pale, pale skin of the black Irish she had a thick black luxurious bush against her white belly. She played a lot of tennis and golf, she said. Her father was a big-time lawyer in Luxor, she told him.

"How old did you say you were?"

"I'm uh twenty-two." The slight hesitation betrayed her. "I will be. Soon."

"How soon?"

"In seven months." She blushed.

"I'm old enough to be your father."

"I think of you as something else. You make me think of a smart, tough, wise, old elephant, who's been roaming his forests forever," she whispered.

"I do, hunh?" Winch said.

She did not seem to mind at all that he was extraordinarily slow in achieving an erection.

"I don't know why I'm drawn to you so, the way I am." Holding his head against her, she added in a breathy voice, "I'll have to go home later, you know. I can't stay out all night."

He found, as he had suspected, that she knew very little about sex at all. He was sure she had not, for example, ever had anyone go down on her before. But he decided that that could wait for some future session.

"Do you think I'm attractive?" she whispered as he raised himself over her to enter her, and stretched out her long-waisted, long-legged pale black-Irish body for him on the bed.

"Yes." Winch didn't feel it necessary to elaborate. In any case Winch was discovering for the first time in his life, to his sur-

prise and disbelief, fatigue in sex. As he worked on her carefully
in the bed. He had always been in good enough shape, before,
that he had never had to worry about becoming tired. Now was
different.

"Oh. Oh. It was never like this." She whispered it with her
eyes closed. How many women had said that line to how many
new men? Winch wondered. To each new man. He had never
been much at long-dicking them but he knew he had a more than
usual circumference.

While they were lying side by side afterward, after he had
come, though he was sure she hadn't, Carol said, "What are we
going to do? What's going to happen to us?"

Winch thought that that, to say the least, was a little bit
premature. "Well, for one thing, we can have a hell of a great
time together for a while," he said softly.

But after two weeks of her he found he too was beginning to
think distastefully about his having to move out to Camp
O'Bruyerre and Second Army some time soon. It was only
thirty miles from Luxor but that thirty miles meant he would
not find it that easy to meet her in town every night.

But by that time Johnny Stranger was back from Cincinnati
and Winch knew about his old mess/sgt that, some way or other,
Johnny Stranger had seen the shit hit the fan.

CHAPTER 17

When he left Luxor for Cincinnati with his two three-day passes in his pocket, Strange was so used to the long crowded bus trip by now, had done it so many times, that he about had it memorized and hardly bothered to look out.

He had hoped to doze but in the moving vehicle full of breathing bodies it was impossible to sleep. The air of the big bus was clogged with exhaled body moisture, and a kind of perpetual murmur. Strange sucked at a pint bottle of whiskey he had bought for the trip, stretched in the cramped seat, and let his mind run over the story and catastrophe of Billy Spencer. His mind had been wanting to do that since the day Billy had first shown up. Strange had known he would have to come to grips with it eventually.

The arrival of Billy at Kilrainey had been as much a torture for Strange as it was for Winch. It was perhaps even worse for Strange, because Strange could not come to terms with it in the way Winch apparently had. Billy Spencer was the first so-called basket case the company had had. And while everybody understood theoretically that such things could happen, nobody really believed it would happen to him. And nobody ever really be-

lieved it would happen to anyone in their company. They had
all heard of them in other companies.

Winch seemed able to cope with that. But Strange couldn't.
The unparalleled distress Strange felt when he thought about
his own having survived relatively untouched, in comparison to
Billy, made the skin on his back twitch, and his buttocks tighten
with guilt.

Whenever he thought of poor Billy a wild irrational hatred
for all civilians who had never been out there and been through
it slammed through him and made him want, unreasonably, to
smash in the face of any civilian that might present itself to him.
It was unreasonable, and Strange knew it was unreasonable.

But even worse than that for Strange was the story Billy had
told them about the disintegration of the company. Strange had
been willing enough to leave the company, willing in fact even
when he knew leaving it and shipping back to the States would
mean being assigned to some new outfit and never going back.
But that did not mean he wanted it to fade away, be broken up,
disappear. It was losing its identity and personality under other
officers and new noncoms shipped in from outside. It was
becoming another, no longer recognizable unit. That was a ca-
lamity.

Somewhere in the back of Strange's mind there had always
been the idea that someday when the war was over they would
all of them all get together again somewhere. Become again the
unit it once had been, only grown wiser and more experienced
by war service.

Strange had been too embarrassed ever to speak of this to
anyone, but he nevertheless had clung to the idea.

The idea had always been a pipe dream, of course. But as long
as the company was still out there, with some semblance of its
old roster and original organization intact, he could still hold on
to and at least play with the idea. Now, with the company no
longer there, and filled up and loaded down with strangers,
Strange felt uprooted, homeless. He suffered from feeling naked
and alone and orphaned with a severity he had never experienced before. Not even when he left home, or when his
parents died. The existence of his civilian wife and her civilian
family where he was accepted as a member was no help for this
feeling at all.

In the wet-aired bus Strange sucked disconsolately at his pint
of whiskey. What the hell, it wasn't something that was going

to kill him. He had been in the Army long enough to get used to changing outfits. He had done it a number of times.

But there was something special about this outfit. And he saw clearly enough that it was the war had done it. Death—death, and maiming—had pulled it together in a way the peacetime Army had never done with outfits. Shared deaths, shared woundings, shared terrors had given it a family closeness it wouldn't be easy to find again.

And Strange did not know if he had the courage to start over from scratch and knowing what he knew now, go through the process a second time.

Outside the bus at the rest stops, when he got down occasionally to relieve himself, there was a chill of October in the fresher air.

When he finally got to the house in Covington it was midafternoon, and almost exactly the same time of day that he had arrived all the other times. Linda's paternal uncle, 4-F older brother, and maternal cousin were all still sleeping preparatory to going off on the night shift. This time when they all began straggling down they found Strange already in the kitchen, drinking beer. Strange sat with them again in the kitchen while they made their breakfast, and had some bacon and eggs himself. None of them seemed much interested that his hand had been operated on and that he now wore the plaster plate on it, since they had seen him last.

He soon found out that Linda Sue, who should have been working the day shift and therefore should be coming home soon, had in fact been transferred to the swing shift. Instead of coming home she had just gone off to work, and would not be getting off until midnight. Strange hung around the house till some of the other women began coming home from work and from shopping, and then had to get out. The women filled up the kitchen so with their gossip and their preparations for cooking dinner that he couldn't stand it. The only other place available was Linda's little chintz-covered bedroom, which was too small for loafing and too small for anything else except sleeping, and maybe fucking.

He went to a lousy war movie. In it some green young Navy kid, stranded in Bataan, kept letting the spoons fly off of hand grenades and counting to three before he threw them, usually just across a coconut log where evil-looking Japanese were shooting point-blank at him. It was so outrageous that finally about halfway through he had to leave. As he walked up the aisle he looked at the faces of the people bathed in the flickering light from the screen as they chewed handfuls of popcorn and watched the fighting with avid eyes, and for a brief insane moment wished he had two or three grenades with him, to toss in among them. And see how they liked it.

After that, he simply went around from bar to bar drinking. When he finally went back to the house at twelve-thirty, he was three-fourths tight and went to bed in the little chintz room. Two others of the family who were on the swing shift were already home in the kitchen, and he talked to them for a while. Linda did not get home until after three.

Of course, she had not known he was coming. She was terribly apologetic when she found him, just waking up, in the little bedroom. Linda was about half-crocked herself, and explained she had been with a few of the girls for some drinks. When he wanted to make love to her, she was warm and kind and receptive. But she certainly wasn't what Strange could call hot. When he was humping her, she stroked his head. He would have preferred her to be passionate.

But there was no inkling of anything else. Not that Strange could feel. Why should there be? Their lovemaking was the same as it had always been. Perhaps it was even just a little better than usual. But when, after he had come, he tried to talk to her about what Curran had said concerning the new, second operation and what this could mean to them with the restaurant, she begged off from hearing about it and wanted to go to sleep. When he went on talking anyway, she broke down and began to cry.

"But, Linda, honey, don't you understand?" he persisted. "You can have your restaurant. All I have to do is say no to this second operation and they'll discharge me."

"I don't want to hear about it now," she wept. "I'm too fuddled and too tired and too sleepy. Can't we talk about it tomorrow? Please?"

"Sure, sure. Of course. Don't cry. Don't cry, for God's sake," Strange said, and stroked her shoulder. After she was asleep, he lay awake a long time with his arms behind his head, thinking. It certainly wasn't the reaction he had expected.

He suggested that he take her out for a nice high-class lunch somewhere, when she came down at eleven the next morning, because he thought she looked peaked and worn down. Certainly the kitchen, with its ebb and flow of family workers preparing or cooking one meal or another, was no place for a discussion. But Linda instead of being pleased gave him a sharp look, and then after a moment said she couldn't have lunch with him. Though she did not say why. Instead, she wanted him to pick her up at a bar near her job after she got off at midnight. She gave him the address. Then around two she got dressed and went off. Shopping, she said.

So Strange found himself with another whole day to put in. He was soured on war movies but there did not seem to be anything else playing anywhere. Across the river the whole town of Cincinnati seemed full of nothing but war films. Finally he found a theater that was showing a rerun of *The Story of Vernon and Irene Castle,* and went to see that. He remembered the outfit had seen that on Guadalcanal, and had loved it. But, now, the richness and wealth and high life of Fred Astaire and Ginger Rogers was so foreign to anything he knew and so out of step with his mood of now that he left that one, too, before it was half over. Hell, even when they were poor they lived rich.

He tried not to drink too much, because he wanted to have his brains sharp. But it was hard not to. It seemed everybody everywhere who wasn't working was drinking. He decided to take a taxi to the bar because he did not know the town well enough to trust trying the bus system.

He had already arranged where to take her to dinner. Across the river in Cincinnati during his lone drinking hours he had checked around, and found a ritzy hotel which had a place like the Peabody's Plantation Roof that served good steak dinners till very late. Strange was proud of the sophisticated tastes he had developed during his two-month stay in Luxor, and decided to take her there and show her. Only when they were arriving and getting out of the taxi did it occur to him that such a high-class place might embarrass Linda and make her uncomfortable. She had never gone to ritzy places, even back in Wahoo. But of course, by the time he thought of this, it was already too late and they were at the door.

He needn't have worried. Linda seemed at least as at home in the place as he was. When he tipped the head waiter three dollars to get them a nice quiet table off to themselves, she noted it with approval. She accepted the big menu with all the French words and ordered her dinner as smoothly and calmly as if she had been doing it right along. Strange ordered drinks for them, and she said she'd take a martini. After he'd ordered the drinks, he sat back and looked around, without really thinking that he had never known Linda Sue to drink a martini before. The big place was jam-packed and they were surrounded by servicemen and their women. The few civilian men in the place appeared drowned in the big sea of khaki and blue.

On the bandstand a sixteen-piece orchestra played through both "Little Sir Echo" and "Racing with the Moon" while Strange sipped at his drink and tried to collect his thoughts. He had never been much of a ballroom dancer so it did not occur to him to ask Linda to dance.

Since she would not mention the operation or bring it up, Strange was forced finally to bring it up himself.

"Well, where shall I begin?" he said finally.

Linda only looked at him. "Don't you want to ask me to dance first?" she said.

"Oh," Strange said. "Sure."

On the dance floor, which though big was crowded, he moved her around to the music of "Chattanooga Choo-Choo," feeling upset and disturbed. The song was almost finished before he realized that Linda Sue was dancing beautifully with him, and stopped and moved her away from him to look down at her.

"Didn't you notice I've learned to dance since you've been away?" she said.

"Yeah. Yes," Strange said. "I just now noticed. How did that come about?" Behind him a sailor still in summer whites bumped into him and he started moving again.

"Oh, well. You know. A lot of us girls go out dancing together," Linda said against his shoulder.

"You dance with each other?" Strange said.

"Chattanooga Choo-Choo" ended and without waiting for applause the band moved into "You'll Never Know," the song Alice Faye had made so famous. Strange had heard it on the radio on both the Canal and New Georgia. And Tokyo Rose used to play it.

"Most of the time," Linda said against his ear. "Sometimes the boys ask us to dance, too."

In spite of his awkwardness and lack of talent Strange found himself dancing better with her now, because of her new expertise, than he had ever danced before. Instead of making him feel good it made him feel more disquieted.

When the song ended, he took her back to the table and ordered them another drink.

"Can we have some red wine with the steak, too?" Linda said.

"Wine?" Strange said, "wine? Sure. Sure, why the hell not?"

"Just ask the man for the wine list," she said, and gave him a funny smile.

"Do you want me to wait until after we've eaten?" Strange said, after he had ordered a twelve-dollar bottle of French wine.

"No," she said. "No, I guess not."

"Well," Strange said, "here's the story."

But as he laid out for her the options Curran had offered him, doing it with that same patient thoughtfulness he had been so famous for and was so proud of back in the company, he began to feel more and more disquiet, more and more distress. He didn't know why exactly. She just wasn't reacting right. She didn't say anything at all until he finished telling it.

"So you see," he wound it up, "I can get discharged—" he moved his shoulders, "almost immediately. We can start working on that restaurant. While the war boom is still on. Probably your folks would loan us some money, wouldn't they?"

"What will happen to your poor hand?" Linda said with a sad smile, and reached across and put her hand over the bound member in its plaster plate.

Strange shrugged. "It'll stay about the same. I'll have only partial use of the two middle fingers. But hell, I've been living like that for almost a year now. It aint so bad. Probly I'll get some kind of a pension, I guess."

"And if you have the operation?"

Strange shrugged again, impatiently, feeling irritable. She knew all that. "He can't guarantee he can fix it. If he does, I'll have to stay in. For the duration. If he can't, it'll be the same, anyway."

"Well," Linda said, sadly, "it's a beautiful offer."

"Christ, aint you happy about the restaurant?" Strange couldn't resist saying.

"Yes, of course. But—" She stopped.

"But, what?"

It was at just that moment, as if deliberately prearranged by some consciously malignant fate, that the waiter arrived with their steaks. Behind Strange the orchestra was playing some dizzy, lilty song called "Elmer's Tune."

"Let's eat, first," Linda said. "Then I'll tell you what's been happening."

If she was upset or depressed or sad it certainly had no effect on her appetite. She put away the entirety of her big, healthy steak except for a thin strip of fat rind, and with it a whole order of French fries, green beans, and a salad. Working so hard made her hungry, she said. Strange attacked his own big steak as if wreaking vengeance on it for the meal's having interrupted them when it did. After putting down three hefty glasses of the red wine with her meat, Linda Sue pushed her plate daintily two inches away from her with her knife and fork laid side by side on it, put her elbows on the table, and looked at him with wide, clear, unguarded, sorrowful eyes.

"Yes," Strange said. "Well, what?"

"Well," she said, and stopped. "It's that—It's because—Well, I've got a, uh, boyfriend."

"You've got a what?" Strange said.

She blushed crimson. "Well. An, uh, lover. I've got a lover."

"You've got a lover," Strange said. He would remember later that the sixteen-piece orchestra was playing the ballad called "I'll Be Seeing You," a song recorded and made popular by Vera Lynn and probably the most well-liked song of the whole damned war, so far.

"Yes," Linda Sue said, over the music. "And I'm not going to give him up."

But, of course, Strange's mind was saying to him. So many things fell into place so suddenly that it was all there in front of him, all of a piece, a consistent pattern, only he had all along just not interpreted it right, was all. How she had been so confused and almost lukewarm, when he had telephoned her from Frisco. How she had decided not to come down to Luxor, because of her job. How she had seemed so distant when he came up to Cincinnati, because she was tired from overwork. How she had slept with him so indifferently, all those times. How she had not cared if he slept with her or not, all those times he had not slept with her. *You should have figured that out, dumbhead,* his mind was saying to him.

"You've got a lover," Strange said. "And you're not going to give him up. Good. Fine. Well, who is this guy?" *Don't talk about it,* his mind warned him. *If you let her start talking about it, you have lost.*

"He's a lieutenant colonel in the Air Force," Linda said promptly, as if she had worked her speech all out, "and he's a wonderful person. He's a Princeton graduate, and he comes from someplace on Long Island called Southampton."

That would account for all the new sophistication, wouldn't it?

"And I suppose you want to marry him?" Strange said. He felt tired suddenly, and he wished they would stop playing that damned song. That fucking "I'll Be Seeing You."

She did not answer him but went straight on. "He does a lot of design work on airplanes," she said, instead. As if from her prepared speech. "And he does a lot of work up at Patterson Field. But his main office is here. And anyway, he flies up there and back whenever he wants to or feels like it. He has a plane, at his beck and call. I met him at our plant when he was there looking at some parts that he thought he might use in some design. And so now, he spends more time here than he does up there, because of me. At least, the evenings. The nights."

"Sure. The evenings," Strange said. "The nights. But do you want to marry him?"

"He's six foot two," Linda went on. "With wide shoulders and a small head, blue eyes, and a long neck. And he's the greatest gentleman I ever met. And he's crazy in love with me."

"Are you going to marry him, God damn it?" Strange shouted, but in a low voice. "You want a divorce. Is that it?"

Linda dropped her eyes demurely, and blushed again. "He can't marry me," she said simply. "He would love to. But he's got a wife and four small children back there in Long Island. And he can't leave them."

"Because they got the money," Strange said grimly.

"Perhaps," Linda said. "Maybe. But he can't leave them. And I don't care. And I'm not going to give him up."

"But, why?"

"Because he makes me feel things. He makes me feel things I've never felt before."

"What kind of things?"

"Sex things." She blushed a third time, completely crimson. "Like what?"

"Lovemaking things," Linda said, still blushing, still looking away.

"I think I'll order us another drink," Strange said tiredly.

"Yes. Please do. I wish you would," she said. "I don't like this any better than you do."

"You must like it some better," Strange said grimly, "since it's not you who's losing anything. Would you mind telling me what kind of lovemaking things?"

She waited till he had signaled the waiter and ordered the new drinks, still blushing furiously, still unwilling to look at him. Only when the waiter went away, was out of hearing range, did she speak.

"He kisses me, down there," she said, her face bright red. "He makes me come. He's taught me how to come. To have orgasms. Do you realize I've never had an orgasm in my life till I met him?"

"Good God," Strange said. "Never?"

"Never once. And you're the first man I ever, uh, went to bed with."

"Not even once?" Strange said. "I always thought—I guess I never thought about it."

"I'm not blaming you. But you can see why I'm never going to give him up. I'm going to stay with him. At least until the war's over."

"Or they move him someplace else," Strange said.

"Yes," she said. "There's that. Have you ever gone out with any other women than me? I mean since we're married?"

Strange raised his eyes to stare at her. But she was still looking down, at the table. "No," he lied.

"Then I'm sorry," Linda said. "I'm truly sorry for you. But that doesn't change anything."

"No."

"I guess you won't want to stay married to me. Under the circumstances."

"No. I guess not."

Strange was thinking that it would be easy enough to put it all down to some form of retribution. That was what he was feeling. But was that really the truth? After all, he had not gone to bed with that girl Frances at the Peabody until long after Linda had her Air Force lt/col. Of course, he had gone down to the whorehouses that one time in Wahoo with the boys, after she left. And a couple of other times, after he'd brought her out and married her, he'd gone down to the whores on a toot with a bunch of the guys. And sweated blood for two weeks after, afraid he might have picked up a dose of something. But in spite of all of that it wasn't really retribution. It was just the war.

"Do you kiss him down there, too?" he asked.

"Yes." She was blushing furiously again. "I'm going to give you all of the money in the account," she said. "It's yours. There's a little over seven thousand now."

"I don't want it," Strange said.

"It doesn't matter," Linda said. "Because I'm not going to keep it. If you don't take it, I'll give it to daddy. So you better take it."

"Okay, I'll take it," Strange said.

He had suddenly become aware of that damned band again. Now they were playing "How High the Moon," another song he had heard on the radio in the tropical islands of the Far East. Tokyo Rose had played that one, too.

"You can see why I can't take it," Linda said.

Strange had hardly heard her. "Well, anyway, you've answered my question for me. You've solved my problem for me," he said, looking up.

"What are you going to do?"

"Why, have that damned second operation. That's what."

Linda did not say anything, did not answer him.

"It's getting really late," he said. "I suppose we ought to be going."

"Don't you want to dance with me? One more time? I've learned to really love to dance," Linda said.

"No, I don't," Strange said. "I really don't."

From the other side of the table she reached over her hand and put it over his claw, bound down on its plaster plate. Agitatedly, he pulled his away.

But there was no fight. Back at the house in Covington, up in her little chintzy bedroom, at five A.M. with the dawn just coming up, they more or less amicably went through the various details that had to be arranged, a great deal like two old friendly business partners who for various reasons are splitting up their firm. She arranged for and wrote out a check for him to cash, closing out their mutual bank account. She would start a new one, she said. Then Linda got ready for bed. And Strange started downstairs, to drink some beers with any members of the family who might be just getting up or getting ready to go to bed.

But when he got to the head of the stairs, she called him back. "I'll sleep with you tonight, anyway," she said. "If you want."

"Jesus, no," Strange said. And then she started to cry.

"Christ, don't cry," Strange said. "For God's sake, don't cry."

She didn't answer.

"Will you tell me one thing," Strange said. "Did you really like it? When he kissed you, down there?"

She looked up from her crying and, incredibly, went right into a deep crimson blush, as red as a beet. "I loved it. I—I adored it," she said. "I've never had anything feel like that in my life."

"Well then don't cry," Strange said harshly, and pulled the door to, gently. Then he pushed it back open. "Do you realize that all that time, since I've been back, when you were sleeping with him, you were screwing me, too?"

"I was your wife," she said.

Downstairs in the kitchen her older paternal cousin, who had just got up to get ready to go on the day shift, was sitting with Linda's maternal cousin's wife, who had only just come home herself after getting off the swing shift. Since they were drinking beer, both of them, Strange joined them. He did not tell them he was leaving. Probably, they would not have cared. Strange wondered briefly why the maternal cousin's wife was so late getting home from the swing shift, herself.

He was waiting at the bank when they opened the doors, with Linda's check to cash. He got a certified cashier's check for $7,140, and put it away in his wallet. Near the bus station he bought another pint of whiskey for the bus trip back, but he was pretty sure he'd have to get another somewhere around Nashville, the way he felt. He sure didn't have much of a batting average for completing his leaves and passes, he thought as he climbed on the daytime Greyhound.

The certified check in his wallet did not seem to make it feel any heavier, or make him feel any lighter, not the way he felt.

But he knew just what he was going to do with the money when he got back to Luxor.

CHAPTER 18

Bobby Prell was in his wheelchair on his ward's small dayroom porch when Strange came down the ward looking for him. He was playing solitaire. Prell had had his final set of casts off only two days before, and was in no mood to think about anything but himself. But he could tell something had happened to Strange, when he saw him.

"What's the matter with you?"

"With me? Nothing. Why?"

Prell knew his new buddy well enough to know when something was wrong. Being thrown together in so many hospitals, Prell believed, had given them a strong sense of each other.

At the same time, the final removal of his casts and a good look at his poor lousy crippled legs had given Prell an enormous shock. He had seen them before, during the first time the casts were off, but they had been covered back up quickly in new, safe plaster cocoons so that he was able to put them out of his mind, not think about them. Now he had to think about them. It did not make for any mood of intense optimism.

Withered, was the only word to describe them. From his hips

down they were nothing but the skin and the bones. Great flabs
of flaking skin hung down from the knitted femurs and the
shinbones. In the middle, his frozen knees were huge red knobs.
Thick red welts and ridges of scar tissue crisscrossed both thighs
where the .50 cal slugs had hit him. The idea that he might ever
walk on them again was a horrible, grotesque joke.

And the pain had started again, immediately the therapy
started. It was not as bad as the pain he had had on the train but
it was with him all the time, never stopped.

"How're you, old buddy?" Strange demanded. He gave a
mean grin as he sauntered on out onto the glassed-in porch. It
was not your normal Johnny Stranger grin. This grin made
Prell think of the last time Strange had had to fire a 1st/cook for
laziness and malingering.

"Not too bad." Prell wondered if Strange would notice the
casts were gone, and if so, how soon. "You been up to Cincinnati
again?"

"Yes. Yes, I have. And I've come into a little money." Strange
whipped out his wallet from his bathrobe pocket and pulled out
a large-sized bank check. He spread it open before Prell.

"Money?" Prell said.

"Money. And I'm itchin' to begin spendin' it."

Prell whistled when he saw the amount. "Your old lady know
about this?" He made himself grin. He was certainly not himself
going to tell Strange about the missing casts.

"My old lady is making a fortune up there in them defense
plants. She don't need this."

"It's a hell of a lot of money," Prell made himself say.

"You bet. And I figured it's about time I started utilizing some
of it." Strange paused, and pushed forward his chest. "You
know about that famous suite of rooms those Navy friends of
Landers have at the Peabody? Well, I thought I'd get me one of
those. For a while. For all of us to use."

Prell moved his head, in disbelief. This was surely not the
Johnny Stranger he knew. Strange had always been the biggest,
most notorious miser the old company had had.

"How long before you think you'll be able to go into town?"
Strange said. "I want you in on the opening." Then for the first
time, he looked down and noticed the missing casts. "Hey?" He
put his hand gently on one of the horrible, scabby-looking,
withered feet. "They're off? For good? How's it going?"

"Terrible." Prell said it without expression or emotion, factually. "I hear they're giving seven for one on the leg wards that I'll never walk on them again."

"They're wrong," Strange said. "I think I'll go pick me up some of that seven-to-one money."

"I know they're wrong," Prell said, in his sturdy, West Virginia way. "They don't know how tough I am. But I think you better wait two weeks and see, just the same. Besides, the odds'll go up. To nine or ten."

"Hey. Listen. There might be a way we could make some money on this," Strange said.

"You mean betting it?"

"Sure. If you were to wait? If you were to work hard at the therapy? And not show anybody? Not let anybody see the results. Make it look bad. Why, hell. The odds might go as high as twenty to one. I'd lay a lot on that."

Prell studied him. "And we could let Landers know." Again, he was struck by how changed Strange seemed. Winch was the one who would have concocted such a scheme.

"What about the other company guys?" Strange said.

"Fuck 'em," Prell said in a flat voice. "I'll tell you something, Johnny Stranger. I don't feel that close to the others. The ones that got here before we did. They don't really seem like the old company. Besides, the more people you tell about a thing, the more it's likely to leak out."

"That's true," Strange said. "And I don't feel that close to them myself, any more. But what about Winch?"

Prell could feel his face get stiff, and flat. His Indian eyes narrowed. Once again, the mere name put in his visual mind that same picture of Winch, standing over him in the bed that day, with his bright eyes and evil grin. Accusing him of letting his squad get shot up because he was medal-hunting.

"I wouldn't give that son of a bitch nothing," he said. "I wouldn't give him floor space in hell."

"Aw, now," Strange said. Coldly, Prell watched him shrug.

"Anyway," Prell said, "I don't know if what you're thinking of would work." Mentioning bringing Winch into it had changed his whole mood. He felt sullen. He didn't care now whether they did it or not. "Look. It's going to be a long time. Three months? Maybe the guys you make the bets with will have left the hospital. How you going to collect?"

"We'll think of some way to secure the money. Put it in sealed envelopes? Leave them with a nurse, or some doctor?"

"I aint got any money," Prell said. He felt stubborn. And sullen. He couldn't help it. "I got here broke. And I aint got my back pay yet."

"I'll loan you money," Strange said. He waved his check, and then put it away. "I've got the money. How much do you want? I'll put up for us both."

"I could invest a thousand," Prell said. "I'll get at least that much back pay."

"Done! I'll start laying off some bets."

"You better wait two weeks," Prell said. "Till we see how I'm doing."

"I'm not worried about you," Strange said. "Listen, how long do you think it'll be before you can get in town on a pass?"

"But I won't have Winch involved," Prell said. He paused a moment, stubbornly, thinking. "Matter of fact, he may just bet the other way. I bet he will. If he does, you cover whatever he puts up with my money. I don't care how much. I'll raise it some way."

"I hate to do that to Winch," Strange said. "But of course if that's the way you want it."

It appeared to Prell that Strange's eyes had grown suddenly shallow, and thoughtful. "No shenanigans," Prell said sternly. "If you do that to me, I'll blow the whole deal on you. I swear it."

"No, no. No shenanigans. Now, how about that trip to town? When can you?"

"I don't know. How do I know? I suppose I could go right now, if we could get me a folding wheelchair someplace."

"I want you there for the opening," Strange said, and drew himself up and grinned. "I tell you, there's more pussy around there than you can shake your dick at."

"I'd like to come," Prell said. "But I aint going to be much good for any fucking. Casts or no casts."

"I suppose not," Strange said. "How you coming along with that little girlfriend of yours?"

"Great. Fine. I've got her jerking me off into a handkerchief every day. I've got her so she'll kiss it a little, but I can't get her to take the whole thing in her mouth yet." He sat and grinned up at the other, mirthfully.

Strange cackled. "Well, I guess you aint hurting any, then."
He waved his arm once more. "I'll look into this about the bets.
I get that suite arranged for, I'll be back to see you. You see what
you can do about borrowing a folding wheelchair."

Prell watched him leave, turning the wheels of the wheelchair
with his hands so he could look after him. He was getting adept
with the damned thing. After a while your mind stopped even
thinking about it. And it was always good to see Strange. But
something had happened to Strange in Cincinnati this time.
Prell would have bet money on it.

Well, if Strange didn't want to talk about it, he didn't have to.
Something had happened to Prell, too. Getting those casts off
was no ordinary everyday experience, either. And he was much
more ardent about the future of his legs, and walking, in
Strange's presence than he had felt before Strange entered, or
than he felt now.

Prell actually had overheard some bitter soul of a double
amputee from the Sicilian invasion, offering seven to one that
Prell would not be walking by the time the amputee left Kilrainey. That would have to be at least three months away. The
amputee had not gotten any takers.

After only two days of therapy, Prell was secretly inclined to
agree with the amputee. That he couldn't do it in three months.
And there was that strong possibility looming there that he
might never be able to do it. That was why, although he had put
a brighter front on it, he had told Strange to wait awhile and see,
before committing money.

He had been equally dishonest with Strange about his girlfriend. He hadn't actually lied. He had been able to get her to
toss him off in a handkerchief. And he'd been able to get her to
kiss his cock once or twice. But, certainly, she didn't really like
it. And certainly she didn't do it every day, as he'd told Strange.
The truth was, he had not tried that hard to force her. For fear
of making her angry. He was afraid of making her so mad at him
she would stop coming to visit him.

She would do almost everything else. She would squirm herself against him by the hour. Kiss and neck with him until he
was hot as a little red fire wagon. Let him play with her tits.
Even let him play with her pussy. As long as her panties remained over it. Play with it till the crotch of her panties was
sopping wet. But as far as Prell knew she never came. A couple
of times they tried to screw, with her getting on top of him,

while he was still in the casts, but it always caused him so much pain in his legs that they had to stop.

Della Mae Kinkaid. That was her name, and she was seventeen. Her daddy was in some Signal Corps outfit in Australia. And her mama worked, to augment the allotments her daddy sent them. Old Della Mae had nothing against screwing. She freely admitted she was not a virgin. The only trouble was, Prell couldn't fuck. And with the casts off now, without their protection, it was even worse.

But everything other than fucking made Della Mae balk. It was either awful, or evil, or disgraceful, or unsanitary. She would never let him get his hand inside her pussy, for example. Unsanitary. And except for those few times when he had forced her to jack him off, she would let him place her hand on his swollen cock only as long as the cock remained inside the Medical Corps pajamas. If any jacking off was to get done, except for those few times, he had to do it himself. Which he usually did, after one of their sessions. The trouble with a damned hospital ward was there was so damned little privacy.

And when he tried to get his thumb on her clitoris, Della Mae disallowed that. That, she labeled disgraceful. Usually she only let it happen when they were out on the dayroom porch, and then she would become quite heated. But of course they were always being interrupted. Damned privacy.

That was one good thing about being a Medal of Honor winner, Prell was learning. People would do you favors. The afternoon ward boy let him use one of the two little private rooms at the front end of the ward for Della Mae's afternoon "reading" sessions. The ward boy never asked any questions. But Della Mae would never let him touch her clitoris, in there. Prell would stay in there alone, with a wad of toilet paper, for a while after Della Mae left.

Another thing Prell was reluctant to admit to Strange, or anybody, was that he was missing old Della Mae more and more on the days she did not come on the ward. And waiting more and more hungrily for her on the days that she did. And lately, she had been talking to him more and more about them getting married.

Prell was well aware that his Medal of Honor had a great deal to do with that, too. Old Della Mae was at least as fascinated by it as everybody else was. It was the Medal of Honor that had drawn her to him in the ward in the first place. And it was the

Medal of Honor that had allowed him to get as far with her as
he had. Prell was aware of all that.

The Medal, with a capital T on the The and a capital M on
the noun—as he had taken to thinking of it—The Medal worked
wonders with just about everybody. It got him extra services
from the ward boys. It got him special meals from the mess hall
when he wanted them. It got him special on-post passes from the
nurses on the ward when he asked for them. It allowed him to
keep a bottle of booze on the ward, with the night man. The only
person it did not seem to work with was Maj Hogan. His Medal
of Honor only made Hogan hate him more, apparently. As
though by putting him in a special category beyond Hogan's
administrative policy, where Hogan could not control or thwart
him, it inflamed the major's soul.

But except for Hogan it worked. The Medal even worked
with his irascible, irritable Chief Surgeon Col Baker. Who had
by now cheerfully admitted publicly that he had made a mistake
in judgment with Prell. The only such of his career, Baker
would hasten to add. It was to Col Baker that Prell went with
his request for a folding wheelchair.

Prell knew that they had them. He also knew there was no use
going to Hogan for one. Shortly before his casts were to come
off for the final time, they had used a folding wheelchair on him.
A request had come down, via Hogan, from the office of Col
Stevens, for Prell to make a personal appearance and a small
speech at a war bonds rally being conducted by the Luxor
Chamber of Commerce.

It was not a direct order. It was in the form of a request, but
the request left little doubt that Prell was expected to comply.
Prell did. And found it was one of the easiest things he had ever
had to do. It was easy because everybody loved him. An ambulance, and this folding wheelchair, were sent to pick him up.
The speech was already written for him, by some writer on Col
Stevens' staff. All he had to do was look it over, and then wheel
himself out in front of the officers and officials on the stage of
the big auditorium and read it into the microphone. Afterward,
there were drinks for everybody at a cocktail party, and people
came up to shake his hand.

It all gave Prell a curious feeling there were two Luxors,
existing side by side, or perhaps one on top the other. There was
the Luxor of his buddies of cunt and cock and booze and parties
that never stopped, going nonstop day and night in the hotels

and bars. And there was another Luxor of businessmen and families, who went to the office and went home to wives and bought bonds without being aware of the first Luxor, which was not aware of them, either.

Prell was aware of both. Because he had visited the second Luxor, to make a speech, in his folding wheelchair. This was the group that paid for the wheelchairs.

So he knew the hospital had at least one folding wheelchair. He brought it up to Col Baker the next morning at morning rounds.

At first, the short-tempered colonel's eyes bulged out and a snarl came over his gaunt lined face. "You want a pass? *You* want a *pass?* Because the people from your old company are renting a *suite* at the *Peabody?*"

"For a celebration. Yes, sir." Behind Baker, Hogan was beginning to fume and splutter and turn red.

"Well, I'll be goddamned," Baker snarled. "And of course you'll have to have a folding wheelchair. That much is obvious. Right?"

"Yes, sir. Well, they gave me one when they took me down town for that war bond rally."

"And just what do you expect to do when you get yourself into the elevator and up to this suite at the Peabody? Get drunk, I suppose."

Prell had planned toward this. His whole idea was that the evil-tempered Baker might somewhere inside him be susceptible to the blunt truth. That might get him, where something else wouldn't. "Well, sir, I'm hoping to try and get myself laid."

"You're *what?*"

Hogan was now red as a beet with outrage. But Baker was beginning to grin, in a wolfish way.

"I know I'm not in much of any great shape for it. With these casts off only a few days. But I'd like to try. I've been laying around an awful long time now without getting any."

"You've got as much chance of fucking some woman as you've got of pole-vaulting six and a half feet," Baker said.

"I don't need to pole-vault anything. Besides, there are other ways of taking care of it," Prell said.

Baker was seriously grinning now, if somewhat reluctantly. "By God, I think you deserve the chance. Damn if I don't. Major Hogan, you see to it, will you," he said shortly.

Prell was still congratulating himself when Strange came by

with Landers in tow that afternoon. Strange had banked his money, and was sporting a new checkbook along with a big wad of cash. But he had not been able to get the Peabody suite. It would be four days before they could let him have one. They were booked that far in advance. Strange had felt badly about it at first. He had wanted it the worst way. Right away. Not only for Prell, but for himself. When you wanted something that bad it was depressing not to get it, he said. But Strange reasoned it would be that much better for Prell, to have four more days of therapy, before trying it. Strange and Landers, of course, would help him with the folding wheelchair and taxi.

"There's just one thing," Strange said. "We've got to invite Winch."

"Yes," Landers said. "We've got to. Everybody else from the company is coming. We simply can't not invite him."

It was clear to Prell Strange had enlisted Landers to help him, about Winch. And from the way his heartbeat speeded up in his ears Prell could tell his face had gone white. Strange knew how much Prell admired and respected Landers' opinions. "Well, just keep him away from me," was all Prell said. "Keep him at the other end of the room. Or I'll brain him with a chair leg."

Strange looked relieved. "He aint going to cause you trouble. Nobody believes that stuff he said."

"No thanks to him," Prell said. He felt frustrated. Suddenly he gripped the rubbered hand wheels of the big-wheeled chair, and rolled himself back and forth a foot or so, repeatedly and furiously. Back and forth, back and forth.

It was much more difficult to go in a taxi, rather than in the ambulance. In the ambulance they had had the big back door to slide him in, and a cot for him to lie on. Prell discovered this right away, at the front gate, before he even got out of the folding wheelchair Maj Hogan had so reluctantly and ungraciously provided.

Landers and Strange were able to get him out of the chair well enough, but then one of them had to let go of him to fold up the chair. At this point the cab driver, when he saw what was going on, leaped out and and came running around the cab, following his paunch like a train following a cow-catcher, to help.

Together, the three of them got him into the front seat beside the meter and got the folded chair into the back beside Landers and Strange. Back behind his steering wheel, sweating and

puffing, the driver shook his head. "Jesus! What you guys won't
go through to get drunk and get laid."

Beside him, Prell was sweating too. But from pain, rather
than exertion. He agreed with the driver wholeheartedly. He
had no more business here than he had in a pole-vaulting con-
test, Baker was right. The four extra days of therapy had helped,
especially in loosening up his knee joints, but he was in no shape
for this. If it had not been for Landers and Strange witnessing
it, he would have given up on the spot and asked to be taken
back.

All he could do was keep his teeth clenched, and his lips
pressed tight together over them. Mainly it was his knees, which
were bent and compressed in the short space of the seat-well
with its meter, but his thighs ached, too. As if he had been an
hour with the therapist. He noted the driver giving him uneasy
looks from time to time, as the cab rolled along through the
Luxor streets Prell had never seen before. In the ambulance, the
only other time he'd been out, he had been lying flat.

It was fall now in the Southland of Luxor and the big maples
were just beginning to turn. In the huge city park men ambled
along the fairways of the golf links swinging their clubs, and
young people strolled under the big trees. In the poorer Negro
sections and poorer white sections men and women sat quietly
on the ramshackle porches, or on the grass of their yards. Every
house, even the poorest, had trees. At one spot they passed a
high school football field surrounded by trees. On it boys in
uniforms scrimmaged and bawled at each other and threw forward passes or punted the ball.

Prell tried to smile with his clenched teeth at the driver.
"Hurtin' you, hunh?" the driver said, and reached down under
the seat and brought up a pint bottle of whiskey. "Here." Prell
risked relaxing one of his fists which were pressed down into the
seat on both sides of his buttocks for support and took a slug of
the raw whiskey that burned his nose and throat and made his
eyes water but felt marvelous. He was afraid of the whole thing
turning into some kind of nightmare.

He had one more bad moment getting out of the taxi, and
another in the elevator. The elevator came the nearest to becoming the nightmare. It was small, and slow, and they had to drop
the chair's leg supports in order to close the door. There was
only room for himself and the black elevator man. By the time

they reached the eighth floor Prell's bent knees seemed to have been in the closed space for a century.

But once out of the elevator the painful parts ended. He waited in the hall with the leg rests up again until the others came up behind him. Slowly the pain subsided. A couple of drunk soldiers and their girls wandered along and said hello and offered a drink. When the other two came out of the elevator they all went in together.

In the suite the party was already going full blast. Though it was only two-thirty in the afternoon. Strange had given Corello a key to come on ahead with the other guys from the company.

Winch was not there. Prell immediately looked all around for him. Later on Winch did come in apparently without Prell seeing him and stationed himself quietly in a corner with, peculiarly, a glass of water. But he did not stay long, and Prell did not see him leave.

Landers had asked his Navy flyer friends and their gang from the floor below and immediately Prell was in the room Jan Mitchell, the lt cmdr, started a roaring chorus of "For He's a Jolly Good Fellow" and the other flyers joined him and finally, in a more embarrassed way, the men from the old company joined in. When the song finished, Mitchell raised his arms for quiet and raised his glass toward Prell in a toast.

"To the only Medal of Honor winner I have ever had the honor of getting drunk with." "Hear, hear!" cried several of the flyers.

Suavely Prell shook hands with all of them, and accepted the first drink that was offered him, something he might not have done a month before.

From Landers he found out that Commander Mitchell held the Navy Cross, won at Guadalcanal.

Prell was about three-quarters drunk when Mitchell began auctioning him off, to the various girls in the suite. Had he not known about the Navy Cross, or had he been cold sober, Prell might have balked. Instead, he went along with it and with Mitchell. Nobody who had won a Navy Cross over Guadalcanal could be all bad.

What he garnered by keeping his mouth shut was to find himself in a bedroom with the prettiest girl, getting himself the best blow job he had had since River Street in Honolulu, if not the best he had had ever.

Mitchell hadn't really auctioned him off. The girls had not

been asked to pay for him. But Mitchell had appealed to their patriotism, using just the right amount of appealing grace and a carefully leavened sincerity, in a way that would have made the hardest-hearted hooker jump in with a gratis offer to take Prell to bed. And these girls weren't hookers. "Here's a Congressional Medal of Honor winner, girls," the lt cmdr called, from on top of one of the little cocktail tables, after hollering for silence. "Do you people know what that means? You may never live to meet another one in your whole lives. This is the highest decoration the good old U.S. of A. can bestow upon one of her sons. Can you do less?"

It was a rhetorical question. Warming to his own oratory, Mitchell clapped his hands. "The problem here is that in order to do and complete the mission he was so carefully entrusted with, our new friend was so thoroughly butchered up in his legs by those dirty Japs that, for the moment at least, he is completely incapacitated in a certain delicate but important physiological, muscular way. Let us say the spirit is willing but the flesh of the thighs for the moment is weak. But what he can't do for himself, just now, can be done for him. In any of a certain number of delicate but immensely laudatory ways. And he is on his first pass in a matter of some seven or eight months. He hasn't even seen a girl close up in that terrible long length of time. Do I have to say more, ladies?

"Just remember. Probably the only chance any of you will ever have at a Medal of Honor winner.

"NOW. What am I bid for him? Who wants him? First come, first served. In that good old traditional American fashion."

Mitchell cleverly had made it a joke, and yet, equally cleverly, it wasn't a joke. Five girls responded. Out of the eleven or twelve. First one, then another, then as the idea became less embarrassing, three others. They pushed their way forward and leaped out into the center of the room, laughing and striking poses. Then two others, emboldened by the five, tried to get into the act but were disallowed by Mitchell. The first five Mitchell decided would have to draw straws. There was a long concerted hunt and confused search for a cleaning broom with straws. This was finally found and brought forward and handed over to Mitchell. The winner was a girl named Ann Waterfield who worked in town, tall, pageboy blonde, stacked, and exceedingly beautiful. Annie had come with one of the Navy flyers, but was not his special girl. Prell suspected Mitchell of having manipulated the broom straws in his favor, but wisely said nothing. Drunk, blushing and embarrassed, and stiff-faced, until Annie rolled his chair away from the others into the bedroom, Prell felt he would owe her a debt for the rest of his natural life.

When they finally came back out, after a long time away there, where under strictest orders nobody was allowed to occupy the secondary bed, and where Annie Waterfield had been so accomplished, tender, and sweet, Annie Waterfield started laughing.

"Y'all been sayin' this young man hasn't had a pass for only seven or eight *months?* He acts like he hasn't had a pass in a year and a *half!* Would you believe three times?"

Three, in the fact of it, was correct. And the second time Annie Waterfield had been able to accomplish something Della Mae Kinkaid never had done. By rolling him on his side and pushing two pillows against his behind for him to roll back on, and then getting her knees astraddle of him, Annie had been able to get onto her feet and squat slowly down over him and fuck his cock without putting any weight at all on his thighs. Della Mae Kinkaid had never done that. The position made his legs ache, but it was worth it.

Back out in the crowded, yelling sitting room she did not leave him. She stayed close to him the rest of the evening, always touching him with one hand or the other. This warmed Prell enormously. He certainly hadn't wanted to let her go. To somebody else.

Della Mae Kinkaid. Prell had thought about Della Mae several times. When he was in the bedroom with the highly accomplished Annie Waterfield. He had wished it was Della Mae doing all these marvelous things to him.

But the main bent of his thoughts about Della Mae was quite blunt. It was to hell with Della Mae and let everybody look after himself. All that talk about marriage. That was a lot of shit. Della Mae was bending his ear.

If Della Mae wanted to marry, she should find herself some other Medal of Honor winner.

Still, it occurred to him it would be great if, relatively quickly, he could teach her that semigymnast's trick Annie Waterfield had used on him that second time.

It was while he was sitting in the chair with Annie Waterfield beside him touching his arm that Johnny Stranger came over from somewhere and from slightly behind Prell put his good hand on Prell's shoulder. Prell turned his head to look up at him and grin. Strange, drunk and red-faced, grinned back down; and then over one drunkenly bulging eye brought down the eyelid with an almost audible click.

"Everything all right?"

"Everything's great."

"Good."

Slowly, swaying ever so slightly, he leaned over till his mouth was almost at Prell's ear.

"We're gonna blow every damn nickel of it. Every fucking dime. Nobody's gonna want for anything, as long as there's one fucking damn fucking dime of it left."

Prell felt the pressure from the hand increase on his shoulder as Strange pushed himself back erect. Then he sensed rather than saw, because he couldn't see that far behind him, that Strange took two paces rearward as the pressure left his shoulder.

When he moved his wheelchair to steal a glance a moment later, Strange was standing there, arms folded, leaning on the point of one shoulder against the wall. The stance was so exactly the same way Prell had seen him stand so many times—leaning against his kitchen wall back in Wahoo; against the tent pole of his kitchen fly on the Canal; against a cocopalm beside his mess tent in New Georgia—that it called up not so much a single memory response as a whole syndrome of memory response.

Right now, the drunken red face was suffused with a peculiar look, both above and below his bulging eyes. It was a look of happiness on the surface. But underneath that butter was something hard and bitter and so flinty it seemed to Prell a bayonet would not have chipped it.

Prell didn't know what it was. And he didn't care very much. It seemed to him now that, without realizing it, out of the corners of his eyes, he had been seeing Strange standing in that same position in one part of the room or another all afternoon and evening. Strange had not been off with a single one of the girls, as far as Prell had noted.

Then, while he was thinking this, the heavy hand pressure came on his shoulder and he felt Strange's mouth come down beside his ear again.

"Did you ever eat a pussy?"

"Well, I—" Prell began, and then stopped, because he realized he was hedging. He did not know what was going on but he knew enough to know that this was not some joke question. The intensity of the voice precluded that. "Hell, yes," he said, and grinned up into the red face.

"Hell, yes. It's great. I loved it," Prell said valiantly. Which was true. Not only with Annie Waterfield, but with a not unworthy number of other girls. But it was not so long ago that he would have refused to admit it to anyone.

The pressure on his shoulder increased again as Strange pushed himself erect once more. When Prell felt he could risk a look, the mess/sgt was standing as before, leaning against the wall. He appeared to be watching what was going on out in the center of the room.

Prell put his own gaze back onto the room. The zany Navy flyer Mitchell was in the middle of pulling off some other kind of a crazy college-boy stunt. Suddenly, without preparation, the old movie roster of Prell's mud-smeared squad, the dead along with the living, began to parade across behind Prell's eyes. He had not had the apparition for so long now that its sudden appearance shook him. Slowly, each hollow-eyed face turned back to smile wistfully, sadly, before it moved on and faded. Faded into whatever Godawful night. God, what they wouldn't all of them have given, Prell thought, just to have been here.

Probably it was the memory syndrome Strange had called up in him which had caused it. The only sane answer to it was to point out forcefully, as forcefully as possible, that he was here and they were not.

On the metal arm of the wheelchair his right hand holding his drink began to tremble, so that the ice in the glass made a faint, constant tinkling. Beside him Annie Waterfield put her own right hand over his and stopped the tinkling, and made a quick motion with her mouth to him that was like a kiss. Prell threw her a wink.

In the cab going back at two in the morning drunk, Prell felt no anguish at all when he was stuffed into the front seat-well, or when he was pulled bodily from it to be stuck back into the unfolded wheelchair by Landers and Strange. The driver of this second cab was not nearly so nice or so helpful as the first driver had been. It didn't matter. "It was one of the best nights of my life," Prell told them, and the driver, again. For maybe the twentieth time. "I wish it had gone on forever."

It was while Landers, drunk too, was pushing him back to the leg wards, with his cane hung over the back of the chair, that Landers told him Winch was going back to limited duty in a couple of days. Winch was going to Second Army Headquarters as chief of the G-1 personnel section, probably with a raise in grade to junior warrant officer.

To Prell, still drunk as he was, the new news about Winch sounded like a deep knell tolling the beginning of the end. On his ward he went about getting out of his new uniform with the help of the night man. Finally in bed and alone, he lay awake a while thinking about it.

What was going to happen to him, when all the others were gone? First Winch would go. Then, Landers. Then, Strange. Finally, Prell would be left. To continue with his painful leg therapy to see whether, finally, he would walk on them again. Still going through the goddam daily therapy. Still trying to learn to goddam walk.

What on earth was going to become of him? All he had ever wanted to do was stay in the Army. How were you going to stay in the Army without legs to walk?

Next morning, as if in answer to his question, he was delivered a typed invitation direct from Col Stevens this time, to go downtown and make another speech. This one was to the Luxor Ladies Clubs, Combined. The first had been hugely successful and the Ladies Clubs had asked for him expressly. It was for that afternoon.

Badly hungover though he was, of course he accepted. There wasn't really a choice. It occurred to Prell that this was to be his future way of life apparently, his future path of duty, if he wanted to stay in the Army. Nobody had said so yet. But Prell could smell it coming, the way an animal can smell snow, or a storm coming.

CHAPTER 19

Landers woke with much less of a hangover than Prell. More used to the heavy drinking luxury than Prell was by now, his body was getting better at assimilating it.

But as he pulled the GI blanket and sheet up to his neck and lay listening to the ward man going down the line waking the guys, he was transfixed by something far worse than a hangover. The big bell at the head of the ward was ringing its short, hard, frightening blasts, but it wasn't that. He was used to that. His whole system was infused with a sharp pure panic.

Landers knew why. There was no need to think back over the whole big party to remember what it was he had done so wrong. It was right there in the forefront of his mind. He remembered that he drunkenly had told Prell all about Winch going back to duty, on the way pushing him back to the wards. And he had been asked precisely not to do just that.

Jerkily, with nerves made jumpy by both hangover and a deep, hollow, awful guilt, Landers yanked on his pajama pants and slippers to hurry up and get to the bathroom first and shave.

It was Strange who had told Landers about Winch's impending return to duty. Landers had been sitting with him outdoors loafing in the fall sunshine, while the two of them waited for Prell to get his folding wheelchair. Winch had told Strange he would be leaving within a week. Then, after telling Landers, Strange had expressly asked Landers not to talk about it. Particularly, he did not want Landers to tell Prell.

Landers had asked him why. Strange had shrugged and moved his head, and in that inarticulate way Landers had come to associate with all of Strange's more complex, profounder ideas, he said he did not think Prell was up to it yet. Prell was still drawn too tight, still too much up in the air. About what might happen with his legs. He wouldn't be able to digest the idea that Winch finally might be leaving them, leaving the company, moving on.

Landers had simply nodded. He was not so sure he was up to it himself. The idea that Winch might not be there for aid and advice when Landers needed him left a big empty hole in Landers. But he had never believed Prell felt that same way about Winch. Astonishingly, it was as if Strange read his mind. Again, inarticulately, Strange had moved his head and shrugged. That Prell hated Winch did not mean Prell thought Winch was an incompetent, Strange said with no prompting. Just the reverse. Prell would never have hated a man whose professional opinions he had contempt for. No; Prell would miss Winch. Badly. Hate, or no hate.

They should give Prell a week, Strange said, or two weeks. Before they told him. He needed sufficient time for the therapy on his legs to start to work. Besides, in the second place, if it was an accomplished fact, with Winch already gone, there would be a fatality about it that would make it more acceptable to Prell.

Landers had nodded again. And had promised he would not mention Winch's leaving to Prell. Privately, he remembered how more than once it had struck him how intricate and complicated these relationships were between these Regular Army men, which seemed so simple on the surface. And he marveled again at the really deep understanding of them Strange seemed to have.

College people. College people, like himself, who had a tendency to think of themselves as more sensitive, and called men like these guys ignorant, and uncomplicated, and insensitive, didn't know what the fuck they were talking about. And had probably never known any. Landers had never known any himself, until this fucking war. But Landers would rather have been like them, than any college people he had ever met. Drunk, happy, he had gone to bed last night after the party thinking these same thoughts over again, a second time.

And had waked up to most unwelcome this.

It appeared that his mind had blanked out, on certain parts of the big, riotously boisterous party. There were whole stretches he had no memory of. But his mind had not blanked out this most awful, most irresponsible thing he'd done. His mind had kept it right there, all ready for him, to stew and seethe and fret and agonize over this morning, with this sense of awful guilt.

How could he possibly have made such a gaffe? How could he possibly have forgotten, ignored his promise?

Shaved, he bolted down his breakfast so fast and nervously, he gave himself a bad bellyache. Then he sat, nursing the bellyache, tapping his feet in their slippers on the polished floor, waiting for morning rounds. As soon as that was over and he was free, he took off across the half-mile width of the hospital to Strange's ward, as fast as his bad leg would carry him, to see Strange and confess what he had done. Maybe there was some way Strange could fix it.

Luckily he hurried. Strange was already in uniform, preparing to take off for town and his new suite. He had already given a key to one of the guys from the company, who had a morning pass and had gone in ahead to round up some women.

"Come on along," the mess/sgt said. "The more the merrier. I'll wait on you while you change."

Landers stopped him with a raised hand. "I've got to tell you what I did," Landers said, and bubbled it all out breathlessly. "It was a terrible thing. A terrible thing. I was drunk. But that's no excuse. It was on the way back to the wards."

Strange took it better than Landers thought he would. All he did was smile a sad little half-smile with the corner of his mouth, and make his shrug. To Landers the rebuke seemed greater because of that. He would have preferred a storm of abuse.

"I guess he'll just have to live with it," Strange said. "A little sooner, is all. We all got things we have to live with a little sooner than we're ready for, I reckon."

"I suppose. I can't tell you how sorry I am," Landers added in a low voice. Nothing he could find to say seemed to loosen that awful guilt.

"I reckon he'll survive it," Strange said, sadly, and laid his good hand on Landers' shoulder with a light slap. "People do all sorts of things when they're drunk they wouldn't do sober. No avoiding that. It aint that bad."

He flexed the fingers of the bad hand, that still wore the plaster brace. "Now you go and dress and get in uniform. I'll wait for you outside at the taxi stand, in the sunshine. We aint going to have all that much more of it, I don't think. Even here in the good old Southland."

It was in the taxi going in that he told Landers about the checking account he'd opened, and the $7000 in cash. He told Landers he intended to blow every nickel of it while he and the remaining guys from the company were still here.

Landers still wasn't over the other thing, but Strange seemed to have forgotten Prell. "That's an awful lot of money to blow, and just burn up," Landers said cautiously. "You can do a lot with seven thousand bucks."

"Like what?"

"I don't know. I don't know what you want. You could start buying a restaurant. You're a cook, and restaurateur, aren't you?"

"Don't want anything like that," Strange said. "Anyway, that amount of money aint going to last long, here. At a hundred bucks a day? For that suite? That's only seventy days of suite, right there."

"Did you ever ask them about paying monthly rates?" Landers said.

"No," Strange said. "I haven't."

"Say," Landers said, "listen. I've got something like two thousand bucks at home myself. What about me throwing mine in with yours?" Suddenly he felt elated, and excited. "That would give us twenty more days of suite, if we needed it."

"All right," Strange said. But then he raised one admonitory horny finger of his good hand. "Make certain you won't be sorry."

"Hell," Landers said.

"Say, I'll tell you what!" Strange said, excitedly. He had been looking out the window, at the big city park, Overton Park, that the taxis passed on their way into and out of town from the hospital. "Why don't we have us a goddam picnic?"

Landers felt astonished. Apparently, Strange had put the matter of Prell totally out of his mind.

"Okay, why not?" Landers said.

"We'll get the booze and the women and whatever guys are

there, and buy some food, rent a taxi for the day, and come out to this damned park for the day," Strange said. "How about that?" He too seemed elated, suddenly. "We'll have ourselves a hell of a damned picnic day, by God."

It was not till they had had three drinks, from the illegal pint Strange bought from the driver, that Strange brought up the other thing that apparently was on his mind.

He glanced nervously at the back of the driver's head, as they moved through the streets of downtown. Then he leaned over to Landers with a conspiratorial air.

"Did you ever eat a girl's pussy?" he whispered.

At first Landers thought he was going to some elaborate extreme as means for a joke. He began to frame in his mind some sort of joke answer. Then he saw, or sort of sensed, that Strange wasn't joking. Strange was asking in deadly seriousness.

"Why do you want to know?" Landers asked in a normal tone, to buy time.

Strange made a violent braking motion with the open palm of his good hand, for softness of voice. "Don't be embarrassed, God damn it," he whispered. "I'm serious."

"Well, if you put it that way. Well yes. I have," Landers whispered.

"Did you like it?" Strange whispered.

"Well yes. I liked it. In fact, I loved it," Landers whispered back.

Strange was nodding to himself. Thoughtfully. "Are you good at it?"

Everything was still in whispers, kept low by Strange's constant admonition.

"Well. Well, I don't know that there's so much to being good at it. There's this girl, Martha Prentiss? Who's around the Peabody? That loves to suck cock."

"I've had her pointed out to me, but I don't know her. Never met her." Whisper.

"I picked her up. She gave me a few pointers. But, hell. All it takes is a lot of gentleness, and a very wet tongue." Whisper.

Strange nodded, but didn't answer.

"I guess you know what a clitoris is, I guess?" Landers whispered.

"Yes, damn it. I know," Strange whispered.

"Well," Landers shrugged lamely.

"Does it smell?"

"Sure. It smells. It smells good."

"Doesn't it smell fishy?"

"It smells fishy. But it's not really fishy. It smells— Do you know the word fecund?"

Strange shook his head.

"Fecund means rich. Like rich earth. Rich for growing. Rich for growing all the rich things of summer. Ripe," Landers whispered. He began to be afraid he was sounding too poetic, and stopped.

"Ripe," Strange whispered sourly. "I'll bet it smells ripe."

Their faces were hardly a foot apart, and Strange stared into Landers' eyes intensely.

"Doesn't it smell pissy?"

"Well yeah. A little bit. But you don't mind that. At least, I don't. But that's only at first. After a little, it doesn't smell pissy."

"Doesn't it taste?"

"No. Doesn't taste at all. Has no taste whatever. Tastes like whatever you've had in your mouth before. A cigarette. Whiskey. A steak."

Strange nodded in silence, his intent eyes not budging from Landers'.

"Say, what is all this?" Landers whispered.

"Oh, there's this girl," Strange whispered with elaborate indifference. "Wants me to blow her. Keeps telling me I'll like it. Says everybody does it."

Landers grinned. " 'Show me the man who doesn't eat cunt, and I'll show you the man whose wife I can steal,' " he grinned, quoting in a whisper the ancient joke. Strange did not laugh. Strange just stared at him.

"I'll tell you one thing," Landers whispered. "Too damn many of them taste like soap."

"Taste like what?"

"Soap. So many girls are so ashamed of them, and so afraid they'll smell, that they're constantly scrubbing the hell out of them. And they taste like soap."

"Aw, shit," Strange whispered, "you're a damned expert."

"No, no. I learned it all right here. Or almost all."

They were so close together, and Strange was staring so intently, that Strange's eyes were like two bright blue searchlights, flooding Landers' face. In that light, just about nothing could be hidden. In front of them, the back of the driver's head was not cocked. By the back of his head, he was going right on driving, totally unconcerned. After a long moment Strange relaxed back into the seat, staring straight ahead. "Times are changing everywhere," he said, to no one in particular. Though said in a normally loud tone of voice, it came out muffled.

The cab was already onto Union Street, still heading in, moving uphill toward Main Street and the big river, invisible beyond it. As the driver swung wide to make the U turn to stop in front of the Peabody, Strange grinned and said, without expression, in a normal tone, the one word, "Thanks."

Strange had not forgotten about the picnic. The picnic, in fact, turned out almost exactly as Strange had imagined it. Except it was even more pleasant, more fun. There were four men from the old company waiting in the suite and they had picked up some girls in pairs and singles, both at the Peabody bar and at the bar of the Claridge up on Main Street. Landers noted that without exception the four were guys who had been at Kilrainey longer, and had run out of money. Strange was obviously concentrating his largesse and his giant spending on guys who no longer had money.

That part was okay with Landers. He was willing to do exactly the same with his smaller sum, as soon as he got it down here. And by that time, he thought, Prell would be further along with his therapy. He badly wanted to do something for Prell. Landers had tried to do what Strange apparently had done so easily with the faux pas of last night, and put it entirely out of his mind. But Landers couldn't do it as well and Prell kept coming back to his mind in some comparative fashion almost all the time. And each time, Landers had the same awful feeling he had had that morning. Even to him, it seemed out of all proportion.

Then, when he had fallen asleep three-fourths drunk on the sunny side of one of the big trees in one of the big glades of the park, the dream or vision of the waterless platoons and his full canteen of water on the dry hill on New Georgia, suddenly came back to plague him. Again they were begging him for his water and he would not give them any. He woke suddenly, choking back a cry. The brunette girl who was with him, he did not remember which one she was or who, quickly grasped his biceps with her five fingers and smiled and winked down at him, and crooned soothingly. She apparently had done it many times before and knew what to do.

Landers sat up, and reached for another drink. It was the first time in a long time that that dream had imposed itself on him and he couldn't help but wonder, Why now?

Fortunately, there was plenty still left to drink. If it had been a great, warm, sunny picnic, it had also certainly been a heavy drinking one. Strange had brought along just about every potable with alcohol in it that he could think of and get hold of. He had, at Landers' instigation, even brought along a couple of bottles of French wine; but the wine had languished. Not even Landers drank it. Like everybody else, he preferred shots of whiskey with cold beer chasers. By the time it began to get chilly and they repaired to the hotel, they were all of them, including the girls, quite drunk.

Strange did not seem to show it as much as the rest. Though Landers was sure he had drunk just as much. Landers had been curious, after their conversation, and covertly watched him with the women. But it was hard to tell about Strange. Strange had divided his time about equally between Annie Waterfield, Prell's girl of last night, and Frances Highsmith. Frances was a girl who had been around the bunch a lot, and whom Landers had made it with a few times, and whom he was sure Strange had been to bed with at least once. During all the booze buying and food buying, Strange had kept Frances with him and had ridden out to the park with her in one of the three cabs they had had to hire, and Landers had thought, Ah ha, that's the one! But then halfway through the picnic he had redirected his attention to Annie and had gone off walking to sit with her across on the other side of the glade from where they had spread the blankets, and Landers had thought, Ah no, it was Annie! But before they left Strange went back with Frances, and rode back with her. But then when they were all settled in the suite, Strange left Frances again and sat with Annie and a bottle of bourbon that was beside them. Frances appeared to be getting irritated. But Annie Waterfield did not. At that point Landers went to bed and to sleep, not knowing who to bet on, or even whether he should bet on either. And not much caring.

He had been afraid to go to sleep again because of the dream. But the heavy drinking all day in the park, and all the hot sunshine, had done him in in a way that was more than he could handle. Even the thought of having the dream again in his sleep could not keep him awake. Besides, the girl, whose name was Mary Lou Salgraves it turned out, was there and went to bed with him, and was willing to hold his head against her naked breasts while he slept. Landers went straight off to sleep. Without even attempting to fuck; without even a hard-on. And Mary Lou seemed to like it as well that way, or like it even better.

He slept for three hours before the dream woke him again, his conscious mind rising befuddled out of sleep but, even befuddled, already trying to choke off any noise or cry he might be making.

As he came awake, he realized Mary Lou had her hand over his mouth, and her other hand was stroking his head. It was she who had waked him, he realized, as his mind began to take messages from outside.

"Ah'm sorry to wake you," she said as she took her hand off his mouth, "but you were beginnin' to make noises and holler in your sleep. I thought you'd want me to." It was curiously as though she had done it all so many times that she knew exactly what to do without asking any questions. They were alone in the big bedroom he noted, and that included the smaller cot-type bed turned endways by the door.

"Yeah. Yeah, sure. Thanks," Landers said in a sleep-roughened voice. "Thanks."

"It was all somethin' about water," Mary Lou said. "Water, water. Are you thirsty?"

"No," Landers said, then corrected himself. "Yes. Yes, I'm thirsty for some whiskey and soda."

"Comin' right up," Mary Lou answered, smiling at him. She got up slowly, and then put her dress on without bothering with the underwear.

Landers watched her and felt a stirring and thickening in his crotch. "You're some girl, you know that, Mary Lou?"

"Why, thank you, sir," she smiled. Her chin dimpled.

Outside in the suite's sitting room Strange was still sitting with Annie Waterfield, talking. His voice sounded a little thicker, but his eyes were quick. The level in the bourbon bottle had gone down appreciably.

"Well," the mess/sgt said from his seat. "You get some rest?"

Landers nodded, stretching. Mary Lou handed him his drink.

Strange and Annie were the only two left in the suite. The four other old-company men and their four girls had disappeared. Frances Highsmith also had disappeared. The door to the other bedroom was wide open, and nobody was in there. It was eight-thirty, and strangely quiet and peaceful.

Strange smiled at Landers fondly, from across the room. "The others all went off to get some nigger barbeque out on Poplar someplace. They were getting a little edgy. I slipped Corello some cash. They going to some movie." He grinned, a little sheepishly. "Frances has left us, too. Frances was the girl, in fact, I was telling you about before."

"I think Frances' nose was a little out of joint," Annie said. "She acted like she had some previous claim on Sergeant Strange." She smiled with sweet feminine bitchery.

"She'll be all right," Strange grinned. "There's plenty of fellows, and plenty of hotel suites, around."

So Annie had won, Landers thought. Or Frances Highsmith had lost. At least, now he knew which one of them it was who had asked Strange to eat her.

All along, Landers had thought it was probably Frances. But he wanted to laugh. If Strange thought he was onto something different with Annie, Strange didn't know what kind of tree he was barking up.

Landers stared at Annie, his mind struck suddenly empty. He had been abruptly penetrated by the blunt realization that these girls had their own fierce little pecking order going here, fought over with just as much blood thirst as any other group of young females. The only difference was that the time span was shortened by the war, and the pride of ownership telescoped to three days or five days, or one night. So they fought over the men night by night. Then they started over, like any divorcée.

Landers wondered who Mary Lou had nosed out, to get him. Or he to get her? Mary Lou had certainly made it a lot easier for him today.

Landers sat down in an overstuffed armchair with his drink, and motioned for Mary Lou to come sit by him on the arm. The new drink, on top of all the booze he'd put away already, hit him swiftly. He sat tasting the strange quiet in the suite, his arm around Mary Lou's hips.

It was such a moment of peace, in all the hot scrambling for cunt, and liquor, and life. He winked over at Strange.

Johnny Stranger, deep in his own cups and already apparently well past Landers, winked back, his one eyelid closing and then opening very slowly. Strange appeared to be savoring the quiet peace, too.

Two hours later the two of them had had their first fight in Luxor, with some Navy personnel. About seven Navy personnel, to be exact. Fortunately, not all of the enemy became engaged.

It would be easy to say it was because of all the booze they had put away. But there was more to it than that for Landers.

The four of them had gone down for a quiet, peaceful dinner in the main dining room downstairs. The old-fashioned main dining room off the lobby, with its wall paneling and quiet old colored gentlemen waiters, had in general been kept back out of the way of the huge influx of wild-eyed, fire-breathing servicemen, and was the place for that kind of dinner. Old Luxor families still took their older and younger generations there for family dinner outings. And Strange and Landers were after a quiet dinner, in keeping with the mood they had had upstairs.

Afterward, they had gone across the lobby to the bar for a drink, Strange picking up a bottle at the package store in the corridor.

They could have gone back upstairs. And none of them knew why they went to the bar. The truth was, they were feeling affectionate and, if not in love, felt warm and close. Like lovers, they wanted other people around for contrast.

Needed the audience, Landers thought sourly, later.

The contrast they got in the bar was immediate and cataclysmic. The whole place was packed. And the noise level was commensurate. They got a table for four, luckily, because a party of four got up to leave as they came in. Right behind them crammed against the wall was a long table filled on the three open sides with these Navy people, ranging upward in rank and topped off with two chiefs, one of them an old duffer in his dress whites.

Strange got up to go out to the john, after they were seated and he had poured a drink. And at the same time, behind him, another sailor came in to the long table. It was then the old duffer in dress whites reached over a huge hand and grabbed Strange's seat away from the table. The white uniform had lots of unfamiliar WW I ribbons above the left breast, and he had gold hash marks literally all the way up his left sleeve from the wrist to his insignia.

Something blazed up in Landers' mind like a fire ball. Though the two girls hardly seemed to notice the theft. Keeping his voice carefully empty of rage, Landers stepped over to the long table.

"That seat's taken."

"There was nobody in it," the old chief said.

"Yes there was. My friend just went out to the pisser." Still politely. But the red fire ball had already exploded.

"Didn't you hear him?" the second chief, who was younger and in blues, said contemptuously. "If it was an empty seat, it was free."

"Yeah. You want it, take it," the old chief said, and grinned down the table at his mob.

"Okay. I will," Landers said evenly. The rage in him was threatening to overflow.

But he held it in. And waited. He waited, until he saw Strange come in through the outside door. A full minute, or minute and a half. Strange of course marked them right away. When he saw Strange had seen them, he signaled him with his eyebrows. Meanwhile, the Navy personnel all just stood or sat, however they had been before, looking at him, waiting too. Waiting for him.

"Well?" the younger chief said, smiling with contempt. "You going to take it?"

They really don't know, Landers thought. Who we are. While Strange came on, he studied them. The old chief in white on his left was still seated. The younger chief was on his right, standing. Landers was between them. Beyond the younger chief was the new man, his hand still on the stolen chair. The others were all seated.

Behind him Landers heard Strange say softly, "Go ahead. Bust him."

He swung with his right hand first at the old chief. It went in accurately alongside the nose just under the right eye, cutting deep. Without bothering to look at the effect, he swung with his left at the chief in blues, rolling his body, like a whip, a punch that was half hook, half uppercut. It caught the young chief two inches back from the point of his chin. Landers heard his teeth clap together. He went down.

Landers swung his body to take care of the third man coming in, but Strange had already accounted for him. Swinging his good, left hand in a hook to the belly that swung the moving man back toward himself, Strange clapped him alongside the head and jaw with the plaster plate bound to the open palm of his right hand. The third man went down.

Meanwhile, Landers' second chief was coming back up, valiantly but slowly. Landers hit him with both hands, hook and short rights, in the belly and in the face. One, two; one, two; one two three four. Faster than the eye could count. And as he landed each punch Landers shouted insanely.

"Pay!" he yelled. "Pay! Pay, goddam you! Pay, pay, pay!"

The chief in blues sagged down.

Beyond him Strange grabbed a water pitcher by its handle from a table, ready to crack it in half on a table edge and turn it into a weapon. His right hand was held ready to slap again. "Just come on," he warned in a hiss, as insanely. "Just come on."

The four seated Navy men looked up at the two insane men, astonishment spread over their faces. None was inclined to get up, and wisely they sat still. It had happened with murderous speed and a blinding violence.

Behind Landers a tall, kindly-looking soldier got awkwardly to his feet, and put one arm half around Landers. Landers spun, ready to hit again.

"No, no. Don't swing. Don't swing," the kindly-looking soldier said. He looked worried. "Don't swing. You guys better get out of here. Right now. The MPs will be here in seconds. I've seen them."

Landers swung back to the table. He had one satisfying look at the old chief sprawled against the wall, his chair overturned, bright blood red from below his eye down over the dress whites. "Pay!" he screamed at all of them. "Pay, you cocksuckers! Goddam you, pay!"

Strange had heard the kindly-looking soldier, too, and carefully put his uncracked water pitcher back on its table. He started backing toward the door, his good hand gripping Landers' arm and pulling him.

"You girls go on, you leave," he called to the table. "Meet us upstairs."

Landers followed him. "Don't forget my cane," he called, "don't forget my cane."

At the door a huge MP already blocked the way, his hand on his black holster, and stopped them. He looked in at the now-quiet bar, inspecting the carnage, then looked at the two of them.

"God damn," he said wearily. "You guys. All right, go on. Git. Out that way." He pointed on down the corridor, away from the lobby. "It goes to the street. Move it, damn it."

"We got a room in the hotel," Strange said breathlessly. "A suite, we got."

"Then go around the block, and come back the other way," the MP said. "My partner'll be here in a minute, damn it. He aint as sympathetic."

Strange was already moving, pulling along with his good hand Landers who was limping without his cane, Strange breathlessly already beginning to laugh. Landers was not laughing.

"Appreciate it," Strange called.

"Go fuck," the MP called back, and stepped inside.

"Those dirty fuckers," Landers was muttering, "those dirty fuckers."

"Come on," Strange said, laughing. "We got to move it."

"Let them see something," Landers muttered. "Let them see something."

It was difficult, going clear around the block with Landers limping so badly. He had pulled or turned something in his ankle, and the pain was bothering him. So Strange led them through an alley beyond the hotel, which went around it and came back out on Union.

Thus as they slipped in through the revolving door and across the lobby, they were able to see the MPs and some medics leading the battered Navy group out from the bar. The old chief in his bloody dress whites was on a stretcher, out.

"You don't think I really hurt him, do you?" Landers whispered anxiously in the crowded elevator.

"No," Strange said. "He was just knocked out." Strange was still laughing, and still breathless. Suddenly his eyes glinted meanly. "And what if you did?"

"He was the one who took the chair," Landers whispered. "Just like that. Without so much as a by your leave. But I wouldn't want to hurt him."

Fortunately Strange had already given Annie a key and the girls were in the suite waiting. And immediately there were all the breathless, laughing recapitulations of battle. Everybody had a viewpoint and story of his own to expound.

Landers came out as the unquestioned hero, but Landers was not taking part. He sat off by himself quietly, nursing his ankle, ministered to by Mary Lou who brought him drinks. He kept popping his knuckles and said nothing. "Let them learn something," he would mutter to no one every so often, "let them learn something." The knuckles of his right hand had been seriously barked but he would not let anybody doctor them. "You must have hit teeth somewhere," Strange said happily.

Very shortly after, the four other old-company men and their girls came back in, and the stories had to be told again.

"I tell you," Annie Waterfield said, "I never saw anything like it. It was all so fast. After you left, that tall soldier? Who warned you against the MPs? He went over to them where they were pickin' up that poor chief petty officer in blues, and tryin' to bring the old one to, slappin' his face, and he told them who you all were."

"What do you mean, told them who we were?" Strange said. "He didn't know us."

"He figured it out because of Marion's cane and your hand plaster. You don't want to mess with them, he told those sailors. Those are overseas men from the hospital, who've been wounded. Don't ever fuck with them. They're all crazy. That's exactly what he said. Someone asked him how he knew, and he made this awful grin and said, 'Because I'm one of them.' Then he pulled up his pants leg, and showed them his artificial leg.

"It was just awful. Terrible."

"Maybe he's seen us around the hospital," Strange said. "But I've never seen him. Have you?" he asked Landers.

Landers only shook his head. "No."

"What did you mean?" Annie Waterfield asked him, "when you kept hollerin' Pay?"

"Hollering Pay?" Landers said. "Pay?"

"Yes. Every time you hit somebody you kept hollerin' Pay! Every time, Pay! 'Pay, you sons of bitches! Pay, pay, pay!'"

"I don't know," Landers said hollowly. "I don't remember saying that. I don't know what I meant." He accepted another drink from Mary Lou.

But he thought he did know. It was easy to say it was because of the booze they had put away. That they were drunk. But Landers knew there was something more. Something inside him. Aching to get out. There was something in him aching to get out, but in a way that only a serious fight or series of serious fights would let it get out. Anguish. Love. And hate. And a kind of fragile, short-lived happiness. Which had to be short-lived, if he was going out of this fucking hospital and back into the fucking war. It had just built up in him.

There was no way on earth to explain it to anybody, though. Not without sounding shitty. There was no way to say it.

It had been building up in him ever since that episode on the train with the Air Force sergeant, on his trip home. It was in his fight with his father over the medals. In that time he had tried to talk to Carol Firebaugh and failed so abominably. It had grown and built in him at an even quicker pace, since his awful boo-boo he had made with Prell.

Landers thought that, probably, it had been building in him even longer. Growing. Ever since he was sitting on that damned evil hilltop in New Georgia, with all those other weeping men with the white streaks down their dirty faces, watching the men below in the valley whanging and beating and shooting and killing each other, with such stern, disruptive, concentrated effort.

Anguish. Love. And hate. And happiness. The anguish was for himself. And every poor slob like him, who had ever suffered fear, and terror, and injury at the hands of other men. The love, he didn't know who the love was for. For himself and everybody. For all the sad members of this flawed, misbegotten, miscreated race of valuable creatures, which was trying and failing with such ruptured effort to haul itself up out of the mud and dross and drouth of its crippled heritage. And the hate, implacable, unyielding, was for himself and every other who had ever, in the name of whatever good, maimed or injured or killed another man. The happiness? The happiness was the least, and best, and most important, because the most ironic. The happiness was from those few moments in the fight, when the bars were down, when the weight of responsibility lifted, and he and every man could go in, and destroy and be destroyed, without fear of consequences, with no thought of debt. In short, do all the things they shouldn't and couldn't want to do, or want others to do, when they were responsible.

What a melange. All tossed up in the air and churned around until one element was indistinguishable from another, and the steam from the whole boiling stew seethed and billowed until its pressure forced a safety crack in even the strongest self-control.

Landers suspected something like that was pushing Strange on, too, from the thin explosive laugh he had heard behind him, as Strange had called in a soft but ringing voice, "Go ahead. Bust him."

It was somewhat the feeling that if all of these awful things had been done to so many of them, somebody was going to have to pay, pay, pay, including himself, themselves. What better way was there for all to pay, pay than in a fight, in which he himself, they themselves, were taking lumps and damage, and getting smashed around, too.

It didn't make any sense. None whatsoever. That was why you couldn't tell it to anybody. You couldn't tell that, even to Strange. Landers was about resigned to never being able to tell it.

Did it mean the two of them had a future of such episodes to look forward to? Landers knew somewhere inside of him that he hadn't had enough of it, even yet. And he didn't think Johnny Stranger had, either. It seemed to promise ill for any future.

When everything in the suite had quieted down, though he had to wait quite a long time, he took Mary Lou (Salgraves, was it?) and hobbled to bed and locked the door and fucked her and made love to her until her tongue was hanging out and even Mary Lou didn't want any more. He was pretty sure Johnny Stranger was doing the same thing on the other side of the suite, behind the other locked door.

That great sage who had said so wittily that a man didn't want sex after he had had a fight, didn't know what he was talking about.

On the way home in the cab at five in the morning, drunk like the others and riding with all four of them, Landers felt Strange lean against his shoulder and put his mouth against his ear.

"She wanted it, too." Strange coughed a drunken hiccup.

"I didn't do it," Strange whispered, drunkenly, so the other drunks couldn't hear. "I didn't do it. I almost did. But I just couldn't quite bring myself to do it."

CHAPTER 20

Johnny Stranger had made up his mind to go back to town the next day. Strange had decided that point before he left the hotel.

He had to get this thing settled with Frances Highsmith.

In the taxi, after he had drunkenly whispered his predicament to Landers, he drunkenly roared his intention to the other old-company men.

"Everybody's invited. Anybody who's free and wants to come, is welcome. On any day. If there are days I can't be there, somebody will have a key to the suite. Enough's been paid for two weeks, and it might as well be used. After two weeks, we'll see. But I see no reason why not keep it. As long as any of us are here. Trynor will go ahead in tomorrow and open up. Trynor's got a morning pass."

Trynor was an old-company pfc, a short blocky muscular man from Springfield, Illinois, who was riding in the front seat.

It was a pretty long statement to declare at a full roar. Strange did it by chunks, waiting to breathe and continue, whenever he was interrupted by the cat calls, Yankee screams, and Rebel yells that kept issuing from here and there in the cab. When he finished, there was a concerted shout of all three types of yell by everyone.

They were all six riding back together in the same taxi. Four were in the back seat, two were with the driver in front. They had bought three bootleg pints off the driver, who didn't carry fifths, and were plying the laughing driver with drink, as well as plying themselves. Arms were thrust out of the open windows waving the illicit bottles, and the calls and Rebel yells followed them down the boulevard like a fading memory. The yells were meant to wake the sleeping civilians whose peace and rest they had all fought so hard for, and paid out so much blood to preserve.

Strange, drunk, looking at them, and squeezed into the back seat beside Landers, felt a choky sensation in his throat, which he swallowed and carefully put down.

Frances Highsmith ought to see this. See and understand it.

It was entirely possible Strange's chief surgeon Col Curran would not allow Strange to go in, tomorrow. Strange had not tried to get in touch with him since returning from Cincinnati, and Curran had not joined the morning rounds group in person. So Strange had not really seen him. Even so, unless he had strict direct orders from Curran himself not to go, Strange meant to go and track down, find, get together with, and have this whole damned thing out with damned Frances Highsmith.

It had been two days now since Strange had acquired his Peabody suite. It had been four more days that he had waited to get it. Add one more day, that it had taken him to get the check deposited in a bank, get organized, start spending money and writing checks, and it was a week since he had last seen Linda, or talked to her, in Cincinnati.

The shock should be beginning to wear off by now. But Strange could not see that it had.

He still was much better off when he was around lots of other people, for example. If the people were having a big drunken party, he was better off yet. If he himself was drunk too, as was usually the case, it was even better. And if he himself had a woman or choice of women to be drunk with at the drunken party among all the people, it was the best of all for him.

But he had to get this other thing, with Frances Highsmith, settled.

It was only when Strange was not with a woman, was sober, not at a party, and not around lots of people, that he brooded.

But, then! Then, it could be a veritable fucking living hell. Brooding over Linda Sue. And her Air Force lt col. Who went down on her, and things like that. And came from Southampton or wherever the hell that place was on Long Island, New York.

Since all this always happened to him when he was at the hospital, Strange had gotten to hate the hospital.

When he checked in at his ward, it was nearly six A.M. All around on the dark ward were the quiet, breathing sounds of deep sleep.

The sleepy night ward man, bent over his check-in roster under the shaded lamp on his desk, shook his head. "Jesus. I don't see how you guys do it."

Strange could have told him, but didn't. Strange felt a little fuzzy at morning rounds. And his face felt puffy. But as soon as he saw Curran wasn't there, only Maj Hogan, he was more than ready to rush into a clean uniform and pick up his day pass and get the hell out of there.

"You're getting in later and later, Strange," Hogan called irascibly. "Since you got back from Cincinnati this last time."

They both knew there was nothing Hogan could do about it. And anyway Strange had this thing with Frances Highsmith that was deviling him, haunting him.

In the cab going back in he was alone. He didn't like it, but there was nobody else waiting at the cab stand. And the thought of waiting around until someone he knew showed up was unbearable.

He sat back and tried to enjoy the delicious November weather, but he couldn't. Pleasant hot sunshine pouring down over everything, drenching the park woods and the trees and lawns. The trees turning their last shades of bronze and yellow and red. The grass still bright green in the expanse of park sward and the private lawns. How long was it going to keep up? Not a cloud in the long stretch of sunny Mississippi sky.

It was no good. He could enjoy it mentally, but he could not enjoy it with his insides. He bought an illegal half pint from the driver, and began guzzling it, taking sips and hot pleasant gut-burning swallows of the raw whiskey. One of the things that rode up on the waves of alcohol fumes mounting his nasal passages was that he had liked the fight of last night. And that he would like another for tonight.

He shouldn't have picked up that water pitcher. And he wouldn't let himself do something like that again. He was glad they hadn't pushed him to using it. Strange didn't want to accidentally kill or cripple anybody. Just a good clean fight.

Strange had put a lot of deep thought on the matter of Frances Highsmith. And why she had to be his first blow job. Even the most superficial analysis spotlighted Frances. She was the first girl he had fucked back home in the States, other than Linda Sue. Frances was also the first girl anywhere to ask him to go down on her. And even more important, at least to Strange, it was Frances who had warned him he could lose his wife if he didn't take better care of her in bed. Frances deserved to be the first. By every moral right. Strange had realized this last night, when Annie Waterfield, too, had asked him to go down on her.

Annie hadn't really asked him, exactly. She had just assumed that he would. When she had started to go down on him, all laid out flat on the bed as he was, she had stretched that long, long, lean, beautiful leg out full length over him, and then had put her knee and her long lean rounded lovely thigh on the other side of his chest on the bed.

Strange had lain looking up at all the exposed woman-flesh, just above his face. She was pretty well exposed, in that position. There was a delicious, beautiful, little hollow on the inner surface of each thigh just where it met the trunk. These shaded into the thick, dark shadow of her crotch hair. In the middle of this thicket was the pink gape of her cunt, the two inner lips, hanging and open, joined to form the sheath, curling and pink, of the clitoris. After a moment, Strange put his hand up and began to manipulate her there.

Annie slowed her sucking, on the upstroke, as it were, and turned her head slightly without losing contact. "You don't suck pussy? All right. Just do that. Ahhh. That's it. But put a couple of fingers inside me." She went back to sucking.

It was certainly tempting. To say the least. Why did he suddenly find it so terribly desirable? Maybe it was that delicious exposure of her position.

But then, like some blocking mechanism lowering an iron inflexible curtain, Strange knew that it was Frances who deserved to be his first one. Deserved it. He owed it. It was easy enough for Strange to see that this was some sophomoric, boy's, or boy scout's, moralism. Easy enough for him even to state it publicly. That did not make it any less binding. He had to back away.

Strange had gone on manipulating her with his hand, doing it as she had told him. When she came, it was with a gush of unintelligible words and an outpour of emotion that was almost shocking and engulfed him. It was the first time in his life, Strange became aware, that he knew for sure he had made a woman come. It was no soft ah-ing and oh-ing, like when they faked it. He realized that making a woman come was one of the better things in living.

None of this changed the way he felt about old Frances. Or the way he felt about Linda Sue.

Strange had expended a great deal of deep thought on the subject of Linda Sue, also. More time and more depth than he had spent on Frances, and almost all of it anguished. One matter he had gone deepest into was the subject of jealousy. He had a lot of that. But only where it concerned Linda Sue.

One of the first things he'd noted about all the girls of Luxor was that, however many times he'd screwed one, and however much he might like her, it did not matter to him who she fucked or might be fucking when he was not with her. This was not the case with Linda.

No. With Linda, his imagination worked overtime, and double overtime. Always, of course, with that Air Force lt col of hers. The "aeronautical genius," as Linda had referred to him more than once. That must have come straight from him himself, to her. Or from some of his buddies, maybe. If he allowed Linda to meet them?

Strange's imagination had a way of slipping little pictures of Linda in passion up into Strange's conscious mind when Strange wasn't expecting them. Linda, with her head thrown back in ecstasy. Linda in the act of coming. Linda, arching and playing with her nipples with the first two fingers of both her hands. Linda with her legs stretched wide as wide, waiting for it, receiving it. All things, of course, which she had never done with Strange. But which Strange had always imagined her doing. And now imagined again.

But always of course with the "aeronautical genius." The lt col was always curiously faceless in these images. But big. Broad-shouldered. Unhairy (Strange was hairy). Long-waisted. Narrow-assed. Beautiful in other words. And he had a huge cock. Much bigger around, much longer, than Strange's own. And a long mobile sensitive questing tongue. Which he used beautifully, to great advantage. On Linda. Driving her out of her seclusion, out of her withdrawal, out of her mind with passion.

And driving Strange out of his mind with thinking about it.

If Strange was with a woman, and was drunk, and at one of those big parties, with lots of laughing, talking, and people, it was not so bad. If he was alone, or at the hospital, it was bad.

The other element he had gone into deeply which concerned Linda Sue was his loneliness. That didn't make much sense, even to Strange. Strange had never been lonely in his life. Never, that is, until now.

Even back before they were married, when Linda was at home single and alone in Texas, and he did not see her except every year or so, Strange had not been lonely. When the war came along, after they were married, and she had been shipped back while he stayed on in Wahoo, he had not been lonely. He had never been really lonely on Guadalcanal and New Georgia. On his way back out, when the restaurant problem and his discharge had become uppermost, about half of the time he wished he was out of the marriage altogether. He certainly had not been lonely for her.

Now, he was lonely with a fierceness and a misery that were unbearable. When he was at a party, drunk, and with a woman, was when he was the most lonely. But it hurt less than when he was lonely alone or at the hospital.

At first, he had attributed the jealousy and the loneliness to love. Lost love. And being in love. Then in his deeper brooding, it occurred to him he had never been lonely away from Linda Sue, as long as he knew he had her there, waiting. And he had never been jealous of her, any more than of the Luxor girls, until he knew he'd lost her.

If these were murky glimmers of truth themselves, then his jealousy and his loneliness weren't due to lost love so much at all, as to a sense of disrupted ownership.

And Strange was smart enough to know that no one had a right to own anybody. That not only wasn't love. It was wrong. It was downright immoral. That was slavery.

And where did that leave him? he asked himself.

It left him a lot better off thinking about Frances Highsmith, and his debt to her. That was where. He got out and paid for his unbearable taxi ride. In the fall sunshine he turned to the revolving door of the Peabody. Its suave old Negro doorman, in

Peabody livery, with his look of thousand-year-old patience, pushed the rotating door leaf for him.

In the frantic, uniform-jammed lobby, Strange looked around. Only, where in hell was Frances? And where in hell in Luxor was Frances to be found?

In fact, it was no trouble at all to find Frances. She was in the suite waiting, when he got there. And she was both drunk and furious at Strange.

"What the hell kind of shit was that?" she began. "Keeping me hanging around. And then standing me up for Annie Water-field. You kept me hanging around till it was too late to pick up any other genuine date. And then you turn me off? Like a faucet? Did you expect me to go out and pick up some soldier boy in the streets? Or the downstairs bar? Do you think I'm some kind of hooker?"

Strange had hardly got the door shut fully. He stared at her pinched little furious face. Apparently the suite of the Navy flyers on the floor below had been closed down for the night, last night. Frances had sat up alone all night, brooding, while doing away with the better part of two fifths of bourbon. Only Land-ers and Trynor were in the place with her. She had burst in on Trynor and begun her tirade when he was there alone, and helpless. Luckily Landers had come along shortly after.

"Well, I'm not some fucking kind of hooker," Frances con-tinued. "I'm a fucking decent girl. I work for my fucking living. And I pay my fucking own way."

Apparently the pickup and use of barrack-room language by girls was another new sign of the times, and the war, Strange realized suddenly.

"What the fuck kind of show do you think we run around here?" Frances demanded. "Do you think we're just easy lays? Just line us up, and bim-bam, thank-you-mam? You embarrassed me. You made me play second place to Annie Waterfield, in front of everybody. Annie Waterfield, who thinks she's such hot shit and number one because she's so fucking beautiful with her tits and long blonde pageboy. You're nothing but a fucking son of a bitch, Strange."

"I've been trying to calm her," Landers whispered. Trynor simply sat, cracking his knuckles, and pushing his eyebrows farther up his forehead, out of his depth.

"Cut off her booze," Strange told Landers. Frances' voice went up another five decibels.

"I'll help myself to anything around here that I want," she shouted. "And none of you fucking pricks will stop me. Gimme nuther drink."

Finally they were able to get her into one of the bedrooms, where she sat on the pillows at the head of the bed, in a sort of last-ditch defensive position, her pretty legs crossed under her.

Strange and Landers sat on the two bed edges by the pillows, on either side of her. Trynor had crawled onto the bed foot and sat there cracking his knuckles and working his washboard forehead.

The three of them were thinking the same thing, which was that if it went on much longer and got any louder, the house dick would be up there, probably with two huge MPs. "I think she's becoming hysterical," Landers whispered.

"Hysterical. I'm not hysterical. I just know my rights," Frances shouted.

Futilely Strange and Landers both flapped their hands at her to be quiet. She was undeterred.

"And you. You son of a bitch," she yelled at Strange. "I know what you'd like to do. Wouldn't you? You'd like to hit me. Wouldn't you? Well, go ahead. Why don't you? Go ahead."

"For God's sake. Shut up, now, Frances," Strange said.

"Yeah, please do," Landers whispered.

She apparently did not even hear them. Strange stared at her. Here he was all prepared to go down on some woman, his very first time, everything arranged, everything all set, and she had to go and throw some idiotic scene. Strange saw it all floating away.

"I know you'd like to hit me. I know your type. Well, why don't you? What's to stop you? I can't," Frances shouted. "Go right ahead. You'd like to bust me right in the nose. Break my nose. Well, go ahead. Why don't you?" She got a deep breath. "I'll tell you why you won't. Because you haven't got the guts, that's why. You're chicken. Chickenshit. Yahhhh."

She shut her eyes and screwed up her face and thrust it forward, sticking her tongue out as far as it would go. "Yahhhh. Yahhhh. Hit me. Go ahead. I dare you. I double-dare you. Yahhhh."

Why not, indeed? The words formed themselves in Strange's mind. Before they could be digested, his left hand shot out, the good one, of its own volition, in a short straight pistonlike punch. Fortunately, he was sitting twisted on the bed, so that he could not put any weight behind it. Nevertheless there was a loud cracking noise, followed by a sharp squawk from Frances, who then collapsed into silence, head down, her hands to her face.

Strange was aghast at himself. Hitting a woman. It was the same sudden violent reaction he had had last night, when he grabbed up the water pitcher. What was happening to him?

At the same time, way down deep under his start and dismay was a tiny bright red tickle of satisfied pleasure. Goddam women. There wasn't one of them who could be rational about anything. At least he had gotten even with them for once. But he was sorry.

"Jesus God," Landers whispered. He got his palm on her forehead, and began forcing her head up. Strange got her hands and pulled them down. A bright red stream of blood was running from her nose, down over her hands, and now down over her chin, into her lap.

"At least it shut her up for a while," Strange said, to nobody, with a silly grin.

Trynor was already on his way back from the bathroom with towels. "You oughtn't to of done that," he said in a mild but shocked voice.

"You big oaf," Frances said, in a muffled but nonetheless loving tone of voice. "A real dumbkopf."

"Put your head back," Landers said. "Way back. Get some ice from the ice bucket," he said to Trynor.

"Go ahead, turn me in," Strange said with a grin. "Just go down to the lobby. There'll be an MP somewhere. I'll wait right here."

"Oh, shut up, you oaf," Frances Highsmith said.

"Do you want us to try and get you a doctor?" Landers said.

"I don't want anything," Frances said. "Just stop the bleeding, and get me out of here. I've got a doctor."

She was much more worried about the blood on the lap of her skirt than about her nose, apparently. The skirt made her look as if she had started menstruating. They got it off of her and Landers washed the blood out of it in cold water, and hung the dress up to dry. By the time it was dry enough the bleeding had all but stopped, but the nose was swelling steadily. "Just get me out of here," Frances said again. They gave her a hotel napkin to cover it and Landers went down with her to the street and put her in a cab. He offered to go with her, but she did not want him to. When he came back, he threw himself down in a deep armchair with a "Whoosh!" of relief.

It was the beginning of the end for Landers and Strange. Trynor stayed on, with a key, in case any of the other old-company men should come in. But Strange and Landers had had enough of partying. Both were ready to go back to the hospital.

But before they did, they stayed on long enough to get good and drunk. Then they drank more in the cab going back. On the main outdoor walkway they parted to go to their respective wards and sleep the night through. It was just suppertime on the wards.

"What's gotten into you?" Landers asked in the cab. "You could have gotten us all into a lot of trouble."

"I know," Strange said. "I don't know. I don't know what's happening to me."

On his own ward he slept the whole night through in an unrestful sleep, but without dreams. In the morning, though Col Curran did not appear with the morning rounds group, Strange went to him in his surgery office and turned himself over to him, with the information that he wanted the second operation.

Strange calculated that in a little over four days he had spent just about two thousand dollars of the seven-thousand-dollar total.

But that, of course, was only if you included the $1400 paid to the hotel for the two weeks of the suite.

CHAPTER 21

Curran wasted little time. Strange told him what he'd decided. Curran smiled his small smile and said he would take Strange the next day, tomorrow.

He had been meaning to get around to Strange, he said. There was not any question of Curran's having waited for Strange to make a decision. He hadn't. He just had been extraordinarily busy. Which was also the reason he had missed making morning rounds. The US 5th Army had been halted by the Germans at the Volturno in October. And had been doing heavy work, was the way Curran phrased it, since then, and in fact had been hung up not far from there since November 1st. And the tougher surgical cases were drifting back, now. He hadn't had time for Strange.

The mention of the 5th Army in Italy shocked Strange. He had seen two of them come onto his own ward with forearm or hand wounds. Sour, dour, silent men. Who knew nobody, and did not even know each other. Strange knew about the Salerno invasion; of course. But what shocked him was that he had not even paid much attention. And how, though he knew about the taking of Naples, he had not bothered to read up on it at all. He realized suddenly he had not looked at a newspaper in weeks.

Was that how it had happened? To the old-company men off Guadalcanal? Who had been here when he and Winch and Landers and Prell arrived?

He left Curran's office, already back on the familiar hospital treadmill. His day pass was canceled for that afternoon. That evening he would get a special light supper. At night at bedtime, which was at nine o'clock, they would give him a light sleeping pill. In the morning they would come at six A.M. with the pisser duck and the calmative hypo, and then wheel him to surgery.

And fuck the 5th Army in Italy. That was how he felt. Was that how the others had felt?

In the surgery, while they were prepping his arm and had not yet put their masks on, he asked Curran groggily, grinning a silly grin, if they would please give him some other kind of anesthetic.

Curran shook his head. Sodium pentothol was the best they had. "Why another?"

"Gives me bad dreams," Strange said woozily.

Curran grinned. "A few bad dreams never hurt anybody." He went on putting up his gauze mask, becoming some kind of an alien with its tie-strap over his cap. Then he turned to his male assistant for his sterile gloves, popping his hands into the rubber.

The dream when it came, the vision, the hallucination, was all very familiar. It was as though it were taking up right where the other had left off. A certain time period seemed to have passed. And Strange, in his mind, was aware of all that had happened, while he had been away.

There were the same flashing lights, and the same distant shouting. As of crowds. And in fact it followed exactly the same physical projection of the other time. First, the anesthetist was talking him up onto it, softly, gently, exhorting, like a trainer talking up a fighter before going down to the ring. Then he was dripping the stuff into the vein, and Strange was counting backward from ten, till the explosion of noxious fumes came in the roof of his mouth. Then with no time lapse at all he was in the great hall. Waking up. Aware he was waking up. Struggling hard to wake up. But committed to the vision, to its complete unrolling, before he would be allowed out of limbo and back to Strange.

It was not the same public hall as before. This hall was some sort of private official chamber, where the public was not allowed. But the public could be heard shouting, outside the building.

It all seemed very Romanesque, to Strange. The robes, the columns, the windowless window openings, the huge drapes, the statuary. Roman, or maybe Greek.

Here, the judge did not sit on a huge plinth as before. He sat on a long raised dais against one wall, behind a long wooden table, which had many official-looking objects and documents lying on it. Once again the judge was shrouded, in a long white robe, that covered his head and hid his face, so that nothing of him showed except his huge, powerful, white hands.

But this judge was not, Strange knew, the same judge of before. An appeal had been made, Strange knew. And this judge, in the privacy of the official chamber, was a much greater authority than before.

Strange watched the shrouded arm and huge white hand come up as before, pointing. Then in a great powerful voice, a huge basso held down to gentleness, to mildness, so as not to shatter all the listening eardrums and shred the heavy fabric of the great drapes, the faceless figure said, "No, my son. You may not stay."

Desolate, Strange turned to walk out of the great hall. Outside, as the word was passed, the shoutings of the crowds grew louder.

Then he was back in the hands of the anesthetist and his assistant, both of whose shoutings suddenly grew softer, as Strange opened his eyes.

Curran was stripping off his mask and his gloves. Under the gauze, he was grinning. There was a feeling of great elation all over the surgery. The anesthetist was grinning. All the assistants were grinning.

Curran himself was in the grip of such an expansiveness he seemed hardly able to contain it.

"I think we've done you a pretty good job of work," he said downward.

"Sure have," the anesthetist grinned.

Strange, who was looking at Curran, managed to lower one eyelid in a slow wink. Then he shut his eyes. As before, he was still so full of the dream that the actual people did not seem real.

What in the hell did it all mean? Where was it he could not stay? What was it he must go back to? It was unbelievable that it could be a continuation like that, like a movie sequel. Where did it all come from? Was it all just lying there waiting for him, every time he had sodium pentothol? What if he never had another operation? Would it just stay there? He would never know the end of the story. And what would happen to it then? He could remember the faces of people he saw in the second hall, whom he had seen in the first hall. It was so real. More real than the operation.

Under him, he could feel them moving him onto the rolling table. His hand was a huge bundled-up package of gauze. He lay still, his eyes still shut, and let them roll him. By the time they moved him from the rolling table onto his own bed in the ward's private room, he was ready to go sound asleep. He woke only for a moment.

The operation was a huge success, apparently. Or so the surgical team seemed to think. Well, he would wait and see. Reserve judgment. They never really knew, till later. It was his last thought before heavy sleep.

The first time he woke it was evening, just at supper time. By then the real pain had begun. They doped him up for it and he went back to sleep, without eating. The second time he woke was in the middle of the night, around three in the morning, and he was hungry. Ravenous. In spite of the pain. The night man was prepared for that, fed him, and gave him more dope for the pain. By the middle of the next morning they were ready to get him out of bed and on his feet. And to hell with his pain. All told, they kept him laid up with it without any passes for a week. The bad pain receded after four days. But on the second day they let him have visitors.

The first visitor was Landers. The first question Strange asked was about Frances. Then, secondly, he asked about Winch. Still high on the dope, groggy in his head, Strange wondered woozily if his putting Winch after Frances meant he was losing interest in the old-company men, in the same way he was losing interest in the battles and the war. If so, that was terrible.

Landers had news of Winch. Winch's orders to leave for Camp O'Bruyerre had come in on the same morning Strange was operated on. By some weird, strange stretch of fate, as Landers put it. Winch had left that afternoon, unable to say good-by to Strange, who was still knocked out and sleeping.

That part had been okay. Unavoidable. But Landers felt Winch had acted odd. The 1st/sgt, now warrant officer junior

grade, had packed his small bit of gear and then come around
to make his expected good-bys to the other old-company men.
But instead of going to see each man, he had designated Landers
and Corello to collect them, and then met them all together sort
of formally, in the snack bar. That meant that Landers had to
go see each man separately, since Corello was so notoriously
irresponsible.

Winch had not given much of a performance in the snack bar.
Afterward, he had called Landers off and said good-by to him
alone. That wasn't much of a performance, either. But he had
sent good-bys to Strange, and said to tell him he would be in
touch as soon as he got settled. Strange should not hold his
breath, though, he said with a snarly grin, because getting settled might take him some time.

"He seemed so distant," Landers said. "He didn't seem like he
cared much of a shit, one way or the other."

"You don't understand him," Strange said woozily, from
where he lay propped up on bed pillows in the tiny room. "It
hurt him too much, to say good-by. It hurt him so much he
sluffed it off."

"Maybe," Landers said, obviously not agreeing.

"He's at his best when somebody needs him," Strange insisted. "I know him. Then he's great. But now nobody needs
him, and there's nothing to do."

"He didn't send any good-bys to Prell."

"Naturally," Strange grinned.

Landers obviously disagreed but he let it drop. And went on
to Frances.

In his woozy head, Strange noted that Landers had given the
news of Winch first, although the first question had been about
Frances. He knows what's important, Strange thought to himself, even if I don't.

The news Landers had to give about Frances was that there
had been no news of Frances at all. She had disappeared from
both Strange's suite and the suite of the Navy flyers. In the two
days there had been no sign of her anywhere. She had not been
in the bar downstairs, or anywhere visible in the Claridge. At
least not to the knowledge of anyone of either group who knew
her. On the other hand, there had been no police coming
around, or MPs. That was all the news of her Landers had to
give.

Strange felt his heart sink in him, but did not let Landers

realize this. Well, maybe she was just resting up, he rejoined. Letting the swelling go down. After all, it was the weekend now. She would have until Monday before she had to go back to work. The swelling might be almost normal by then, mightn't it?

Landers raised an eyebrow wryly, and didn't answer.

"Well, mightn't it?" Strange said.

Landers did not answer. Landers had not mentioned the nose-breaking to anybody, and had cautioned Trynor not to either. In the two days since Strange's absence Landers had by a kind of consensus become the administrative head of Peabody Suite 804. Or Strange's Suite, as it had come to be called by all of them. Fortunately Landers' own money had come in, and he was able to lay out what sums were necessary.

"No, no. No, no," Strange said with great upset, rearing up in the bed and then falling back as his right arm twinged. "I mean, you can't do that. This is my thing."

"Shit on it," Landers smiled. "Fuck it." He passed across a sour, hard, unreadable look. "I guess if I want to get rid of my money too, I can."

Landers had been forced to forbid the other old-company men from inviting just any soldier up to the suite. They none of them seemed to have any real judgment of people, and they wanted to show off. He had been forced to lay down the law after last night that any stranger who was invited up to the parties must first be screened by Landers himself.

"Last night we had a couple of meanies, mean drunks," he said. He had had to punch them and throw them out bodily.

Strange looked at him tiredly from the pillows. "You've become a leader," he said.

Landers gave him the bitter look again. "Yeah." He didn't smile. "It's funny, aint it? Right after I've chucked the whole thing. Now the Army'll never be able to use it."

"Maybe they will," Strange said.

"No. The Army doesn't want my kind of leadership. The Army doesn't want imagination. They don't even like a limited imagination."

"Don't be too sure of that."

"I'm pretty sure," Landers said equably.

To Strange's woozy head it seemed pretty clear Landers had made some decision about something, had moved from one plateau of thinking to some other.

"What do you mean, chucked it?" Strange said.

"I've chucked it," Landers said. "Given up on it. From now on I'm only going to do exactly what I'm told to do. No more and no less. And as little of that as I can get by with safely."

"Then you're officer material," Strange grinned. "You should put in for OCS."

"Not me," Landers said briskly. "I'm not going to tell some poor son of a bitch under me to go get killed."

Strange only laughed. But the whole thing set him to thinking, and to fretting, about Landers. And about the change in Landers. Whatever it was, and Landers did not say what, it had changed Landers in some very basic way. He had a lot more authority. And a lot less dedication and commitment, to go with it. In town, he went on spending his own money, over Strange's protests. And he also went on administering the minor problems of Strange's Suite 804. He also became Strange's eyes and ears in town, for the week that Strange was laid up.

Everything that happened in the suite, or around the suite in the hotel, or around the hotel in the town, was reported to Strange by Landers. Landers reported in such detail that it was about as good as Strange being there himself. Sometimes Strange thought it was even better. Not participating had a lot of points in its favor. The reportorial sessions took place usually just before Landers went off to town, right after lunch.

Lunch was what they both called it now. After so much going to town on day passes, Landers had dropped the Army meal designations of dinner and supper, and had gone back to lunch and dinner. Strange had followed his example, almost unconsciously.

But sometimes Strange wondered what Linda Sue called her midday meal, now. Had she stayed with the old, family and country names of dinner and supper? Or had she gone on to lunch and dinner, like her "aeronautical genius" from Long Island must call them?

Linda had not telephoned Strange since he left Cincinnati with the money. And certainly Strange had not called her. Strange wondered sometimes if she was perhaps waiting for him to call, first? If she was, that was tough shit. He wasn't that interested. He was much more interested in Frances Highsmith.

But repeatedly, day after day, the only news Landers brought about Frances was that she had disappeared. Nobody had seen her in any of the places where the men of the two suites hung

out. Neither in the low-down bars, nor the high-class. She had
not shown up at any Navy suite parties. He and Strange discussed this, but could come up with no answer of what to do.

Another of the things they discussed at great length was the
frequency with which Landers was getting into fights.

Since the day of the breaking of Frances' nose, Landers had
averaged a fight a day with somebody. It seemed to Strange, as
Landers said it had to him, that the first fight with the two Navy
chiefs and their bunch in the Peabody bar presaged a period of
fighting for them both. Landers felt that Strange's hitting
Frances and breaking her nose was part of the same syndrome.
Landers said he had felt it, though he hadn't done it, as far back
as his furlough home when he had become enraged at the Air
Force sgt on the train.

Strange was inclined to agree. Though he had no answer as
to why, any more than Landers had. Strange pointed out one
thing, which was that they were both in better physical shape
now, more nearly healed, and so were able to fight. At least he
himself had been, until his new operation. Landers nodded at
this, and accepted it. Landers pointed out that also they were
both much closer to going back to duty and combat, probably
in Europe, with their accurate foreknowledge of what that implied. Maybe that affected them.

Landers said that he himself did not like to fight and did not
want to, but that he was constantly becoming enraged. Landers
had never been much of a fistfighter or brawler, and had not
wanted to be, though he had learned a little boxing. But he used
to go out of his way to avoid a fight, walk around it. Now, the
slightest thing, and Landers was not only ready to fight. A fight
was just about guaranteed. All they had to do was show the
slightest lack of respect for himself, or for any of his overseas
buddies, or for his old outfit, or for his branch of service even.
And Landers didn't even care that much, about the Army.
Nevertheless, a kind of intense, awful rage that tinged everything in sight with red would leap out from some unknown
place in Landers and demand retribution. Landers did not know
where it came from, or what was causing it.

One day, for example, Landers had gone alone across the
street to the little hashhouse restaurant opposite the Peabody.
The suite upstairs had been empty and Landers had wanted
something to eat in the presence of other people, without bothering with the goddamned room service. A quick little quiet

bite. Standing in the line to go through the cafeteria counter, he had had three soldiers come in behind him.

The leader of the three was a small, muscular man with a cocky, cruel face. Landers had disliked him immediately and turned away. But the small man marched right up to him, and tapped him condescendingly on the shoulder, twice.

"Looks like a GI messhall, don't it, Mack?" he demanded in a truculent voice.

"Don't put your hands on me, Mack," Landers said. His voice had hardened instantly, and down deep inside him he felt the red tickle begin to grow. He swung half around. He hadn't yet picked up a plate.

"Don't call me Mack, Mack," the small man snarled, and leaned his head forward with a sort of eager, mean, fighting smile. "I don't let people call me Mack."

Landers hadn't answered. There didn't seem to be any point. He completed his swing around, bringing his right hand around in a sort of tight, rising right hook that hit the man perfectly on his thrust-out jaw.

The man went down. Landers immediately went on top of him, the peculiar red tide rising in his ears with the noise of an ocean breaker, and tingeing everything that peculiar red. He had hit the man six or eight times in the face and sides of the head before one of the man's buddies and some stranger soldier pulled him off. The little man was hardly conscious. His face was bleeding, his nose was broken, three of his teeth were out, and one ear was torn loose where a punch had grazed it.

Around them the civilian customers had scrambled out of the way, looking horrified and talking about soldiers. Landers stuffed in his khaki shirttail and blew out his cheeks. But the red rage in him had not receded. It wanted more.

"You want some of it?" he said to the other two.

But fortunately neither of them was as truculent as their leader. They backed away holding up their friend, one of them carefully picking up his three teeth, and left.

Landers did not know why he had done it. Telling it to Strange, he said it seemed stupid to give the other guy the first shot. Then thinking deeply, Landers added that the guy was obviously a mean, cruel, petty guy. Used to bullying people. But Landers was sorry about the teeth.

Another time, at the Plantation Roof on top the hotel Landers had, personally and all alone, beaten up three warrant officer pilots from the Army Ferry Command. It was the same stupid kind of a story.

Landers had gone up there alone, mainly to get away from the crowd and noise in the suite. He hadn't taken a woman, but had taken a bottle. In the customary brown sack. The huge place was crowded but by now Landers knew the headwaiter, who knew Landers tipped well and gave him an empty four table with a "reserved" on it. It was about then Landers noticed the three young warrant officer pilots, sitting at a table nearby and watching him. Perhaps because he had an expensive table all to himself.

The table was a good one down near the dance floor and Landers sat at it alone watching the dancers and getting steadily more drunk, and feeling lost, and lonely, and blue. With a kind of irascible self-pity, as he later said to Strange. There was one of those huge revolving mirror balls, with tiny mirrors that flashed spectrum lights in his eyes.

It was no time to have a woman with you, and Landers was glad he had not brought one. But he enjoyed watching the dancing couples, as they moved through the colored lights spraying the floor. It was near to closing, and the band as was customary was playing a set of sentimental numbers. Songs like "As Time Goes By," and like "Red Sails in the Sunset," and "Harbor Lights," and like "We'll Meet Again."

Landers found them all so in keeping with his mood that it was unbelievable. At that moment there wasn't anything in the world Landers hated, or detested. Everybody suffered. That was one thing you could count on. Stray, wispy shreds of thought ran through his head before he could catch their tails. About honor, and death, and tragedy, and love. Misguided honor, searched-for death, tragedy that was embraced, love that was hopefully lost. Everybody died; some younger, a part of his mind said, as Landers later told Strange, and someday all of us would look back on these lovely sweet darling times and remember all these songs. Yeah. Yeah, the other part of Landers' mind said, as he explained to Strange, those of us who survived would. But at least he wasn't mad at anybody.

At closing, which was one o'clock, they played "The Star-Spangled Banner," as they always did. Landers did not get up. It was almost force of habit by now, since so many of the wounded out at the hospital did the same thing. The general, if perhaps irreverent, joke out at the hospital was that the wounded did not need to stand for the national anthem. There had been talk of fights over it, but Landers had not seen any. But Landers had always been with a group when he did it.

Almost before the music ended, as the place was beginning to clear out, the biggest and apparently highest ranking of the three w/os appeared at his table.

"I think you had better learn to stand up for the national anthem, soldier," he said.

Landers glanced up at him, and then down. The red tickle was beginning to burn in him. "Fuck off, bud," he said.

"Okay. I want your name, rank, and organization," the w/o said, "and that's an order, soldier." He pulled out a pencil and notebook.

Inside, Landers was beginning to chortle. Down deep underneath, the red ocean breaker was swelling and growing in his ears. This time, he looked up and didn't drop his gaze. "How would you like my fist in your face, instead?"

Without a word, the young pilot put away his notebook, turned on his heel, went back to his table, and sat down. He began to argue with his buddies. One was on his side, and one apparently wasn't. Landers sat and grinned at them.

By this time their two tables were the only two still with occupants. At the entry, the two elevators were swiftly siphoning off the crowd. Behind Landers, the civilian headwaiter was hovering nervously. "Who are them bums?" he asked. He had a New Yorkese accent.

"Out-of-towners," Landers said, "flying through. College boys from the Ferry Command. Don't worry." He paid his bill and left the headwaiter his big tip with a wink. He got almost as far as the elevators, before he was hailed by the same w/o.

"Hey, soldier. I want that organization of yours. And your name."

The three of them were coming toward Landers, all in a resolute row. The biggest one had won the debate apparently.

Landers pushed the elevator button, and then stood, quietly watching them. His mind was totally blank, totally empty. When they were almost at punching range, he drove himself at them like a catapult. Some belated instinct told him to go for the reluctant one first.

From that point on, things happened very fast, though they seemed to be in slow motion. They weren't expecting a rush and scattered, away from him. A mistake. He hit the reluctant one, who went down, and stayed down. As Landers'd hoped. He swung around, and the big one was rushing him. Landers stepped to meet him, and hit him with everything he had, a left that knocked him sideways back against the elevator doors.

But just as the w/o touched them, his arms flung wide to catch himself, the elevator Landers had summoned arrived, and the doors opened. The w/o stumbled back across the elevator interior, his feet working fast, a look of surprise on his face, and hit the back wall of the elevator with a crash, and started to go down.

Landers was almost as surprised as he was. He stepped after him, hoisted him by his shirt, hit him hard on the jaw, and saw his eyes glaze. He turned, pushed the ground-floor button, and stepped back out before the doors closed.

The third one was rushing him, but looking reluctant now that he was alone. Landers hit him once, twice, three times, four, driving him back across the entry and following him, until he went down, lolling against some antique loveseat.

Landers' drive was so hard it carried Landers clear on past him. The red roar was in his ears, and inside him the huge, red ocean breaker was topping over. He could hear his own voice shouting something or other.

Then he saw the elevator arrow was rising again and went past the third one who was struggling to get up, kicking him carefully in the side of the head as he passed, and met the elevator as the doors opened. He hit the biggest w/o as he came out, followed, and hit him twice more, then pushed the ground-floor button again, and stepped out.

Everything was silence. The one elevator was still going down. Landers pushed the second elevator button, stepped into the empty elevator when it arrived, got off at the eighth floor, and went back to the suite. He was limping from where he had hurt his bad ankle again, one side of his jaw was sore, and the knuckles of both hands were barked. But the MPs would never find him. He did not tell anybody in the suite what had happened, he said to Strange. And he was sorry that it was over.

Strange had been moved from the semiprivate room back out to the open ward, by this time. Landers told him this particular tale on the fifth day after the operation. Strange sat on his bunk, flexing his weak fingers inside their new plaster cast, and watched Landers' calm, matter-of-fact face, wondering what was going on in Landers' head while he told his fight tales so matter-of-factly.

Strange was having trouble knowing what was going on in his own head. Certainly, one part of him wished hungrily that he had been there, and in it. Another part of him devoutly was glad he had not had the chance.

Strange did not know what was happening to himself, either. Any more than he knew what was happening to Landers. Strange only knew he no longer had his old self-control. That frightened him a little. He was unable to judge, for either of them. And that made him a little scared.

Landers did not know it, but Strange had had another version of the fight with the three pilots. Two of the old-company men had slipped away from the suite and gone upstairs to look for Landers, to make sure he was all right. Everybody was a little worried about him, so with the benediction of everyone Corello and Trynor had gone after him. They happened to be standing against the back wall with the headwaiter when it started. Landers had not seen them. It was Trynor who told Strange since, naturally, Corello never told anybody about anything, if he could help it.

"I never seen nothing like it," Trynor said, with a kind of unwilling, irate protest. "I don't think nobody could of stopped him. Five men, seven men couldn't of whipped him. It was like some unbeatable power or force in him. When he went at them, them three fellows didn't know what hit them. It was like they had grabbed a damn tiger by his tail."

Trynor cleared his throat. "Do you think maybe he's losing his mind, Sarge?"

Strange did not answer. He did not trust himself to. He had felt the same power or force in himself.

Trynor held up his hand. "I'm not sayin' he wasn't right. He was. But it was the way he went about it. I know all of us got some of that feeling in us," he said, in his lumbering way. "But not like that." Suddenly Trynor laughed, reluctantly. "My God, them fellows scattered like a covey of birds."

"I don't know," Strange had said to Trynor. "Anyway, as long as he was right," he wound up, inconclusively.

And sitting with Landers, Strange felt just as inconclusive. Strange did not know if he was equal to bringing it up, and going into it. In depth. Smart, Landers was. He knew Landers was smart. But he did not know if Landers had his, Strange's, powers of analysis.

"Anyway, Marion," Strange said, "I'll be out of here in a couple of days now. We'll go in together. You've done a wonderful job of taking care of things." It was the first time Strange had ever called him by his first name.

Landers grinned at him. "We'll have to find old Frances Highsmith." He shrugged. "I don't have any idea where she could be. But for the two days I'll keep looking."

"Yes," Strange said. "Well, I guess that don't matter so much," he said. "As long as she's all right."

Of course, he was lying. It did matter. Strange did not know if Landers knew he was lying. But he did not want Landers to know, or want to admit to Landers, that Frances Highsmith and the idea of going down on her had become an obsessive preoccupation with him. To an unreasonable degree.

In the end it was Strange himself who found her, finally. Landers had not turned up any signs of her. The day Strange went back into town, the two of them together hunted but did not turn her up either. Frances Highsmith had disappeared off the face of the earth as far as the Peabody and Claridge hotels were concerned. For four more days Strange hunted for her, half-heartedly, by himself. The most of his hunting was confined to the night hours. During the day he assumed she was working. Somewhere. Wherever it was she worked. It was on the fifth day, the night of the fifth day, that he found her.

Strange had left the suite and its nonstop party, then after a quick look in the bar had left the hotel, and walked the two blocks up Union to Main St. He was looking for her, and he was not looking for her. He had about given up. He no longer expected to find her. But the suite bored him. Landers had given him a quick wink as he left.

At the corner of Main, he turned vaguely by the big Walgreen's to walk the five blocks to the Claridge. But not because of Frances. There was a melancholy hunger in him that was palpable, in the night air. There was nothing of love in the melancholy. No love of a lost Linda Sue, no love for a misplaced Frances Highsmith. The hunger was so general, so diffuse, so a love for all females, all women, that it was essentially without object. It was a hunger for unknown, forbidden, sexual adventure.

The fall air was chill against his summer uniform. He crossed the street to look in the unlighted shop windows. Strange felt exactly as he used to feel as a boy when he got all dolled up and went into Houston to hit the whorehouses.

The shop windows on the other side, the Claridge's side, were loaded with stuff for women. Hundreds, thousands, tens of thousands of dollars worth of stuff. For pretty women, pretty girls.

Who the hell could afford to buy it all? Businessmen. Only the businessmen, who had stayed home, and were making fortunes off the good old war.

Strange walked on along, looking in the women's shops' windows. He had not been without women the past four nights. Each night he had had at least one, out of the Peabody covey. But it hadn't worked. He had performed well enough, but there was no excitement. The irony was that now there was the excitement, but no girl.

One of the first things he had found out from them was that not all the girls were sexually as free as Frances, and her pal Annie Waterfield. They didn't go down on you and they didn't expect you, didn't want you, to go down on them. Strange would even have gone for Annie Waterfield this time, but Annie had gone off with some new officer from the Navy flyers' suite. For an unspecified period. Annie had become somebody else's girl for the moment. For this week.

Strange ambled on along. So here he was, Frances-less, and Annie-less. His head had just finished the thought about Annie when his eye caught a figure. It had detached itself from among the figures on the opposite sidewalk and moved out into the street to cross it diagonally, going away from him.

His eye recognized it as Frances before he himself did. Automatically, he filled his lungs and bellowed. "Hey! Frances!"

The excitement in him swelled. Strange couldn't believe his luck. Inside his belly, something got all slippery and greasy and seemed to slide around with grease on it. A thickness filled his throat until it altered the sound of his voice.

The figure had stopped and was looking at him. It was Frances. But how he had recognized her he didn't know.

She was dressed presentably enough, in a light dress with a light fall coat. But there was something furtive and scuttling, something crablike, about the way she moved and stood. No longer was there the free-swinging stride and breast-jutting posture. She was hunched down inside her coat as if trying to hide.

Strange's heart gave a huge, twinging lurch. He hoped there was nothing wrong with her face, to have caused the change in her. He gulped air. Jesus, that would be terrible.

His eyes moved away sideways to go over the façade of the low-life bar she apparently had just come out of. It was one they had not even bothered to look in for her.

"Oh, it's you," she said in a low voice when he got close to her. She seemed to straighten up a little. "How are you?"

There was nothing wrong with her face structurally, he saw. And a great, silent whoosh of relief sprouted in him. The broken nose had healed perfectly, not twisted, no flattened bridge, no ugly lump.

Only in the very deepest bottoms of her eyes, when he was close, was there any indication of change in her. Down there, way down, something slippery seemed to move and change shape, and refuse to let him come close to it or put a finger on it.

"The important thing is how are you?" Strange said. He was smiling hard.

"I'm fine," she said. But there was no give in her, no letting down.

"I've worried like hell about you," Strange said, in his noticeably choked-up voice.

"You have?" A sudden strange, wise, greedy grin cracked her face from side to side. "Well, I'm fine. I'm in great shape. I don't think I could be better."

"I've been looking for you." When he thought of why, his throat got choked up more. It sounded in his voice. And the grin on her face seemed to get wider and greedier. She stared straight at him, and the slippery thing in her eyes moved. She didn't answer. "Why didn't you ever come back to the hotel? To the suite?" Strange asked.

The grin did not go away, but her words were hard and cold as iron. "I don't ever want to go back to that place again."

"Oh, come on," Strange said. "Why not?"

Her eyes looked away from him, then her face turned away. She was no longer smiling. "Everybody knows everything about what happened."

"No, they don't. Landers and I haven't told anybody. And we swore Trynor to secrecy. He hasn't told anybody. None of us have."

"Well, they know about your having chosen Annie over me."
She seemed to slump again, into that crablike position, half
turned away. Ready to scuttle.

"Oh, come on, now," Strange said, uneasily. "You girls have
never been that way about anybody else. You've never cared
who had who first."

"I don't ever want to go back there," Frances said, anyway.

"Fine. Then don't." Too angry. Strange could see himself
blowing the whole thing sky high. Nothing was coming out
right, and he didn't know what to say to make the proper effect.
He tried again. "I don't like it much any more myself. That's
why I'm out here. That's why I left it."

She did not respond.

"Come on over to the Claridge with me and have a drink and
let's talk about it," he said.

She did not answer. Neither yes nor no.

Flattery, damn it. Always remember flattery, Strange bela-
bored himself. Flattery always works with women. Always.
When nothing else will. Simple flattery. Even when they know
it.

"That's a lovely outfit you've got on," Strange said. "Listen.
I've been going nuts, looking for you. I've been looking for you
for a whole week. Come on. Have a drink?"

She did not answer that. "What were you doing the other
week?" she said.

Strange suddenly felt dumb, and empty. "What other week?"

"The first week," she said.

Strange felt reprieved. He held up his cast. "I was getting my
hand operated. The day after the— The day after I last saw you,
they pulled me in and did my hand again. I've been in the
hospital. I was laid up for a week. They wouldn't let me out.

"But I had Landers looking for you."

"He never found me," Frances said.

Somehow, without having answered him, without having
ever said either yes or no to his offer of a drink, she now had him
by the arm, and they were moving. Toward the Claridge. It was
the right direction.

"You're the most attractive girl I've seen," Strange said, in a
husky whisper. "You're the most attractive girl I've met since
I've been here."

"You want to go down on me," Frances said.

There was an audible pause. "Yes," Strange whispered in a choked-up voice. It seemed to him the answer had been torn out of him.

"All right," Frances said briskly.

Against him Strange felt her pace quicken in a brusque, purposeful way. That oddly wise, greedy smile was back on her face. Everything seemed to have gone into a pink haze of unsubstantiality in front of his eyes, as if his blood pressure suddenly had risen alarmingly, and motion took on a slowed, languid quality that made everything dreamlike and unreal. They hurried slowly toward the Claridge.

"I knew you would," Frances said with her greedy smile, holding on to the arm tightly. "I knew you'd want to, eventually."

The sense of dreamy unreality stayed with Strange through all the preliminaries. Luckily, there were rooms available at the Claridge. He did not have to call Jack Alexander upstairs at the poker game. Luckily, the liquor store had not quite closed. He was able to get them a bottle. In the room, Frances did not even wait to get her stomach a drink, before she began taking off her clothes.

She did not have a bad little figure. Strange made drinks of bourbon and ice and a little water, and noted as he did that she was not wearing either a brassiere or panties. Well, she didn't need a bra. And maybe she didn't need the pants. Vague thoughts of the low-down bar he was sure she had just come out of tipped dreamily through his mind, and whether she had been with somebody already tonight. He thought briefly about the clap, and syph. But it didn't matter. Nothing mattered. He didn't give a damn. He could feel his heart beating slower, and slower, and slower in his ears.

He handed her the drink and, nude, she drank it off in one long pull and put the empty glass down and sat down in an armchair. She pulled her legs up, opening herself, and put her heels on the chair edge against her buttocks, experimentally, and then put her legs down and crossed them.

Strange was almost frantically getting out of his own clothes. The tie, the shirt, the T-shirt, the shoes, the pants, the underpants, the sox. It seemed an endless process.

It occurred to Strange, as he toiled, that nude photos and paintings of women did not matter and did not really expose women, and that secretly women knew this. A woman was not really exposed until she opened herself, as Annie—as Frances, had just done. But men did not know this about women and women were never going to let out the secret.

From her chair Frances held up a warning finger. "I just want to get one thing straight, before we start," she said with the authority of a 1st/sgt. "Did you go down on Annie?"

"No," Strange said. "No, I didn't."

"You didn't? Scout's honor?" She nodded emphatically. "Because she's the only one besides me up there who does it, who likes it."

"No," Strange said. "But how did you know that she—"

"From the men, of course. You dumbhead," Frances said scornfully.

"Do you talk to each other about—"

"No. We only talk to each other about the men. But we know everything about everybody."

She pulled her nude legs up and set her heels against her buttocks, in the position she had tested before. "Now, listen. You can go down on me. But I'm not going down on you. And I'm not going to let you fuck me afterwards. After I come." She paused to look at him, and closed the admonishing finger into her hand. "I may let you jerk yourself off. But I may not let you come at all. I haven't decided yet."

"All right," Strange said.

She stared at him. "I may make you sleep all night right there beside me, and not let you come," she said, and watched him.

Strange didn't answer.

"Or I may let you jack off with your nose in me." She stared at him more. "I want you to understand it all beforehand," she said, "before we start. I'm not as big and strong as you. But if you hit me or start to beat me up, I'll scream for cops so loud they'll hear me in St. Louis."

"All right," Strange said again.

Still staring, but as if she were satisfied about him meaning it, she let the strange grin crack open her face again, as though it had been split with a razor. And the slippery little wormy things in the bottoms of her eyes seemed to move around.

"You've got it coming to you," Frances said. "You owe it to me."

Strange guessed she was right. Anyway, he had never been so

hot for anything in his life. He would have agreed to anything. He could not remember ever having had such a full, hard, throbbing erection ever.

She had one hand down there touching herself, pulling it open. "All right," Frances said. "Come on over here. Come on. Yes, come on. Yes. Yes. Yes, that's it. Yes. Yes," she said as she twined her fingers into his hair. "Oh, the little piggie. Oh, the little piglet. Oh, the greedy, hungry, snorty, little piggie." Strange felt her take a deep, long breath. "That's it, yes. Yes, that's it. Oh, he loves it. Oh, he does love it. He wants it. He wants it. They all want it." Her voice went on, talking things to him, or to herself. But Strange wasn't listening.

It was not true that it did not taste. There was a faint taste of urine, which was not at all unpleasant, and a faint odor of it, but this disappeared almost at once, presumably because he himself had licked it off and swallowed it, and then it was true that it had no taste. The faint odor of urine combined with an even fainter smell of perfume, and perhaps of sweat, and mingled with the odor of what for lack of a better word Strange could only call "Woman," which got stronger, and then stronger.

But the really delicious thing about it was the textural quality. It had all the benefits of deep kissing, but was a hundred times more delicate. Strange had never felt anything with his mouth that felt so delicious. The smaller, delicately formed inner lips seemed to cling to his face. The texture of the roll that covered the little organ felt like an inner lip of the mouth but was more sensory, and moved from side to side under his tongue. The hairs along the heavier outer lips tickled the sides of his nose.

"Do it up at the top more," Frances said in an unsteady voice. "Do it up at the top more. Do it up at the top mowwW-WWAARRGHNNNNNnnnNNHHH!" She seemed to go on talking in disconnected syllables that did not seem to say anything, for quite a long time.

Strange did not know what she was saying, and did not care. When her body stopped quivering, he rolled away and sat on the floor, breathing as harshly as she was. His cock felt like some kind of monstrous club. It was so charged with blood he felt it might just blow up like a grenade, explode outward spattering himself and her and the walls of the room with red drops. It wanted something around it, a hand, a mouth, a rubber glove, a pussy. Anything. And yet he was all prepared, all psyched, to abide by whatever decision she made, even if it meant going to bed beside her with this swollen red, flamboyant thing un-touched.

Strange had discovered he was a pervert, that was the truth. There wasn't any other way to look at it.

As if responding to him, Frances, who had put her legs down and crossed them in a sort of self-hugging, pussy-hugging way, opened her eyes, staring at nothing. "There are so many things we can do," she said dreamily to the ceiling. "Hundreds of things."

Abruptly she brought her eyes down, to Strange, looking at him in a way as if she had never seen him before.

"Oh!" she said. "You! I don't care about all that other stuff. I want you. I want you inside of me." Quickly she got to her feet from the chair, and headed across the room to where the bed was.

Strange almost beat her to the bed. Although he felt a faint disappointment in him.

"God," she said. "I never had it like that before. Most men, you know, most men don't really like it. They want to do it but they hate it. They're rough, and mean, and brutal. When they do it.

"Oh, there's so much we can do," she said. "Strange. Johnny. Johnny Stranger."

When he had come, and after she had quieted and gone sound to sleep, which wasn't long, Strange rolled over on his back and tried to think it through.

In the first place, it was such a flattering, ego-pumping thing to have somebody say your name so lovingly. So he had to discount, because of that.

In the second place, he was not in love. Not any kind of love he had ever heard about. And he was sure Frances Highsmith wasn't either.

On the other hand, they had it pretty damned good together in the bed. That wasn't to be sneezed at. Anyway, it wasn't going to last that long. Not if his educated guess about the new hand operation was correct. He would be going back to duty.

But in the third place, there was the new undigested knowl-edge. He was a pervert. A sexual pervert. From some deep well in him where he had never been, this thing had risen up and taken him over. In one fell swoop, he had become an addict of eating pussy. Just like it was some damned drug or something. Jesus, in most places it was even against the laws. Specifically against the laws. Like fucking animals. Or homosexuality. And he didn't even care. Laws simply could not stop him. Addict or not, unlawful or not, he would never want to be without it again. And that made him a real pervert.

For the first time in what seemed a very long time, lying in the cool bed, between clean, smooth sheets, with the hump of Frances Highsmith's sleeping ass under them beside him, Strange thought about the old company's mud-hungry platoons, still out there, still fogging it, still sweating, still dying.

Nobody, until he had been out there with them, could appreciate sheets. And clear, clean water flowing out of a tap, on demand. Or the smell of a woman that wasn't really his, sleeping next to him.

Strange wondered what they would say, if they ever found out that their old mess/sgt, Mother Strange, was a cunt-eating pervert.

Strange felt very undeserving. He was afflicted with a terrible guilt. But the guilt wasn't sexual. It was military. Or, maybe it was both. He could no longer tell.

Finally, having decided nothing, he rolled over on his side and went to sleep, replete. More replete, more fulfilled, than he could remember ever having been in all his life.

To think that all those years, he had . . .

The next morning just at dawn (he had left a call downstairs in the lobby) Strange hoisted himself, and joggled Frances awake just enough to say good-by, and took off for the hospital and the regular reveille. It was still the prime guiding principle in his life.

At morning rounds, when Curran told him they would take the cast off in a day or two and see how successful they had been, Strange wondered if the surgeon, looking at him, could tell he was a pervert.

BOOK
FOUR

THE CAMP

CHAPTER 22

Mart Winch had been at Camp O'Bruyerre three weeks when he first heard Marion Landers had been fighting people and was in trouble because of it. By that time winter finally had set in, it was the first week in December, and Luxor had had its first cold and its first light snow.

The word on Landers came to Winch via a telephone call from big Jack Alexander at the hospital. Landers had gotten into a fist fight with an injured, wounded 1st/lt, had beaten him up in the post recreation hall, had then proceeded to have a violent altercation with Maj Hogan, the administrative chief, in which he had threatened and verbally insulted the major, and then had gone AWOL for five days.

Landers was now under ward arrest, Alexander said. Maj Hogan was preferring charges, on all four counts. The 1st/lt had declined to prefer charges. But Hogan's charges would be enough to get Landers a special court-martial and a three to six months sentence.

If Landers had not come back on his own, and instead had been picked up by the MPs and been brought back, he might easily have drawn a general court.

"Well, what the fuck am I supposed to do about that?" Winch said, in a kind of exasperated bawl.

For a second he let his eye go to his office windows outside which so much was going on at the moment.

"I dunno. Nothing," Alexander said. "Nothing at all." His clipped, hard, thickened voice came over the phone in exactly the same way his blue eyes fixed you. Winch had a sudden wild vision of his hard-edged turtle's mouth, eating its way up the phone mouthpiece crunch by slow, ruminative crunch. "He's one of your original bunch of boys, aint he? I thought you'd want to know."

"Wait a minute," Winch said. "Don't hang up. What is there I can do about it? What does your Col Stevens say?"

"Col Stevens," Jack Alexander said, very slowly and very precisely, "aint said anything about it." He did not say "his" Col Stevens, this time, Winch noted. "I don't know he even knows about it."

"He must know about it," Winch said. "If Hogan's preferred charges."

"I suppose he must know about it. Yeah," Alexander's voice said. "But he aint said a thing to me."

"Do you think it would be worthwhile to talk to him?"

"I don't have an idea."

"Well would it be bad, if I talked to him?"

"I don't see how it could do Landers any harm. But I don't know."

"Now what the fuck is that supposed to mean?" Winch cried. He was getting frustrated. Here was supposed to be one of the most important men the US Army in the middle area of the United States was supposed to have. A man who could get done just about anything he wanted done, the word said. A man who was supposed to be making deals and money right and left and backward. And Winch was soliciting him. Begging him, and asking him not to hang up. And he—after making the call in the first place—was playing footsie and being coy. "Do you think I can be of any help to him, or don't you?"

"I don't know if you can be any help to him, or not be any help to him," the hard, scarred, old sea turtle's voice said. "I only called you. You know as well as I do, just how uptight things have been getting in all the services lately. All around the Horn. And you know why.

"Don't you?" the voice said sharply.

A little thrill ran up Winch's back. But he did not want to think about any of that, right now. He glanced again at his windows.

"Yes," he said. "Yes, Jack. I know why. You think that might affect this thing on Landers? Well, do you think if I came in there to see you?"

"I'm not in this," the voice said immediately. "Not in it."

"Okay. Then I'd better see Col Stevens here at the club. If I want to get involved. He comes out just about every evening, at cocktail time."

"Fine. If you want to get involved. And I'll see you in town up at the Claridge. I'll be coming in the next few nights."

"I'm not sure I do want to get into it," Winch said. He thanked him, for the call, before he hung up. For a moment he stared down at the black instrument. Then he went over to look out his big picture-glass windows. They were among the only third-floor windows in the only three-story building on the post.

The view that met his eyes was a little breathtaking. As far as his eyes could see from his third-floor windows, through the rising mists of a sunshiny winter morning, collections of one-story hutments and two-story barracks stretched in various lines, encompassing muddy drill fields and parade grounds. Secondary gravel roads and streets, their holes and low spots glinting back watery reflections of the winter sun, divided them. A few main arteries of asphalt, streaked with muddy vehicle tracks and smeared with the snail-like exudations off the feet of marching columns, weaved among them. Over everything lay a pall of coal smoke, adding to the mists. Far off over the huge rolling plain that seemed to begin at the foot of his building, but in fact began some two miles behind him out of visibility, clumps of taller treetops were apparent in the horizon-band of the woods. That was what all this area was like, before some astute citizen had got hold of his congressman and sold his piece of badlands to the government for a camp. Among the distant trees, way beyond the newest group of tarpaper hutments that they were building, geysers of black cloud rose silently, blowing up dirt and chunks of trees as heavy artillery units practiced range firing. Nearer in, companies and platoons and occasionally a full battalion of drab-clad men, helmeted and under slung arms, moved along the gravel streets of wet holes, exhaling streams of steam that matched the steam emitted by the strings of vehicles.

And Winch was, theoretically at least, the chief overseer of them all. At least until they left Second Army Command.

Everything had happened just as old T.D. Hoggenbeck had said it would. Just as old T.D. had envisioned it and set it up. The perfect sinecure. All you had to do was keep your nose clean.

It was everything Winch had dreamed about, back in his misspent youth, back when he was bucking for his first staff rocker, to add to his stripes. Now he had it.

Below his hands on the low sill a radiator sent a stream of hot air up at him. It merged with others, to warm the air of the office so that he would not feel the cold the men outside were feeling. Warmed enough to where his trim winter blouse with its new w/o insignias could be hung neatly over a chair back, the two rows of ribbons throwing color splinters.

Winch continued to stand at his windows, rapt.

If he had it, had it all so handily, so nicely, why didn't it make him happy?

Two full divisions were under training out there. Getting ready to go to northern Europe—not Italy.

Two full divisions. That was 18,000 men. And God knew how many other single, autonomous QM and Ordnance and Signal units.

Winch could let himself think now about the allusion Alexander had made on the phone. Because Winch was looking right at it, out there. Canny, closemouthed, old Jack Alexander, the ex-pug, had alluded to the tightening-up that was going on in all of the services.

The same little thrill ran up Winch's back again. The United States was finally going into Europe. The United States, helped by Great Britain, was going to invade France. A few thousand men involved with command knew it. The public announcement, and the command designations for it, was going to come any day now. Men like himself and Alexander were not even told and taken into the secret. But they knew. Just about everybody knew.

The public announcement wasn't supposed to come until around Christmas time. But these civilian draftees out there in the winter mud of Camp O'Bruyerre knew where they were going, and what they could expect.

European invasion. There had been rumors of it as far back

as September, before the Salerno landings. Light rumors and heavy talk had flowed up and down the corridors of Kilrainey General about it. Any man who went back to duty would be getting back just in time for it.

Now it was no longer rumor. It was definitely coming next spring or summer. In about six months or so. With it coming, as Alexander had pointed out, every service was tightening-up on AWOLs and insubordinations.

That was the time Landers had to pick to get himself in trouble. Still staring raptly out his windows at the steam-exhaling marchers, Winch watched the winter Mississippi rain begin to fall on them as the winter sunshine clouded over.

It seemed almost the last straw to lay on them. But a lot worse than that lay ahead of them. He wondered how many of them would die in the coming big affair. Go down, disappear forever. A lot.

Winch didn't really care. His overlordship was only theoretical; on paper. And only temporary, at that. Let them die. Somebody had to.

He cared more whether Marion Landers got his ass in trouble. Just as he cared more about damned Bobby Prell. And his mess/sgt, Johnny Stranger.

Winch did not feel that strongly about the other old-company men. Perhaps it was because the rest had already been back awhile and had changed, before he and Strange and the other two had arrived. Or perhaps his life had become entangled with those three, on the long road back.

The three of them meant more to him now than all these other men outside his window, sweating and blowing steam like broken-down, ruined horses in the winter cold.

These others must have problems. And disrupted private lives. And wives, and kids, and maybe parents who lay awake nights worrying over them. Winch didn't really give a damn.

Prell and Landers and Strange were what was left to him of his real life.

Somewhere down in the deepest part of his mind, in some place he wished neither to investigate nor explore, but consciously knew was there, was a strong feeling, a superstition, that if he could bring Strange and Prell and Landers through, without them dying or going crazy, and make them come out the other side intact, he himself might come through. And Winch's nightmares had been getting worse and worse, lately.

It angered him into a fury, that Landers would let himself get into a bind at a time like this. Winch did not know whether he ought to get involved or not.

Even Jack Alexander didn't want to be involved with it. Not right now.

Any fool should know better. Times like this were the times when everybody's righteousness came into play. Every cheap, mean prick like that Hogan got all puffed up and went looking for a victim, just to make himself some points. Hell, even honest men couldn't help doing it.

Maybe, probably, it would be good for Landers. Let Landers serve his three months, or six months, and learn a lesson.

That evening, after work at cocktail time, Winch cornered Col Stevens just the same, and held him captive against the bar at the Camp O'Bruyerre officers club.

Stevens knew about Landers and his special court, right enough. And he didn't think much of it or of Landers. That came out at once, as soon as Winch brought the subject up. Winch did not bring the subject up until he had bought the old man at least three drinks.

Winch had learned long ago how to handle officers in their own terrain. And being a warrant officer, with club membership privileges and the right to mingle on privileged ground and be an equal, was only carrying the old principle one step further.

Respect was the secret. No matter what you really thought. All any old West Pointer wanted from you was the right to be fatherly. The higher the rank, the greater the father. All you had to do was keep on Sir-ing them, and not be cocky because you had moved up into officer country. Cockiness was something they watched for narrowly.

Respect. Not with obsequiousness, either, but with charm. Fortunately, Winch had not been standing behind the door when the charm was portioned out. He used all of it on Col Stevens. As he had been using it on everybody, since moving up into this rarefied atmosphere.

"He was one of your old outfit, I guess. Wasn't he? On Guadalcanal?" Col Stevens said dubiously. He leaned against the bar familiarly, at his ease. He liked to come out here from town because of all the old West Point buddies he had in Second Army Command.

Winch was not unwilling to lie. When it was absolutely necessary. In a way, lying might be called the history of his life. "Yes, sir. Guadalcanal," he lied. "But he was hit on New Georgia."

Stevens nodded. That had to count. "We have a lot of men out there who've been hit on some island or some continent," he added nevertheless, mildly.

"True, sir. And most of them are a little goofy for a while."

"But not quite like that. Just what is your point, Mart?" Stevens picked up his glass, and smiled at it. "Do you mind if I call you Mart? I've heard a great deal about you, here and there."

"My pleasure, sir," Winch said promptly, and smiled his most charming smile. Till his jaws ached. "I've heard a good deal about you too, sir, or I wouldn't have approached you. My point is, I hate to lose his ability and his intelligence. That's it, in a nutshell."

"Yes, of course there's that," Stevens murmured. "And what you tell me carries a lot of weight. I don't want to do any good man in." He shook his head. "But I've decided that I don't intend to interfere. I don't really think it's my place."

"Nor would anybody ask you to, sir. Least of all me," Winch said. "But we all of us know, all us old Regulars, that the good civilian doctor Maj Hogan is—shall we say—a little overzealous."

It was funny how you could pump yourself up till you fell into their way of talking; their language. It was just a different way of saying things. Less direct. But you had to be careful then not to overdo it, and let them catch you.

Stevens had smiled, then broken into an unwilling laugh, and now he blushed a little, embarrassedly. Cleared his throat.

"Hogan's certainly not a Regular," Winch said. "Nor does he know how to handle Regulars."

"Your man Landers is not a Regular, either, I think, is he?" Stevens smiled.

"No, sir. He's not. And as a matter of fact, he's a three-and-a-half-year college student. That's another reason I hate to see us lose him. But he acts more like a Regular than a draftee."

"I don't know what to make of a man like that," Col Stevens said, his brows knitted. "He ought to be putting his shoulder to the wheel. Especially at a time like this." He eyed Winch, narrowly.

"He probably doesn't even know anything unusual is going on, sir," Winch said.

"Everybody knows," Stevens said. "Even my wife knows."

He bit his lip, then exploded. Politely. But his gray eyes, which matched his hair, flashed. "I've only had two courts-martial since I've been out there. And both were only summaries."

"Well, there's another way you could do it. You could bust him down to private, sir." Stevens' glass was on the bar, empty, and Winch signaled the enlisted barman for another. Stevens held up his hand and shook his head, demurring. Winch motioned the barman to bring the whiskey anyway. "If you don't want it, somebody else will, sir."

"You're not drinking, yourself?"

"No, sir," Winch said cheerily. "I'm not. I can't. The doctors won't let me. But don't let anybody tell you it isn't missed. I miss it like hell."

The old man snorted his laughter softly.

The glass delivered, Winch suddenly stood away from the bar and held his arm out toward the room. It was getting more crowded now, more smoke-filled. "I'm not keeping you, am I, sir? I didn't mean to do that," Winch lied.

"No, no. No, no," Stevens said. "Go ahead. I want to hear your point out."

"Well, it wasn't much, sir. I just thought that you could bust him to private," Winch said. "He's a buck sergeant, you know. I made him myself. He was my company clerk for a while. Before my battalion colonel stole him to make him his communications sergeant." He smiled again. Winch did not wink, but he did something with his eyes that was almost that. To clinch it, he added, "That was only a few days before he was hit. The battalion colonel didn't even have time to promote him."

"I'm afraid busting him is beyond the authority I have," Stevens said faintly. "These men are all transit casuals, you know. I don't have unit authority over them. It would have to go all the way to Washington."

"It would still be better than a court-martial, sir," Winch said.

The colonel smiled. "I suppose it would at that," he admitted. "But the point. You haven't made any point, Mister Winch."

"I don't have any point, sir. At least, no point except the one I made, which is to save the man." Winch studied his half-finished glass of ice cubes and grapefruit juice on the bar. "It did seem a little strange to me though that the first lieutenant who was involved, the other man in the fight, did not think it worthwhile to prefer charges himself."

Stevens was staring at him, and continued to stare. "That's

true. You're right. He didn't, did he?" he said after a moment.

"Did you talk to him at all, sir?"

"No. No, I didn't. Perhaps I ought to talk to him."

Winch picked up his lousy grapefruit juice and drained the glass to the ice, staring straight ahead. "It might be worth a shot, sir," he said as he set the glass down. "Under the circumstances."

That was the way they left it. Winch knew when to quit. Col Stevens offered a promise that he would talk to the 1st/lt patient who was involved, tomorrow. Then he smiled a slightly crooked smile, before he spoke.

"You know something, Mart? I would be pleased to have had a commanding officer like you. I did have one, for a while once."

"Why, thank you, sir," Winch said, and put up all that he could raise of the humility they thought you were supposed to have, into his most loving, most respectful smile. All he could think of at the moment was how quick he could get the fuck out of there.

"Did you ever think of trying for a commission?" Col Stevens asked.

"No, sir. I didn't. I'm not sure my health would be up to it," Winch smiled cheerily. "Anyway, why should I start taking orders from everybody as a second lieutenant, when as a w/o I can give them."

Stevens smiled. "I suppose you're right, at that."

"I think so, sir," Winch smiled, with the same cheery smile.

Outside, he walked to his little Dodge through the cold winter rain. It was still falling. The Dodge was in the middle of the big new asphalt parking lot for the club. Winch felt as though he had expended as much energy as if he had played the full sixty minutes of a football game, and his knees were shaking. In the car he turned on the windshield wipers and just sat a minute. Grateful he did not have to compose his face into a cheery smile, again. The lights from the club, where he could not stand to be, shown out at him and glinted across the wet asphalt, and prismed through the rain-smeared windshield glass, sardonically promising comfort where he already knew there was none. He could not remember ever having felt so desolate. He would have given everything he had ever owned for a drink, right now.

Out in the air the rain had felt good on his face but in the car he was chilled. He was wearing his new $150 tailored trench coat and one of those brimless overseas caps which were required by regulations now (called *cunt cap* by the troops, because of what the seam across the top made them think of). Ruefully Winch thought about the old campaign hats of before the war, and wished he had had one in the rain. The trench coat had a longer skirt than was usual and was green, the color that was "in," now. The Dodge was the result of a deal Jack Alexander had engineered for him. In town in Luxor was a cozy apartment Alexander had known about, and Carol Firebaugh should be waiting for him there, soon. He should be saving his money, and not spending it on all this ritzy shit, Alexander had told him, or else how could he buy in on anything? Any of the deals?

After a while, he started the car and the heater and drove home to his quarters. In the tiny room he drank the two remaining glasses of white wine in a bottle he had there, and without taking off any of his clothes except the trim winter blouse, fell on the bed and went sound asleep.

He was awakened by the phone, ringing. He woke confused, thinking it was the sound-power field phone from the battalion command post; Col Becker. He was out in the big open field again. And fuck Col Becker. Col Becker couldn't help. Col Becker couldn't even see them, from where Becker was. The mortars were falling on them fore and aft, again. He could see that from where he stood. He was shouting and waving at them frantically and screaming again, "Get them out of there! Get them out of there! Can't you see what they're doing? They're bracketing in on them! Get them out of there!" He bit it back with his teeth, as he sat up and looked at the ordinary, everyday phone as if it were some foreign, alien object on the little bedside stand. Even from this far away, he could see the great white eyes of the platoons, white-white in their muddy faces, looking back at him. For help.

When he picked up the black phone out of its cradle, and cautiously asked who it was, clearing his throat so it would not sound husky, it was Jack Alexander.

He had not cried out. He was sure he hadn't. As long as he didn't cry it out loud, the sentence, as long as he didn't tell anybody about it, or need to tell anybody about it, as long as nobody knew, he would be all right, he was sure he would be.

"Well, what do you want?" he said, more sharply than he had meant to say it.

"Don't bite my head off," the thick voice said. "I just called up to congratulate you. I don't know what you said to the Old Man but you sure sold him."

"I got him to promise to talk to that lieutenant," Winch said.

"Yes. No, I don't mean about Landers. I mean about you. I don't know what you said, but he came away thinking you're about the greatest guy that ever lived," the voice said dryly.

"I didn't tell him anything about me," Winch said.

"I of course did not tell him the truth," the heavy voice said coyly, in a ponderous try at a joke.

Winch tried to get hold of himself. "Yeah. I'm glad you didn't give me away."

Alexander didn't waste breath on any laugh. "I'm to get hold of that lieutenant tomorrow. The Old Man even called me at home. But I'm on call to him all the time, anyway. So we'll talk to the lieutenant tomorrow. Things are looking a good deal better for your boy Landers."

"But what we've got to do is to get Hogan to withdraw all those charges. That's the main thing."

"That asshole," Alexander said. "He's so anxious to get in good with Stevens, he'll squat and strain if Stevens hollers 'shit.' Don't worry about him."

"Well, then it looks pretty good."

"Yeah. Yeah, it does. Say, listen, are you coming on into town tonight? Because—"

"I wasn't planning to," Winch said cautiously.

"There's a couple of guys from out of town going to be here," Alexander said. "Important guys. It would be a good thing for you to meet them."

"I don't know if I can," Winch said. "But I'll try to get in."

"Do it if you can. We'll be at my game at the Claridge. They carry a lot of weight in certain places. Know senators and people." The voice seemed to know that he wasn't going to come, anyway, but nevertheless felt required to go on and do its duty just the same. "Okay, I'll talk to you tomorrow, otherwise." The voice and the phone went dead.

Winch put the phone down and sat and looked at it. The nightmare, so familiar now in all its details, was as strong in his mind as the real conversation. He had no desire to be with Alexander tonight, and no intention of going to the Claridge. Desolation ran all through him and was like the taste of biting on some old copper coin, in his mouth. In this mood he wanted only to be with Carol.

His uniform was wrinkled from being slept in. He put the new winter blouse on over it anyway, without changing. Outside, it was still raining.

It was about thirty-five miles in to Luxor. In the rain, peering out through the slow fan of the wipers, it would take him fifty-five minutes, driving on the old-fashioned, white-concrete highway. Alongside the concrete ran the two-lane blacktop road the government was building. Together they would make a four-lane highway for the convoys into the city's railroad station from O'Bruyerre. Winch settled into the driving, not wanting to think, wanting not to think. About Carol. Or about Alexander.

Alexander was right, of course, with his advice. There was nothing very tricky, or even very dishonest, about the way they were all making money. They did not do anything that your average businessman, after a government contract, didn't do. Mostly it was just knowing the right people. Knowing the right people, and passing along or picking up the right piece of information at the right moment. Occasionally, very occasionally, it might mean slipping a small chunk of money along, too, at the same time.

But mostly it was just knowing the right thing to buy. And to buy at the right time you had to have money, cash. Somebody had to own the Coca-Cola and Budweiser delivery systems that carried all the Coke and beer to all the PXs in the area. Somebody had to own the beer and soft drinks distributorships that supplied them.

T.D. Hoggenbeck had explained it all quite clearly. Buy a bar, he had said. People will always drink. Come hell or high water, depression or boom. People will drink. But before you could buy a bar you had to have that kind of money. And Jack Alexander had the means of acquiring that kind of money. That was why T.D. had sent him to Jack. Jack had the contacts, he knew the people involved. Jack was also, Winch knew, dead right about his advice.

His advice, mainly, was to put by every nickel you could get your hands on. Then when the chance came to buy into some item, you would have the cash. Parts of enough such items, and you would begin to have the kind of money that could buy a bar, or two bars, or three, and pay off the politicians under the counter to get your package-store licenses, and pay for the high-priced licenses themselves. That was all there was to it. It was easy. And, all that was just exactly what Winch was not doing.

Alexander apparently knew there was some woman involved. But he did not know who Carol was. And he wasn't interested in finding out. He wouldn't even ask Winch about it. As far as Alexander was concerned, it had to be some woman. What else would make Winch spend all his cash like some drunken dock-side sailor. Who she was did not matter.

"You're going to regret it," he would say mildly, with his scarred larynx. "Now is the time to buy in. These deals will all be gone, before long."

Winch would always shrug, and promise that the next time he would have the money. Faithfully, Alexander would come and tell him when the next deal opened. Faithfully, Winch would say he didn't have the cash again.

"A cunt aint worth it," Alexander said phlegmatically.

Tacitly Winch agreed. A woman wasn't. None of them was.

"If it wasn't for old T.D., I'd write you off," Alexander said mirthlessly. "And let you go to hell."

Winch could not disagree with that, either. If it were not that he felt he owed T.D. some favors, Alexander would probably do it, too. But it was T.D. who had helped him put it all together.

It was not that Winch was buying Carol fur coats and jewelry. It was not even that he cared that much for Carol, or was madly in love with her. Winch knew, now, already, how all that was going to end.

Winch did not know where all the money went. He knew he spent it. Mainly it was spent in maintaining a certain life-style. A life-style which made his affair with Carol comfortable, and easy, for both of them. A life-style which made their affair, in a word not usual to Winch because he didn't think that way, un-dirty. Un-grubby.

And underneath that truth was another truth, which was that Winch did not really give a damn. Down deep, half of him was glad whenever he could tell Alexander truthfully that he did not have the money for some deal. Half of him was pleased he did not have it. So why not dispense it all on and around Carol? What difference did it make? It was not that he expected some return from it.

Carol. She was quite an interesting girl, Carol was. In her own right. And so now, sitting over the wheel, behind the sweep of the wipers in the rain, he was thinking. Exactly what he had hoped not to do.

Was there ever a woman who did not always already have some man on the string, in her own right, that she was committed to? None. Or very damn few. They were just like men. The idea of being alone, really alone, terrified them. So they clung onto whatever man they had, until they found another that suited them better.

So, the only real alternative to taking a woman away from some other man (who might not want her any more than she wanted him, until he found her being taken away) was the rebound. And she was rare. A woman who had broken up with someone, and was really free. For a short while. Usually the life-span of a rebound did not exceed three months, at the outside. By then she would have found a new one. Rebounding was all in the timing. You had to know, quickly, when not to waste your time. Winch had been quite a rebounder in his day, back when women really meant something to him.

It was right after the first time he had gone down on Carol that she had first mentioned her boyfriend to him.

They were both lying nude on the bed in the Claridge hotel room. He had not yet taken the little apartment. Carol was lying all sprawled out flat, arms and legs spread wide, staring at the ceiling. "Most men don't like to do that," she said faintly.

Winch had to smile. "You mean, most American men. I suppose not. I like it. I like doing it, and I like giving pleasure."

She had such a magnificent young body. Young breasts, flat hips, prominent crotch bone mound. So unworn by living.

"Why do you think they don't like it?"

"Oh," Winch said lazily. "I suppose it's our American religious training. American Christianity. Sex is all scrambled up in with our religion. Evil, dirty, filthy. Guilt. It shouldn't be. It's all very primitive. Medieval. But it's all tied in with our puritanism."

"I never thought of it quite like that," she said. He felt a certain pause of intensity in the air, before she spoke on. She was still staring at the ceiling. But stiffly now. "My boyfriend—up at school—doesn't like it at all, and won't do it," Carol said.

Instinctively Winch sensed he was expected to react to this. A test balloon. From where he lay on his elbow, looking over, looking down at her, he saw her eyes roll toward him once, then flick back to her close scrutiny of the ceiling. Her one cockeye seemed to waver around for a focus up there, on it.

He smiled. "He won't?" he said, easily. "He doesn't?" He let a little pause develop. "Well, he's very young yet."

"Yes he is!" Carol said vehemently. Her eye focus never left the ceiling. "Did you ever go to a whorehouse?"

Winch had to laugh. "Me? Yes. Sure. A lot of times."

"He goes to a whorehouse a great deal."

Winch chewed on this a moment. He was, for no reason he could isolate, enjoying himself immensely. No jealousy, no anguish. No pain. "He probably tells you he goes a great deal more than he actually does," he said.

"Why?"

"To show off."

"It's the only way I can climax," she said. "What you did. Unless I play with myself."

"In my experience, my vast experience," Winch smiled, "very few women can come from simple fucking."

"Really?"

"Yes."

"You don't think there's anything wrong with me, then?"

Winch shook his head. Climax. That must be one of her college words. He had noted that she never would say the word *come*. It had struck him, suddenly, that perhaps she might be lying to him about the boyfriend's whorehouses. Could she be lying to him about the boyfriend, too, then?

She wasn't lying. "I like to do it that way, too," she said. "Like it. Like to do it. But I'd never dare try it, with him. Never dare even suggest it."

"We can arrange that easy enough," Winch grinned.

"Do you mind if I talk to you about him? Tell you about him?"

"No," he said. "Not at all."

He had learned a great deal about him. Then, and since then. He had been Carol's boyfriend, off and on, since high school. He was the second boy she had ever slept with. The first was a secret. Still a secret, even now. She had pretended to be a virgin with the boyfriend. She thought he had believed her. She had quit him once in high school for a while. For an older boy, a college boy. Then she had gone back to him. She had gone to Western Reserve up north largely on the suggestion of the college boy, who did not go to Reserve, but who was studying to be an actor. The boyfriend had followed her. He had intended to go to Mississippi down at Oxford. But he had found out he could study business administration at Reserve. And he said he could not stand to be away from her. At Reserve, she had left him twice, after stormy quarrels, but had always come back to him.

It had been hard for the boyfriend. The men of his family had always gone to Ole Miss. Once he decided to follow her, though, he had fought his family hard. But he was so insular. And so fixed. And stubborn. He was exactly like all the parts of Luxor she had wanted to get away from.

At school both times she had left him she had had affairs with older persons. Once with a senior boy, when she was a sophomore. Once with an English instructor, a married man, when she was a junior. Both, of course, had been impossible situations. Untenable. Both times the boyfriend had accepted her back, without any questions. He had been a perfect gentleman. Half of her, or some fraction less than half, had wished he had not been.

He always had wanted them to marry, as soon as they both graduated, when he came back home to go into business.

She had never agreed. She had refused to become engaged officially.

He was just so damned insular. When he was drunk, he was absolutely crude. That was when he talked about going to a whorehouse.

Lying naked on the bed beside Winch that first night she talked about him, Carol had suddenly blushed, all the way down into her breasts.

Once at a party, when he had gotten drunk and crude and jealous, and had passed out, in a fit of anger she had gone off with a lone dateless man, and had slept with him, outside, in the back seat of one of the cars. The boyfriend had never suspected.

"I've never told that to anyone."

"It's safe with me," Winch smiled.

"I don't want to be a Southern belle," Carol said. She paused a moment thoughtfully. "But I'm afraid I'm a Southern belle, anyway."

"You're a beautiful Southern belle," he said, emphasizing the descriptive adjective.

She raised her head off the sheet and looked appreciatively

down along her nudeness, blushing again. "Not like in any of the War of the Rebellion lithographs, I'm not," she said.

This had been in mid-November. And quite soon after, it came out that the boyfriend was coming home from school for Thanksgiving. She would not be able to see Winch for a few days. Perhaps a week. She hoped Winch would not mind. She hoped he would not hold it against her. She hoped he would not be jealous. And that it would not—change anything.

Winch had smiled. "No. It won't. I've got plenty to keep me busy."

"You won't be lonely?"

"No, I won't be lonely."

Suddenly she laughed. "Damn you."

He smiled. "Well, maybe I'll be a little lonely."

That was better, she had said. "You see, I can't help being a Southern belle."

When she came back from Thanksgiving, the first thing she said was that the boyfriend had said he "knew I had a lover."

Winch laughed. "How do you think he knew?"

"He said he could tell by the way I acted. I was too happy. Of course, I denied it."

And now the same thing had come up again lately, about Christmas. The boyfriend was coming home for Christmas vacation from school. She would not be able to see Winch for quite a while. Maybe three weeks. And of course by now Winch had the apartment.

"I'll try to sneak away and slip off at least once," Carol said.

"Don't worry," Winch had smiled. He was back to duty by now, out at O'Bruyerre, and busy in a very real way.

He did not really know what he thought about the boyfriend. He apparently was just a good, solid, generally good-natured, thoroughly fucked-up, upper-class Southern boy. Winch certainly did not envy him his marriage to Carol—if and when it came to pass. And Winch felt pretty sure it would come to pass. He felt a certain sympathy for the boy, more than anything.

"He wants me to be like his mother," Carol said about him once. "And at the same time, he halfway wants me to be his whore."

"But if you're his whore, you can't be like his mother," Winch smiled.

"Exactly!"

But it was curious Winch was not jealous. He wasn't. The time she spent with the boyfriend at Thanksgiving did not bother him. He did not conjure up painful pictures of her in bed with him, and brood about them. Instead, he felt he was very lucky. More than anything. A lucky weekender.

Perhaps it was just age. And his physical condition. But, what the hell, he was getting it up with her now more than he ever had with any woman, for quite some time. She was blowing him well, he was teaching her. And he was blowing her well. Apparently. And the fucking they had going was of a superior quality.

What better deal could a man of his years ask for?

Suddenly, a picture of his white-eyed platoons, wherever they were, blossomed in his head. And with it, screamingly, came up the single, silent sentence of his nightmare. *Get them out of there! Damn it! Get them out of there!* Winch bit it back. But on the wheel, his hands were slippery.

The apartment Alexander had found for him had been the biggest single item of expense. He had had to pay a large sum under the counter, in cash, to get it. The monthly rental was high. The next biggest item was the car Alexander had put him on to. And the black-market gas Alexander had made him privy to.

Lately, after her revelation of the expected Christmas visit, Carol had begun asking his advice about various things. This tickled a fatherly perversity in Winch. For the moment, it was the boy's military status. He had a deferment, until he graduated in the spring. Then, his father had it fixed to keep him out on a bogus local deferment. But the boyfriend wanted to enlist right now. Quit school and enlist. It was going to be the big fight of their Christmas.

Winch had told her to tell him to stay out. Whatever else happened, stay the hell out. And if he did go in, he should get his father to get him some kind of a commission, preferably with a job in Washington attached to it.

Suddenly, under the wipers, a white picture formed on the windshield glass in the rain, as though it had been etched by Steuben or one of those big glassmakers. It interfered with Winch's vision of the road in the headlight beam. Winch stared at it, engrossed, as it took clearer shape, and recognized it.

It was Jacklin. Pfc Freddie Jacklin? He was one of the men, one of the dead, from the platoons. The forever beleaguered platoons of Winch's mind. The glass picture of him was an exact replica of the way Winch had seen him last. Winch had been going down the gently sloping forward slope of a knoll. Not much grass. Winch had glanced back once, a scanning look, before going into the jungle that came part way up. Jacklin had been lying there.

He was facing downhill, on his back, his head thrown back, one arm out one arm in, a grimace of intense effort on his face, above the open mouth and eyes, his big chest extended as if still trying vainly to draw air. Winch had not known where he was hit. Had not even known he'd been hit.

Now he was on the windshield, etched in white bevels and lines and grooves, and he was obstructing Winch's vision. Wherever he moved his head or eyes, the figure moved in front of them. A fucking obstructionist!

By peripheral vision Winch could see the car was edging toward the road edge. He tried to adjust his steering, but could not do it fast enough. The right front wheel, then immediately the right rear, caught in the soft, rain-soaked shoulder.

There was the scream of rubber, and the rending of metal, and then the car was halfway in the roadside ditch, front end down, but turned clear around and there was silence, the motor turning over and ticking in the quiet.

Automatically, Winch turned off the ignition. Then just sat in the stillness for a while. It was the first time any of his nightmares had actually impinged upon his outside physical world and affected it. That would bear some thinking about.

As he sat, he realized slowly that there was nobody at all around, anywhere.

Fortunately, he was able to back out. The metal damage was negligible, mostly a bent headlight, fender and bumper. He could still drive it. Luxor was still five miles off.

Nothing happened the rest of the way. As if satisfied, the figure of Jacklin did not return.

At the apartment, which was the upstairs of a private home downtown not too far from the Peabody, he parked the damaged car and hurried up the outside stairs in the rain to the upper floor.

Inside, Carol put down the book she was reading and stood up. All the lights were on, the way he liked it. She was fully clothed. She hated to undress herself or lie around half-nude, and always waited for him to come and do it. She looked very young. Incredibly young. She held out her arms for him to come and begin undressing her. Winch did so.

"What happened? What's wrong?" she said when she saw his face.

Winch did not answer and buried his face in her young, unwounded, hungry shoulder.

"Oh, whatever is going to become of us?" she said, in her emotional child's voice.

"Nothing," Winch said. "Hush. For God's sake, just don't talk."

CHAPTER 23

The summons to report to Col Stevens in his office came when Landers had been on ward arrest for over a week.

Landers had no way of knowing Winch had gotten involved in his case. And if he had known, he would not have been elated. Landers had decided lately he no longer liked Winch so much. He wanted no help from Winch. He did not know Winch had called Strange about him that same morning, on Strange's ward, and that in fact Strange was supposed to get him a message about the developments. So he went up to the lion's den with a daredevil's, I've-got-nothing-to-lose attitude that was not really in keeping with all that had transpired.

Strange would kick himself in the tail, later in the day, for not having gotten to him before he went. But then later still, Strange wondered whether it could have helped.

Being on ward arrest was not actually all that bad. Even Landers had to admit that. There were no chains or handcuffs to wear. The ward door was not locked. It was more like some sort of school honor system. But if you stepped outside the door, or went off walking away somewhere, you immediately became officially a fugitive. In practice, it did not work out that way and

Landers was often outside the door, talking to somebody or other, and when he was sent to his medical appointments outside in the hospital he went alone, not under guard. If he stopped off a few minutes to see somebody, nobody checked up on him. He was required to eat all his meals on the ward, and not allowed to go and stand in the long line at the big messhall, but this was a gain, a great boon, as far as he was concerned. He had total freedom of the ward itself. And he was allowed to have visitors.

On the other hand, he was not for some reason allowed to make or receive phone calls. He had never made or taken phone calls on the ward, nor wanted to. So the restriction didn't hurt him. But it irritated him because of its unreasonable, Army nonsensicality.

Another thing that irritated Landers was that his uniforms were locked up, in the lockup closet with the uniforms of the medically restricted patients. If he did walk off the ward without permission, where the hell was he going to go? In pajamas and bathrobe and slippers?

But mainly it was that he had no more all-day, all-night passes which got to Landers the most. He had grown accustomed to getting fucked every night, at least once. And the absence of human females afflicted him sorely. He had become used to these exceptional, wounded-patient hospital passes, they seemed one of his natural rights. Now it struck him, forcibly, that when he did go back to duty with the ordinary, everyday Army, even on limited duty, he would no longer have them.

He did not like the attitude the others on the ward had developed toward his incarceration. His restriction had become a joke to them, instead of the basic, mean tragedy that it was. "Hey, Landers," one would call, "I'll think of you tonight, when I'm deep-humping my big juicy wet slippery pussy." Or, "Hey, Landers. I'll dip a finger for you tonight. Bring it back and let you sniff it. A dollar a sniff."

Then they would finish dressing, and all troop out into the noon day in uniform and Landers would stay behind in the empty-seeming ward with the medically restricted, who could not go out, and who were continually coming in with new batches of lower-leg wounds from some battle front or other, but who were certainly not much sport, no great shakes, to talk to.

The winter weather change affected him strongly, in his

locked-up state. Affected him very adversely. Free, or relatively so, with the hospital day passes, he had moved into town and around the city, watching the lingering Southern fall change to the rains of winter, with a melancholy that matched the drooping leaves, and whispered to him privately that this was the last autumn he would be seeing. There was no question now that he would go back to duty. And no question in Landers' mind that he would do so just in time to be killed, murdered, in the big European push that had to be coming. Mournfully he accepted it. But Strange's suite at the Peabody, with its kaleidoscopic changing of women, was a great, if temporary, antidote for this.

Now that was gone and lights were being left burning longer and longer in the mornings, and being turned on earlier and earlier in the late afternoon. And Landers would sit around on the little, glass-enclosed dayroom porch, playing solitaire or trying to read, and watch the lights being switched on in the other porches down the way, on his own side, and across the way, in the other bay.

Midmornings his archenemy Hogan came in, with the other doctors, for morning rounds. Landers sat his chair at attention like a good soldier. But he stared his dislike and hatred across silently at Hogan, and Hogan glared his own dislike and hatred back at him. Neither ever spoke.

It was little wonder to Landers that he felt mean and gross and flamboyant, as he walked up to Col Stevens' office. In full uniform, and under guard.

Make an example of him. What did he have to lose? Might as well be shot for a mean wolf as for a shitty sheep dog.

It was some wonder to Col Stevens, though. The arrogance, the cockiness, of the young man was a palpable force in the room of the office. Stevens thought all that already had been taken care of, by Winch.

The boy was even wearing all his ribbons, including his Purple Heart and a Bronze Star. Stevens felt guilty enough about his age and where he was, without being reminded. The whole of it irked him exceedingly.

Stevens had meant to say how he had found extenuating circumstances in Landers' case, and that he had been given a highly laudatory recommendation of Landers. It had been his intention, up to now, to let Landers off without even breaking him, because of Winch. Now, instead, he spoke shortly, and much more sharply than he'd intended.

"Well, what have you got to say for yourself?"

In fact, Landers' arrogance had been shrunk a great deal from what it was originally, only a moment before. That was the moment when he opened the outer door, and came into the presence of the statue-like, giant figure of Chief W/O Jack Alexander.

The w/o had looked huge, just sitting behind the desk. Then he had stood up. Landers thought he was the biggest man he had ever seen. The icy blue of his pale blue eyes bored into Landers' soul. The bone edges of his hard mouth looked ready to physically take bites out of Landers. On the square bald head the giant face was as without expression as the eyes or mouth, as without expression as expressionless could get, neither contempt, nor pity, nor liking there. Combat service meant nothing to this soldier, his whole life had been one long war. It was the natural state of things.

The message seemed to be, if Landers was getting it, something like: Whatever the fuck it is you're doing, you dumb punk kid, for God's sake try to do it like a soldier.

But he hardly said ten actual words. Landers had seen him around the hospital compound at a distance, and at the medals awards ceremony, but he had never thought of him as so big, or so formidable.

It took every ounce of power Landers possessed to pull back any arrogance at all, in the short time he had, between Alexander and the opening inner door. And he did not lose hold of the message the huge, room-filling ex-heavyweight, ex-1st/sgt seemed to be communicating.

Certainly it affected his first answer. Probably it affected all the others.

"Nothing, sir," he said staunchly. "I don't have anything to say for myself." He continued to stand at attention, since Stevens had not ordered him to stand at ease.

"At ease," Stevens said. "I expect you know," he said thinly, but much more mildly, "that Major Hogan has preferred four counts of charges against you."

"Yes, sir," Landers said.

"And from what I can gather in investigating, Major Hogan is well within his rights. More than."

"Yes, sir," Landers said, ungivingly. But he was glad Jack Alexander was not in the room. Alexander would have made it harder.

"You attacked and struck an officer, then engaged in a *fight* with him, in the recreation hall in front of twenty witnesses, and when Major Hogan remonstrated with you in the hall outside, you cursed him, insulted him, and physically threatened him. Then you disappeared, and went AWOL, for five days, before returning."

"Yes, sir."

"And you have nothing to say to any of this?"

"No, sir."

"You have no defense to make, at all?"

"No, sir," Landers said, unbendingly. This would have been the moment for abject apology. He let it pass. He didn't feel like an apology. He was boiling mad. At the unfairness of all of it, and he did not care now whether Alexander was in the room or not.

"If I sit back, and let this thing go through," Stevens said, "you'll come before a special court-martial. And that you'll be convicted, with a sentence of three months or six months, with loss of grade and forfeiture of pay and allowances, there's not much doubt."

"No, sir," Landers said, unwavering. But he hadn't thought it would be quite that bad.

"Major Hogan has indicated he might be willing to withdraw the charges," Stevens said, and waited.

Landers did not answer.

"I think I might be able to talk him into doing that," Stevens said, and waited again.

"May I speak frankly, sir?" Landers said. "Frankly, sir, I don't give much of a damn one way or the other." There, so it was out. He wondered if Alexander would have approved the manner. Or Winch. Probably not.

Stevens sat back in his chair, and moved some papers, noting abstractedly that his hands were shaking. With anger. He was trying so hard to be completely fair. To this dumb punk kid.

"Have you ever been in an Army stockade, Landers?"

"No, sir."

"They're tough," Stevens said, more mildly, now that he had more control. "They're not easy."

"May I speak frankly, sir."

"Go ahead," Stevens said, and nodded.

"The lieutenant involved insulted my old outfit. He had no business doing that. He said we ought to come over to Europe if we wanted to see some real fighting. Besides, he didn't have any business in there. In the recreation hall. It's an enlisted man's hall. He came in there looking for a Ping-Pong game.

"Major Hogan, when he stopped me in the hall, accused me of malingering. He said if I could play Ping-Pong like that, and fight like that, I ought to be back to duty, and that I was malingering by staying in the hospital. That's why I cursed him, and that's why I insulted him. As for threatening him, I said I'd like to beat him up. But I didn't."

"Why did you go AWOL?" Stevens said.

"I was sick of the whole thing, that's why. I was sick of this place, and the people in it, and the war, and everything else. Major Hogan doesn't deserve to be an officer. He's never treated anyone fairly here, and everybody knows it. He's probably a bum as a doctor, on the outside. He's never been shot at, he's never been in danger, he's never seen men blown up beside him. I'll probably be killed in this war. Certainly I expect to be. But he won't be, and you won't be, and neither will most of the people here. He doesn't deserve the job he's got, and he shouldn't be where he is. He shouldn't have it. And if there was any justice at all in this Army he'd be canned."

He stopped.

"Is that all you have to say?" Stevens said.

"Yes, sir," Landers said.

"All right then, Landers. You may go."

"Yes, sir. I just want you to know that I don't expect to get any square deal. And I won't get one in this trial. That's why I don't really give a damn. The whole thing is a big fat joke. On me." He drew himself up to attention and saluted and about-faced.

He didn't know, as he left, that Stevens behind him in the office was wanting to jump up on his feet and yell with rage, and was instead resolutely studying his pale fingernails. Landers didn't know because he was doing all he could to maintain his ego and combat the enormous, reproving presence of Jack Alexander which filled the outer room.

Back at his own ward Strange was waiting for him. With the message "to play ball" that Winch had asked him to deliver. When Landers gave him a detailed account blow-by-blow, quote-for-quote of the interview, Strange began to curse him.

Despite Strange, Landers had a weird sense of growing elation he had not had when he left the big office. When he left

Stevens and Alexander, he had been suffering a deep depression. He had heard enough about stockades, one place and another, to picture graphically what it would be like for him when he was delivered to one. That was what he had done to himself. But slowly, as he walked back, the armed guard marching behind him, the strange elation had begun, and then had grown and grown. By the time he reached the exiling ward door, it had completely transformed the depression. While Strange railed at him, he simply sat and smiled beatifically.

"What the fuck are you smiling about?" Strange demanded. "Well, we'll just have to wait and see," he finally finished lamely. "See what he does."

They had to wait two days. Then orders came down from the administrator's office, one copy to Landers, one to be posted on the ward bulletin board, to the effect that the special court-martial had not been called, and that orders were being cut to be forwarded to Washington for approval that the transit casual Sgt Landers, Marion J be reduced to private and all pay and allowances of sgt be withdrawn and discontinued.

"I think you got off damned lucky," Strange said. "Considering." There was an urgency in his voice, and on his face. "I don't think you got one damn thing to complain about."

He then proceeded to tell Landers, who did not know, about the two days of phone calls and talks that had gone on, to avoid the court-martial. Winch had been the prime mover, behind it. Alexander had been for the court-martial, but hadn't really cared.

"If he had cared," Strange said, "believe me, you'd have got it."

Col Stevens had been against the court-martial, when he got over being angry. He did not think what Landers had done was all that terrible. The whole thing had rested on the conscience of Stevens. And Winch had played on that. Though he did not like Landers personally, in fact detested him personally, Stevens did not think what he had done really deserved the special court Hogan was after.

"You can thank your lucky stars that that old man has a conscience," Strange said, urgently. "Hell, if you hadn't acted up like you did, you wouldn't even have got busted."

Landers was curiously disappointed. Though he did not tell this to Strange. He had geared himself up emotionally for the trial. And its conviction, which he knew would be a foregone conclusion of it. And for his three to six months sentence, which he felt he had readied himself for. Being busted to private seemed like a ridiculous, terrible anticlimax after the possibility of all that. He had proved to himself, to his own satisfaction, an important moral point, moral issue, about the whole US Army —only to have the damned schoolboy conscience of that one old man ruin it and throw it all out.

Also, his nightmares had stopped. The dream about the platoon and Landers' one canteen of water which kept recurring to him had ceased on the night of the day of the interview with Stevens, and had not come back until several days after the administrative order had come down. That in itself had been a blessed boon to him. At least, while it lasted.

"I can understand his disliking me," he said to Strange at one point in their discussions. "But do you really think he *detests* me? That was the word you used. Where did you get that word?"

"It was Winch's word," Strange said. "He used it." The odd look of urgency had come back over his face. "Winch would never use that word himself. So I reckon he heard the old man use it."

"But detests," Landers said. "That's pretty strong." He looked into Strange's eyes, with their urgency which still did not make any sense to Landers. "If he detests me, it's because I showed him what hypocrites he and the Army are," he said righteously, "for not firing Hogan.

"He's never been shot at, neither has Hogan," he finished inconclusively. "None of them has. Or ever will be."

"No," Strange said. "I don't reckon they ever will be." The silent look of urgency, Landers noted, had not left his face.

"What's this with Winch?" Landers asked him. "I didn't ask him for anything. I don't want any help from him."

"You better be damn glad you had help from him," Strange said. "Without him you'd be in jail."

"Fuck him. He never comes around. We never see him. We never hear from him. He never comes up to the hotel."

"He's busy out at O'Bruyerre. He's back to duty, and holding down a whole new job," Strange said. "But he keeps an eye on us. Besides, he's got some little girl he's shacking up with."

"Who? Not that little girl I tried to make?"

"I don't know, honestly," Strange said. "And I don't care. Why? Does that make you sore?"

"Me? Are you kidding?"

"Well, what's eating you then?"

"Nothing," Landers said. "But fuck Winch."

With his tentative bust to private in the works, Landers was no longer on ward arrest. He was able to go back to the suite at the Peabody. Until the demotion was approved in Washington he was not required to remove his sergeant's stripes, so he didn't. He found he had a really serious reluctance to part with them that was totally unanticipated. Especially around the Peabody.

But getting back to the Peabody was not the great thrill he had imagined so heatedly, when he was being kept away from it. The girls were all pretty much the same girls. And the few new ones were not that much different. The fellows were all still the same fellows. Corello, and Trynor, and the others. Strange apparently had developed a permanent relationship with Frances Highsmith, and no longer came around to the suite much, though he still saw to it that all its bills were paid, as did Landers himself. With Strange gone, Landers became the leader. He developed a semipermanent relationship himself, with Mary Lou Salgraves. But none of it was really that exciting.

Landers had lied to Col Stevens only once, and that had been during the interview when Stevens had asked him about his ankle. Stevens understood that Landers had reinjured his ankle in the fight in the rec hall with the lieutenant. He was given this impression by Landers' surgeon, Curran, who had examined the ankle after the fight. Actually, the ankle had been reinjured in the first fight he and Strange had had with the Navy petty officers in the hotel bar, and then reinjured again when Landers had kicked the Air Force ferry commando in the head. But Curran had not known about this, and had not examined the ankle after the first fights, had assumed the ankle was reinjured in the hospital fight, and Landers had not felt up to telling either Curran or Stevens the whole truth about it.

It was not until after the whole thing was over and the court-martial had been canceled that Curran told Landers he had known about the ankle all along. They were together in Curran's little office, after the most recent examination of it.

He had grinned. "Yes, it's not too hard to tell from the swelling, or lack of it, if a muscle or a joint has been injured recently. It's harder to tell how long ago, or how many times, something has been hurt, if the injury was at some time in the past. I just knew, was pretty sure, that you hadn't done it in that particular fight."

"Why didn't you tell that to Col Stevens?" Landers said.

Curran was still grinning, that funny little private smile of his. "Well, you obviously hadn't told him yourself. For some private reason of your own. I just wanted to back you up, and give you some maneuvering room if that was what you wanted, or felt you needed."

"I just didn't want them to know about the other fights, back then at the beginning," Landers said.

"I figured it was something like that," Curran said. He shrugged. "Sit down, Marion," he indicated the chair on the other side of the desk. "You and I have known each other quite awhile, now. Enough to get to know each other pretty well."

Landers took the chair gingerly. And sat in it a little stiffly. Then he proceeded suddenly, without having thought it out, to tell Curran about the two earlier fights, in detail. By the time he finished they were both of them laughing. On the strength of that he told in detail about the other fights he had had over the past months, the ones in which he had not hurt anything. Except a barked fist, or a jammed knuckle or two.

Curran made a large, elaborate shrug, and then held up his two surgeon's hands. He wiggled the eight fingers and two thumbs in the air. "I simply can't do something like that. I'd be out of a job."

"I don't think it's all that great," Landers said, lamely.

"I've been wanting to talk to you, Marion." Curran hitched his swivel chair a little closer to the desk. For intimacy. "Normally I don't talk to anybody except about their surgical problems. But you're on the verge of getting into serious trouble."

Landers stared at him. "You mean like going to the stockade?"

Curran nodded.

Landers grinned. "I'm already in serious trouble. I'm going to get killed in this war. I'm futureless."

"Think beyond that. Think about after the war."

"I can't."

"You don't want to get into trouble with the Army and wind up with a dishonorable discharge that will dog you the rest of your life."

"I can't think about after," Landers said again. "There's no after there. There's nothing. A blank wall. A curtain of fog, that I can't see beyond."

Curran peered at him piercingly. "You really mean that?"

"Sure," Landers said. "There's no after the war. Not for me. It's easy for you. You'll go on. You'll go into surgery, have a big career, become famous, you'll help humanity and make lots of money. Incidentally. It's easy for you."

Curran pursed his mouth, still peering. "Yes. I guess it is. I guess that's exactly what it will be like. I feel guilty enough about it, as it is, without your mentioning it." He stared at Landers again. "But you really do feel that," he said. "How did you say it? That there's 'a curtain of fog' you can't see beyond."

"Sure," Landers said. "That's exactly what it's like. There isn't anything there."

After a moment, Curran's hand reached out and pushed his chair back, back a little way, from the desk. Didn't take long, Landers thought with an inward grin.

"You'll be going back to duty, before long," Curran said in a different voice. "I'll be sending you to the rehab cen soon."

Rehabilitation center, Landers the old-timer translated. His outfit hadn't even had those words. That was the barracks off in the far corner of the paved central compound. Everybody with atrophied muscles went there for a while for toning up, before going back to total duty.

"Your ankle's all right. It's not in bad shape," Curran said in the changed voice. "You're lucky you didn't do it more damage. But you can't get in any fights with it for a while. Ping-Pong's all right, you can play all the Ping-Pong you like. But the sudden, enforced, disruptive violence of fighting could damage it again, much worse. I want you to remember that," he said sharply. "If you came in with it hurt again, it would not look good to Stevens."

"Injustice and insults bug me," Landers said.

Curran ignored that. "You'll be classified limited duty. Don't thank me. That's your true classification. That ankle's no good for infantry, that's for sure. Anyway, limited duty isn't all that different. About two out of every five wounded we get are limited-duty men. Quartermaster Gasoline Supply Companies, in the tank fighting. That kind. Even that isn't accurate because in the QM Gas Supply Companies the biggest number of casualties are never found. If an eighty-eight shell hits a truck that is loading."

"I may not be in that."

"No." Curran stood up. "I'm Irish. I'm a superstitious man. I even believe in leprechauns. If you tell me you see a curtain of fog in front of you—" He shrugged. "What can I say? There's nothing I can say."

Landers grinned. "I'll tell you something else. I no longer believe in humanity, either. Or care about them. I think we're a doomed race. Like the dinosaurs. We just don't know it. I guess the brontosaurus and tyrannosaurus didn't know it either, when they were feeding. We've overspecialized ourselves out of existence. Like they did."

"When did you decide all this?"

"I don't know. Sometime after I was hit. I was sitting on a hill, watching them all fighting, down below in the valley."

"It's pretty bleak," Curran said. "I hope you're wrong."

"Yes. Well, I'm not," Landers smiled. "It's pretty bleak, all right," he agreed. "Especially when you find you don't care. We've overspecialized ourselves in war. A war will do us."

"You think this war?" Curran said quickly.

"No. Probably not. But it doesn't matter. Some later one will. The human causes no longer matter."

"You think human causes no longer matter?" Curran asked quickly.

"Nope. Not as long as we continue to kill each other over them."

Curran nodded.

Still standing behind his desk, Curran moved his feet, and shifted his weight, awkwardly. Hesitantly, he brought his right hand halfway up.

"You should be out of here by the first of the year. We'll probably have a chance to talk again. But in case we don't—" He held the hand out shyly.

Landers took it and shook it. It felt warm and cool and dry. But then, his own hand was, too.

As he closed the glassed door, he looked back and grinned inwardly again, over what he saw. Curran was already seated back at his desk, writing furiously, on papers out of Landers' file.

Fuck him, he thought with vast amusement. Let him write it all down for the bastards.

He felt pretty much that same way about everything else. And everybody. Except for Strange, and occasionally Bobby Prell. Certainly he didn't give a damn about Winch. Or the people at the Peabody suite. None of them cared, really, about anybody else.

And now Strange had more or less dropped him, and dropped everybody else, for this woman. This Frances Highsmith. That he was hanging out with.

And Bobby Prell appeared to have dropped them all, too. Including himself and Strange. Prell was getting around a little bit now on his legs, the least little bit, but he never came into town with them, and never came up to the Peabody. One day, riding into town in the taxi with Strange, Strange told Landers that Prell had told him that he Prell was going to get married.

"Married?" Landers said, and then grinned. "Married? Who the hell to?"

"To that little girl on his ward he's been doing. Been hanging around with."

"When?"

"I don't know," Strange said, staring out at the slow winter rain. "He didn't say when."

"He's crazy," Landers said, definitively.

"Probably," Strange said, softly.

But in the taxis riding in was about the only time Landers got to see Strange. Or so it seemed, any more.

He didn't mind. It was as if he were saying good-by to all of them, in a finite way. Their time together was running out. Their common interests changed. He would be alone, when he went back into the fire. As they all would be. If they went back at all to it.

At least he knew how long he had. Curran had told him he had until around the first of the year. That was less than a month. That wasn't too long. On the other hand, Landers did not know what he wanted to do, or could do, for a whole month.

It was funny but in each case it was a woman who had pulled them away. Females. Pussy. Cunt. Had split the common male interest. Cunt had broken the centripetal intensity of the hermetic force which sealed them together in so incestuous a way. Their combat. Cunt vs combat. In his cups Landers decided he had discovered quite by accident the basic prevailing equation of the universe.

If the universe is represented by a floating compass, and the cock is a sliver of iron rubbed on a magnet, it will always point due North to cunt. Always. No matter what.

This was the equation modern man had broken, to his peril, with his creation and introduction of mechanized, social, group combat, for some fucking damned cause or other.

But sobered up he didn't think so much of it.

And half-sobered up he suddenly remembered when he was a boy his father when he was drunk had this song he sang, "Those Wedding Bells/Are Breaking Up/That Old Gang of Mine." That was the only line Landers could remember. But he remembered the rest of the tune. He went around whistling it to himself, for a day or two. Until he wore out its poignancy.

He saw no reason why he should not do it, too. Since the others were all doing it. Even if only for a month. But his new dislike for and distrust of humans included the females. It was not that there were not opportunities. One night at the Peabody, during their two hours allotted time on one of the beds, Mary Lou, cuddling up to him with her breasts and pubes after a rousing fuck, said, "I think I could fall seriously in love with you."

This was very flattering. Too flattering to refuse totally. "Don't," Landers said immediately, and then quickly amended, "Or at least don't too much. Just a little."

"Why not?"

"Because I don't know where I'm going, or what I'll be doing. You don't want to be in love with a combat infantryman, do you?"

"Maybe."

"You wouldn't marry one, would you?"

"Maybe. I might. What are your allotments?"

"Very low. And don't forget, I'm not a sergeant any more. I'm back to base pay."

She laughed. "That's true. That's an important point," Mary Lou said huskily. "Oh, I think I am, falling in love with you, Marion."

"Good," he said. "Let's leave it at that." He brought his raised arm down gently onto the top of her head. "I'll be gone soon, and you can fall in love with another one."

This new cynicism about females served as a braking mechanism, in the month he had left. He did not fall in love. But it was hard to tell whether new types of female-related experience were created by the cynicism, to hunt him down; or whether now he simply saw the new experience standing there, where before he would have passed blindly by, protected by innocence.

Some of them, outside the Peabody, were pretty bizarre. None of them featured poor Mary Lou. But Landers had no time to think about them, then. The days passed with a swift inexorability that was the essence of a tragedy in a drama. Like some Shakespearean play, or some dumb war movie. He would have plenty of time to think about the woman-experiences later, when he was mired in the muddy depths of Camp O'Bruyerre. Plenty of time, with no passes except on weekends. By Christmas he had long been out in the rehab cen, doing GI calisthenics and running in the mornings. His ankle seemed in fine shape. Much better than Curran had made it sound.

Landers ate Christmas dinner in the rehab cen barracks, alone. And in a self-castigating, tooth-biting way he enjoyed it. Nobody there knew anybody else, or tried to. They were all on temporary assignment, before shipping off to various destinations. All of it was so familiar. The turkey and dressing and cranberries, and mashed potatoes and yams, lay like a lump of lead in his belly.

Landers, a pvt now, with the traditional dark spots on his sleeves, could have gotten a three-day pass to go home for Christmas, but chose not to. Besides, he did not want to miss any of his nights up at the Peabody or off alone in downtown Luxor. At the Peabody he wanted to eat another, real Christmas dinner but couldn't, because of the undigested one.

On Christmas day the papers carried the names of the commanders of the European expeditionary forces, and their assignments. It was the big, lead story. IKE TO LEAD ALLIED INVASION OF FRANCE. Eisenhower, Omar Bradley, and Patton were off to England. President Roosevelt, everyone's great hero, had shrewdly chosen December 24 to make his announcement, so that correspondents would have time to cable the news home for the Christmas papers release.

By the tenth of January Landers was reporting to the chief of Second Army Command G-1 Personnel Section, for reassignment. The chief of Second Army Command Personnel turned out to be W/O Mart Winch, his former 1st/sgt.

CHAPTER 24

Strange had told Winch on the phone, "I think he's going crazy, if he aint already crazy." But then Strange had not been able to explain what he meant, and had simply fumbled it around. He said he didn't mean crazy in any ordinary, accepted sense. "He's not cutting out paper dolls or anything." But his ideas were not tracking. His thoughts were not following each other in any reasonable manner. "It's hard to explain," Strange ended lamely, "or even see. Unless you've spent as much time with him as I have."

"Well, I'll have to watch it. I'll just have to watch for it," Winch had mumbled. He was wondering if Landers was having nightmares, like those he himself was having. Strange of course couldn't know that. And Winch wouldn't ask.

"I aint spent as much time with him as I ought to have," Strange said guiltily.

"Fuck him," Winch said. "Everybody has to do a little something for himself on his own."

Winch had not changed his mind about that. He still felt the same way, when one of his twenty-three clerks brought Landers

320

into his private office in the Command's three-story headquarters building.

Landers clearly did not know that he was receiving special treatment. Usually hospital reassignments never got past one of the twenty-three clerks. Winch himself never saw them. But he was not going to tell that to Landers.

Nor, Winch received the distinct impression, if Landers had known, would he have been very interested, impressed, or moved. Or affected.

But Winch had given explicit instructions that he wanted to see Landers, when he reported for duty. Landers obviously could not have cared less. Also, Landers was three days late, three days AWOL, Winch noted when he examined his papers.

Landers on the other hand, which Winch could not know, was surprised. He knew from Strange that Winch had made w/o and had moved into a big important job. But he had not guessed at the magnitude of the importance. This was at least the office of a colonel, that Winch was installed in.

"I see you're a little late," Winch said to him.

"Yes," he said. "I took myself a three-day pass. To say good-by to my girl. They wouldn't give me one."

"Say good-by?" Winch said. "She's only thirty-five miles away."

"Yes," Landers said. And would say no more.

Winch stared at him. Landers smiled. If Winch couldn't figure it out, to hell with him.

"I see," Winch said. "You don't have a car, and wouldn't be getting any passes except weekends. If then."

"Yes," Landers said. "But also, she's one of the girls that hangs around up at our suite in the Peabody."

Winch continued to stare at him, and nodded.

"She's in love with me," Landers explained reasonably. "But I couldn't ask her to be faithful to me. Not up there. Not around that bunch."

"And you couldn't ask her to move out here to the village," Winch said.

"I asked her," Landers said. "She didn't want to. I couldn't blame her for that." He felt very equable.

"So you took three days off to say good-by to her," Winch said. "All lovey-dovey."

"Yes," Landers said, stiffly.

"Great," Winch said. "Fine. Beautiful."

"I view it as just another casualty of the war," Landers said.

"Casualty?" Winch said. "Well, we can fix that AWOL up," he said. "Right here in this office. We can fix up a lot of things here in this office."

"Oh?" It was all Landers would let himself say. He did not expect, or want or need, any help from Winch's shitty office. But Winch apparently did not understand that point, either. Because he went on.

"There are a lot of things this office can do, for certain people," Winch said. "If you know me, you're a friend of Jack Alexander. And if you know Jack Alexander—" He let it trail off, and grinned.

"Besides," Landers said, "she doesn't know where I'll be, or what will happen to me. When I leave here."

"You may never leave here," Winch said.

"We can only assume it will be bad," Landers said. "And that's no way to leave a girl. Especially a Peabody girl."

"Yeah. Well, I said you may never leave here," Winch said, a lot louder. "You may even have your own car yourself. And all the passes you can handle."

"Yes?" Landers said. "Ah, how? How so?"

"Very easy. Just assign you to myself here. You're more than qualified. And nobody's going to protest it anyway. You'll have your three stripes back in no time, and maybe a couple of rockers. Hell, that was the whole plan from the beginning. When I first went to Colonel Stevens about you."

"I think that's indecent and immoral," Landers said.

"Hell, didn't Strange tell you all that?"

"No. And if he had I'd have told him the same thing. With all these poor fuckers going overseas and getting their ass shot off. I don't want any part of that. Or anything like it." He could feel a cold, brilliant, hardened diamond point of determination in him. Winch could not affect that.

"I grant you it may be indecent and immoral," Winch grinned. "But that's the way things get done around here, you'll find. And the way they get done in the world, too, you'll find. Too. Someday."

"Maybe," Landers smiled. "I still don't want any part of it."

"And I don't want any part of you," he suddenly said more sharply. "Mister Winch." It suddenly was all threatening to pour out of him, and he had to bite it back. He had to keep his coolness. "I don't need you, and don't want you, don't want any help from you, and don't need help from you. I can pull my own weight. And I intend to. Do just that. On any line."

"Well," Winch said. "All right." But he wasn't grinning any more, Landers noted. He sat down behind his desk and began to look at the papers Landers had turned over. "You want a drink, kid?"

"Sure," Landers said.

Winch put up on the desk top a bottle of Seagram's which he took from a desk drawer. "I'm sorry I haven't got any ice. But there's water," he pointed at a glass cooler.

"No ice is fine," Landers said.

"Paper cups, there," pointing. "Help yourself. I'm not drinking." He riffled through the papers and examined them while Landers made his drink. "They've given you a royal decking with these papers, kid," he said after a moment, and threw them down. "I could send you to the infantry if I wanted, on these papers."

Landers turned on him sharply. "What do you mean?" he demanded, his voice even sharper than the turn. "Where?" He leaned over the papers. He had never been able to trust Winch an inch. Nobody had.

"Right here," Winch said and handed him the papers.

There were six sheets of them, which had been in the large envelope with his service record and his 201 File. "Look on page two. You're marked *fit for Limited Duty only*. Now look on page four. It says fit for *infantry duty*. See there? That's a direct, bald contradiction." They were signed officially by the officer who had headed the Medical Board Landers had gone before, a colonel he had never met except the once.

Landers was in a fury. "How can that be?" he demanded. "How can they do that?"

"They can't," Winch said. "Like I said, it's a contradiction. Some fool clerk, or pair of clerks, who made it out made a mistake. But that wouldn't have made any difference, here. One of my clerks, say, who processed this, would have sent you to the infantry." He accepted the papers back from Landers, and threw them down again. "I didn't have anything to do with that, kid."

"Those dirty fuckers," Landers said in a quivering voice. "Dirty cocksuckers."

"You want to go to the infantry, kid?"

"No," Landers said. "No. I don't want to go to the infantry."

"Okay. Where do you want to go? Since you don't want to stay here." Winch spread his hands. "You can have your choice."

"I don't want any choice," Landers said, trying to get hold of himself, and of his voice. "I want to go where I'd have gone if everything were straight. I want to do what is decent and honorable—

"Don't you see? That that's the only way I can live with myself, damn it?" He was trying desperately to hold his voice down to normal. But on the last phrase it sailed upward, almost getting away from him.

"Noble sentiments," Winch said. "Noble sentiments, I'm sure. Well, we won't send you to the infantry. (Remembering that I could, if I wanted.)"

"They're not fair," Landers said furiously. "It's unfair."

"Fair? Unfair?" Winch said. "You're dealing here with forms. Forms made out in triplicate. Somebody just happened to make your forms out wrong. Make a mistake.

"But we won't send you to the infantry. We'll throw you up to the lottery. We'll turn you over to one of my clerks. I don't know, I have no idea, what's coming up right now out there. And he probably doesn't either, until he looks. There's no fix. How's that?"

"Fine. That's fine," Landers said coldly.

"There's no way to be decent, and moral, and honorable in a war, kid," Winch said softly.

Landers refused to answer.

The clerk Winch turned him over to certainly was unbiased. He picked off the top reassignment listing from the stack that was on his desk, then paused to take two slow, bored drags on his cigarette. The assignment was to the 3516th QM Gasoline Supply Company, a brand-new, newly organized outfit, limited duty only.

Landers took his processed assignment orders and left to go report in, without pausing to thank Winch for fixing up his three-day AWOL. Winch watched him leave.

On his way down there Landers remembered his last conversation with Curran at the hospital, about limited duty in general, and QM Gas Supply outfits in particular. Their high rate of unsung casualties.

The hutments assigned to the 3516th as quarters looked like

a natural disaster had struck them. Built at some time in the distant past of nine months ago, they were already coming apart at the seams and threatening to fall. The day's quota of new men fresh from the comfort of the hospital stood around with their gear, looking at them disbelievingly.

One-story high in the gray cold, they were heated by pot-bellied coal stoves. The stoves were inadequate to the cracks in the clapboards, and sheet rolls of tar paper had been nailed up inside by desperate former inhabitants. They were filled with old double-decker wooden bunks which threatened to splinter when an upper bunk was used. The latrines were worse. In separate buildings, yards from the hutments, they were built over concrete slabs on the ground which were freezing cold. Half the faucets did not work, and one-third of the toilets were out of order. Dirt was everywhere. Old dirt, new dirt, and dried mud. The accumulated dirt of men living together in confined spaces. Nobody could ever really get it clean.

When they had all inspected their new home, they were called outside to listen to a lecture by the new company commander. He too did not look very happy. The subject of the lecture was cleanliness. It sounded as if he had given it numbers of times.

The cold, wet winter weather was the worst part of it. The ungiving, unrelenting cold kept on, boring in from all directions, until nothing and nobody was ever really warm. And the constant daily scrubbings at the encrusted dirt, while never seriously diminishing the dirt, made the walls, floors, and ceilings colder.

Landers existed in an almost constant state of anger and outrage, over his hospital reassignment papers. It was so typical of the Army. Nobody had read them. Who the fuck had read them? Had Curran? Had Stevens? Had the man who signed them? That colonel heading the medical board? Landers did not even know whether these papers were to be part of his permanent records. What if he were shipped to Europe, and over there, on the strength of these papers, was suddenly transferred over to some infantry unit? Where would he turn for authentication? He had not remembered to ask Winch about the possibility of such a thing happening. Landers did not even know if it could. He should have asked Winch to correct the mistake. But to go back up there now and ask him would be awful, as unseemly as Winch's indecent grin. So he went on living in a kind of limbo, combined with fury, not knowing.

The new outfit was a catastrophe, as bad as its quarters. Newly activated, around a cadre of five men and three officers, it was receiving shipments of from ten to thirty men a day. Most days it received none. Landers arrived on a day when it received twenty-five, none of whom the cadre knew how to process properly. The cadre did not know their jobs. The officers did not know how to help the cadre. Meanwhile, the new men went on scrubbing at the quarters until enough new men arrived to fill out the company strength and begin the training.

Slightly more than half of the men were from one of the two infantry divisions in training at O'Bruyerre, which had just had its final division medical exam before shipment to England. Having squeaked through their lucky failure of that, they were very happy to be here and made no bones about saying so. At least not until they saw what an abysmal fuckup their new outfit was. A fair percentage of them were noncoms, transferred in grade, and these were quickly snatched off the lineup by the cadre officers to fill the vacant NCO slots in the new company T.O.

The rest of the men were hospital releases like Landers. Mostly they came from Kilrainey General. Landers recognized a few faces he had seen along the corridors. But a lot were from other hospitals in the wide area serviced by O'Bruyerre's Second Army repple depple. (Another new word.) Some were more crippled than others. They were the "barrel scrapings," as one tobacco-chawing country farmer with a mean smile put it, succinctly. One man whom Landers could not get out of his mind had had the whole ball of his left calf taken off in the Italian campaign, so that it looked as though some large animal had bitten it.

With very few exceptions these men were overseas wounded, who were now going back. They were not happy with anything. Not with the new outfit, and not with anything else.

In such a situation Landers as a pvt could hardly be noticed, and wasn't. Landers was relieved that he was not. He wanted time to think. At this point, he had decided never to seek promotion again. He would do what he was told as a pvt, but no more, no less. His fury and righteous indignation at the way the hospital discharges were being treated was high, and pure. He did not care so much about the infantry division men. But even they should not be put in barracks like these. He explained all this to Strange up at the Peabody, the first time he got a pass.

"Nobody cares," he said, trying to make it simple and easy so Strange could understand. "Except the unsophisticated. And they're just being used. Look at that medical board. Those five old men. All good citizens. Not even your shitty West Pointers. And they all sit there and give me their spiel. About how they need me. They want to use my experience. So I agree. What experience? And look how they're using it. Tell me they want me to train people in infantry fighting. I don't know infantry fighting. What am I agreeing to? Am I crazy? And look where I am. And they didn't any of them read those papers. None of the doctors read them. Or they'd have found that mistake. No, sir. I don't see any other way for me. Except to run away. And there's no place to run to."

"Good," Strange said, with that urgency, "fine. But I still don't understand. All you got to do is go to Winch, and get a good clerical job, and sit it out for the rest of the war. You've got *that* experience. You'd be good at *that*. I don't understand, I honestly don't."

"But then I would be like all the rest of them," Landers protested. He shook his head. "I won't do that."

Mary Lou had already found another serviceman for boy-friend. Strange went off with Frances Highsmith, as soon as he could. Landers could have stayed on and taken one of the other girls. He preferred to go off by himself in the city, just wandering around. Bar to bar.

It was the only pass Landers was to get for quite a while. Back at O'Bruyerre, when he reported back in, he found the 3516th had received orders it was to go through the standard six weeks of basic training.

That this crew should go through basic training was ridiculous. Even the new company commander was embarrassed, and half-apologized when he read the order to them. The chorus of bitching which greeted the announcement might have been funny. Except that it carried so many serious results. Twelve men went over the hill in the first week after the announcement, and as the first weeks of basic training got under way, more followed.

Landers did not go. But he thought about it seriously. And in fact was invited to go, by two other hospital cripples, who had decided the whole thing was more than they could stomach. But they did not know where they were going, or how long they would stay away, and had nobody really to go to. Also Landers did not much like them. All this decided him against going with them.

And in the end he decided not to go alone, by himself. Where would he go? He couldn't go home, that was the first place they'd look. He did not want to go back to the Peabody, like his first AWOL, and lie around day after day. This time, when he decided to go, it was going to be for good. For desertion. Not for any piddling AWOL. And he did not think things had gotten quite bad enough to warrant that, yet. Partly he did not go because he had begun to have a tenuous, sneaking affection for this befuddled fucked-up outfit, and partly he did not go because he had begun to take a serious liking to the new company commander of the 3516th.

The new company commander was a 1st/lt named Harry L Prevor. Prevor was a Jew from Indiana, with high cheekbones and Mongolian eyes, who had been sent down here to the boondocks to take over and build this scumbum outfit for that very reason, according to his cadre. If so, he took it very well. Prevor was a French name, he said, probably a corruption of *prévoir*, which meant to see ahead; foretell the future. The wry way he said it always got him a laugh. He had not let the new assignment deck him. Prevor was a self-effacing man, of low physical authority perhaps, but with a sense of humor, and a man of considerable decency.

The cadre said the other officers had fucked-up in some equally catastrophic way, though both were *goyim*. Landers formed no opinion of them, but grew to like Prevor more and more.

The cadre themselves were not at all in the same situation and were not being punished. For them this was a definite step up. They were all very happy to be where they were, and anxious to keep their promotions. The only trouble with that was that they were all so terrible at their jobs. And the promotions were not permanent yet. They were "acting" 1st/sgt, "acting" co/clk, until the time when Prevor was to finalize their positions, which was supposed to be in two months. This tended to make them even more nervous and anxious.

Landers learned how really bad they really were when he applied for the job of assistant company clerk, after suffering and struggling through his third week of basic training.

He still had not given up his decision never to seek promotion. But the suffering he incurred going through basic training with his bad ankle warranted some kind of counterattack. And the only way he could get out of the basic training was to get back into administration. The only way he could be useful enough to them to be shifted into administration was through clerking.

He was not all alone, in his reaction to the physical stresses of the basic training routines. Men were dropping out all around him like flies, going on sick call, trying unsuccessfully to turn themselves in to the camp hospital, actually falling down and failing in all sorts of the training exercises. The man from Italy with the crippled calf fell down and simply lay on the ground four times in one morning, before being allowed to go over and sit on the sidelines in dour silence.

Landers did not think the man from Italy was putting it on, faking it. The reactions of his own ankle to the physical strains, swelling up, turning out on him, simply refusing to move, were too painful. Curran certainly was right when he told him it was no good for infantry work. And his crippled ankle was a nothing, compared to that mutilated calf. But the man from Italy was not transferred.

The physical jobs the 3516th would be performing in combat were loading and unloading five-gallon gas cans from high-bedded two-and-a-half-ton GI Army trucks. The beds of the two-and-a-half-tonners were about the height of an average man's shoulder. Each truck carried one "bay" of 125 cans. Speed in loading or unloading was considered essential. For two men to load or unload a bay of empty cans was not a difficult physical feat. But for four men to load and unload a full bay of 125 cans full of gas (or water, during their first practice sessions) was no mean feat at all. And to do it all day long, six times, eight, ten, twelve times, was more than most well men could handle. To think the hospital cripples who had been siphoned off to this outfit could do it was ridiculous. Most of the men who had come down from the infantry division after its physical exam found it just about impossible. To send all these same men through the infantry training exercises of basic training was doubly ridiculous. No one knew where the order originated.

The complaints about the basic training came to a kind of a head near the end of Landers' third week in it. It was a night training exercise. And of course it was raining. Not a hard rain, but a steady uncomfortable cold drizzle. Landers could imagine some Plans & Training colonel with a nice big Scotch and soda in hand sitting at his warm desk in his warm office, and saying

in his deep, manly, tough voice what a good thing it would be
for the men, the rain. Teach them more about what it would be
like in France.

The exercise was the old live-fire exercise. It was designed to
show green men what it was really like to be under fire. To this
end seven or eight machineguns were set up on a small bluff,
their barrel ends wedged between stakes and two-by-four cross-
pieces so they could neither elevate nor depress nor traverse.
Behind these, machinegun crews were to fire tracer ammo off
across a low area. The trainees (that was Landers and company)
were to crawl across the valley to the bluff, the MG fire spar-
kling with tracers every five rounds four feet over their heads.

Landers did not know who began the protest. But ten yards
from the bluff, where they were supposed to stop, the man on
Landers' right leaned toward him in the rain and shouted at his
ear in the racket of fire pouring over their heads, "Look at here!"
In his right hand was a rock, about the size and heft of a hand
grenade.

In the near dark, lit eerily and unevenly by the burning tracers overhead, Landers after a moment recognized him as the
man from Italy with the ruined calf. His face and uniform were
covered with the mud, and the piece cradled in his arms was
going to take hours of cleaning. The man from Italy grinned and
made a gesture with the rock as if chucking a grenade at the
MGs.

They had arrived at the end line among the first, and had
nothing to do until those behind crawled up to them. Landers
looked around him and saw that the ground was strewn with the
grenade-like rocks. Plenty for all. Landers did not know
whether the idea had come from the right of the line, or the man
from Italy had thought of it. He seized a rock for himself and
shouted at the man on his left, made the same gesture of chucking a grenade. The man nodded happily and turned to pass the
word.

In two minutes each man of the forward end line was lobbing
his grenade-like rock over and up at the bluff line of firing MGs.
As men crawled up singly through the mud of the little valley
in the dark, they were incited to join in.

At first there was no appreciable effect from the line of machineguns. Then the throwers began to repeat, concentrating
their lobs on the seven or eight MG positions. They were easy
enough to see in the dark, with the tracers spouting from them.

There were some squawks of dismay from the little bluff, and strings of cursing which could be heard but were not readable in the noise of the fire. In the pauses in the firing a clank or two was heard, as if a rock had hit metal: an MG receiver or a helmet. Then there was one loud shout of consternation from the bluff, and in half a minute three loud blasts of a whistle came from behind the crawlers where the officer commanding them was placed with his radio. The exercise was over, called off before half of the men had completed the crawl. When they climbed up the bluff, they found one of the machinegunners had had his jaw broken when hit in the face with a rock. There was a lot of cursing and grumbling and complaining up on the little hill.

For Landers it had been a wild, bizarre, eerie scene: the crippled, muddy veterans of the Pacific from Lae, Guadalcanal, New Georgia, the European vets and survivors of Sicily, Salerno, Naples, lobbing grenade-sized rocks into the line of their own fixed machineguns manned by their own green men. Landers had not expected or thought about someone getting seriously hurt. He was not so sure about some of the others. When he climbed muddily up the bluff in the cold drizzle, shaking with cold, and watched the injured man for all the world like an injury in a football game being walked away by medics with flashlights, Landers had already made up his mind about applying to the new orderly room for an assistant clerk's job. Any job.

There was a minimal investigation of the incident. But nothing came of it. The men looked at each other with wide, innocent eyes. No one knew who had thrown any rocks. No one had seen any rocks thrown. Nobody was prosecuted. The investigation died of malnutrition. The basic training schedule continued. The next time a live-fire exercise was laid on, it was placed in a terrain where no rocks or stones or other debris littered the ground. Just mud and grass.

Landers applied for the job by presenting himself at the orderly room and asking for it. "My God!" Prevor said, overhearing, and coming to his own office door, "do you know something about clerking?" Landers nodded. He said he had run an entire infantry company on New Georgia. "Service records? Morning report? Sick book?" Prevor asked. Landers nodded. "Come on in here," Prevor said, and shut the door to his office behind them. Outside, his acting 1st/sgt and clerk were sitting with their heads down.

A batch of morning reports had come back from Second

Army Hq as unacceptable. They had been improperly completed and would have to be done over. Prevor grimaced. "My damned 1st/sgt doesn't know what's wrong with them." The sheaf comprised the first two weeks of the company's existence and that meant almost certainly that other batches would be following them, to be done over also. The sick book was in a like state, perhaps worse. It was being sent back almost every day, though the doctors were actually taking care of the men who reported sick. "They more or less have to," Prevor said. "We've got more men on sick report almost, than we have for duty."

The service records were a different matter. Prevor launched into that. None of them had been completed with the remarks of transfer. The 1st/sgt and the clerk were both afraid to touch them. One mistaken entry on a service record could require a week's work to straighten out. "And the first payroll is coming up soon," Prevor said. "Without properly completed service records we can't make out the payroll."

Landers nodded. Then after a moment he thought to rub his hands together briskly, like a man ready to go to work. The office was pleasantly warm, and a pot of coffee was heating on a hot plate in the corner. It was one hell of a lot better than going through old-hat basic training exercises out in the cold rain.

"Have you got enough experience?" Prevor said. "To straighten these things out?"

Landers nodded. "Yes, sir." A picture of Winch's long thin leather morning report book on New Georgia came into his mind. Winch always had it with him in his musette, up on the line. The mahogany leather cover was smeared with mud and so were some of the pages. But it was always correctly filled out and the drills Winch had put him through on it, so Winch would not have to do the job when they were back in bivouac, had been many and harsh. A sick book was about the simplest form there was, only a moron could fuck it up. Service record remarks he had been trained in by both Winch and the regimental S-1 sgt/maj. "Yes, sir. I can do them all. But I've never done a first payroll off the service records."

"Never mind that," Prevor snapped. "If you can do the others, there's a sergeancy in it for you."

It took a week. Landers asked for a new book of blank morning report forms and a new sick book. He got up in the freezing dark with the troops, but while they were bitching and getting into cold field uniforms, he dressed in his garrison ODs. He ate in the freezing cold kitchen messhall with them, but when they went off to freezing training formations, he reported to the warm orderly room, with its pot of coffee on the hot plate. It seemed the greatest of luxuries.

While he was working on the old morning reports, others came in from Second Army to be redone also. When he had time to spare from that, he worked on the unacceptable sick book sheets bringing them up to date, and at the same time doing each day's new sick book entry correctly for the clerk. When he had a spare moment, and in the evenings when he could be alone, he worked on the service records remarks, which required such absolute accuracy. After supper he worked alone in the lighted orderly room, which was the only warm place in the company area anyhow. Landers didn't mind it at all. Every so often Prevor would stop by late, to compliment him and see how he was coming along.

By the time ten days had passed he was running the company for Prevor. Just as he had run the old company. (God love them, God help them, wherever they were, he added quickly with a pang of guilt.) Except that now he was functioning as 1st/sgt too, doing the 1st/sgt's fatigue rosters, and training rosters, and plotting out the basic training schedules for the various sections.

"Do you think you could handle the payroll, too?" Prevor asked him one night. "We've got to have it in in three days' time, or they'll redline the entire payroll. And nobody will get paid."

Redline. A red line of ink through a soldier's name on the payroll, because of a mistake in his line on the roll, or in the remarks under his name, was just about the cardinal sin in the Army. It meant the soldier did not get his pay that month.

"I'll try it for you," Landers said. "But I told you, I've never done a payroll directly off the service records. I always had a previous payroll roster to work from."

"If you can do it, by God," Prevor said fervently, "you'll have your sergeancy before the next month is out. And as soon as I can swing it on the T.O., I'll get you a rocker and staff sergeancy to go with it. If I have to put you down as a section leader, by God."

"Frankly, I don't want any goddamned rating, Lieutenant," Landers said, and stared at him. "Quite frankly, I've made up my mind that I don't ever want another rating in this shitty miserable Army."

Prevor stared back at him a moment. "Well," he said, "*I* want it. And *I'm* going to give it to you. So you're going to have to take it."

Landers looked away, back at the service record he was working on. "Well, you had better understand that I don't believe in this Army any more, and I don't believe in this country any more, either, and I don't believe in this race that you and I happen to have been born members of. Fucking *human* race. I don't like it, and I don't give a shit for it, and I don't believe in it."

Prevor did not answer for a long moment. Then he said, "Never mind that. You get this payroll out for me, and you're a staff sergeant. I don't want to break my cadre. I can't do that to them. They care too much, and it would ruin them. Anyway they'll be all right, after they get worked in."

Landers nodded, in support of the sentiment. "I respect that." But then he shook his head, against the opinion. "But they won't be all right. Unless I teach them. I could teach them, if you want. I know a pretty good bit about supply and about mess. I could work with them all, if you want me to."

Prevor's Mongolian eyes opened wide. "Would you really do that?"

Landers nodded. "Sure. Anyway I don't want their fucking jobs. I just don't want to go through basic training, and I don't want to be cold."

"I can certainly promise you both of those," Prevor said, with a grin. "But you're also going to have that rating, Landers. If I have to run shorthanded a section sergeant in one section."

Landers smiled. "Besides, it would make you look bad up at Second Army Command, if you fired your cadre."

Prevor gave him a peculiar look. "Yes, it would," he said simply. He turned away, but then, with a spur-of-the-moment gesture, turned back. "The truth is, I *can't* fire them. They're Second Army Command men. I fire them, I lose this company. Like a shot."

"You'll have to give me a place where I can work around the clock, and not be disturbed," Landers said. "I won't be able to do the daily sick book and morning report."

"We'll take care of that. And you can have my office here," Prevor said. Then, hesitantly, he stuck out his hand.

Landers took it, without much enthusiasm. "It looks to me like somebody up at Second Army is trying especially hard to do you in. Is it because you're a Jew?"

Prevor didn't answer for a moment, and it looked as if he wasn't going to answer. He made a shrug, a very Jewish shrug, and then a rueful grin. "That's what it is, all right," he said finally.

"Well, we'll see," Landers said. "But I won't guarantee that a few men won't get redlined."

It took the full three days to do it. Landers worked two whole nights and the three full days without sleep, to get it done, and on the third night between half-hour snatches of sleep spent most of the night going over it and proofreading. The next morning he submitted it, all properly signed and initialed by Prevor. Two days later it was back, all properly okayed, and the company was paid. Not one man was redlined.

You could walk out anywhere on any parade-ground street and stop a soldier and tell him you had just completed a forty-page first payroll directly off the service records without getting a man redlined, and the soldier would nod without comprehension and give you a nervous, puzzled smile. The only words he would really hear would be the words *no redlines*. Very few people knew the amount of work that went into even an ordinary everyday payroll. The Finance Office allowed not even the slightest deviation. No strikeovers, no erasures, even a bad smudge of a single letter or serial number numeral would cause the unfortunate soldier whose name it appeared in, or after, to be redlined. And Landers had been working with blocks of six to eight lines of remarks under each entry's name, taken directly from the service record.

But Prevor knew, and caused the entire 3516th to know. Prevor bought a bottle of champagne and with the rest of the officers and the clerk force opened it and drank it in the orderly room, toasting Landers. Landers walked out into the company area in the drizzle to find he was the new hero of the 3516th. In the messhall he was cheered. Every man who had his pay stuffed in his wallet wanted to shake his hand and pat him on the back, and by the end of the next month he was a buck/sgt and nobody begrudged him the promotion.

Only Landers was not elated. If he had told Winch what he felt, Winch would have snorted and then cursed. If he had told it to Strange, Strange would have said that he was seriously crazy.

But only Landers knew. He had an instinctive feeling that all this was not going to last. Not for him. Not for Landers. Just as he knew Prevor the Jew was not going to last, was going out. And when Prevor went, God only knew what would happen to the 3516th.

Landers wondered if Winch up at Second Army Command, the place where all the morning reports had been returned from, was following his progress.

CHAPTER 25

Winch had kept track of him. As he had all of his boys. In his job there was not all that much to do, that he did not have time to do outside things, too.

Also, Winch's contacts had grown. In the time he had been at O'Bruyerre. With important help from Jack Alexander, he had extended his contacts until by now he had a web of informers, spreading out through all of Second Army Command here at O'Bruyerre, through all of Second Army HQ in Luxor, through Alexander's hospital, and through all the various areas and aspects of O'Bruyerre itself.

Winch hated to use that word *informers*. But that was what it was. Pals, or buddies, would have been a better word. But that wasn't what they were, they were informers. For vanity's sake, and for pride, the whole thing was built and structured to look, and to seem, as if they were buddies. Nobody wanted to be an informer. First-three-graders from the QM from here, first-three-graders from Signal from there. All coming in singly to report from time to time, but looking like they were coming in really to say hello and have a beer.

Winch had set up in the first-three-graders area of the big

main PX beer hall, at a big corner table. This was part of the bigger NCOs' section, which was separated from the rest of the huge hall by a low fence of aluminum poles. At early evening every evening, just after work (what would be called the cocktail hour at the officers' club) the big table was reserved for Winch, and there at his corner table Winch received.

The topics of conversation were always the gossip. That was how his informers conveyed their information. Junior first-three-graders came into Winch's table for beer from just about everywhere on the big post. I don't know if anybody can believe this, but I heard. So and so may not know what he's talking about, but he said. So and so said this. Some other so and so heard this.

Winch presided, buying the various beers, easily, laughing, but filing away in the dark file cabinets of his head everything that might be pertinent somewhere or other. Almost everything was. For a while at first he kept a half-full glass mug of beer in front of him which he never touched. Later on he dispensed with the untasted beer. He would drink a glass of white wine or two now and then, from bottles he himself brought the barman.

Winch hated the aluminum-post fence. Just as he hated the two huge chrome-and-colored-lights Wurlitzer jukeboxes which stood in the big hall and were constantly being paid fortunes in nickels and quarters to play at top volume all the popular war songs. If they were going to put in a fence, why couldn't they have put in a fence of turned wooden posts, like a beer hall should have? And he was heartily sick of Jo Stafford's "I'll Never Smile Again"; Dinah Shore's "Sentimental Journey"; Vera Lynn's "I'll Be Seeing You"; Dick Haymes' "I'll Get By"; Alice Faye's "You'll Never Know"; Frank Sinatra's "All or Nothing at All"; Helen Forrest's "I've Heard That Song Before." Sentimental hogwash. And "Avalon," "Elmer's Tune," "Ciribiri-bin," "Chattanooga Choo-Choo," "The Jersey Bounce," "I've Got a Gal in Kalamazoo." They rattled and banged, or moaned, all over the place without cease, hanging up high in the huge room like a second cloud of tobacco smoke. But they made a good screen cover for the information that was passed to Winch in the form of lighthearted gossip.

So Winch knew all about Harry L Prevor and the 3516th, long before Landers showed up and drew that assignment. He also knew immediately it happened how Landers had saved Prevor's ass twice, or three times, if you counted the payroll, with his superior clerking ability, learned right here at Mother Winch's tit. He also knew, as soon as it came through, about Landers' promotion back up to buck sergeant. And a month later he knew about his promotion to staff.

In spite of promotions Winch shrewdly suspected Landers was a long way from being out of the woods yet. It was Winch's hunch that Landers had taken up the cause of Lt Prevor, and the saving of his company for him, as a moral cause. If so, Landers was shit out of luck. Winch had followed Lt Prevor's progress since Lt Prevor had arrived in Second Army, a week after Winch himself. The anti-Jewish discrimination practices utilized against Prevor and two other Jews who had come in in the same batch of young officers were constant and unbending.

There was nothing in it for or against Winch and his command. But Winch found it an interesting thing to watch. There were other Jews in Second Army, quite a few of them, and some of them quite high-placed. But none of these were new, and strangers, without friends. And none of these established Jews came forward, either openly or behind the scenes, to help Prevor and the other two. According to the gossip received by Winch from their various sergeants, the established, accepted Jewish officers seemed to be more against Prevor and the other two than the white Anglos. In the sergeants' opinions, the accepted Jews were doing it to stay "in."

That made sense to Winch. He had long ago given up making moral judgments against Jews, or anybody else. But he did not think Landers had. And if Landers had decided to throw in his moral indignation behind Lt Prevor, Landers was on the losing side from the start. Because poor Prevor was a lost cause from the beginning, and his ouster from command of the 3516th was a foregone conclusion from the moment he got the command.

Second Army was allowing only two alternatives. One, if Lt Prevor got the command working and whipped it into some kind of good shape, Second Army would put some well-liked unassigned captain in over Prevor's first lieutenancy to command it, and sop up the gravy poor Prevor had sweat blood to create for him. Second, and much more likely, if Prevor turned out an inept and shady outfit that was malfunctioning and in lousy shape, Second Army would relieve him and put him to work on some other cadre, with several black marks against him. And would then let some unloved young officer take the outfit overseas.

The only other possible alternative, the worst of all, would be that Prevor would be able to do nothing at all with this soured, motley crew, and would wind up with an undisciplined, morale-less gang of crippled stockade figures. In that case Second Army would let him take them overseas himself, caught up in the midst of his own death trap he had created, to be rid of him. Any way it came out Prevor stood to lose.

And if this was the cause Landers was putting himself and his talents behind, there was no way Landers could do anything but lose, too. What Landers would do, when one of these bad alternatives came up to be faced, was something Winch had to think about.

Meantime Winch had his own life to live. Mostly, his life consisted of Carol. Carol, and his nightmares. And the nightmares were gaining ground, on Carol, and on everything.

There had been a time, when Winch first got back from overseas, that he had had a very strong, almost uncontrollable desire to sleep with a bayonet or .45 pistol under his pillow. There was no sense to it. It was just comforting, like a kid with his security blanket. Winch had kept his pistol from the old company, writing it off as lost or stolen, and it was easy enough to come by a bayonet. He had used one or the other a few times, self-consciously, at the hospital in San Francisco, but then had stopped it. But both pieces still reposed in his gear and now the desire had come back so strong that only the presence of Carol in the apartment and in the bed at night kept him from doing it. The few nights he slept alone in his quarters, he did sleep with one or the other. There was something immensely comforting about the feel of the warm metal under your hand under the pillow as you fell asleep.

The nightmares had nothing to do with the desire for a weapon, at least not as far as Winch could see. But lately the nightmares had started to win. There were three of them now. Three separate and different nightmares. There wasn't a night, or a nap, or a half-hour's doze, that there wasn't one of them there, bedeviling him. And recently the original nightmare had broken through into the outside world, into the conscious awareness of other people. The thing he had tried most to avoid.

One night in a deep sleep Carol had awakened him saying that he was shouting something in his sleep. Something about "Get them out of there! Get them out of there!" The same sentence, over and over. It sounded as though it had something to do with the war, she said. But it was all so garbled. Was that what it was? Something about the war?

"It was nothing," Winch said. "No. It wasn't about the war."

But the eager look on her face of concealed delight was so apparent, and so strong, that he felt sorry he couldn't tell her. It would give her something romantic to remember about the war. When she was older. An older woman.

"It was nothing," he said. "Just a bad dream." But he was shaken, by the fact that he had yelled it aloud.

"You really are upset," Carol said.

"A little. It'll go away."

Instinctively, or almost instinctively (it was always hard to tell with her), she had shoved one of those delicious breasts of hers up to his face, lying beside him, as if to comfort him. Winch had begun to nuzzle it, then kiss it and lick it, then suck it, the puckering nipple. Detesting himself. But it was so soft, so tender. Then she began to pant.

So he had wound up fucking her. It was probably the best thing. But his way, not her way. She liked it hard and driving, like a piston, beating against her spread crotch and crotch hair. He liked that, too. But he liked better the slow, long insertion and withdrawal, softly, gently, over and over, feeling every tiniest quiver along the barrel of his blood-swollen organ. When he came, it was all he could do to pull it out. But he remembered she did not have her diaphragm in, and he had to. Afterward, he lay rubbing his loosening cock into the wetted cushion of her pussy hair while she clutched his shoulders.

He fell asleep to be awakened by one of the other nightmares, some unknown time later, and lay looking down at her as she slept, for a time. He had a hunch she was not going to let it drop and he was right, she didn't. The next time he saw her she brought it up, and kept on bringing it up, asked about it. And once the nightmare had broken through the one time, as if a gate had opened, it began to happen more times. Before long she was waking him every night, from one of the nightmares or another. Winch got so he hated to drift off to sleep. He became what he had never been before in his life, even on Guadalcanal and New Georgia—an insomniac.

The two new nightmares were totally different. In both texture and quality. Different from each other, and different from the familiar one. In one of them he was being attacked by a Japanese, either an officer with a sword or a tough, mean, old-hand sergeant with a Nambu which was out of ammo but was armed with a bayonet. The Japanese was coming on, intent on killing him. Winch had his .45. Winch knew he would get him, but that was not the point. The point was that they were in the middle of a mortar barrage, and the Japanese ignored it. But each time a mortar round landed nearby, which was every couple of seconds, Winch would find himself flinching. The Japanese did not flinch. Winch would fire two or three times, flinching and missing each time because a mortar had landed. There was no question he would get the Jap, he would save his last round until the Jap was right on him. This made no difference; the Jap had won. Because the Jap was ready to die, and Winch wasn't. So he would stand, waiting, and flinching, ready to kill, but stricken with a boundless terror at his own inadequacy, uncontrollability.

The other was of a wounded man. Winch could not recognize him, and never knew who he was. It was not Jacklin (whom Winch had actually seen dead, and always remembered in the dream as a comparison), but he was lying in the same manner as Jacklin had lain. Stretched out, arms widespread, head back, but looking uphill this time, instead of downhill like Jacklin. And he wasn't dead. A long way from dead. But enemy fire kept them from getting to him. Winch could hear him crying piteously, bleating for help, whenever the fire slackened. And there wasn't a thing Winch could do about it. The company commander was dead, Winch commanded the company (Winch had never actually had a real company commander killed), he had a hundred and sixty men at his back, and there wasn't a thing he could do. He couldn't send one, or two, of these men down into that fire. And he could not go himself, he was needed to command the company. Below him the man cried out piteously. The enemy fire swept across, giving him a new wound. Again, and again. But never a killing wound. The man would never die.

Winch never did tell Carol the nightmares, could not tell her. He still believed, even though he had in his sleep let them outside himself inadvertently, that if he did not tell them to anyone, didn't talk about them, he would be able to wriggle out of it somehow, and get back his control. And Carol was too delighted by the idea of them. Too delighted to tell them to.

There was something about her that seemed to enjoy gruesome, monstrous war stories, with an almost sexual thrill. It was like a kid loving and hating Dracula movies. That was because she had never had to live them. When you had lived them, they weren't gruesome any more. They were just sorry. Sorry tales. But there was no reason she should be expected to see that. Far too many civilians were like her, Winch had found.

Carol was having her own troubles, anyway. They had begun with the Christmas vacation of her boyfriend. He was still hot to go into the Army, and he had come home for Christmas with nothing but that on his mind. He was determined to quit college and enlist. His own family was against it, particularly his mother. And Carol's family was against it: they were not going to have her marrying some enlisted soldier just off on his way to Europe, no matter how well-bred and well-connected. But only Carol's opinion carried any real weight with him. She had brought the problem to Winch again.

She had not seen Winch but once all through the Christmas vacation, as she had promised she wouldn't, so it was not until January that he heard the story.

"Well," Winch said, with the crispness of command, "Do you want him to go? Or do you want him not to go?"

Carol made an anguished little face, and then sort of wailed. "Well, I don't want him to go. But I'm not sure I want to marry him. I don't think I'm in love with him. I'm in love with you."

"I don't count in this," Winch said. "Leave me out of it."

"How can I?" Carol cried. "But I don't want him to go. I mean, his whole family doesn't want him to go. His poor mother. And his old dad. He's got it all fixed for him to get a business deferment. I have to respect their wishes. I'm just not sure I want to marry him.

"And if he stays, I'll surely have to marry him. Won't I?"

It was easy enough to tell what kind of answer she hoped for. Was demanding, in fact. "Not necessarily," Winch said.

Carol turned to stare at him with her large, dark eyes, for a long moment. The cocked one rolled off a little bit, then came back. "Anyway, he won't stay just because I ask him not to go. I don't have all that much influence on him."

"It's very simple," Winch said immediately. "That's the easiest part. Just tell him you have a lover."

The dark, cocked eye made her seem extraordinarily sexy.

"Oh!" Carol said. "Do you think that would make him stay?

It might work just the opposite. Make him run off and enlist," she said. "In deep despair."

Once again Winch suddenly had that feeling he had been getting more and more lately with all sorts of things. Was it real? Was it really real? Did she really mean it? Evidently she did.

Did these men really mean it, when they got together, and got all this explosive together, and killed all these other men? Evidently they did. But were all these men killed? Were they really dead? Or was it all just sort of one big kids' game?

If you built a house, was it really a house? Or was it just a bunch of wood stacked up together a certain way and nailed, and everybody got together and said it was a house.

The frightening concept, and the bottomless feeling he had, stumped him. She had stopped him. Again.

"I just hate to do something like that," she said. "Unless I'm absolutely sure." Then after thinking a moment, she looked up resolutely, the one eye rolling away, and said, "I'll do it."

"Maybe I'm wrong," Winch said lamely. "But it would certainly make me stay around."

"I'll do it," she said again. More resolutely.

But then she hadn't done it. She told Winch later, the next time she saw Winch, that she had been too afraid to do it. Instead she had agreed to come up to school and visit him for a week, if he would agree to go back. He had agreed. She had promised she would come up to Cleveland near the end of January.

After that she and Winch had had their four or five nights a week together for several weeks. Till she left for Cleveland. She still got up resolutely every night at four in the morning, dressed herself all up carefully, and put on all her evening makeup, to go home and be there by four-thirty. Nobody ever waited up to meet her. Nobody ever got up early to see if she came in. But it was a gamble she did not want to take. And she was always home in bed, when she had to get up at eight-thirty and her mother called her.

Winch, who at four did not have to get up for another three hours, would lie in bed and watch her go through her meticulous ritual. A lot of times he badly wanted to make love to her in the mornings. She was so cute. So adorable, with her unrelieved ritual. But there was never any chance. The ritual must never be broken, or even slowed.

It was when she got back from Cleveland that she told him she had found a new boyfriend. She had stayed away almost three weeks, instead of the one week she had agreed upon, and the new boyfriend was the reason. He was from a small town in Ohio, and the same age as the other one. "He loves it when I go down on him," she said, without even blushing. "And he loves to go down on me. Gamahouche, he calls it. It's an old Victorian word. He loves all the sexual things." They were in the apartment, and it was freezing cold out. She stopped to take off her coat. "Maybe, I'll marry him, instead." He had even more money than the other one, and more social prestige. And his family was marvelous, very genteel. Especially his mother. "Oh, you've taught me so much, Mart!" she cried, and swirled her coat onto the couch and whirled herself off across the room.

Winch felt he had heard the final accolade.

Then she stopped. "But I don't love him!" she cried, in another tone, a wail. "I love you!" She came across the room and put her arms around Winch and rubbed both her breasts against his chest. In high heels she was nearly as tall as he was.

"Whoa. I'm not a competitor in this competition," Winch said. "Remember? I told you that from the beginning."

He put his palms, flat, on the round of her back under the arms, in the sweater she wore, then moved them down her to the flat on her hips, his finger paps pressing themselves alternately into the round of her bottom. Storing up sensory impressions. To be remembered some time later.

"Oh, what's going to become of us?" she said, rubbing the side of her head against his ear. "What are we going to do?"

"Let's try going to bed. How about that?" Winch said.

For quite a long time after he had begun fucking Carol, he had had this feeling of extraordinary breathlessness, panting, afterward. A result of that heart condition. Then for quite a while it had gotten better, almost gone away. Lately it had come back, almost as strong as at first. Winch did not know why. But this time it was there, exceptionally strongly. He had to get up and walk around the room, to hide the fact that he was panting.

It was while Carol was away that three weeks in Cleveland that Bobby Prell's marriage took place.

Winch had known it was coming. But he hadn't expected to get an invitation. He had kept in touch with Strange by telephone, and even once, during the Christmas school holiday, had spent an evening with Strange at his Peabody suite. Strange had kept him filled in on Prell.

When the invitation came, he was nevertheless surprised. The

engraved invitation form could not have been filled in by Prell's
crabbed handwriting. The rolling, back-slanted, schoolgirl hand
could only have been that of little Della Mae. Della Mae—?
Kinkaid? And there was no reason she would send him one.
Winch at once suspected Strange was behind it, and got on the
phone to him.

No, Strange had not told her to invite Winch. Nor had he told
Prell, either. But she had come to Strange when he was visiting,
and taken him off to one side, and asked him whom she ought
to invite. Strange had mentioned Winch, but told her Prell
might not like it. "You leave that to me," she had told Strange.
Landers was invited, too, Strange said. And Corello, and Trynor. And the rest of the old-company members. Though there
weren't that many left, any more.

"So then he didn't stop her," Winch said. No, Strange guessed
not. "Well, I guess I'll come," Winch said. "Why the fuck not?"
He cleared his throat. Some strange powerful emotion in him
had risen up suddenly, unclaimed, and unanticipated, and shook
him violently, like a large dog shaking a rat. "What the fuck is
he getting married for, anyway?" he demanded. "A guy as crippled up as he is? How's he going to support a wife, when he's
outside? It sounds crazy, to me."

There was an almost Mephistophelian, low chuckle over the
phone, from Strange. "Didn't you know? Didn't I tell you? She's
knocked up." Winch exclaimed. "Yes. Higher than a kite,"
Strange said. "He aint got a whole hell of a lot of choice."
Another near Mephistophelian note crept faintly into Strange's
voice. There were going to be quite a lot of people there. People
Prell knew. It was going to be quite a big shebang. And Winch
might not have to worry, about what Prell would do on the
outside to support little Della Mae. He might be staying in.
There was even talk of their making him a lieutenant, Strange
said. A first lieutenant.

Winch snorted sourly, said good-by, and hung up and forgot
about it. Had he been thinking, as he ought to have been, had
he been the Mart Winch of old, he would immediately have
called Jack Alexander. But he didn't.

So he was surprised again, when he arrived at the wedding.
Which was being held at the hospital chapel. But it did not take
him long to catch on. The Army, Col Stevens officiating, was
giving the wedding. And picking up the tab for it. If Winch had

hung out a little more at the officers' club, as he should have done, he would already have known about it.

The other people Strange had referred to were all civilians. The reception after the ceremony was in the rec hall, which had been taken over for it, and milling around with drinks or champagne glasses were members of the Chamber of Commerce, the Lions Club, Rotary, Kiwanis, the Elks, and their wives, and even a contingent from the Luxor Combined Ladies Clubs. They were all people from the organizations Prell had given official war bonds speeches to.

They were all having a good time at the party, liked and admired Prell, and were all obviously happy to be where there were so many newspaper and magazine photographers, and reporters, all around. When Prell and Della Mae cut the huge wedding cake with a black, GI bayonet, there were a lot of flashbulb pictures taken and the civilian guests loyally made a hearty round of applause.

The Medal of Honor was much in evidence. With its neck ribbon. When the official wedding picture was taken, Prell was asked to put it on. He was asked to put it on when he and Della Mae cut the cake. When news photos of him and Della Mae and of him and Col Stevens were taken, he was asked to put it on. After each time, he folded it and put it carefully away in its box.

"Well, what do you think of it, Mart?" Col Stevens said from beside Winch's elbow.

"It's all right, sir," Winch said, and grinned. "Are you getting lots of war bonds sales?"

Stevens made his embarrassed, unwilling chuckle. "No. Not today, of course. But we will."

Winch was glad he had worn his tailored dress uniform, and his ribbons. He talked to some of the civilians. Without any exception they were great admirers of Prell, and all said the same thing when they found out who Winch was. Wasn't he proud to have been his first sergeant? Winch said he was. Johnny Strange worked his way over to him and the two of them stood together in a protected corner off to one end of one of the bars.

"You didn't bring your girl?" Winch asked.

"Naw. She don't go in for things like this," Strange said. "Didn't you bring yours?"

"She's away," Winch said. "But I don't think it would have

been a good thing for me to bring her. Not out here where she works."

Strange told him that Prell had become an enormous success as a war bonds speaker. People loved his simplicity. So much so that Col Stevens had recommended to Washington they should pull him out of Kilrainey and Luxor and send him on a tour. It would not be for a little while, until he got a little better on his legs, and stronger. But then they were going to send him out. Strange said the rumor was, to Hollywood. And the Hollywood Canteen. And all that. That was the how and the why of the deal, Strange said, that was going to keep him in the Army. At least until after the war was over.

"Then I guess he's all fixed up in pretty good shape," Winch said, feeling heavily relieved. It was hell, not being able to drink, at these parties. Winch stepped over to the bartender to see if he had any white wine. He did have.

"I wouldn't be too sure of that," Strange said. He shook his head. Because Prell wasn't too happy about it. He wanted to stay in the Army. But he wanted to go back to regular duty. "We all want to go back to regular duty," Winch said sourly. Strange nodded. But it wasn't the same with Prell. Prell really meant it, and believed it. Every day he was down there in the therapy rooms with the whirlpool bath and the exercises, pushing himself and his legs to the absolute limit. That was why he had made such incredible progress.

"But he's never going to have normal legs," Winch said, "an infantryman's legs, again. He's crippled. That's crazy."

"I know," Strange said.

Winch looked off to where Prell was, still with little Della Mae. He was back in his wheelchair again. He had been up on his feet for the ceremony, and for the pictures and cake cutting, and had walked a little bit. But even that little bit was obviously too much for the legs.

When he had first come in, Winch had gone straight up to him and shaken hands and congratulated him, and kissed little Della Mae on the cheek. The look of innocence on Della Mae's face had not changed a bit. Prell had reacted properly. He had shaken the hand and said, "Thank you." But he hadn't smiled.

A couple of times later Winch had caught him looking over at him across parts of the room, unsmiling, expressionless. The second time Winch had winked at him. Prell had simply stared back without expression, then had looked somewhere else. Winch could not even be sure he had seen the wink.

"The last time I saw him," Strange growled, following his gaze, "when we were alone, he told me that the first time he was physically able to put it in her, he knocked her up. He wasn't able either physically or mentally to pull it back out."

Winch snorted. "Yeah." He moved his gaze elsewhere. He suddenly realized Landers was not here. He hadn't seen him anywhere. His gaze fell suddenly upon the not-badlooking Gray Lady who taught the cripples their basket-weaving course in a corner of this very same rec hall all week long. She was clearly one of the Combined Ladies Clubs delegation, and she didn't have on her Gray Lady's uniform. She had on a very expensive dress, was obviously wealthy, and her middle-aged shortish blonde hair had just been marcelled into a very sexy, seductive hair-do. There was no Gray Lady's cap on it. She was a little dumpy, but she didn't have a bad ass at all, and had very nice tits. And Winch was suddenly afflicted with an immediate and totally uncontrollable need to go over to her and seize one of her tits gently, and pour all of his new, second glass of white wine onto her brand-new hair-do.

The need, the desire, was so strong Winch felt his feet tensing in his shoes preparatory to walking off in that direction. Instead, grasping himself and turning his already begun motion side-ways, he drank off his glass of wine and set the glass down.

"I got to get out of here," he growled to Strange. "I can't stand parties like this."

"Me neither," Strange said. "I'll go with you."

Outside, in the so-familiar corridor Winch had walked along so many times, Winch could feel sweat standing out on his forehead. He reached for a handkerchief in his pocket to wipe it off. His hand was trembling ever so slightly. It had been a very near thing. And he had not even been expecting it.

"What's your wife say, about you spending all that money up at the Peabody?" he suddenly said to Strange.

"Nothing. It aint her money. It's mine."

"Yeah," Winch growled.

"She's making a bundle up there in Cincinnati in her defense plant."

"Yeah. What's she say about this new girl of yours? This Frances? Or don't she know about that, either?"

"I don't guess she knows about it," Strange said, slowly and precisely. "But I reckon she suspects it." Strange did not go on for a long moment. "Anyway, we've split up," he said finally.

"Oh?" Winch said, "you have?"

"She's got some colonel, some lieutenant colonel, that she's been running around with up there for quite some time."

"I see. Another casualty of the war," Winch said, suddenly remembering Landers.

"Yeah," Strange said, "yeah. Yeah, I guess you could say that. That's pretty good." He paused. "Except I guess this goes a lot farther back than that. Than the war."

"Sure," Winch said. "They all do."

"Whatever happened to that wife of yours?"

"Oh, she's around," Winch said. "Somewhere."

"Yeah? Where?"

"Somewhere," Winch said. "Not in Luxor." Suddenly he grinned. They had long since passed out of the closed-in corridor into one of the open walkways, and were now out approaching the front gate, where the cabs were. "You ever get around to eating that pussy you were asking everybody about, awhile back."

Strange's face took on the look of a blatant lie, and he cleared his throat. "Well," he said, "no. I meant to. I just never did. I will, though. I will."

Winch signaled for a cab. "Just remember," he said as he got in, and grinned, "eating a cunt is the best thing there is for a broken heart."

"You can say that again," the cab driver put in.

"See you soon, Johnny Stranger," Winch said as he rolled up the window against the drizzle.

"See you soon, Mart," Strange called as he signaled for another cab.

Winch did not look back. He gave the driver the address of the apartment. Strange was all right. There was nothing to worry about over Strange. Strange was as solid as a goddam fucking rock. But Strange was worried about Prell. Winch's tired mind did not know if that meant ill for Prell or not.

The train of thought brought him back to Landers, and why he had not been at the wedding. That didn't sound good at all, to Winch. In the cab he fell asleep on the way into town, but woke dreaming the dream of the Japanese sergeant.

"Hey," he asked the driver. "Did I say anything just now? In my sleep?"

"No," the driver said, "I don't think so."

Winch relaxed and slid back. They were almost at the apartment. His mind felt like half-dried mud.

He did not know whether he would be able to cope with Landers, or not.

Unfortunately, it was just one week after the wedding that Harry L Prevor was shipped down, and a captain named Mayhew was sent in over him to command the 3516th Gas Supply Company.

CHAPTER 26

There was no way not to be involved in it, for Landers.

They had had vague rumors about Mayhew. So they were not unprepared. And the night before, Prevor had talked to the company noncoms. But Landers was both stricken and infuriated by the sick, sad smile on Prevor's face, the afternoon when Mayhew appeared in the orderly room to take over Prevor's company.

The reason Landers had not gone to Prell's wedding was that he was working. Now that he was a s/sgt and section leader on the 3516th's T.O. he had a section to take care of as well. And all his late afternoons, which was when the wedding was, as well as his evenings, were spent teaching the cadre their jobs, and checking or doing over the paperwork of the day. To keep the 3516th with Prevor, and away from the Mayhews. His emotional commitments were no longer with Bobby Prell, they were with Prevor and the 3516th. Though he often felt Prevor had been unwise in giving him a staff sergeancy, and a section to handle.

But his heart went out to Prevor with a violent lurch, when Mayhew arrived.

At the same time a little thrill of recognition slid through Landers, exciting him. Here was something really happening. To somebody else. This wasn't the heated imaginings of some psycho-neurotic. Here was a case of Hitler's Germany, and the world of the Japanese, alive and kicking, breathing and well, in the good old US of A. Here was something that could be acted against. Landers' excitement was almost greater than his sorrow for Prevor.

And next morning, when the company tumbled outside into the cold dark for reveille, the same sick, sad smile was on Prevor's Mongolian face, when he was forced to stand as executive officer, five paces behind the new captain as the captain took the reports. By then Landers was in an outrage of righteous fury.

The night before the takeover Prevor had called his little clerk force and his mess sergeant and supply sergeant together in the orderly room (his cadre plus Landers, in effect), and given them a lecture and a little speech. Then he called the company noncoms together with them, and gave them another, slightly watered-down version.

He told them, in essence, that he did not want them to make any trouble. "I don't know how much of your personal loyalty is to me. I've never asked. But I don't want any of you to let personal loyalty to me get in the way of your loyalty to the company. That's what's important. We've taken a bunch of unattached, uncommitted fellows . . . not all of them too happy with what was happening to them"—he smiled his wry smile—"and we've made a dependable outfit with pride in itself and each other. Men who can depend on each other. That's the best anybody can do, and we've done that. I don't want to see us, the outfit, lose it. We're getting a change of command, and a change of command means a change of style. That's natural. But a change of style is only modal. It doesn't affect the essentials, and we've got those. Let's not lose that."

Landers thought it was a nearly perfect speech. Prevor may have used a few big, intellectual's words like *modal* that the rank and file would not know, but the quality was there, and the heart of it was the truth. Landers couldn't fault him. He himself would certainly not have been so generous.

Prevor was a little less circumspect with the cadre. "I know you guys can cause him a lot of trouble, if you want to. I'm asking you personally, as a personal favor to me, not to do it. I don't know what he's like, any more than you do. But he can't be all that different and bad."

Landers found out, almost immediately, that this was wrong. What Mayhew was like was about as bad as you could get.

He was one of those tough-guy officers. The ones who would not ask their men to do anything they wouldn't do. The trouble was Mayhew would do anything. And he had a company of men who could do very little, and wanted to do even less. He apparently never understood this. His arrogance was insufferable.

He, too, made a little speech. It alienated the company immediately. His central theme was: "We have played around enough. We are going to shape up around here." In the first place, they hadn't been playing around. In the second, they knew there was nothing much to shape up. He was not talking to a bunch of green men. He was talking to men who had been through the mill, over and over and back again. Nevertheless Mayhew expanded on this at some length to the company standing at attention on the freezing parade ground. Mayhew did not stand at attention but moved around, and a couple of times even slapped himself with his arms against the chill. When he did stand at attention, for a little while, nobody gave a damn.

Mayhew had come up from the ranks, he told them. So he knew how enlisted men thought. So nobody need expect to get by with anything. Landers, standing at attention and listening, had a vivid mental picture of the crowds of heads Mayhew must have stepped on, crushing a number, during his climb.

He must have been on the defensive. Coming into an outfit with a relatively well-liked commander and taking over, as he was. But it did not matter. Certainly not to Landers. And not to much of anyone else. The result was only to make Prevor, who had not been all that well-loved really, seem like a saint.

One of the things that distressed the whole company more than anything else was the leaving of Prevor in it as its executive officer. There was no need to have done that. There was no way the former commander could avoid losing face, in such a position. Simply being there, with nothing to do, was a loss of face. That Mayhew was a captain, and therefore able technically to come in over Prevor, meant nothing to the company. Whatever it meant to Second Army. The company had to look at Prevor's face. And it made them angry. The whole deal offended them, and offended their sense of fair play. Even Second Army should have known better than to do that. That was not the kind of reward a man should receive.

The company began to disintegrate immediately. Performance levels dropped in the training exercises. Formations became sluggish. Bickering and insubordination with noncoms grew. And the noncoms did nothing about it. There were always plenty of ways to drop a monkey wrench in the machinery and not get caught, and everybody now had the same common enemy. When Prevor had made them do stupid things, like the basic training, they had had Second Army to hate. Now they blamed Mayhew. Guilty or not. And were swiftly on their way back to being an unorganized gang of malcontents.

Landers sat back and watched and kept his mouth shut. He still had in front of him his tacit promise to Prevor not to make trouble. But he felt ready to make trouble.

The second or third day after his takeover Mayhew had called him into the commander's office for a private talk. "We have some things we have to straighten out," was the way he began.

The commander's office had changed. Under Prevor it had been a place where the noncoms dropped in for a cup of hot coffee and a discussion. Now noncoms were not welcome, and the coffee was reserved for officers. Unfortunately, the only telephone was in there and Landers or the 1st/sgt had to go in there to use it. But the coffee was not free even to the clerk force.

"I know what a key man you are around here, Sergeant," Mayhew said from behind his desk. "You have not," and he smiled, "escaped even the eyes of Second Army.

"But I am not happy with that rating you wear. The rating for an assistant clerk on the T.O. is a corporal. You're on the T.O. as a section sergeant. But you're not really handling the section you're assigned to. You're mostly in here, doing clerical work. We're going to have to do something about that. Lt Prevor was inclined to be sloppy with his designations." He smiled again.

Landers did not trust himself to answer for a moment. Rage was charging through him. "Yes, sir," he said evenly, after a few seconds. "I suggest you bust me back down right away, then. I didn't ask for the rating I'm wearing. And in fact, didn't want it. You can bust me to corporal, and I'll function as your assistant clerk. Or you can bust me down to private and I'll go back to straight duty.

"Matter of fact, I'd just as soon be a private doing straight duty, in your outfit, sir."

Mayhew's face could not help registering surprise. Then it stiffened sharply. "No. That's not what I want. You will continue as you are. We'll see about all the rest, later. Do you think the first sergeant and clerk are capable of handling their jobs yet?"

"No, sir," Landers said. "They're certainly not. Nor are the mess sergeant and supply sergeant, without help."

"Then I want you to keep on what you're doing. Forget about your section and spend your time teaching the cadre. That's all, Sergeant. You're dismissed."

"Yes, sir," Landers said. Then he decided to be sarcastic. "Thank you, sir." But it appeared lost on Mayhew.

Landers had to go somewhere by himself and sit down to cool off. Was the man stupid? Was he some important person's nephew? He clearly knew, from Second Army if from no other, how much Landers had done and was doing to keep the 3516th running. Then why go out of his way to antagonize a man he needed?

From that moment on there was a sort of generic hatred between them, hidden and covered up by Landers, but open and openly expressed by Mayhew. Landers began to slack off in his evening work, and evening teaching. There was no way in the world Mayhew or anybody could order him to do office work after supper, not without risking an investigation. Anyway, the 1st/sgt and clerk did not relish working evenings, unless pressed to it by Landers. Besides, Mayhew kept the commander's office locked by key, and that was where most of the work material was. Landers began going to movies in the evenings, or getting drunk on beer at the small sectional local PX, or just sitting around thinking about women. The lack of women was beginning to get to him now, after all these weeks.

One time he was able to talk to Lt Prevor about it, out in the freezing cold company area, just at dusk one freezing cold evening. Landers wanted to be released from his tacit promise not to make trouble. Prevor reluctantly released him, but at first refused to.

"What do you mean, make trouble? What more trouble can you make, if you've stopped teaching the cadre? Anything more would have to be open sabotage of the office work. You can't do that."

"I can quit. Go back to straight duty as a private," Landers said. "That would make plenty of trouble."

"But you'd be cutting off your nose to spite your face."

"No, I wouldn't."

"You don't want to go back to straight duty."

"I wouldn't mind straight duty. Tossing gas cans around in the trucks would be heavenly, compared to working for that son of a bitch."

"You wouldn't feel like that after you'd been doing it a little while," Prevor said.

There was something else, too, he could do. But Landers instinctively shied away from mentioning it to Prevor. He could go over the hill: desert. That could cause Mayhew the worst trouble. Landers felt like laughing. But he did not want to mention it to Prevor. Anyway, after talking to Prevor, he did not feel quite so bad. Although Prevor in effect released him from the so-called promise, he decided not to do anything for a while.

It was the fucking telephone that was the last straw, and finally drove him over the line. Since the beginning it had been situated in the company commander's office. In the days of Prevor it had not been a problem. When it rang, whoever was near it picked it up and answered it. Since his very first arrival Mayhew had taken to never answering the phone personally. Even when he was in his office alone at his desk, where the phone sat, doing nothing, he would call out, "Sergeant, get the phone." And whoever was in the outer office, usually Landers or the clerk, would have to stop whatever work they were doing and go into the commander's office and answer it. Just about always the call was for Mayhew.

One day, a week after Landers' talk with Prevor, Mayhew did this, "Sergeant Landers, get the phone," and Landers exploded. That the explosion was entirely internal did not make it any less powerful. Maybe it made it more. Mayhew was leaning back in his swivel chair with his boots up on his desk, smoking one of his cigars. It seemed to Landers that he looked at Landers with hatred and amused contempt.

After he had answered it (it was for Mayhew) and handed it over, he went back to his own desk in the outer office and sat looking at his trembling hands. "What's the matter with you?" the cadre clerk whispered nervously. He had been looking at Landers more and more nervously, lately. "Are you all right?"

"Me?" Landers said. "Me? Fine. Just fine. I'm just fine. Why?"

It was nearly five-thirty and quitting time, and when Mayhew left, locking the inner office, and the 1st/sgt and the others left the outer office, Landers did not even go back to the barracks but walked through the cold down to the little local PX and from one of those freezing cold little pay telephone booths outside under the front door floodlights, called Johnny Stranger in Luxor at the Peabody suite.

"I'm coming in," he said, the phone beginning to shake against his ear with cold. "I want you to have everything ready for me."

"You're what?" Strange asked. "Have you got a pass?"

Landers did an abrupt about-face. He hadn't even been think-ing about Strange. Strange would only try to talk him out of it, if Strange knew he was going over the hill. "Of course," Landers said scornfully. "Do you think I'd come in if I didn't have a pass? Is Mary Lou there?"

There was some rustling.

"I'm taking off," Landers said harshly, as soon as she came on. "I'm going over the mountain. Do you want to run away with me? Have you got someplace to go?"

"You're what, you're what?"

"Hush!" Landers barked. "I don't want Strange to hear this. Or even know about it. Are you where he can hear you?"

"No. No, I'm in the bedroom."

"Then, listen. I'm skipping. Pulling out. Do you want to go away somewhere with me?" She must have somewhere she could take him that was safe, some home, some place.

"But, Marion, I can't do that," Mary Lou wailed. "I've got a boyfriend. I'm in love. He's on his way up here, right now. We're going to get married, I think. We're— We're in love."

"Oh," Landers said, "well." He stopped, at a loss. It had not occurred to him Mary Lou would not go, and he had no other resources. He should have guessed it about Mary Lou. But there must be somebody. In the world. Who was willing to hide him. The cold was beginning to get to him so badly his teeth were chattering into the phone. But he couldn't think of anyone.

"I could maybe get Annie Waterfield for you," Mary Lou said. "She's back."

"Is she there?"

"No. But she's supposed to be coming over. I could try to get hold of her for you."

"You have her phone number?"

"I have her home number here in town."

"All right, get her for me. And I mean, get hold of her. Don't fuck around. Don't tell her I'm going AWOL. I want to tell her. But you get hold of her for me, hear? Or I'll— Now, give me Strange. And keep your mouth shut. To Strange and everybody."

Cold as he was, and shaking uncontrollably, he talked to Strange for several minutes, to kill Strange's suspicions. If he had any. It appeared that he had some, and when Landers hung up he did not think he had allayed any.

He was too cold now to stand out on the cab stand and wait for a cab. He went inside the little local PX and drank three cold mugs of beer at the bar. They warmed him and gave him some spirit. He had a full half pint of whiskey back at the company barracks, and wished he had brought it, but did not want to go back there after it. Luckily he had on his regular ODs and had his GI overcoat, instead of a field jacket uniform.

The little local PX, one of five on the big post, was nowhere near the size of the big main PX beer hall. But it still had plenty of room, and plenty of beer drinkers. It was warm and funky with the smell of tobacco smoke and damp GI wool and stale beer. There was a magnificent feeling of safety in numbers about it and its crowded interior. It was an illusion. But at least these guys here, bitter and sour or happy and acting up, were on the right side of the line. They would at least die in bunches and groups, not alone. Landers had a distinct feeling of hating to leave its warmth, as he buttoned up his GI overcoat and turned up its high collar. He went outside.

It was a long, chill ride in the taxi. There was no trouble getting out of the post's main gate, in a cab. He found nobody had kept their mouths shut to anybody, when he got to the Peabody.

Rather than argue it out with Strange, Landers claimed his rights with Annie Waterfield first. Mary Lou had gotten hold of her and she was there waiting. Nobody could argue against that with him. When they had locked themselves in the bedroom, he thought he had better tell Annie the truth. Until they made their way to the door and got inside, and shut the door and locked it, he took refuge in the statement that he was only taking a little AWOL vacation of a few days, or maybe a week, and that he was being covered for, in his company. But inside he told Annie the truth.

He did not tell her before the sex was taken care of, though. Annie had her own rights. "You're in much better shape than you were before you went out to O'Bruyerre," she said, running her hands over his bare shoulders. Landers had to admit he did not require much urging, mental distress or not. After they had sixty-nined awhile and come that way, and he had gone down on her while she had a multiple orgasm of at least two or three, he fucked her and came again himself and they lay on the bed side by side replete while he fondled one of those gorgeous breasts.

"Have you got any money?" she said.

"A little over eight hundred dollars. In a bank."

"That should last us a week or ten days," Annie said. "We can go up to St. Louis."

"I can probably get a few hundred more off of Strange," he said.

"Say two weeks, then," she said. She sat up and leaned on her elbow, and her young breast became heavy in his cupped palm. "But I have to say," she said, looking down at him, "that I don't think it's such a good idea. I don't think you ought to do it, Marion. Besides."

"Besides, what?" Landers said.

"Besides, I've got this trip to New Orleans I can take, if I don't go with you. That's what. I've got this Navy flyer I met here who's being transferred to New Orleans. He wants me to go down there with him and stay three weeks or a month. I hate to give that up to go off with you, with practically no money, and the chance of you getting picked up always hanging over our heads. I have to admit it."

"Have you got anyplace we could go and be safe? Some kind of refuge, or place only you know about? That was more what I had in mind."

She didn't answer. She continued to sit, leaning on her elbow. "Don't do that. I'm trying to think." She took his wrist and moved his hand away from her breast.

"You know," she said, "it's kind of crazy, but I do have a place like that. I don't go there much."

"Where is it?"

"It's my dad's."

"No good," Landers said. "If somebody here told on us, that you were with me, that'd be the first place they'd look."

Annie's voice trilled with a young, bright laughter. "And a fuck lot of good it would do them. My dad's the sheriff."

It was almost square in the middle of west Tennessee, way west of Nashville. No cities around anywhere. Did Landers have any idea how country west Tennessee was? There was no reason why Landers couldn't go up there and stay as long as he liked. All she would have to do would be to call her dad, and give Landers a note to him. Her daddy had been sheriff there since before she could remember. Actually, since the county law was that a sheriff could not succeed himself, her daddy and his number-one deputy traded places every four years, and the deputy would be sheriff for a term. "But there's never any question who the real sheriff is," Annie laughed. "That's my daddy." Barleyville was the county seat, her hometown. "A great name," she laughed, "for the county seat of a dry county. In Barleyville, the saying goes, there're two kinds of people. Baptists and drunks." There were also a lot of Holy Rollers.

"It doesn't sound like the swingingest place in the world," Landers said.

"You'd be surprised. Booze and juke joints may be illegal, but there are plenty of them around," Annie laughed. "And my daddy knows them all. He owns half of most of them."

"Any Army camps around there?"

There was one. Fort Dulane. About fifteen or twenty miles from Barleyville. But that wouldn't matter. Her daddy would know every provost marshal and MP there. "He'll get you a pocketful of blank pass forms, if you want them," she laughed.

"But you wouldn't be going with me," Landers half asked.

"No, I don't think so." She really wanted to make this trip down to New Orleans. And she didn't go up to Barleyville much any more. She had taken a boyfriend up there for a week a couple of different times, but it upset her daddy so and made him so sad she had about stopped it. "And if I go up there alone, there're five or six old flames of mine from back in high school, who come buzzing around like bees around a sugar cube," Annie laughed. Her bare breasts swayed deliciously, and quivered. "Of course, they're all of them married, if only to stay out of the draft. It tends to create a certain havoc. While I'm there."

Landers studied her. "Do you fuck them?"

Annie laughed again. "Well, it doesn't really matter if I do or not. Believe me. It doesn't."

"I guess not."

"I have," she said. "Have fucked them all. At one time or another. In the past. And all that kind of upsets daddy, too."

She got up off the bed and went to the spindly little hotel desk and got a sheet of hotel stationery out of its drawer. Carefully she tore the hotel letterhead off the top, using the big desk blotter edge as a straightedge. Then she tore off the bottom line that carried the hotel's name, address, and phone number. She held what was left up to the light. While she did all this, she went on talking gaily, about her family.

"I never knew a man who understands women like my daddy. But maybe that's natural, with him having four daughters." She was nineteen, her next youngest sister sixteen. The two younger ones, who had come along ten years later, were now nine and eight. "Love babies," Annie laughed. "You know. When people almost break up and then get back together, they often have a baby or two." That was what happened to her folks. Her daddy had had a mistress, or at least that was the local story. Now they were separated, though still married, and her mother lived on the other side of town with the two younger girls in a fine old expensive brick house, and was the mistress of one of the local politicians who was a bigwig in the state senate in Nashville. His wife, a Barleyville girl, and their kids lived in Nashville. Loucine, the sixteen-year-old sister, lived with their daddy in their big old house across town that their daddy had bought for them when Loucine was born. Loucine, at the moment, was about eight months pregnant and still unmarried.

"Sounds like a wild wide-open place, Barleyville. For a country town," Landers said from the bed.

Annie stopped writing the note to her father and looked up, nude, her face laughing. "Are you kidding, country town? It's country people who really know what people are like. That's why they're all Baptists."

"Or drunks," Landers said.

"Or drunks." She finished the note, and signed it and folded it up. "I don't want to put this in a hotel envelope," she said. "It would just make daddy sad. Will you get a plain white envelope and put it in it?"

Landers took it and put it away carefully. When he looked back up, Annie still in the desk chair, still nude, had begun to laugh outrageously. "What's the matter, now?" he said.

"Nothing. Nothing. Just laughing. I was just thinking how you won't be there three days probably, before you'll be fucking my pregnant sixteen-year-old sister. Old Loucine." She began to laugh again.

Landers felt shocked. "Oh, no. No, no. I wouldn't do something like that."

"I don't see how you're going to avoid it." She stared at him, her face grinning more. "You're shocked," she said.

Landers felt irritated. "No, I'm not. Not shocked." He made himself grin. "But I don't want your daddy the sheriff to throw down on me with his shooting iron."

"My daddy would be more likely to throw down on you if you didn't," Annie laughed. "I told you he understood women, didn't I? Well, women are going to get love made to them. One way or another. And it doesn't matter what they call it. Or if they don't call it at all. Or don't mention it even, which is more likely. Well, my daddy was born knowing that, from a baby. I guess that's why women have always found him so attractive."

Landers found he had no answer.

"Come on," Annie said. "We might as well get dressed. I still have to call daddy for you."

"Listen, don't call from out there. I don't want Strange and those others—"

"Don't worry. I read your plans. You don't want Johnny Strange to know where you are, or to tell your Sergeant Winch." She smiled. "In actual fact, I was planning on taking you home with me to my place. I'll call daddy from there, and you can listen. Then I thought I'd see you off at the bus station."

"Well," Landers said, at a loss, "fine. But why are you so nice to me?" He felt perturbed. There had been whiskey available up here at the suite, and now he had drunk enough to make his courage considerably reinforced. But he was upset by the extravagance of her help. It made him want to look around for exits. "Why?" he said, and made himself grin. "Tell me why?"

Annie laughed. "I suppose it's partly because I'm not going to Barleyville with you. I feel a little guilty." She paused. "But I've had to run a couple of times in my life," she said more seriously, "and I know what it's like. Especially if you have no place really to run to."

"Let's get something straight," Landers said stiffly. "I'm not running anyplace. I'm leaving an untenable position."

"That was what I meant," Annie smiled. "Besides, you're a nice boy." She took a deep breath, and sighed. "But before you go through with this, I wish you'd think twice, Marion."

"I've thought twice," Landers said shortly. "More than twice."

While they dressed, she went on talking to him, about her sister Loucine. Now that they were moving, Landers wished that she would shut up about it all. It was as if having once got started talking about her family, she did not want to stop. Loucine had come down here to Luxor for a while to stay with her, she said, when the baby began to show, but Loucine had hated Luxor. After two months she had gone back home, to face it out. She preferred that to staying in Luxor.

"Nobody said anything to her?" Landers asked, tying his shoes.

Annie laughed. "What are they going to say? They've all seen unmarried pregnant girls. About as many as married." She was putting on her lipstick. "You know, times have changed, even since you've been away overseas. This old war has changed everything a lot."

Landers guessed that was true, but didn't care very much. He did not answer her. "Now you just let me handle Strange," he said.

But it wasn't that easy to handle Johnny Stranger. Landers pretended that he was just going off somewhere for a few days with Annie, and that he was being covered for in his outfit at O'Bruyerre, but Strange wasn't buying that.

"Listen, you crazy son of a bitch, Landers. I know exactly what you're trying to pull. And you're never going to get the fuck by with it. They'll trace you down, and they'll get you. They'll get you, and they'll do you in. So I'll goddamn follow you, if I have to." He reached and grabbed his own GI overcoat. "You crazy son of a bitch, I'll follow you and camp right outside your fucking doorstep, until you come back."

By this time it had all become a big joke to just about everybody in the suite, except Strange and Landers.

"You can't do it. You'll never get away with it," Strange half shouted. "You're ruining your fucking life. I'm not going to let you."

Several people tried to shout him down. In the end Landers had practically to tear himself out of Strange's arms, to get out of the door. It was only through the ministrations of Annie, plus some help from Frances Highsmith, that Strange was kept from following.

"I'm only taking him to my place, Johnny. I promise I'll call you from there. I swear I promise."

"Where is this place that's your place?" Strange demanded, shouting. "Nobody knows where the fuck you are. I'd never find him."

"No. And not just anybody's going to know, where my place is. Either," Annie said. "A girl's got to have some privacy. In her life. Around this stinking mess."

It was only on the strength of the promise to call that they were finally able to get outside.

And they did call him, after Annie had talked to Charlie Waterfield in Barleyville. Strange insisted on talking to Landers. Landers talked to him for five minutes, but was unable to convince him he was only taking a small AWOL vacation. He could only get off the line by promising faithfully that he would call tomorrow.

"I hate to lie to him," he said heavily, when he finally hung up.

"Come on," Annie said. "If you don't hurry, we'll miss your bus."

At the bus station he waved to her in the sea of faces until the bus turned out from the stall, and her face swung away with the others into invisibility. Then he was off on his single-handed, one-man adventure, alone. As soon as she was out of sight, it was curiously as if she had never existed. And deep down, he felt very righteous and very Christian, if a little sick.

But he couldn't help wondering what kind of a looking guy Charlie Waterfield must be.

CHAPTER 27

It was three in the morning, when the Greyhound pulled up for
Landers in Barleyville. Landers hadn't the least idea of what to
expect. And didn't much care. The windswept little town
square was empty, nothing was open. The driver had some
bundles of newspapers to deliver, depositing them against the
closed storefront of the newsstand. Then the big door closed,
and the hissing of the big bus's air brakes whispered, fading
across the square.

Almost at once, a tall figure in a sheepskin coat and a semi-
Western–style hat stepped leisurely out from the shelter of a
storefront, into the cold wind.

"Marion Landers?"

Landers said he was. "Charlie Waterfield. Annie's dad," the
other said. He was a lean man, but even in the heavy sheepskin
you could see he had the paunch of a heavy drinker.

"Might as well go somewhere where there's lights and people," he said.

There was an official sheriff's car parked across the street
against the courthouse square. The courthouse was a red brick

and white clapboard affair. It had a Sheriff's Office sign on it, and Landers realized Waterfield could have waited for the bus there, in his own office, where it was warm. Instead of standing alone out in the cold and wind, in a darkened storefront.

Waterfield was squinting up at the courthouse, through the bare branches of the big trees, from beside the driver's door of the car. "Damn grackles. Roosting in the eaves again. Do it every winter." He got in and slammed his door.

By the time Landers was in, he had a pint bottle of whiskey out. "Want a snort?" Landers accepted gratefully. Waterfield took one, then slipped it under the driver's seat.

But then he didn't start. Instead, he sat with his ungloved hands on the wheel, staring out across the country square. Landers got the impression of an immensely inarticulate man, tongue-tied not so much by dumbness, as by the terrible complexity of saying anything at all. After a minute, without a word, he turned the ignition key and jerked at the gear lever.

Somewhere in the outskirts of the town he pulled up to what up north would have been called a roadhouse. It was dark, and looked deserted and closed. Waterfield rapped on the door, anyway. A man in an open shirt and a woman in a long gown opened it. The two led them into music, warmth, low lights, and a long bar along the lefthand wall with a dance floor behind. Vera Lynn was singing "The Umbrella Man." There had been ten or twelve cars outside in the parking lot. All the people from them were in here.

Waterfield got a chorus of affectionate greetings. Somebody said, "Say, Charlie, who's your friend?"

"Friend of Annie's come to visit. From Luxor."

The point wasn't pressed, but it was an announcement. Any friend of Charlie's had better be a friend of Landers.

In the light, he had circles under his eyes so pronounced they gave him the look of an alert, very patient hound dog. The eyes looked at you with that same look of a smart hound, alert, patient, waiting.

They fixed a table for him, in what was apparently a ritual. Off by itself, with a bottle of whiskey, glasses, ice, and a pitcher of water. The two of them sat at it and talked as they drank, mostly questions by Charlie and answers by Landers about Annie.

How was she doing down there in Luxor? Was she in good

shape, healthy? Was she having a good time, was she happy? How was that job of hers holding up? Did she look good? Did she have decent friends?

Here was the only place he stumbled, over the adjective decent, which he half hesitated on, then changed to nice. So that the final question read: Did she have nice friends?

Landers answered the best he could, not knowing much about Annie. Landers did not know, for example, whether Annie had a job or not. He did not see how she could, going off for a week or a month with servicemen all the time. But he did not tell this to Charlie.

"She doesn't have to work," Charlie smiled, from below the perpetually alert hound's eyes. "I send her all the money she wants. But I guess she enjoys working." Landers thought it best not to make an answer to this at all.

There wasn't much question that Charlie was at least part owner of the joint. The lady manager in the gown came over to ask his advice on a technical question about the bar. "I don't want to talk about it now," was all he said, raising those alert, patient hound's eyes, and the lady faded. Charlie went back to his questions about Annie.

It was six-thirty and the daylight was coming up in the east, when they finally got home. Landers was both drunk and exhausted. Charlie showed no signs of either. He showed Landers to his bedroom in the huge derelict house, but he himself did not go to bed. He changed into his day uniform, and went out to do his morning inspection tour he did every day at this hour.

Changing into his day uniform meant taking off his navy blue pants, and the white shirt with shoulder straps, with its black four-in-hand tie; and putting on khaki pants and a khaki shirt with shoulder straps, and a khaki four-in-hand tie. The sheepskin coat and semi-Western–style hat he did not change. He walked out of the house, telling Landers that Loucine would be around the house when he woke up, to make him breakfast.

This was the pattern life took, in the big Main Street house. It was Charlie's pattern, but day by day Landers' pattern fell more and more in line with it. He got up at noon, had breakfast, then read the papers in the dark, unused living room. Then he went for a walk in the business district, hitting all the poolrooms, and in one of them he usually found Charlie. He would have a sandwich and a Coke laced with illegal whiskey for lunch in one of them. It was amazing how much whiskey there was

loose in this county seat of a dry county. Then he would go back
to the tall, spindly house and sleep or read for a couple of hours.
They almost always had dinner out with Loucine. Then when
Loucine went home to bed, the two of them would start
Charlie's late evening rounds that would last till dawn.

It was not such a terrible deal. At the very least he was safe
here. The only comment Charlie Waterfield ever made on his
being a deserter was to hand him a full book of blank pass forms.
"There's plenty more where these come from. And you're welcome to stay here as long as you like."

But of course that didn't solve anything. The problem was
somewhere else. Whenever Landers thought of Captain Mayhew and his fucking telephone, and what he had done to the
3516th, he went into a rage that was murderous, and which he
carefully hid, and he swore he would never go back.

But the sworn oath was always followed by a monstrously
deep, black depression, which drove him out to wherever there
was whiskey. He had not been there more than a week when he
knew he would not be able to stay.

When Landers woke that first morning at noon, it was to the
smell of bacon frying. When he could get dressed and downstairs, he found Loucine in her winter nightgown and a not very
sexy robe, cooking and eating her own breakfast. She did not
seem surprised to see him. She was enormously pregnant. She
was a small, slender girl, but she literally waddled around the
kitchen. It was a big, comfortable kitchen, sunny at the end
where the table was, on a sunny day. The plate of yellow scrambled eggs laced with red-brown strips of bacon and tan squares
of toast she placed before him looked and tasted delicious, in the
winter sunshine. Then she went off to get dressed.

Landers had to grin sourly two days later, when Annie's
prediction about how long it would take for him to end up in
bed with Loucine came true, a day ahead of schedule.

It happened suddenly. The second noon at breakfast she was
not in the flannel nightie and unsexy robe, and instead wore a
thin shorty nightgown and a knee-length negligee, also thin.
When Landers went into the living room after he'd eaten, and
sat down with the papers, she sat silent on a windowseat near
him and looked out over the town, which was under a thin
snow, granular and sifting like flour. The next afternoon she
was suddenly in his lap, between him and the papers, crushing
the Louisville *Courier-Journal*, although Landers never quite

knew how she arrived there. Charlie seemed to make it a point
of not coming home at this time of day.

So Loucine was added to Landers' daily life pattern in Barleyville. Her time was the early afternoon, or the early and late
afternoon, depending. Loucine would screw him as many times
each afternoon as he felt he was capable of screwing. The record
was ten, in four hours of one afternoon. Landers wanted to see
just how far she would go, and what her limit was, and also
whether he could get her to talk, besides just saying hello and
good-by. Besides, he had nothing much else to do. But he never
found out. And afterward she had to make him a big raw-
eggs-and-milkshake drink, to help his shaky legs, before he went
out for his daily walk down the street and a half of business
establishments and pool halls.

Charlie introduced him to lots of other available women, during the nights. Almost all were married, or at least engaged, to
guys who were away overseas, or at least off somewhere in the
Army. All of them were lonely, and hungry for a cock.

Landers had a sneaking feeling that Charlie already had made
out with each of the ones he himself went off with. But Charlie
never talked about it, or about women. The women never talked
about it, either. Any more than Loucine did. It was as if the
women all felt that if they did not talk about it, it would seem
not to have happened. And they all would still be getting the
release they all needed.

So there were plenty of women. But Landers began to resent
being the out-of-town stud for all the juke joint ladies. Besides,
he got tired. Serving as stud to a pregnant lady was not all that
easy. After the first couple of times the novelty wore off. Especially if like Loucine she didn't talk. He discovered it required
an enormous amount of physical energy, because you had to be
careful to keep yourself up off her stomach. What it amounted
to, finally, was a sort of series of unlimited push-ups, until either
you came or your arms gave out, whichever happened first. But
Landers felt he owed it to Loucine. He certainly owed them
something for taking him in. And after his afternoons with
Loucine, he was not up to other ladies. He took to spending
more and more of the nights just with Charlie, getting drunk
and just talking.

They talked about everything, excepting women. There was
something about Charlie that seemed to insist on seeing all
women as ladies. He was prepared and willing to make excuses

for all of them. Most of his Southern confreres, Landers had found—indeed, most Americans—divided women into two distinctive categories: ladies and whores. With no shadings of gray in between. But not Charlie. He had only the one category.

Twice while Landers was with him in the sheriff's car he drove over across town in the late afternoon to see his wife. Charlie, it turned out, brought her every afternoon the groceries she wanted for that evening and the next day.

Landers was curious to see her, knowing what Annie had told him about her down in Luxor. She was a good-looking woman for her age, about forty-five, and she had not lost what they called bloom. She still had a figure. But for a roundish face such as she had there was a peculiarly elusive ferretlike toughness to some part of it. She had a soft, gentle, delightful Southern smile, which went all the way up to and deep into her eyes, with a kind of ropy, sexy charm of innocence. She almost never relaxed this smile in her eyes, even when her face wasn't smiling. The few times she did, the very few times Landers caught her at it, Landers thought he saw behind it the eyes of a shrewd, hard-hitting poker player. The kind he would not want to play against, in any serious game.

She took one look at Landers, and decided immediately Landers was sleeping with her second-oldest daughter. Both she and Landers knew what this conclusion she had made was. Both knew there would be no revoking it. While Charlie was unloading the car of its groceries, Landers sat with her in the parlor and talked politely.

Her first name was Blanche. She was, it came out quickly in her talk, a pillar among the local Baptists, and wanted to know if perhaps Landers would come down to the church to some of their meetings. Landers said he would be delighted to. She smiled her thanks. But she carefully did not press him for a specific time.

Apparently Annie in Luxor was the only one who knew she was the mistress of the local Nashville politician, Landers thought. But then he revised that. Charlie knew. Then he revised again: Everybody knew.

The two little girls of nine and eight were abominable. They were both spoiled totally rotten. Worse, even at eight and nine they were both already well aware of being females, knew that this carried special privileges, utilized these shamelessly, and just did not have the finesse yet to hide it. They flirted outra-

geously, just as if they were already women, and thrust out their
little buds of breasts as though the breasts had already grown
into what they would someday become.

Outside in the car, when Charlie had delivered all the groceries, Charlie stared off through the windshield again. As if he
were about to say something. But he thought better of it, and
threw the car violently into gear. Before he released the clutch,
he took a deep breath and let out one huge sigh.

Sitting there, watching and saying nothing, not even involved, Landers had the impression he was with a man who in
the course of his life had had to learn the hard way to cope with
a great many disarrayed and enigmatic things, and had done it;
but in the course of doing it, had found a great many other
darknesses he would never be able to cope with ever. Not ever.
Never.

Landers never had found out when Charlie slept, and never
did. It wasn't in the morning. And it certainly wasn't in the
afternoon, because he was never there. Landers finally decided
he must exist by catnapping. Like a combat soldier. Sleeping a
half hour at a time, in his big swivel chair at his desk, in the back
room of his office at the courthouse.

When they had taken Loucine out to eat and brought her back
home, Charlie brightened up. As the two of them set off on his
evening rounds. And that night it was Charlie who went off
somewhere with one of the lonely juke joint ladies. Leaving
Landers behind for an hour or two. Landers could almost hear
him sighing. Simplicity, simplicity.

It was near the end of the third week he had been there that
Landers told him he couldn't stay. It would not have been true
to say that his final decision was due to their two visits to
Blanche and the little girls. But it was possible meeting them
caused him to make the decision earlier.

He tried to explain to Charlie how there was just too much
going on, too many things that had not been resolved; too much,
too, he hadn't solved for himself. Charlie apparently had already
anticipated this. He had a sad, rueful smile and said he suspected
as much, but he must add that he thought it was a mistake.

"You know, this war's not going to last forever. May seem like
it to you, but it aint. We've won it, now."

"A lot of good men are going to die before the Germans and
Japs believe that," Landers said somberly.

"I know, and that's sad, but what I say's the truth, just the same. Soon's this invasion of France gets under way, sometime this spring, it's not going to be too long in Europe. And the goddam Japs're already whipped. Just going to take a little power."

Landers thought this was an awfully large and conclusive statement to swallow, without water. Especially coming from a Tennessee country sheriff. What he felt must have shown on his face.

"Believe me. Just believe me," Charlie said. "A year in Europe. Another six months for the Japs. I've got friends in Washington. They know. They're already planning.

"Anyway, I think it would be pretty silly for you to get killed in this war, now. You've already done your share.

"So you just think it over a couple days. And in the meantime, let me make you a proposition."

"What kind of a proposition?"

"You just stay here with us. Forget about going back to the Army. That's the proposition."

Landers was staring at him, and didn't answer.

"Just think about it," Charlie urged. "That's all I ask. In a month you can start putting on civilian clothes. I can even get you a job, if you want. But you don't need it.

"Nobody's going to say a word to you. Nobody'll pick you up. Not in my county."

For Landers it was a little breathtaking, that the law could be so grandly circumvented so totally, and with such confidence.

"You think about it," Charlie said.

"What about my citizenship?" Landers asked. "I'll get a dishonorable discharge out of it, finally, in the end. As a deserter. Lose my citizenship. Lose my right to vote." He wrinkled up his face. "Not that I give a shit about voting."

"I'm telling you, that can all be taken care of. Maybe not right now. But certainly after the war," Charlie said. "And maybe right away. I told you, I got friends in Washington."

"Well!" Landers said. "It's some proposition. Why?"

Charlie made a squeezed, painful shrug. "Well, we like you. I certainly do. And Loucine has gotten to like you a lot. I even suspect that she's in love with you."

"In love with me!"

Charlie held up a big hand. "Young women her age fall in love, Marion. If you happen to be standing close to them, and are in focus at the right moment, they fall in love with you. You move away a few feet, they fall in love with another one, that happens to be closer. That's just the way it is."

Landers did not trust himself to answer. No mention had been made of his sleeping with her.

"You could do a lot worse than Loucine," Charlie said. "You wouldn't have to marry her, of course. Unless you decided you truly wanted to. And that kid's my property. The one she's carrying. I'll take care of him, and I'll raise him. You wouldn't have to take on that responsibility unless you truly wanted to.

"Have you ever thought about how you'd be as a deputy sheriff? I think you'd be pretty good. You've got natural authority, and you stand right." Suddenly he grinned, impishly. "Anyway, all you have to do is walk around and look important, look like you know things. And have a piece of a bunch of the right kind of investments."

Landers still did not answer.

"You could grow up to be a good sheriff yourself. In a very few years. And Loucine is going to make somebody a fine wife."

"Charlie, she's hardly said ten words to me since I've been here," Landers said.

"That's why she'll make a good wife," Charlie said solemnly.

Landers thought briefly that vaguely, like some transparent apparition, he could see the fine faint hand of Blanche in this somewhere. But then he thought he couldn't.

"Well, Jesus, Charlie. I don't know," he said finally.

"You think about it," Charlie smiled. "Let me tell you something. I know you're a friend of Annie's. But that won't matter. Annie's a rover. Always been. She's always going to be on the run. Loucine's not. Loucine's a regular homebody. You give Loucine a home and she'll never stir. She just aint got any home, yet.

"Let me tell you something else. About being a father. A father is the garbage pail of a family. Everything that's getting a little old, or getting to smell a little, or is going bad, or is upsetting, is dumped on him. Just like a garbage pail. That's what he's for."

"I don't know if I'm ready to be a father."

"Well, nobody is," Charlie said.

It was a munificent offer, in its way. Almost unbelievable. Charlie didn't even ask that he marry Loucine and give the kid his name. Of course, Charlie probably figured that he would, if he simply stayed around long enough. Landers promised that he would think it over for two days. But even before he promised, even from the very beginning of it, he had known he was not going to accept. He did think it over for the two days. But nothing he thought changed.

"Charlie, I just can't," he said when the two days were up. "Too many things aren't finished. I've got to run out the string, you know?"

"You're going back?" They were in one of the four or five joints Charlie had first introduced him to. It was late in the night. The Tex Beneke Band was singing "Chattanooga Choo Choo."

"I have to, Charlie," Landers said.

"Well, the offer still holds. I don't know how long it'll be open. Like I said, you move away a few feet, and they focus on somebody else."

"Sure. I know. And if it had all happened a month from now, well maybe." But he didn't really believe that. "I'll leave on the bus tomorrow."

When he said good-by to Loucine, she put her arms around his neck, and began to cry. "Oh, I'm going to miss you so, Marion." Landers was startled.

Charlie delivered him to the one o'clock bus. As the big door closed, and the bus's air hissed, Charlie called one last thing to him.

"Remember!" he yelled.

CHAPTER 28

There was an awful, frightening depth to the depression that hit Landers when the taxi from Luxor carried him back inside O'Bruyerre. The sprawling, grimy, coal-smoke-smeared, mud-greased areas of the huge camp stretched for miles. From miles away, the pall of coal smoke that hung above it was visible like a flat, gray umbrella. The place seemed to have grown in even the weeks Landers had been away.

To come back into it as an unidentifiable nonentity among tens of thousands of other nonentities was unbearable.

And yet, under the depression was the orange-colored pick of excitement in his chest, as his frantic adrenal glands poured into him the juices for his coming combat. He wouldn't have missed it for anything.

Landers hated himself for coming back to it when he could have stayed away. But he could no more have stayed away than he could have changed himself into a genuine deserter.

There had been no trouble getting in, at the main gate. On the ride out from town he had thrown away the precious block of blank pass forms, in case he should be searched, and kept only the current one, filled out for the past three days. But the MPs at the gate paid no attention to him, and he hadn't even needed it.

Once back inside under his own steam he was no longer a deserter. He was only an AWOL.

Once inside, he told the driver to drive him right on down to the 3516th's barracks. After the expense of the ride out from town, it didn't cost that much more. In Luxor, he had not even gone around to the Peabody to see Strange, partly out of shame for having lied to him, but partly because he did not want Strange to get on the phone to Winch, and have Winch involved with planning his return. But now some instinct of self-preservation, once he was back inside on his own, made him change his mind about Winch.

He told the driver to take him up to the Second Army Command building, instead. The numbers of men and vehicles and amounts of matériel that were on the move in the camp were overwhelming. When they passed the section of camp where the old Division had been which had left for England, he saw that a totally new Division with a different patch had moved in.

On the third floor of the Command building, Winch came out to get him. He led him past the acre and a half of clerks outside his private office, then shut the door and looked at him with a somber grin.

"So you're back." His voice sounded strangely faint.

"Back," Landers said. "Yeah. I'm back."

"At least you got back on your own hook. That will help some." Winch hauled the bottle of Seagram's up out of its desk drawer. "Make yourself a drink."

Landers had intended to refuse a drink. But now it was in front of him, he accepted. "Thanks," he said stiffly. It was so hard to know at any given time exactly what Winch was really thinking. It always had been. "Just how much do you know about all this?" he asked.

Winch stared at him a moment, with what appeared to Landers to be irritated disbelief. Then he said mildly, "I only know what Johnny Stranger told me when he phoned. And what Mayhew told me."

"Mayhew!" Landers said. "You know Mayhew?"

"I went down there and talked to him, after I talked to Strange."

"A shit," Landers said. "An absolute shit."

"Listen," Winch said, "wake up. I've known everything about

you since you went to that outfit. Where do you think those fouled up Morning Reports came, when those boys filled them out? Who do you think sent them back? Where do you think that payroll came, before it went on to Finance?"

"I don't know," Landers said with bravado. "Where? Here?"

"Do you have any idea at all of what is going to happen to you?" Winch said.

For the first time since he had come in the outside door, Landers looked at him seriously, the way he should have first looked at him. Winch looked pallid to him. He had lost the too thin, sharp look he had had. His face looked heavier, and his paunch had begun to come back. Office life was agreeing with him. Or wasn't agreeing with him.

Landers grinned. "No. I don't."

"Mayhew wants to make an example of you. He's going to send you to the stockade, and have you transferred overseas immediately, as a replacement. A recalcitrant replacement, is what they call them, secretly."

"Fine," Landers said. "Even better than I'd hoped."

"You got any idea what it's like to be shipped overseas like that? I don't have to go into it, do I? A new outfit? You don't know anybody? The dirtiest jobs. The most dangerous assignments. You'll be on probation. No rewards, or thanks. No fucking Medals of Honor. You're a marked man."

Landers made himself grin. "All this was your idea?"

"I tried my level best to talk him out of it. To no avail. You hit him right where he lives. His outfit has fallen apart all around him."

"Well," Landers said. "At least there's that. Second Army will—"

"Second Army will nothing. Mayhew is the favorite pet of some clique at Second Army HQ in Luxor. Nothing's going to hurt him."

"What about Prevor?"

"Prevor? If Prevor's lucky, he'll be sent overseas with the outfit, as Mayhew's exec. If he's unlucky, he'll be reassigned right here. If Prevor's very lucky, he'll be able to hang on overseas until that fool Mayhew gets himself killed, and then Prevor will reinherit his old outfit and, if it isn't totally ruined, make it back into something. But you won't be there to see any of it."

"I don't care," Landers said, and forced another grin. "At least I'll have made that asshole Mayhew think a little."

"No. Men like Mayhew don't think much. They more run on pure instinct, like a dog does. The only trouble is, right now all that instinct is in hatred, and directed right at you."

Winch suddenly turned clear around, turning his back on Landers, and sat down at his desk. He appeared to be breathing heavily. Angrily, Landers thought. But after a moment he leaned back in his expensive-looking swivel chair and appeared to grow calmer. Landers wanted to kick him in the balls.

"There's only one way to get you out of this," Winch said.

"Yes?" Landers breathed, sarcastically. "How?"

"We've got to get him to agree to let you go up to the hospital first, for a few days."

"Hospital? What for?"

"For observation," Winch said, calmly. "Before he sends you to the stockade."

"Oh, no," Landers said. "Oh, no." He was standing, but he thought he was sitting down. So that when he put his hands behind him and pushed, and jumped up to his feet, he actually simply jumped straight up in the air and came back down on his heels. It looked peculiar, to say the least. "No, sir. Not me. You're not going to pull any of that shit on me."

"Well," Winch said reasonably, "it's either that, or off you go to the stockade immediately."

"Not me," Landers said. "No, sir. I'm not going to play psycho. Not for you. Not for anybody."

"Well," Winch said, "there's not much to doing it."

"I wouldn't even know how to go about it."

"Just act crazy," Winch said. He was staring at him mildly. His face was wide open, receptive.

"Mayhew's the one who's crazy, not me," Landers raged. "Look at the way he came into that outfit, and balled it all up. Antagonizing everybody."

"I agree. But unfortunately we don't have any way to handle Mayhew," Winch said. The blandness left his face, and it knotted up. "Listen," he hissed, "I haven't mothered you fuckers, and babied you, all this time and all this way, for you to go and get yourself into a sure-death situation. I won't goddam fucking put up with it. See?"

"Do you really think I could do it?" Landers said. Despite his bravado, he did not really want to ship out like that. He knew what it meant, as well as Winch. What he wanted was to creep into somebody's arms, and be held. "You really think I could?"

"Tell them about your nightmares," Winch said, his face calm again.

Vaguely, Landers wondered how Winch knew about that.

"Now listen," Winch said, fast. "You go on down to your outfit. Take one of these camp cabs, outside the office here. No use in walking up, and letting them spot you a mile off. You go straight on in to your own barrack, to your own bunk. You fall out for the next formation, just like you never were away," Winch looked at his watch, "next formation ought to be evening chow. If they don't come for you, you fall out for evening chow. Okay?"

Before Landers could answer or even knew what was happening, Winch had him by the arm and was shooing him out. "I'm going to call Mayhew. And ask him to meet me. I'll talk to him as best I can. I think he will agree. Okay? Now, scoot."

"I can't do it," Landers said hopelessly, at the door. "I don't know how to act crazy." Once again he thought how impossible it was ever to know what Winch was thinking.

"Well, just try," Winch said, looking at him. From the doorway, he watched Landers thread his way out through the desks and desks of clerks.

He went back inside and called Strange at the Peabody. He wasn't sure Strange would be there, but after a moment Strange came on.

"I got him to go," Winch exulted. "He's agreed to go up to the hospital. Now I've got to talk fucking Mayhew into sending him." He listened as Strange gabbled on, on the phone. "Hold it, hold it." Strange asked an urgent question. "No, I don't think there's any doubt they'll think he's crazy. I think he's crazy." Suddenly Winch felt like giggling. He suddenly wanted to let his voice go deep and begin to talk gibberish, in a profound tone, to Strange on the phone. "Listen, I can't talk now. I've got to call Mayhew. I'll call you later. Will you be there?" He hung up and asked the operator to get him Mayhew at the 3516th.

In his way Winch had been preparing Mayhew for this moment. Mayhew had been belligerent, and excessively aggressive, at their first meeting. Winch had made himself stifle his own natural anger until he could get a fix on things. What he found out was that Mayhew was surprised and a little shaken that Landers would dare to go AWOL on him. Mayhew was much more concerned with what Second Army HQ would think of Mayhew. And Mayhew was more than a little impressed that the famous W/O Mart Winch would come to talk to him about it. Winch had let him run on a little bit and simmer down, then he had hit him with the story of Landers, Mayhew, and the telephone. Strange had told it to Winch. The reaction on Mayhew was phenomenal. His neck got visibly thicker, and he began to bristle again. Not a man who took well to criticism. At least not from anyone not his immediate superior.

Winch had all this well in mind, when he telephoned him this time. He said only that he had news of his wayward AWOL. And he suggested they meet at the officers' club bar. Mayhew said he would meet him right away.

Winch had the barman set them up at a two-table off by itself, where they could talk. But it wasn't where they would not be seen. It was just at the close of the working day. That fit in, too. He did not waste time on any amenities. "I've brought your boy back."

"Yeah, I know. I saw him come in on my way out to come meet you."

No element of surprise. Winch had hoped to have that. "Are you going to let him go up to the hospital for observation?"

Mayhew shook his bullet head. "It's a stockade case. Already made up my mind. He deliberately did it to make me look bad."

"I think it would be wise to let him."

Mayhew shook his head. "In my mind there's a question whether he's a deserter. He was gone three weeks."

"Nobody's a deserter, if he comes back on his own and turns himself in."

"That's not an absolute regulation."

"It seems to me," the celebrity Winch said, "that you're more concerned with what Second Army HQ will think of you, than you are with anything else."

Mayhew's jaw came out and he began to bristle.

"Don't be angry. But it seems to me a stockade case would make you look worse than having a nut, a real psycho, on your hands."

"I don't care. He did it deliberately. To make me look bad. I want him to get what's coming to him."

"All that's personal," Winch said sternly. "A personal vendetta."

Mayhew shook his head. "Legally I'm right."

But he was not as at ease as he seemed. Mayhew kept looking brightly around the bar. Winch knew he did not frequent the main officers' club bar. A lot of colonels and lieutenant colonels were coming in now, most of them waving hello to Winch. Almost all of them knew him because they had to work through his Personnel office. Winch waved at a couple of colonels from Second Army, then waved for them to come on over. He stood up to introduce them to Mayhew, who jumped up right away.

Then what he had been waiting for came in the door. It was Col Stevens from the hospital. The thin, white-haired, dignified old West Pointer walked in. There was an air about Stevens that stood out everywhere. But now he was wearing the single star of a brigadier. His generalcy had gone through a month before. And he came right over, right away, without being waved to. "Hello, Mart," he smiled warmly. "How are you? I haven't seen you in a long while." There was no question of the depth of his liking. When Winch introduced him to Mayhew, he nodded politely. "How is that young protégé of yours, Mart? What was his name? Landers?"

"Just fine, sir," Winch grinned. "Just fine."

When he went on off and the two of them sat back down, Mayhew's round head was stubborn.

"Then I'll tell you what I'm going to do," Winch said. "I'm going to go over your head, Captain. You send him to the stockade as an overseas replacement, and I'm going to put in for him and have him transferred to me."

It was a grand slam poker bluff. Winch did not himself believe he had that much pull anywhere.

Mayhew looked disbelieving. "You'd really do that?" Then he stumbled over what to call Winch. And he chose the formal address. "Do that, Mr Winch?"

"I sure would. I trained him. He was in my old outfit with me."

Mayhew's neck was redder than when he had been angry. "All right," he muttered, as if to himself, "okay." He downed the rest of his drink. "Okay. All right, Mr Winch. I'll go down to my orderly room and have them take him to the hospital." He looked as if he badly wanted to stay, and have another drink or two. And meet another general. But he got to his feet. "I hope we'll see each other around, Mr Winch."

"We will," Winch said. Like hell. He watched him walk off to go to his orderly room. He was thinking that he must go and call Strange right away with the good news, from the pay phone in the club foyer. But he felt unaccountably worn down and tired.

Landers was already in Mayhew's orderly room, under guard, when Mayhew got back. Landers had done everything exactly as Winch had told him. But Mayhew had come hustling out of the orderly room on his way to see Winch just as Landers was crossing the frozen mud to the barracks, and had seen him. Mayhew had sent a man back.

Landers had gone on. But when he got inside to his old bunk, he found it completely dismantled. Blankets and sheets gone, mattress folded on the bar springs. The sight brought on Landers an acuter sense of homelessness than he had ever felt. The guys around the barracks, who had their blankets and beds, looked at him with noncommittal faces. The two guards Mayhew had ordered sent met him by the bunk.

Mayhew, when he came in from Winch, was his own inimitable self. He was hard and cold and tough and businesslike. "I've agreed to send you up to the hospital for observation. Some people seem to feel you should do that." Mayhew himself did not agree, and he made that clear.

All of this was said in front of the other company officers who were clustered around, warming themselves at the space-heater stove, just in off duty. Landers thought he caught a sympathetic glint in the Mongolian eyes of Lt Prevor; and Lt Burns, Prevor's former exec, gave him a genuine if terribly fleeting smile. Landers wondered if he had sensed a wave of relief pass among the officers at the mention of the hospital, or if it had come from just himself.

Young Lt Mathieson, one of the newer officers, was told off to the assignment of delivering him to the hospital prison ward, with the two guards.

The ride up in the jeep seemed to pass before Landers in a series of humiliating flashes like still-camera shots flashed on a screen.

And if you had seen and been in one hospital, you had seen and been in them all. They weren't that different, Landers decided. Then the big steel door of the prison ward down at the end of the main corridor on the top floor clanged shut behind him.

At one point in the trip, as they descended from the jeep outside the hospital, Mathieson got a chance to speak to him alone, and did it quickly, looking around to see if he was being observed or overheard.

"I've been authorized to tell you that we're all behind you. I was told to tell you we all know why you did it. And that we're all going to do everything we can as officers, to get you out of this."

Landers stared at him. If they knew why he did it, they knew a lot more than he did. Then he felt a powerful surge of emotion roll up through him to behind his eyes which almost brought tears to them. He managed to grin, and only nodded.

A little later when Mathieson was signing him in, one of the guards spoke to him. There was little or nothing the men could do but they wanted him to know. "The guys are all for you. That cocksucker should get every fucking kick in the balls he's got coming." Landers made himself grin and said to thank them.

He ought not to feel so terrible, going in the way he was. He was going in with lots more people behind him than most men going to jail. But the truth was, he did not feel much like grinning, on the prison ward. After the big door clanged shut. And once he was fixed there.

He tried hard not to let anybody know that. One of the worst things was the being cut off from all the local war news and developments that went on in the camp, and with all of the outfits. The ward had newspapers and the radio speakers over the doors for the general war news. But the big iron door cut off all that other, individual news, as cleanly as it cut off the illusion of freedom that circulated on the other side of it. Freedom? Landers had to laugh sourly. It seemed like freedom from here.

Another bad thing, one that had to be fought against every minute if you wanted to avoid despair, was the sense of total abandonment you got on the prison ward. Outfits went on, the war went on. People in your outfit might have cared for you, yesterday. But the yesterday you remembered so vividly when locked up here was receding into their past. They couldn't go on caring about you, even if they wanted.

In spite of what Mathieson had said to him, in confidence beside the jeep, there was no word at all from the officers of the 3516th. Nor was there any word from Winch. Or from Strange. Neither was there any word from Mayhew, or the stockade provost marshal.

He had almost no visitors. A good-hearted noncom or two

came up and sat and talked awhile, embarrassed, obviously making duty calls. None of them knew what was happening with his case. Landers was intensely relieved when they left. They didn't come back.

Time, the days, passed in a hurrying unidentifiable slide which could hardly be marked off on a calendar, punctuated only by the almost daily sessions with the psychiatrists, who asked him if he had ever sucked a cock, or if he had ever wanted to suck one, and whether he hated his father. Happily Landers got his weekends off from these, when all the doctors went in town on Saturdays and Sundays.

The life itself was not so bad, and not all that different from life on any hospital ward. The prison ward was one of four lockup wards in the hospital, all situated together at the end of the same corridor in a wing, two above, two below. The other three were the nut wards, for the psycho cases, called NP wards for neuropsychiatric, and while they were also restraining wards, their patients were not legally prisoners.

At night sometimes, when he had first come in, Landers heard a man screaming faintly from one of these wards on the floor below, and yelling over and over something like, "Get them out of there, goddam it, get them out of there." It seemed very much in keeping with the whole place. But then one night he did not hear it any more, and the scuttlebutt came around that the old-timer 1st/sgt who had been doing the screaming had been discharged out of the Army and moved out to a Veterans' Administration hospital somewhere. The rumor said he had been a sergeant in a company on Guadalcanal in Landers' old Division.

Things like this made life a little more interesting.

The prison ward had its share of mental patients, of which Landers was one. But it also had prisoners who officially at least weren't mental patients, and were there because of illness or some violent injury. This tended to liven things up a little, too. Most of the knife cuts from the knife fights on the post tended to end up there. So did the bad results of fist fights or club or rock fights, until their injuries healed enough for court-martial. It was sometimes difficult to know whether these men were also mental patients. A couple of times men were brought in badly injured from the stockade itself, where it was reported they had fallen off the back ends of trucks. When they were well enough to talk, they made no bones about saying their damage was the result of beatings. But nobody much listened. And Landers had to admit, after looking at their shifty faces, that they could easily have been lying. Another interesting item was a German Nazi prisoner who was on a hunger strike, and drank only one quart of milk a day for nourishment.

Landers took an insanely violent, murderous dislike to the German. The German had worked on one of the prisoner-of-war farms nearby, but now refused to because he wanted to be repatriated, to fight for the Führer and the Fatherland again. Heavy-footed, stolid, completely self-assured, he made Landers think more than anything else of Mayhew. To Landers the German was representative of everything about the human race that had sickened him since that day on the hilltop in New Georgia. His hatred reached such a point that he would have killed the German if it were possible.

The German had a habit of marching up and down the ward while he drank his one bottle of milk. Landers made up a fantasy in which he leaped on the German, smashed the milk bottle on the German's head, and cut the German's throat with the jagged edge of the neck. He would sit on the edge of his bed and play his fantasy while the German walked back and forth with his milk. In the night, the German was kept locked in a special cell, which doubled as a padded cell when needed, so that none of the Americans like Landers could get at him.

Another thing which could provoke Landers to instantaneous rage was the fact that on Sunday mornings the radio loudspeakers played Christian religious sermons. The sermons were blasted all over the ward, everywhere, and there was no escape. Being forced to listen to such honeyed bullshit and obvious falsehoods about love of man threw Landers into such a state of fury he could not sit down, or stay still. After the first time, he went to the ward man and complained about it. He was an atheist, and his rights were being infringed on. The Sunday ward man hastened to agree with him. But he pointed out that he did not have control over radio volume or the choice of programs; all that came from hospital HQ. All he could do was send them a note. He doubted it would do much good. Landers noticed that while he talked, he was also writing detailed notes on sheets of paper which went into Landers' thickening file.

"What are you doing that for?"

The ward man shrugged. "Orders. From the head head shrinker."

The sermons were never stopped. But after three Sundays of violent complaining, Landers was allowed to shut himself up in the padded cell on Sunday mornings—the same cell in which the German prisoner spent his nights of protective custody. The sermons did not bother the German. Who it turned out was an ardent Catholic, and anyway spoke no English. In the cell Landers could still hear the sermons, but a lot less clearly. It was a minor triumph of sorts, to sweeten his days.

There was also the problem of where to masturbate when it became necessary. There was not a lockable door in the place. The toilet stalls in the shower room did not even have doors. There was nothing for it but to do it in bed at night and try not to make the springs squeak, then lie with the cold wetness of drying semen on your belly so as not to have telltale spots on the sheet. Only a desperate man would jerk off that way, and slowly bit by bit the greatness of Christian thought triumphed.

Then, suddenly, Strange came to visit, and things began to open up very quickly. Strange brought words from Winch.

Winch was not coming himself because he didn't think it would look good for the case, Strange said. But Winch could now assure him that no punitive measures would be taken. In other words, he would not be court-martialed or sent to a stockade and he would not be sent overseas as a cannon-fodder replacement. What he must do, though, now, was some serious thinking. What he must do the serious thinking about, was whether he wanted to be discharged out of the Army completely, or not.

To be discharged would be the easiest, Strange said. But if he wanted to stay in, Winch could guarantee him with a seventy to seventy-five percent surety that he would be transferred to Winch's outfit. But Winch would not guarantee it one hundred percent. Too many other things might still happen.

Surely, Landers had the time and place for some serious thinking, Strange grinned as he left.

The discharge, Strange hastened to reassure him, would not be dishonorable. Not a yellow one. Not a Section Eight. Not even a blue discharge. It would be clean and clear and a white one. A Section Two Medical, Winch said to tell him. A Section Two was for neuropsychiatric reasons, service-connected; no loss of citizenship; no loss of voting; no taint, in other words.

That kind of a discharge, Landers realized, really would require some serious thinking.

The place Landers used for serious thinking was the window behind his bed. Fortunately his bed butted against a window in the ward. Only one out of every four beds got a window. That was where Landers did his serious thinking, usually late at night, after lights out. He would sit on the pillow at the head of his bed, his arms propped on the sill, and look out through the heavy wire grid at the lights of the camp and think. Think seriously. About all of it. Everything.

Although he never came up with any satisfactory answers. Or even any unsatisfactory ones.

It had taken awhile to get permission to do it. The first week the night ward man kept making him get back into bed, and trying to give him a pill. Then finally he gave up, and became more sympathetic. Or else was ordered to by one of those wily psychiatrists.

But the thousands of lights of the camp through the window gave Landers a pleasant melancholy. They left him with a tranquillity and sense of objectivity he never had in the day, when he was constantly reminded how insane everybody and everything was, and kept flying into rages because of it. Out there, thousands of men were going through lives at least as bad as his was.

Up until Strange's visit, he had not trusted Winch. All this time there had been no word from him, any more than there had been word from the 3516th's officers. From his window Landers could see one corner of the tall three-story Command building. The lights in the third-floor corner office were on late every night, and Landers liked to think he was watching Winch's office. It was too bad the venetian blinds were closed. Even so, if he had a rifle he could put a round just about where the desk chair would be, closed venetian blinds and all. Having been there.

But he didn't really hate Winch.

What Landers hated were the war and humanity. And people. People like Mayhew, and the German prisoner. He thought a lot about Mayhew, and the German, and what it was that made them like they were. Landers guessed he would never find out what that was. But there were certainly a great many more like them in the world, than there were people like Strange, say, or Prevor. And they were the human race which sickened Landers, and filled him with this despair, and made him into this terrible, lonely thing of being an outsider.

The ones who wanted power. Who cared about having power, more than they cared about how they got it, or what they did with it when they got it. Like Mayhew. The ones who wanted to die for some glorious cause. Like the German.

And Winch? Winch did not count. Winch was an anomaly.

But now he had something else to think about. A discharge. A real discharge. A clean one, a white discharge. And Landers did not really know if he wanted a discharge or didn't.

When he thought about Mayhew, and that German, he wanted a discharge. He wanted nothing to do with humanity, or with humanity's war.

But when he looked at those thousand lights out there; and thought about Winch, and Strange, and Prevor, and those two good-hearted sergeants who had come up to see him; when he thought of all that, he did not want the discharge. He wanted to be with them.

Landers simply could not make up his mind if he wanted the discharge from Winch or not.

And he wasn't given all that much time to mull it over. Two days after Strange's visit, one of the officers from the 3516th was brought in to see him.

They talked sitting on his bunk. The officer was Lt Drere, a thin, blond, slight man in his thirties. He was one of the newer officers brought in later to fill out Prevor's company, like Mathieson. Drere was quietly incapable of coping with anything physical or manual, but always in good control of his head. As out of place in the 3516th as it was possible to be. He had wound up as the company intellectual, whom the other officers always went to with their paper problems. That he was also warm, genuine, and generous was just an extra.

"I'm sorry we couldn't get up to you sooner," he said. "But we thought it was best to wait until we had something specific we could do."

Landers just nodded. "Yeah, well. How are things going down there?"

"We're surviving." Drere smiled. "Your case is coming up before the Medical Board for review and a final decision. All of us officers have been asked to write personal reports on you. To go to the Medical Board."

"Yeah, great. I know these fucking Medical Boards," Landers said sourly.

"No, no. Don't be discouraged. By the way, how are you?" Drere said kindly.

Landers shrugged. "I'm all right. It's not the best place for a vacation."

Drere looked around the ward curiously, and nodded brusquely. "Naturally, we all know what kind of report Capt Mayhew will write. And we pretty much know what Lt Prevor will write, which will be laudatory. The rest of us have decided among ourselves we will write the best reports we can to help you. According to what you want to do. To do that, we need to know how you want us to slant them."

"How do you mean?"

"Well, if you want to stay in the Army. Or if you want a discharge. We can write them either way, and slant them toward either objective. But we need to know from you which way you want us to write them."

"This was your idea?"

"Mine," Drere assented. "More or less. But the other officers all created the idea. I only formulated it."

Landers was looking out of his window. From here it was a different angle, and he could not quite see the Command building. But he could see the thousand hutments. "I don't know," he said disconsolately. "I just don't honestly know. Which way. I don't know whether I want out or not."

"Well," Drere said. "We have to know. If we're going to write the reports."

"Can I tell you later?"

"I don't see how. We need to know today. That's why I'm here. The reports have to be written tonight. They go in tomorrow."

Landers still did not answer, for a long moment. "All right," he said, looking up. "Tell them to slant the reports toward a discharge. I'd rather be out of this fucking mess. Than in it." He sighed. "As long as the Mayhews of the world are in it."

"I'm afraid the Mayhews of the world will always be with us," Drere smiled. "That's the human race. Imperfect, to say the least."

"Always?" Landers said, and he began to laugh. He was able to get hold of it in a moment, the laughter, and choke it down.

Drere was looking at him curiously. "You're sure, now? You sure that's the way you want it?"

"No, I'm not sure," Landers said, beginning to get angry. He shrugged, swallowing down the anger, too. "Look, Lieutenant. What I'm thinking is that if I want to change the decision, in front of the board, it will be a lot easier to change it toward staying in the Army, than to change it toward wanting to get out. Right?"

"Yes. That would certainly be true," Drere said. "So you want the reports slanted strongly toward a discharge?" he said. "Then that's what I'll tell them?" Drere said.

"Yes."

Drere made a small precise note on a paper, then put all of the unused papers together in his little briefcase. His preciseness irritated Landers, and he stood up.

Drere got up with him, and thrust out his hand. "I'll be on my way, then." His face took on a peculiar look, for him, of embarrassment. "You know, you're a real hero, Marion. In the 3516th."

"Some hero," Landers said sourly.

"It's nice to know, I think," Drere said. "I just want you to know it's been a pleasure knowing you."

Landers watched the big steel door shut behind him, wishing too late that he himself had said other, nicer things. But that wouldn't have mattered to Drere.

It was amazing to see the change that occurred on the ward, almost immediately. Nobody ever knew how the word got around on these things, but it always did. Somebody always knew, somehow, and told somebody, and that somebody told somebody else. It was the same jungle telegraph that existed in every outfit. Landers told no one but by evening everybody on the ward knew: Landers was on his way out, to a clean, white discharge. An honorable.

Landers was disgusted, and infuriated. Particularly since he himself did not know whether or not he wanted out of the Army. Even the mean, crazy-headed stockade prisoners began treating him differently, with great respect. To the other mental patients he was a sort of shining example, a real American success story, that they could look up to, and model themselves after.

Even the ward boys were kinder to him. And the night man offered to sit down and go over his file with him, on the idea that there might be something in it Landers could use to help him with the board. Landers refused this categorically. In the back of his mind was the idea that this, too, might be another ploy of the crafty psychiatrists, testing him.

In the end it did not even take as long as Drere had suggested it might. It took more than the week, but less than the ten days Drere had postulated.

The ward boy came to him, grinning hugely, on the Monday. He would go before the board tomorrow at their regular Tuesday meeting. A clean new pair of MC pajamas, a clean maroon robe, clean duck slippers would be waiting for him in the morning.

It was so similar to the previous time at Kilrainey that Landers had a weird, eery sense of déjà vu. There was the same dark, formalized room. There was the same group of five civilian-looking men wearing lots of hardware on their collars, behind the same long table. It had the somber smell of a criminal courtroom. And Landers suddenly knew he desperately wanted out of the Army.

It had the distinct feel of a repeat performance. Except that now as Landers went up against this kindly, middle-class, bourgeois enemy, it was with all the pessimism and experience he had not had at his fingertips the first time out. Landers knew now that all the fine promises they made would have nothing to do with him once he was out in the field again, in the real world. They might not know that, but Landers did; now. He was prepared at any moment to tell them he wanted to stay in the Army.

But the moment would not come. That was apparently what they were trying to get him to say. But everything they said to him, every question they asked him, seemed to drive him away from the point of wanting to say it.

All the questions they asked him about his abilities and intentions were the same questions the five men at Kilrainey had asked him. All the statements they made about wanting to use his talents, his experience, were the same statements made at Kilrainey.

Finally the round-faced, jowly man in the middle wearing glasses, a full colonel among three other full colonels in the five but plainly the chief, asked him in a perplexed, slightly amused voice, "Well, Sergeant, what kind of job in the Army would you like?"

Drawing himself up, his voice fluting with the rage he was trying to hold down, Landers gave the only answer he felt he could give them. "Sir, there's no job in the Army I want," he said stolidly.

"All right, that's all. You may go," the bespectacled colonel said.

The word was around the ward almost before he could get back to it. Landers was out. The board had voted, unanimously, to discharge him. So many other prisoners, who saw this as a major triumph, rushed over to him to congratulate him and slap him on the back that the morose Landers finally insulted them and ran them all off, cursing.

After that, he was even more of a marked man. Not only was he out while all of them were still in, but they did not like it because he had rejected their well-meant congratulations. All of them left him strictly alone.

It didn't really matter. The winding-down, the mechanics, took only five days. Five days, from the meeting of the board till Landers was out on the street, a free man. The wheels ground slowly, but once they got started, they rolled very fast. And much of the last three of the five days was spent out of the ward, signing releases in first one office then another. Landers wasn't in the ward that much to suffer his new rejection. Anyway, he didn't care what they thought. He wasn't like them.

He went to the Finance office, to sign his last payroll. He went to the QM office, to turn in the last of his gear. To the Insurance office, to keep or cancel his GI insurance. Landers decided to cancel his. If he was going out, he did not want any more to do with the Army than was obligatory. Most of the rest was done in offices in the hospital HQ section itself.

As was required by the regulations, everywhere he went an armed guard had to go with him. He was still a prisoner. But it was indicative of his status that the pistol-wearing MP joked with him and hardly bothered to watch him. No guy who was going out in two days was going to run off from a guard.

In retrospect it seemed like a wild, fantastic rush, the last five days. Then on the morning of the sixth he was signing his last paper, which was the receipt for his engraved, pure, white Honorable Discharge which was tendered to him. That took place in the hospital clerical office itself.

Then, totally unprepared for it, he was suddenly out in the street in front of the hospital, in uniform, with an old blue barracks bag half full of personal gear, a free man able to go anywhere he pleased to go.

He walked the three blocks down to the bus stop, and waited there. After a moment, he set the bag on the frozen ground. A bus for Luxor should be along in a little bit. It was a dry day, but cold, and a little snowy on the ground.

Landers huddled down into his GI greatcoat. In front of him on the asphalt main street a long column of men in fatigues and field jackets marched by, wearing the Divisional patch of the new infantry Division, their faces gaunt and haunted and worn-down looking. It took them a long time to pass, and Landers watched them.

It had been running through his mind all the places he was now free to go. Places these guys couldn't go. He would proba-bly wind up going home, to Indiana, in the end. To his lousy family. The thought of going home filled him with anguish. But he didn't have to do that yet.

Normally he would have gone into Luxor to the Peabody to see Johnny Stranger. But Strange had told him during his visit that in two or three days' time, from then, he would be coming back to duty himself. Somewhere here on the post at O'Bru-yerre. That meant Landers would have to go up to see Winch at the Command building and say good-by to him, in order to find out where Strange was. And Landers didn't have the stom-ach for that at the moment. Of course, he could always go in to the Peabody by himself. Though Strange was giving up the suite, Strange had said, having run out of money.

In front of him the last of the troop column had made their right turn off of the main road, and were dwindling away down one of the hole-pocked gravel side roads. Behind them on the main road, coming fast, was a civilian car, but with post plates. Driven by a woman. Women were so important.

Landers watched the last of the troops dwindle, getting smaller and smaller, their breaths throwing out the same plumes as before, but now at this distance the plumes seemed bigger than they were. Landers was devoutly glad he wasn't one of them. On the other hand, he had no desire really to go in to the Peabody all by himself. Even if he could get a room, this late.

Landers watched the woman coming on in the car. She was very good-looking, even at a distance. Probably some officer's wife. But she was really going too fast. Landers bent with the tie rope of the barracks bag he was holding, and rolled it meticu-lously down and around onto the top of the bag, and then stood teetering on his heels and watching her.

Just as she was about to come level with him on the road, Landers stepped out off the curb in front of her.

As he stepped out, he realized he would not have done it if she had been a man, driving a jeep or a GI truck. But she really was so beautiful. Her coat was thrown back open in the heat of the car, and in the sweater under it her breasts swelled out thrusting their weight against the lapels deliciously. So delicious. And her hair fell to the collar of the coat with an equally delicious feminine grace.

Landers heard the wild squeal of the brakes. And perhaps a cry. And then the crash of glass and tear of headlight metal. And a loud thumping thud.

He saw or thought he saw the look of horror that came across her face in back of the windshield. Because she thought she was doing something wrong, and he wanted to laugh. The mouth a wildly spread O of lipstick. Eyebrows arched up. Eyes staring. He hated to do all that to her. But, by God, at least she knew she had hit something. Then the helicopter moved away from the ship.

The big red crosses were still on its white flank. And the sea still moved backward along its waterline. Everything was still silence.

Far off, the great blue continent still stood. Uninhabited. Green with the silent, unpeopled forests and soft grasses. The breakers clashing on the white, unpeopled sands. And the silence of home.

BOOK
FIVE

THE END
OF IT

CHAPTER 29

Bobby Prell heard about it at the Muehlebach Hotel in Kansas City. Strange called him there long distance to tell him.

Prell was on his first bonds-selling tour, and in fact the call took several hours to reach him because he was out and running around. It was their first day in Kansas City, and the first day was always spent running around. Setting things up. "Working," was what the people in the tour staff called it. Though Prell found it hard to think of what he was doing as work. He was also doing some real running around on his own, with some of the tour staff, chasing women. Something the tour staff boys apparently always did in every city. When he got back to the hotel after an all-day, eight-hour absence, it was to find six little white call slips waiting for him. That someone from Camp O'Bruyerre had been calling. A Sgt Strange.

All that seemed so far away. Prell had difficulty recalling who the caller was. If the slips had said Kilrainey General and Della Mae, or Luxor where Della Mae's mama had moved in the past month, the call would have meant something was wrong with her damned pregnancy probably. But not Strange, from

O'Bruyerre. Strange had only been at O'Bruyerre now for a month. Prell could not imagine why Strange would be calling him.

Prell was supposed to go out with a couple of the "crew" and the "producer" of the "show," Jerry Kurntz, for drinks and dinner that night. They were meeting some of the women, or "broads," they had collected like a comet's tail during the course of the day and the day's meetings. The tour staff were all Holly-wood "types," and Prell was learning a whole new "show-biz" vocabulary from them.

But in the big, old lobby with the six call slips from the desk clerk in his hand, Prell begged off. He would take a rest in his room, and eat there, and find out what this phone call was and maybe he might meet up with them later. He had no idea what could be so important that Strange would telephone him. And no idea how soon the call might come.

"Okay. But listen, kid," Jerry Kurntz said. "You're missing a big opportunity. I aint never seen a bunch of broads as ripe as this one. And aint you the star of our show? Without you we won't any of us stand as good a chance."

Kurntz was a college graduate who was not only not ashamed of using *aint.* He was proud of using it, and other bad grammar. Something else that was new to Prell.

"My legs are tired," Prell said, and made his eyes go flat. All of them knew how he disliked referring to his legs.

"Oh, fine, fine," Kurntz said quickly. "You go on and rest, then. The legs are more important." The group broke up quickly, to go to their own rooms.

Prell had learned there were two things they were afraid of. They were afraid because he had killed people, and nearly been killed himself. They thought that somehow made him different. And they were afraid because he came from the West Virginia coal country. And knew how to make his eyes go flat.

Prell ordered some bourbon sent up to his room, and went on up himself. Beside the desk was his wheelchair, and he dropped into it gratefully, and let the bellboy push him to the elevator.

His folding wheelchair was always kept near the desk, out of sight, no matter what the hotel or the city. This was a strategy he and Kurntz had worked out at the start of the tour to satisfy Prell. The wheelchair was never taken along in the cars at the start of the day for the day's outings and meetings. Not unless there was a speech to be made that night, before they came back to the hotel. They took the little half-crutches, and if Prell had to have help during the day, he used those. But Prell hated the wheelchair, with a rabid dislike. He refused to have it in the cars, or to use it, during the day. But there were times, like right now this evening, when he simply could not stay up on his feet any longer and had to use it.

The room was big, and comfortable. But Prell had to get up onto his feet again, out of the wheelchair, in order to make himself a drink at the little table bar. The bellboy brought in the new bottle, and Prell double-locked the door and put the chain lock on. With his impassive face, nobody was aware of the effort it took for him to get onto his feet from a sitting position. With the door secured, he took off his pants and sprawled down on the bed to ease his legs, while he waited on the phone call.

His legs were worse than tired. They were like two tooth-aches. Using them was the only way to make them better. But then the pain was always there. It was like one of those tooth-aches you so learned to live with and got so used to, that when the dentist finally got to you and stopped it you felt there was some part of you missing.

He was so uncomfortable on the bed, turning on his side each time to drink from the glass, that after a couple of tries at it he got up again, and sat in the damned wheelchair until he finished the drink. Then he lay back down again.

He had fallen asleep when the phone rang loudly in the room and he made a large scringe in both thighs as he rolled convulsively over onto his belly and put his head down, thinking Mortars. A part of his mind was already saying how ridiculous he was. What was it? eight months? nine months now? It took him a little while to get up off of the bed and the phone rang four or five times before he could get to it.

"Yes?" he said cautiously. "Yes?"

It was Strange, all right. And he didn't fiddlefuck around. He came right to the point. Had Prell heard that Landers had been killed?

"What? Killed?" Prell said. "Killed? How?"

Strange went on to tell him. A woman. In a civilian car. But with post plates. Some officer's wife. Had hit him. Killed him instantly. He had only been discharged just an hour before. Was on his way off the post. The woman was all broken up by it.

"What a dumb way to get it," Prell said. But why call him up, all this way, to tell him about it? he wondered. His first, natural reaction had been to think it was some drunken fight. In some poolhall or bar. "Sure a dumb way to get it," he said.

"Yes," Strange's voice said. "But there's even some question about that. The woman claims he stepped right out in front of her. She couldn't miss him. And he was looking right straight at her." The voice stopped.

"What's that supposed to mean?" Prell said. But why call me up? he wondered again. He was beginning, as his sleep confusion lifted, to catch a peculiar urgency in Strange's voice.

"Well, there's no reason for her to make it up. Nobody's blaming her. They were already calling it an accident. Not her fault. Why make up a story like that?"

"Wait a minute. Then you mean a suicide?" Prell suddenly felt wide awake. But he wondered still again, So what? Why call him? If old Landers wanted to knock himself off, he had the same right everybody else had. "A suicide, Johnny?"

"Well, nobody's saying that. And certainly officially it's going to go down as an accident. Maybe she's just feeling guilty anyway. Even if she's not responsible?" Strange said. "We all do that sometimes. Otherwise why would she make up such a story?"

What was coming through to Prell was that Strange had not called him because of him, but because of Strange. Prell had never been a buddy of Landers'. Had hardly known him, really. Landers hadn't even been Regular Army. But Strange had been a buddy. If Strange needed him, he had to be there.

"Would she?" Strange's voice said urgently.

"I don't know," he said. "She might have. But anyway you can't solve it all right now, Johnny. Hell, maybe it's something we'll never know.

"What does Winch say about it?" he asked cautiously. "How is Winch taking it?"

"Who knows," Strange said. "With him? He's pretty upset, I guess. Hell, I'm pretty upset. But I didn't mean to upset you, by calling you."

"I didn't really know him all that well," Prell said calmly.

"I know. But the four of us were all on that same ship together."

"Yeah. He came in to see me there in that main lounge a bunch of times, I remember." As he talked, he was casting around for the right thing to say that would ease Strange.

"Yeah. Well." He heard Strange swallow. "Well we were working on that discharge for him. Or Winch was. He thought that was what he wanted. He said that was what he wanted. To one of his lieutenants." Strange's voice was getting higher, and threatening to crack.

"Yeah, you told me," Prell said. "I thought it was all fixed up."

"Well, how would you feel? If you suddenly walked out of the hospital, with a discharge out of the Army?"

"I'd feel terrible," Prell said. "But I wasn't him. He wasn't a Regular Army type"—then he changed that word—"Regular Army guy. I am. That was what he wanted, wasn't it?"

"Yeah. That's true," Strange said, sounding unconvinced. "He was no RA soldier."

"Listen, Johnny. I'll be back at Kilrainey in a couple weeks. You just hang on to it. Go talk to Winch about it."

"Winch won't talk about it."

Of course he wouldn't. That fucker, Prell thought, furiously. "We'll go over it when I get back. We'll talk it all out."

"Sure," Strange said. "Sure. I'm not flipping out, over it. I just thought you'd want to know."

"Of course I'd want to know. I'm glad you called me," Prell lied. "Call me here tomorrow, if you want. The day after tomorrow we'll be in Lincoln, Nebraska."

"Sure," Strange said. "Don't worry. Don't worry about me, I mean. I'm fine. I'll see you as soon as you get back."

"How's the new outfit doing?" Prell asked.

"Fine. It's no great outfit. Signal Corps, I'm in. But at least I'm seeing they get some decent hot meals, for a change."

"I bet they love it," Prell said, and found he was grinning frantically, at the phone. Idiotically. As if Strange could see him.

"They do. They do. Okay, so long." The question that followed was a polite afterthought. "How are you doing, out there?"

"Fine," Prell said. "I guess I'm a natural-born speechmaker."

"Good."

The phone clicked off, dead. Prell realized he had been standing up on his feet all this time, and that his legs had begun to hurt him seriously again. He went back to the bed. Then, after he had sprawled back down, the guilts began to attack him.

Guilt because he had not helped Strange as much as he might have on the phone. Guilt because he had not cared more about

Landers. Then, guilt because he had not been a better friend to
Landers. Why hadn't he been?

Then finally, the biggest guilt of them all. What was a man
like him doing here? Making speeches for a living. He had become an entertainer. Him, and his Medal of Honor. They were
a vaudeville team. It was something he had to wrassle with and
defeat every day. And every new day it was back again, stronger
and more powerful, to be wrassled with and defeated again.

Usually it hit him at this same time of every afternoon. After
a day of loose pussyfooting around. He would come back to
some hotel, with something great to look forward to, like an
evening speech. Or another night of revels with the jolly fun-
sters of Hollywood. All now in US Army uniform. He would
lie on his bed, trying to give his legs a couple of hours of rest,
and try to battle it.

An entertainer. Get people to pay out their money to buy war
bonds. Playing on their emotions. A "performer." With "lighting experts" and "sound experts" and "script writers," and a
"director" and a "producer." All telling him what to say and
how to say it, and how to "act" it. What on earth was he doing
here?

Prell had no new answers to the question. The old, simple
answer to it was he was here because he wanted to stay in the
Army. If he wasn't here he would be a civilian out on the streets
somewhere.

Prell had been over it all before. Long before. He had been
over it back when the final decision was made, back in early
December. General Stevens, then still only a colonel, had called
him in and presented him with the alternatives. There were
only the two. Discharge; or sell war bonds. Stevens had kindly
been willing to discuss it with him. The two of them had decided it then.

"I know how much you dislike the idea of it," Stevens said.
"But if you want to stay in the Army, I don't see any other way.
There's just no other way to keep you in. In the shape you're
in."

The slim, white-haired old West Pointer smiled, and behind
his desk pushed back his own chair, looking at Prell in his
wheelchair.

"I have to admit I feel a certain personal involvement in this,
Bobby. It goes back to when you first came in here, in danger

of losing your leg. We discussed the various options then, you and I, if you remember."

"Yes, sir. I remember," Prell had said, huskily.

"Back then, you didn't have any Medal of Honor, and we weren't even sure you were going to have the leg," Stevens smiled. "Even then all you could say was that you wanted to be a twenty-year man."

Prell had nodded, but hadn't felt up to smiling back.

"I've looked into it for you carefully, as much as I can," Stevens said. "W/O Alexander and I have. I can tell you pretty much what to expect. I'm not sure you'll like it."

He was a hospital casual right now, not a member of any outfit. He would be assigned directly to the AGO Washington, his provisional HQ here in Second Army, Luxor. His actual authority would be Stevens himself here at Kilrainey, at first. If he was as successful on the first couple of tours as they had every reason to think he would be, and if physically he was up to it, he would then be reassigned, probably to Los Angeles on the West Coast. And after that perhaps to Washington. Out there and in Washington he would work with these professional theater people who ran this kind of thing for the Army. He would become a member of a unit that traveled all over the country selling war bonds.

"That ought to keep you in business at least until after the war," Stevens said.

"What about after the war?" Prell said.

Stevens held up his hand. "Now, after the war," he said, and cleared his throat. "After the war is something else again."

After the war, there were going to be an awful lot of men hanging around looking for work as soldiers. And there weren't going to be that many jobs for all of them. At the same time, there were going to be a lot of bread-and-butter assignments lying around, for men who qualified for them and could get their hands on them.

One of them would be all of those ROTC assignments, at all of the various colleges and universities across the country. Usually they were held back for old-time master sergeants. But they had been known to go to lesser ranks.

"I don't see any reason why you couldn't qualify for one of them," Stevens smiled.

Prell had sat listening, suddenly wanting to weep. A kind of

wildly inarticulate love, out of all proportion to anything he was
used to feeling for anybody, had seized him for this elegant old
soldier. He was such a fine example of the old-time, old-line,
gentlemanly school of Army officer who once had existed.
Those were the school of men Prell had wanted to serve under,
back when he first enlisted, but he hadn't found too many of
them. At the moment, he would have done just about anything
the old gentleman might have asked of him.

"I'm not saying you'll love it. But it's the best that can be
done," Stevens said. "I've asked around and found out what I
could, both W/O Alexander and I have, about placing you in
one of these posts. And I think you can get one, after the war,"
Stevens smiled. "Particularly with that Medal of Honor you
have tucked away under your web belt."

"I only have one question, sir," Prell said, huskily. "I'm not
sure it isn't degrading the Medal."

Stevens glared at him piercingly. "Nothing on earth can de-
grade that Medal. Or what you did to earn it. Don't you ever
forget that."

"Aye, sir," Prell said. And then decided to go one step further.
"But I've always felt I didn't really deserve the Medal."

"If you didn't deserve it, you wouldn't have gotten it. That's
why the system of recommendations is set up the way it is, to
make it difficult. And since you have gotten it, you deserve
everything the Army can do to help you." Slowly, he smiled
again; but his eyes were still piercing.

And that was the way they had left it. Back in early December. There were a few little strings attached, to getting Prell one
of the coveted ROTC posts, Stevens said. One of them was the
problem of rank. If Prell wanted to come out of the war a
master/sgt, so that he would be truly qualified for the ROTC
post, it meant he would have to make at least 1st/lt. Once the
war was over, everybody made during it would be reduced two
grades in rank. Stevens was beginning to do what he could about
that. "As of right now, today, you're a staff sergeant." And at
the successful conclusion of his first war bonds tour, he would
be moved up to tech/sgt. And then up to master. Once he was
with AGO Washington and on the West Coast, he would be
given a commission to 2nd/lt, and then promoted to 1st/lt.
"There's a little trick to this rank problem," the old colonel
smiled. "That's right." He nodded. "If I want to retire as a
colonel, I'll have to make major general during the war."

He had pulled his chair back up to the desk. "You understand, there are no absolute guarantees to this. I can't guarantee you all of this. It's much too soon, for anything like that. And it would be dishonest to say so. But it is certainly something to work toward, and I think it's something you should plan toward."

Prell had simply nodded, too dazzled to make an answer. He was as dazzled by the old gentleman's honesty and sense of honor, as he was by the prospect of so much swift promotion.

And it was these traits, Stevens' honesty and sense of honor, that sent him back to the old West Pointer for advice when his problem arose with Della Mae a month or so later.

There wasn't really anybody else to go to. He did not want to go to Strange with it. Anyway, what could Strange tell him? And in the month since their first talk he had been back three or four times to see Stevens, whose door as Stevens said was always open to a Medal of Honor winner. Prell had come to think of him almost as a father. It was as close to a father, anyway, as a West Virginia orphan boy had ever had. Winch or Strange had never been that to him.

If it had not been precisely as he told it to Strange at the wedding, it had been very close to that. Perhaps he had not knocked her up the very first time his legs had been physically able to get on top of her and seriously fuck her. But it had been damn close to the first time. It had been in the first five days. All that time his damned legs had been too damned weak, and painful, to pull back out. And they had been going at it like a couple of minks. Then in two or three weeks she had come to him with looks of chagrin and fright darting over her face and told him that she had missed her period. But even then on her face there had been that look, that glow, of triumph, victory and success. It shone out openly and with total shamelessness from under the other looks, a glow saying that she knew she had trapped him.

"Of course, you must marry her!" Stevens exclaimed, without preamble or qualification, as soon as he was told what had happened. "It's the only honorable thing you can do."

Prell was ready to accept this. But he needed a little time to digest it. "Well there are other ways to solve it, sir. I mean, as a problem. If we were thinking of it like a mathematics exercise. Several other ways."

"What ways?"

"Well, I could just not marry her at all. That's happened a lot more times around this area than you might think, sir. She'd just go on off home and have the baby. And her mom would work and she'd take care of it. Or she'd work and her mom would take care of it. That's happened a lot. Particularly in cases like this, when I'm about to ship off from here."

"Good God, son! And that's what you propose? What about her father? What's he say? Where is he?"

"He's overseas, sir, in the Army. In New Guinea, I believe."

"MacArthur," Stevens murmured, to himself.

"Some Signal Corps outfit," Prell said.

"Well at least it isn't the infantry. What other brilliant ideas have you got?"

"I could take her to an abortionist, sir. There's one of these sleazy doctors who does them, down on South Main. Down below Beale Street, near the black section. I have lots of friends who have the address. She has the address herself."

"No, no! Great Scott, boy!" The old West Pointer looked seriously shocked. "You're destroying a human life."

"I don't really think of it as a human life yet," Prell said. "She's only a month and a half gone."

"A human life is precious," the old soldier said. "Um, how did she get hold of that address?"

"She said a friend gave it to her. In case she ever might need it."

"I see. Well. Are you sure you're the father?"

"It would be easy to say I'm not sure. But, honestly. Between us, sir. I'm pretty sure I am."

"Well then, you've got to do the right thing by her," Stevens said staunchly. "We men. We men like to have our good times. But we don't like to pay up for it. We are supposed to look after women, and take care of them. Protect them. They need that from us. Our whole civilization is based on that.

"What about her mother? Does she know?"

"Yes," Prell said. "She knows. She told her mother before she told me."

Stevens stared at him. "She did? Well. Well, what does the mother say?"

"Oh she's all in favor of the marriage," Prell said. "She thinks I can become a movie star."

"She *what?!*" Stevens said.

Prell shrugged lamely. "She said since I'm going off on this war bonds tour, I should make all the contacts I can with these

Hollywood people. Then I can get started through them. She has this idea of a series of movies where I can be the owner of a ranch in the West somewhere, in a wheelchair. She seems to think I can become another Hopalong Cassidy or John Wayne."

"Great Scott!" Stevens said.

"Well, she's a little crackers, sir. The truth is she's got this boyfriend in town in Luxor, older fellow, who is stationed at Second Army, and she wants to move into town with him. She figures if she marries Della Mae to me, she'll be free to do that."

"Does her husband in New Guinea know?"

"I don't think so, sir."

"Hasn't the daughter written him about it?"

"No, sir. I don't think she has."

Stevens was staring at him, kind of unbelievingly.

"She's sort of in the middle," Prell said.

"Yes," Stevens said. "Do you see much of this, uh, mother?"

"Only when I can't avoid it."

Stevens continued to stare for a minute, then sighed. "You've gotten yourself into a bad bind, haven't you, son?"

"I'm afraid so, sir. Yes."

Stevens stared down at his desk, frowning at it furiously as if it were responsible for this, before he looked up. "Well, if you're asking my advice, I think you should marry the girl. In spite of all. I think you owe her that. Besides, you don't know. She may love you with all her heart."

"She loves the fact that I'm a Medal of Honor winner," Prell said.

"I think you must marry her. You want to give your child a name." He had commenced to doodle on a pad on his desk.

It was somehow what Prell had expected to hear. It was almost as if he had heard it in the air around him, before he had even come in. Perhaps he even had come here hoping to hear just that.

"Well, sir. I'm ready to do it," Prell said. "If you think that's what I ought to do."

Stevens made a big circle over his other doodles, and ran it around three times, and then threw his pencil down. "I do. And you've given me an excellent idea. I think there is at least a way that we can make a lot of capital out of this for you, just in publicity alone." And he had commenced to lay out his ideas for the hospital wedding.

Prell himself, in Kansas City, still did not know how much

effect the idea of the wedding had had on his final decision to marry. It certainly had had some. Also, as Stevens had said, "If it doesn't work out, you can always get a divorce. But at least you'll have given your son your name." He did say son. Although how he thought he knew, Prell had no idea. Della Mae was about five months into her pregnancy right now and nobody, including the doctor, had any idea boy or girl.

In the big hotel room Prell pulled himself laboriously up onto his feet again and, haltingly, walked across to the table for another bourbon.

He looked at his watch, which said ten-thirty, and realized room service would cut off serving dinners soon. If he didn't order, there would be nothing but damned white turkey meat sandwiches.

But he wasn't hungry. He took the straight bourbon back to the bed and sat down on the bed edge to drink it. Then he stretched back out and tried to burrow back into the sleep the ringing phone of Strange's call had brought him up out of.

The sexual cutoff had begun almost as soon as the wedding itself was over. She was too tired, her back hurt her, or she was nauseous. He tried to point out that she was only two days more pregnant than she had been two days before the wedding, but it had not made the slightest difference. Stevens had arranged for them to spend four days at the Claridge free, paid for by the hotel's public relations account, as a sort of honeymoon. Prell actually had gotten less sex during that four days than he had had at any time since he had first met Della Mae on the ward, when he had felt a hell of a lot worse.

It was as if all the hot sexuality in her, which she had hated secretly all this time but had never admitted hating, had run down out of her like mercury out of a broken thermometer, leaving only the glass shell and the etched numbers as sort of ghostly reminders of the heat that had once been measured there.

It was as if now, with her back areas and lines of retreat safely stabilized and covered by a marriage certificate, she was ready to stand and fight for her principles. Whatever the fuck they were. One of them was clearly that genu-wine high-class ladies wasn't supposed to like sex.

Prell burrowed his head down deeper into the bed's pillow.

The sleep came slowly, in little spurts. It came like small snow flurries, sweeping an area with their stillnesses, on the light

winds of a steadily thickening snowstorm. Then when the full
sleep came, with it came the nightmares. Immediately. Or so it
seemed. It seemed only half of him was truly asleep, because it
seemed half of him was awake watching the nightmares.

They were all involved with the squad again, and the patrol.
They went all through it again, over and over. The half of him
that was not asleep was aware that he had not had them in quite
a long time, and was a little shocked at seeing them. And this
time Landers was with them, in them.

It was as though Prell could never quite spot him. But he was
with the dead, and at the same time he was with the wounded.
Whenever Prell looked back from his own improvised stretcher
to check, the two dead, both Crozier and Sims, would be there;
but Landers would be one of them, or sort of with them. Whenever he looked at his wounded and counted them to check, all
of them would be there, the count exactly right, but one of their
agonized faces would be Landers. When Prell looked at their
faces individually, each belonged to its owner. But he would
know that there was another one hanging around, hovering
somewhere.

He woke sweating. He had not had any of these dreams in
quite some time. And never had Landers been in any of them.

His watch said it was after midnight. He knew he would
never go back to sleep now. He didn't want to go back to sleep.
Heavily, he got himself back onto his feet and walked teetering
over to the phone, and on the strength of a pretty solid hunch
called Jerry Kurntz's central suite. Sure enough, they were all
there.

"Shit, kid," Jerry Kurntz cried at him from the phone.
"Didn't I tell you this bunch was ripe? All you got to do is pour
some booze down them, and loosen up their inhibitions. And
they all of them got the hots for you. One of them thought she
was your date, and got so mad when you didn't show up, she
went into a sulk. But she's beginning to loosen up now."

"Well what about the other guys?" Prell said. "Are there
enough to go around?"

"Hell, baby, nobody cares," Kurntz roared into the phone.
"You come on over and you can take your pick."

Prell's pick was the one who had sulked over his absence. She
was a good-looking blonde lady, who by the time he arrived had
had more than enough to drink, but was still a lady. None of
these ladies was the kind of bimbo you would find down around

4th Street in Luxor. And, usually, almost always they were married.

"Married and harried," Kurntz liked to say, laughing.

Kurntz always liked to point out that it was because the tour people were out-of-towners, only there for a night or two, that they made out so well. They represented no strings, no embarrassing reappearances.

Kurntz's suite was laid out more or less on the same principles as Strange's suite at the Peabody. Except that there was only one bedroom, and there was no "preparation station" bed in the living room. These ladies would never have gone for, would have been shocked by, something as open as that. But since the tour guys had their own rooms in the hotel to take the "Damsels of their choice," as Kurntz called them, there was no problem.

Prell had ridden over in his wheelchair, and had the bellboy push him. He had found the wheelchair worked wonders of sympathetic limpness on the ladies, once the ladies realized he was no paraplegic and not paralyzed from the waist down.

The Kansas City lady's name was Joyce. "Joyce, would you mind pushing me back to my own room in this thing?" he asked after they had talked awhile in Kurntz's loud, crowded living room.

They always loved pushing him in the wheelchair. And they loved talking to him about the Medal of Honor, and how he had gotten it. Prell didn't mind telling them. He simply soft-pedaled his own feelings of inadequacy about the whole thing. A feeling of inadequacy was not what they were after, at a time like that. Sometimes when he was telling them about it, it seemed that was the way it really was, had really happened.

Most of them liked undressing him, too. Prell always let them. He wasn't ashamed of the scars, and if they wanted to inspect them and ask questions about them, well, the scars were very close to where he wanted to get their faces. And that almost always worked, too. If only with passionate kissing.

"What kind of outfit's your husband in? Where is he?" he asked Joyce.

"He's in England," Joyce said drunkenly. "He's in the Air Force. He's an air-crew ground mechanic. He doesn't fly. But he's written me," she said, running her fingertips over Prell's thigh scars, "about some of the boys who've been flown back to base all terribly torn up. They've had two Medals of Honor in his squadron, he wrote me."

They went to sleep with their arms around each other, Joyce performing a sort of contortionist feat, by keeping her breasts pressed against him up above, while lying away from him down below so as not to hurt his legs. There were no nightmares.

She woke up around five, cold sober. Prell had gotten pretty used to this, too. Her eyes were full of panic.

"My God. What on earth am I doing here?" she demanded, and pulled the sheet up over her breasts.

The lines were almost always the same. So was the action with the sheet.

"What ever will you think of me?"

That line was usually the same, too. Prell had learned how to handle them by talking gently and affectionately and sensibly. He wasn't even sure they heard the words he said, only the tones. He wasn't even sure they saw him.

The next little scene was to leap from the bed stark naked, while enjoining him not to look, which he always did, with pleasure and regret; and then rush for the bathroom to wash themselves, put on makeup, and dress. Usually with their clothes in arm. Or at least panties and bra.

Prell had the perfect excuse not to get up. A cripple didn't have to get dressed, and see them home. But he would always offer to call down for the night bell captain to have a cab waiting. They always accepted that.

Then all he had to do was roll over, go back to sleep, and sleep until Jerry Kurntz would call him at nine and ask how he made out. To which Prell would always answer that he had not made out at all. To which Kurntz would laugh.

This time however, after Joyce blew him an affectionate kiss from the door (they always seemed to be in better control, once they got their clothes and makeup back on) he did not want to go back to sleep because of the nightmares. He got up and, smelling the delicious scent of sex all over him, sat in the wheelchair in his robe with the bourbon bottle. He was careful not to drink enough to incapacitate himself for tomorrow, just enough to relax. He must certainly have dozed some in the chair, whose wheels he had locked, but it was not enough to let the nightmares back in.

That night was his main talk from the stage of the big downtown auditorium. There was quite a large crowd and Joyce, who was one of the ladies helping with the invitation list, was there. When they had a moment alone, she wanted to know if they were going to see each other again that night. Politely Prell begged off and told her no. Women and sex were the furthest things from his mind right then. He had brooded about Strange all day. Strange, and Landers. But Strange had not called at all. Prell was still hoping to get a call from him.

Prell had had another, smaller talk to give in the afternoon, but that night in the auditorium his rehearsed speech got away from him and he suddenly found himself telling them the story of Landers. In the middle of talking, he found himself changing the story all around, to fit the circumstances, to fit the audience, so that Landers' wound came out in his version as much worse, a leg amputation, and he told them that Landers had died as the result of an additional amputation operation. His points for the story, he told his audience, were two. One, that Landers had received no medals for his sacrifice, nor had wanted or expected any. And that two, Landers had not become famous for it and there were going to be a lot more like him. Who, if they survived at all, were going to take a lot of work, here at home.

Prell had no idea at all why he had done it, and thought he might be losing his mind. It was, he supposed, his own personal tribute to Landers, and had just popped out of him.

Kurntz told him later it was a huge success and there wasn't a dry eye in the house when he finished. The pledges and sub-scriptions which Joyce and the other ladies were taking in the lobby were the biggest of the tour to date.

"Jesus, fella," the producer said earnestly, "it was a very moving little routine. You even had me shedding a tear. But you got to tell us about these little ideas when you get them. Before you try them out. We got to write them in, and prepare for them."

"Well it just came to me while I was up there," Prell said, "I didn't know I was going to do it."

Kurntz nodded sympathetically. "Luckily, the lighting man up in the back was listening to you, and was able to follow your mood." Kurntz coughed. "Listen. Was, uh, was that what that phone call was all about last night? That had you so upset for a while?"

"In a way, yeah," Prell said. "Yes. It was."

Kurntz patted his back lugubriously. "I thought maybe so. Well, we'll just work it in. Into one of the speech variations. I'll get Frank on it tomorrow."

Prell was not sure whether he wanted his "Thing" on Landers incorporated into his speech or not. But he did not feel much like discussing it right then.

The worst fight he and Kurntz had had on the entire tour had been over the wheelchair, whether they should use it to wheel Prell onto the big auditorium stages. Jerry wanted to use it and have Prell get up out of it himself, and then walk three or four halting steps to the reading lectern. Prell was furiously against it.

But Kurntz had made a strong case for his idea. "Look, kid. I know how you feel about the wheelchair. And I know you think it's phony to use it. But those people don't have any way of knowing that you *have* to use a wheelchair. I know it. But they don't. Don't forget we're here to *move* these people, to *entertain* 'em. And *instruct* 'em. When you get up out of that wheelchair and walk bravely to the lectern, there's not a person in the crowd who's not going to love you. And that's what we're here for. If we make them love you, they'll buy more bonds. That's why we're here. That's our assignment."

There was no arguing with the logic. It was easy to see why Kurntz was a major. And Prell finally had agreed. And once he began doing it, there was no question that it worked.

Now the same thing was going to happen with his little Landers story. He was going to have to go on telling it. The oftener he told it the less it would be his. The less it would really mean, to him.

Even so, Prell didn't feel like fighting about it right now. All he really wanted was to get back to the hotel and find out if Strange had called.

But there was no call. Strange had not called while they were away at the auditorium, and he did not call after they got back.

So instead of another affectionate night with Joyce and no nightmares, Prell spent the night with the nightmares.

The newly reactivated dreams woke him three times, sweating and fearful, during the course of the night. In the morning they, the whole tour group, flew off in the big Army plane to Lincoln. Two days later they flew on to Denver for their engagement there, last stop on the outward leg of the tour.

Lincoln was a pretty small town, so there hadn't been much hanky-panky there. But Jerry Kurntz was promising a rousing debacle for Denver.

By Denver the nightmares had begun to dim.

CHAPTER 30

Strange had not called Prell back because he hadn't thought it was worthwhile.

Besides, his new outfit was going out in the field for ten days of field problems and he had an enormous amount of work to do then and the next day getting his field kitchens ready.

Prell's indifference over the phone had shocked Strange. It had never occurred to Strange that someone, especially among themselves, wouldn't care about Landers. He might have expected it among the company remnants as a whole, but not from the old hard-core nucleus. It meant that now even the nucleus was breaking up, its parts going off in different directions, pushed by new interests, new loyalties.

The worst part of all that was that it made Strange find his own loyalty suspect. It wasn't really loyalty, apparently. It was a commodity to be sold, traded off, exchanged, according to the whims of the Army in a war, an Army too big to worry about loyalties except in very large bundles. Winch had told him this once.

What was it he had said? Where had it been? On the hospital

ship. The day of the big home landfall. They were pulling into San Diego.

What had he said? *Johnny Stranger, all that shit of the old outfit is over. You better believe it. You better get it through your thick Texas head.* Something like that.

Winch had been right, as he always was. He had just been ahead of time, ahead of everybody, was all. As he usually was.

It must be hard on the sanity, seeing things ahead of time like Winch. Seeing. And knowing. And telling people. Who never listened. Damned hard on the sanity. Strange was glad it was a talent he didn't have.

But now it was catching up to Strange, like a slap in the face. While Winch was already prepared.

Strange had no loyalty to his new outfit at all. It was just a bunch of people, brought together from scattered parts. Officers, some ambitious, some not. Enlisted men, some ambitious, the rest just putting in time, hoping to survive. The ambitious ones, officers and EM, kept moving on, out and upward to somewhere, but of the outfit.

The outfit itself was a communications unit. A bunch of wooden switchboards (they would get metal ones in England, they were told), destined to be set up out in the woods somewhere, and become the link between some Division and its sister Divisions, or some corps of tanks and another corps. Nobody knew exactly what yet. That was the kind of stuff they were going to be practicing on their field maneuvers. Strange was one of the company mess/sgts.

How could you have any loyalty to that? You could have loyalty to your work, but that was all. Perhaps the fire and the strains of combat would combine them and squeeze them into one big self with one big loyalty, when they got to Europe. But they weren't that now. And Strange felt no loyalty to any of them.

He had had some loyalties left, back at the hospital. He had developed a strong loyalty there to Col Curran, for example. And there had been the loyalty to the old-company men who had met at his suite in the Peabody; it was a thinning and diminishing loyalty, true, as more and more of them went back to duty and were scattered, and as he himself got more involved with Frances Highsmith, but it was still a countable loyalty. Frances herself was a serious loyalty, if not an Army one. And then there had been his prime loyalty of all, to the nucleus of four he had been a part of and had come back home with. Strange had never believed that that could break apart.

But the hospital appeared to have been the breaking and thinning point of all a man's loyalties. His own last session with Curran was indicative of all of Strange's, it seemed.

Curran had called him in, one morning during morning rounds, for what he laughingly said might be their last conference. Strange's heart had begun to beat in his ears. He had wondered, lately, about the fact that only he and Prell were left. First Winch with his heart problem or whatever it was, then Landers with that really bad ankle of his, both had gone. Even Prell with his two horribly crippled legs was being set up for hospital discharge to start his war bonds tours. All of them had been worse off than Strange, with his minor hand wound. And yet Strange still languished on his ward, with no word one way or the other. How come?

Curran wasted no time disabusing him. "Your hand hasn't healed as well as we expected. That's why I've kept you as long as I have."

"What do you mean, hasn't healed? It isn't sore, isn't infected. It feels fine to me." He held it up and wiggled it, clenched and unclenched it. A panic ran all through him at the idea of being discharged from the Army, now.

"I don't mean the physical healing. That's fine. I'm talking about the internal healing, the mechanics, the thing we went in there to correct. We had such a success with the operation we thought we had every right to assume it would heal perfectly. But it hasn't." Curran held out his own hand for Strange's wrist.

"Here," he said. "Clench it. Now unclench it. You feel that little pull, that little hesitation?"

Strange had to nod. "Yes."

"Well that's what I mean. It could be," Curran looked at him a moment, as if he were about to list every possible thing it might be, then shrugged, "—it could be a lot of things. It could be something that will go away.

"But my hunch is that it won't. My hunch is it'll get worse. Certainly it's going to bother you later in life."

"Well, what does that mean for right now?" Strange asked. "Does that mean I'm not going to get out of here and back to duty?"

Curran began to laugh. "You still want to get overseas to England, like you said?"

"That's what I'm after," Strange said stiffly.

"I'm not going to keep you here. Just what your hand does not need now is another operation. No, I'm sending you back to duty in a day or two."

"That's great," Strange said. "You had me scared."

"But I've got to warn you about the hand," Curran said sharply. "It could start up tomorrow. Or a week from now. My advice to you is to favor it because of this."

It was Strange's turn to grin. "I can fake it. I went on working with it for six months the first time."

"I wouldn't advise you to. You saw what happened to it in six months the first time."

"I ought to be able to fake it a year this time."

"In any case, I have to send you back as limited duty," Curran said.

"Actually my job as a mess/sgt isn't all that much different," Strange said cautiously, "whether I'm with an infantry line company or some limited duty outfit."

Curran smiled, and shook his head. "Makes no difference. I've got my orders and I follow them."

"Sure." You couldn't argue with that.

"If it starts to act up, you'll be right back in the hospital."

"I've got a question," Strange said.

"Shoot."

"Say it did start to act up. Say, while I'm still on this side. In the East someplace. Where would they send me?"

Curran shrugged. "Theoretically, to the nearest hospital that had a good hand-surgery man. In actual practice, to your post hospital and if you refused to let some joker there play around with it and operate on it himself for fun, then you'd go to the nearest general hospital. Whether they had a good hand-surgeon man or not. And they would operate on it there."

"What if it happened right here, at O'Bruyerre?"

"Then you would come back here."

"And you would handle it."

Curran didn't answer for a moment. "No. I wouldn't."

"Well, Jesus. Why not?"

"Because we're undergoing a reorganization here. We're expanding. We're getting ready for D-Day and the European campaign." Curran shrugged. "The surgery department is being doubled. That means Col Baker and myself are going to become the administrators of two whole new surgery sections. We're being pulled off the operating tables, to do it. We're being kicked upstairs. You know the phrase? I doubt if either of us will have the time to handle any operations at all."

"Well, Christ. Then whatever I do or don't do isn't going to make that much difference anyway, is it?" Strange was angry.

"No, I suppose not, in reality. At least you have learned enough here so that you can say no to some eager young wise-ass who wants to operate you."

"You know how far that will get me."

Curran had grinned. "I'm not even supposed to be telling you this much. There are no bad surgeons in the Army. You know that."

He had stood up from his big black swivel chair Strange had become so familiar with, and thrust out his hand. "Of course, if you do come back here, I'll see that you get everything I can get for you."

"Sure, of course," Strange said, and shook the delicate strong hand. "But I don't expect we'll be seeing each other again, Colonel."

Curran had looked at him a long moment. "No, I expect not," he said. "Not in this war."

And it seemed to happen like that with all of Strange's loyalties. When he left Kilrainey for O'Bruyerre, they all were cut. Precisely, sharply. Even his relationship with Winch, which had been mostly by telephone and about Landers for some time now, seemed to diminish and be cut when he moved to O'Bruyerre.

But of course Landers was already on his way out then, his final decision made. Or so they had thought.

His last, his only visit with Landers in the prison ward had been just a day or two after his conference with Curran. And Strange hadn't moved to O'Bruyerre yet. As usual in the Army, everything was a week later than calculated. Even then Landers had looked so peaked, and pale, with such huge circles under his eyes that Strange should have known something wasn't right.

Then his own move to O'Bruyerre had gone through and he had been so busy getting himself oriented and settled in that he hadn't had time to go back up to see Landers and talk to him.

Strange, of course, in his move to O'Bruyerre had passed

through Winch's office too, like everybody else. And Winch had come out to meet him, also.

Landers had told him about the hidden whiskey bottle. Now he got the chance to see it for himself. He accepted the drink Winch offered, with alacrity.

"Well, what kind of an assignment do you want, Johnny Stranger?" Winch said expansively. "I'm in a position to give you just about anything you want."

Strange had grinned. "Well it don't really make much of a difference, old First Sarn't."

"It's likely to," Winch said thinly, "in a very short time. Now, listen.

"If you're willing to take a bust from staff to buck sergeant, I've got a place I can put you here, in my outfit. As a first cook. But I can't very well take you on as my mess sergeant. I've already got one. That will take two or three months. Will you take the bust?"

Strange hadn't even had to think. "No, I don't think so, First Sarn't." He grinned again.

"Then you mean to follow it right on through." Winch's eyes narrowed, and got a mad green glint in them. "All the way."

"I aint got nothing much else to do," Strange heard himself say. "And I aint never seen Europe."

Winch said no more, didn't argue. He sat down in his big chair and punched a button on his intercom phone. He asked into it for all the reassignment request forms for a mess/sgt in full grade of staff/sgt. There were only four of them, when the clerk brought them in. Together, the two of them went over all four. The communications unit was one of them.

"That's not a bad outfit," Winch said when Strange held the paper up. "At least it's not a rotten one."

"Then that ought to be just fine," Strange said.

Winch called outside for another file and, when the clerk brought it, leafed through the sheets in the folder. "They're due to go out on some field maneuvers some time soon. Then, not too long after that, they'll be shipping out. For England."

"That sounds perfect."

"Then I guess that's your slot. Is all your gear here?"

"Two barracks bags. They're out there in that big barn you call a clerks' office."

"Well I guess they're safe there," Winch said dubiously. He looked outside through the curtained window. "Just sit down there for a minute and have yourself another drink. I'll call the outfit for you. They can send a jeep up. For a man of your stature."

"Why, thank you, First Sarn't."

They talked about Landers a little. Winch seemed to feel Landers was getting exactly what he wanted. And needed. "He's come all apart at the seams," Winch said. "A discharge is the only thing will help him. Otherwise. If he stayed in. Hell, he'd be no good to nobody.

"Besides," Winch added, "a discharge is what he's asked for. That was the way he told his company officers to slant their reports."

"How did you find that out?"

"From the officer. Who went up to talk to him."

"Then I guess you got everything pretty well lined out for him."

"I tried to. I hope so. Now, what about you?"

"What about me?"

"Have you told your wife? Have you told Linda Sue about what you're doing?"

"No," Strange said. "I haven't."

"Well, don't you think you ought to?"

"No. Not especially."

"Has she still got your GI insurance?"

"Yeah. Why?"

"Are you still married?"

"Yes. Still married. Legally. Officially."

"You're not divorced yet. Then it would seem to me that you owe it to her to tell her what you're doing, what to expect."

"I'll decide that," Strange said. Then, because he felt that sounded too harsh, he added, "Maybe I'll drop her a little note. Before I pull out."

"I think you at least owe it to her to tell her face to face. Or at least over the telephone."

"I don't owe her a fucking thing," Strange said.

"I think—" Winch began, but was stopped by the buzzing of his desk phone. He picked it up and listened for half a minute. Then when he put it down, he spread his arms. "Your jeep's there." He stood up, his arms still spread. "I don't know what I think. That's the fucking truth."

"Me neither," Strange said. "Join the club."

"Come on down to the main PX some night. I'm there almost every night. Five-thirty or six," Winch said.

As with Curran, there was the finalizing handshake. Both of them seemed to know it was the end of some era or other. As he and Curran had known.

But as he picked up his two bags and followed the jeep driver down the stairs, Strange remained surprised at how much Winch knew about his personal affairs. Winch hadn't seen or talked to Linda since back in Wahoo before the sneak attack. Yet here he was, seeming to know it all.

Strange had already made his good-bys to Frances. That had happened in town in Luxor, the day after his final conference with Curran. But it was something that had seemed to be coming on for a long time, too.

Partly that was due to his having run through his $7000 savings and allotment money, and having had to give up the suite at the Peabody. Maybe. Maybe it was partly that. Or maybe it wasn't?

Strange hadn't been staying there much for quite a long time, and had taken to renting a double room at the Claridge for himself and Frances, which Jack Alexander, Winch's old buddy, had got for him. The only two old-company men who still frequented the suite were Corello with that ruined shoulder of his and Trynor who had come into Kilrainey a few days after Strange himself. The rest of the time now, when there was a party there, all of the other people who were there were strangers and outsiders. Strange no longer really wanted to go to the parties. He much preferred being off alone with Frances.

But Strange was not about to let go of the suite till he had spent on it every nickel of the $7000. He didn't care who came to the parties every night. He didn't care if he himself didn't go to them. Not one dime of that $7000 restaurant money was going to walk away from the Peabody in Strange's pocket. And not one dime of it did.

Fortunately, or unfortunately, for Strange the money ran out swiftly after Landers went over the hill, and then came back and turned himself in and went into the prison ward. It was really only then that Strange began to realize how much money Landers himself had been pouring into the Peabody suite. Without Landers and his money, the funds in the bank account he had opened with the $7000 began to dwindle with a wild speed.

Strange hadn't wanted money from Landers. He and Landers had talked about it that one time he had visited Landers, and Landers had laughed and told him he had spent almost $4500 himself. All of his own allotments, all of his other savings. Until he was broke himself, or just about. Landers certainly hadn't seemed upset by it. No more than Strange.

In any case, it was when he closed out the suite at the Peabody, and the bank account he had created for it, that Strange learned how much Frances Highsmith had been depending on that money.

"Does that mean you're broke?" she asked him, cautiously, "if you have to give up the suite?"

"Not exactly broke. Badly bent. I still got my salary as a staff sergeant. And a little bit of gambling money."

"But that's all? I thought you were a friend of Warrant Officer Alexander."

"A friend. But not a business associate. Why? You want me to introduce you to Alexander?"

"That great big hulk? Are you kidding? Who would want to fuck him? He's the least attractive man I ever saw. But he's certainly making a lot of money around Luxor."

"He is. But I'm not one of his partners."

"He looks like some kind of huge turtle."

"You better believe it. If he ever gets hold of you and clamps down, you'll think he's a turtle."

Frances tossed her head, irritably. "Then all those expensive lunches? And all those big dinners and shows at the ritzy places around town?"

"Yep. All gone," Strange grinned. "Of course, I can probably still afford a night a week. Or two."

"Listen, I've got a little bit of money of my own," Frances said, cautiously. She smiled. "But all I've really got is my job and my little apartment. And the job doesn't bring in all that much." She smiled again. "Of course you're welcome to whatever I've got."

"I wouldn't think of taking it," Strange said. He had learned enough about her in the past three months to at least know what her job was. She was the buyer and assistant manager for a women's store on Main Street called Three Wives, part of a chain through the South and Middlewest. Her apartment she shared with another Luxor girl whose husband was overseas and who didn't run around, not very much.

"On the other hand," Frances said, "I don't want to just sit home every night and listen to the radio. Or go out to dumb movies." She looked at him shyly.

"Of course not. You'll just have to find yourself some other dates."

"No, no. I'd never do that. But on the other hand, how long do you think this war is going to last?"

"Oh, two years?" Strange said lightly. "At least two years."

"Exactly. Then everybody will have to go back to ordinary living again. To being—" She stopped.

"Sure. Cinderella. Like in the fairy tale. And the coach turns back into a pumpkin, and the horses turn back into mice." Strange grinned at her. "I understand that."

"It is a little bit like that," Frances said. And that was how they had left it.

So there wasn't much doubt in Strange's mind what would happen when he took her the news of his move to O'Bruyerre.

"I don't much see you wanting to move out to that village that's near the camp," he said.

"Oh, that little town?" She was trying hard not to say a downright No, immediately. "I'd have to give up my job. And my apartment? I'll bet the living arrangements there are horrible. I don't see how I could give up my job."

Strange didn't say anything. The back of his throat hurt, a little.

"And you've never said anything about marrying me," she said, cautiously.

"No," Strange said. "I haven't."

He thought she looked relieved. "I don't see how," Frances said, "I can give up everything I have here, and have worked to build, to move out there."

"No," Strange said. "I don't think it would be fair to ask you."

"Sexually, I'm not so full of discipline I could sit on it and wait and wait. How often will you get off out there, to come in? Weekends?"

"Every other week. For one night."

"You see?"

He nodded.

"But you could call me," Frances offered. "Ahead of time. Any time. So we could make a date."

"Sure. Sure, that's it," Strange said. "That's what I'll do."

But he had no intention of ever doing any such thing. That

night they had one of the most rousing sexual performances they had ever done. After it, Frances cried. Strange almost cried. She did not see how she could change her mind, though.

One of the odd things was that Winch had never mentioned her, Strange thought as he left Winch's office behind the jeep driver. Winch had only talked about Linda. His wife.

It was as though he was looking into Strange's mind.

Because if there were any love leftovers in Strange's thinking, the residues were of Linda Sue. Not of Frances. If he was still in love with anybody at all, a proposition Strange devoutly wished he could respond to with an unqualified negative, it was with Linda. Strange didn't know why he was. But Winch seemed to know that he was.

If he had any sexual fantasies about anyone, after he was installed at O'Bruyerre, they were about Linda. Not about Frances. If any angers and rages struck him and shook him, and some did, they were over Linda. Not Frances. If any fits of jealousy and highly graphic fantasy of one of them sleeping with somebody took him over, they were always of Linda and her goddamned Air Force colonel, not of Frances and some guy.

Anyway, sex took up very little of his time and thought at O'Bruyerre. Strange was too busy organizing his new kitchen and new kitchen force and getting them to work together. As Winch had said while they were looking for a unit for him up in Winch's office, no outfit that requested a new mess/sgt to come in in grade could have a top-rated kitchen; otherwise they would have promoted one of their own first cooks and picked an apprentice second cook out of the ranks. This was almost exactly the case. The other mess/sgt had been badly burned by a pot of cooking grease, something that should never happen in a well-run kitchen anyway; and he left behind him a shambles that could not have been much better when he was there. One of the first cooks was fat and one was thin, but they were equally ineffectual, equally bad. It took a great deal of cajolery, flattery and complimenting, as well as a lot of order-giving and meanness that almost came to fistfights a couple of times, to get them into some kind of shape. But by the time orders came for their ten-day maneuver out in the field Strange had whipped them down and had them working as a team.

It was just three days before they were to move out that Winch called him about Landers.

It was one of the most emotional moments Strange had had

since seeing the Golden Gate. It was just ten o'clock in the morning. Landers had been killed at about eight-thirty. They had taken him back up to the hospital, not knowing where else to take him. Then they had called Winch and Winch had gone up there. That was why he was so late in calling. "Can you meet me at the main PX?" Winch asked hoarsely. "In the senior NCOs section? Have you got a ticket to let you in the PX this early in the day? Never mind. I'll make one out for you, and forge it." When Strange turned away from the phone, his new 1st/sgt was looking at him with a distressed face.

"What happened? You look like you seen a ghost."

"What? Oh. Yeah. Almost. Old buddy of mine from the Pacific just got killed here at O'Bruyerre."

The 1st/sgt's face got jumpy. "What was it? Artillery? MG ranges? Hand grenades?"

"No. No. He just got hit by a car."

"You old guys." The 1st/sgt shook his head. "Your old combat buddies are closer than family."

"Here, sign this, will you? I got to meet my old first sarn't," Strange said, getting from the clerk's desk a ticket that said he could be allowed in the PX bar before noon. The 1st/sgt looked perplexed, as if about to say an officer must sign the ticket, which Strange already knew; but then he signed it, with an illegible, scrawled flourish.

"I'll be back in a while," Strange said. "Anyway, everything is in shape in the kitchen and they've all got something to keep them busy."

But he might as well not have bothered with the PX pass. No one stopped him, or asked to see it. This PX pass ticket was a new thing, put into effect since the training had gone up into high gear for the European D-Day. Finding Winch was easy, as uncrowded as the place was now. It was only the second time Strange had been in the big main PX.

Winch was alone. Strange sat down beside him at the big round table.

"Well," Strange said. "Tell me."

Winch did. Strange listened as he ran through all that the woman had told the authorities, and what she had said about it looking like a deliberate suicide. They talked about the possible suicide awhile. Winch did not think it was possible. But Strange was not so sure.

"What the hell?" Winch said harshly. "He was getting exactly what he wanted. That's what he told that company officer of his he wanted. That's not a suicide position."

"I don't think he knew what he wanted," Strange said suddenly. It was as if he had seen it and read it, written on the pressed paper Budweiser coaster under his beer mug, and was reading it off the circular paper mat. "I think he wanted both equally. Exactly equal. That's an unsolvable position." He looked up from his coaster.

Winch looked at him, his eyes wondering. "Then there wasn't anything anybody could do for him."

"No," Strange said. "Nothing."

"So it was all of it . . . And I was just wasting my time," Winch said, to himself.

Some man in the big empty hall got up and put some money in the tall, bubbling, whirling, lighted Wurlitzer machine. "Ciribiribin" by the Andrews Sisters began to play in the huge hall.

"By God, I hate those fucking Wurlitzers," Winch said viciously.

"Did you see him?" Strange said.

Winch drank down the glass of white wine that was sitting in front of him. Then he signaled the barman over behind the mahogany-colored bar for another. He drank two more in quick succession. Then he began to hem and haw around about how, and whether or not, he had seen Landers' body. They wanted another identification signature, besides just the hospital people. They didn't want to call his old outfit. Anyway, he didn't have an old outfit any more. Somebody knew Winch had known him.

"Did you see him?" Strange said again.

"Yeah, yeah, I saw him. Or at least his face. Was no great thing. Just another dead guy. He had that pale, greenish color they get. Face wasn't smashed up. Just one big bruise on the right cheekbone."

"What are they going to do with the body?"

"Send it home to his family, I guess."

"He never liked his family that much."

"No. I know. He told me that, too. But they can give it one of those big old local military American Legion funerals, out in the old cemetery. Beside his grandfather, and his great-great-grandfather, and all that. Fire a couple of volleys over it."

"Have some Boy Scout play his bugle over it."

"What the hell?" Winch said. "It's only a body. It's as good a way to dispose of it as some other."

"You going to write them a letter?"

"No," Winch said.

"Me neither. I wouldn't know what to say to them."

Winch signaled for another white wine. "Listen, you never come down here. Come on down some evening, at five-thirty or six. If you get the blues or anything."

"We're going out in the field day after tomorrow," Strange said.

"Then come down when you get back," Winch said, harshly.

Strange had nodded. "Sure. It's only ten days."

He had telephoned Prell that night. Winch had found out for him from Jack Alexander that the tour was in Kansas City at the Muehlebach. But Prell's reaction made him decide right away that there was no point to calling Prell back.

The ten days out in the field were probably the best thing that could have happened to him at the moment. First, it was an abrupt switch from the garrison living. And existing under canvas that had to be pulled down and put back up twenty miles farther on in some other patch of woods every two days did not allow you much time for thinking, except in snatches. Strange could handle snatches. From 3:30 in the morning to midnight he was constantly on the run; cooking, stretching kitchen flies, feeding, overseeing that the flies and tents were ditched properly against the rain on the wooded slopes. Strange loved every minute of it.

And spring came while they were out there. For the first three days it rained, dismal winter rains at first, then each day warmer and more humid. Then, suddenly, the sun came out, and stayed out for the remaining seven days, and the leaves popped out and everything turned green.

It was absolutely beautiful. And the incredible speed with which it happened was unbelievable. Strange would stand outside his kitchen fly in the soft mud of some bare woods, checking his Lister water bags, and look off at some western Tennessee hill farmer's rough slab cabin through the hard black lines of the bare hardwood branches. Minutes later the cabin would be invisible through the screen of leaves which had popped out, uncurling on the budded limbs.

Not many of the other men seemed to notice, or to give much

of a damn. When it rained, they complained about the wet. When the sun came out, they complained about the mud. But to Strange it was unbelievably beautiful. This was the first time in six years that he had seen an American spring come on. Before the war he had spent four years in Wahoo, where there was no real winter or spring, then another year in Wahoo after the sneak attack, then a year in the South Pacific in the tropics. He hadn't seen a real American spring in a long time.

They were out in the western Tennessee hill country, west of the Tennessee River. It was nothing like the primitive mountain country of eastern Tennessee, but if you got back into it far enough, where they were, you still found the home-built cabins covered with home-split shakes, the well and the outhouse outdoors around them. The farmers in their dilapidated hats and gum boots had eyes like wild, secretive animals. They were always willing to sell you a pint or two of homemade white lightning, yellowish and oily and evil-looking. Inside above the front door there were always some home-grown tobacco twists hanging, rolled and bent double and the ends twisted around each other. They would not sell you the tobacco but would give you a twist. The women with their hatchet faces always looked at you with gentle, tender eyes above the seamed, tight slash of their mouths. Strange had not chewed home-twist tobacco since he'd been a boy in Texas.

In almost every home, behind the home-set, swirly glass windowpane, hung one of the blue star flags with one, or two, or more blue stars in its center indicating the male members of the family in the service.

If there were any daughters, you never saw them.

On the single Saturday night of their ten-day field assignment orders came down giving them the Saturday afternoon, the night, and the Sunday morning off. The nearest town was a dinky little burg called McSwannville, three miles away. Those who could not catch a ride in on some loosened company vehicle walked it, along the muddy country lanes. Strange had control of the company's freed kitchen jeep, and was able to take his entire kitchen force in on it. Men hung from it like overfull grapes dangling from an overladen garden cluster. After he parked it in the town, Strange wisely walked to the one hotel, intelligently thinking he should have some place to take any windfalls, and it was well he did. He got the very last room.

Men had centered on the one available town from all over the maneuver area. Infantry. Artillery. Quartermaster. A few raucous, tough paratroopers; tankers; other Signal Corps units. They all were there. It did not look like there were going to be many windfalls. But there was plenty of booze. The town was the county seat of a dry county, but there were three bootleg joints on its outskirts, where you could get real bottle whiskey instead of the always available, powerful white lightning. Each joint clearly had been alerted to stock up. Each was crowded, with a line of servicemen that came out of its door down to and along the muddy edge of the county road. As Strange walked down the one main street in midafternoon, the fistfights had already begun. One here. One there. Another starting, as still another stopped.

Not many women were even visible. Most of them stayed completely indoors. A few local bad girls and hookers hung around the two little eating places where much of the "concealed" drinking was done, or sat at one of the few tables the bootleg joints had inside, always with some soldier. The men of the town went about with a sort of business-as-usual attitude, but apparently trying to stay off the streets as much as possible. MPs with jeeps hauled jeeploads of lax drunken bodies off to some staging area where they would be collected by their outfits. Strange decided quickly there weren't likely to be any windfalls, and concentrated on drinking. Even bad bottle whiskey tasted delicious after the white lightning.

There was this odd feeling everywhere that it was one week before the end of the world, and Strange let it pick him up and carry him.

He no longer thought about Landers with pain. People, like the seasons, all had to end sometime. In one manner or another. Somehow, seeing the spring had straightened that out for him.

Amiably drunk and at peace with this ending world he wandered through, he ate some food somewhere. Then about eleven P.M., as he walked along the one main street, he was accosted by the fat first cook of his company. The cook was sweating profusely and breathing heavily, and came out of a darkened alley.

"Hey, Sarge. Is it true you got a hotel room?"

"Yeah. I got one. Why?"

The fat first cook had been the biggest troublemaker Strange had had to deal with in the company. Naturally, he had wanted

Strange's job, and had thought he was in line for it. Strange was not about to give him half an inch. But none of that seemed to be bothering the cook, now.

"I got these two cunts, two broads, down here. I'd like to trade one of them for half a hotel room."

Strange paused to stare at him. Strange never had liked him. If he had brought his complaints out, and had done his fighting in the open. But he hadn't. He had done it all under cover, using other people to do his dirty work, and getting them into trouble. Strange intended to break him as soon as he could.

"How much do they want?"

"They don't want any money. They just want to get fucked."

"Do they know you're trading one of them off?"

"Oh sure. It was them that suggested it. They'll go off in the woods, or the park. But if we had a real place to take them, they'd stay all night."

"How'd you find them?"

"I didn't, really. They found me," the cook said. "I was sitting out in the grass, drinking. By myself. And they just sort of came up out of the shrubbery. I don't think they're townie girls. I think they're off some farm."

"How old are they? Are they of age?"

"How the hell do I know? They look the right age."

Strange looked down the dark alley. "What the hell are they hiding down there for, then? Why don't they come on out here into the light?"

"They're not hiding. They just don't want to come out here where all these guys are. They'd have a mob of guys all over them, if they came out here with no men."

"That makes sense. Okay, let's have a look."

Strange had made his mind up so strongly that there weren't going to be any windfalls that he was finding it hard to shift gears.

In the dark of the alley the girls were waiting. They both wore faded print dresses that came just to the knees of their shapely legs. Each of them wore a shabby girl's coat against the spring night's chill. They certainly weren't women, but they certainly weren't underage girls, either.

Strange knew when he saw them that he wasn't going to turn it down. The thickness in his throat when he swallowed and the breathlessness in his chest when he breathed told him that.

They didn't mind walking along the lighted street when they

had men with them. One's name was Donna and the other's was Ruby. Neither of them wanted anything, except to go to the hotel. Both Strange and the cook had bottles, but the girls didn't want a drink. Neither girl drank. Nor did they want something to eat. Thinking of all the girls he had squired so grandly at the Peabody, Strange grandly offered to buy them a meal at one of the hashhouses. Neither of them wanted it.

At the hotel the boy behind the old, tiny, ramshackle desk in the tiny lobby looked at the girls with carefully widened eyes which did not seem to see them, and gave the key to Strange. In the room, which Strange had not inspected, there was one bed. This did not seem to bother the girls. Fortunately, it was a double bed. The fat cook began to get out of his green field uniform immediately. He was apparently already counting the available hours he would have.

Up to now the girls had not said more than three or four words apiece. Now they began to giggle over the naked cook with his erection, and made it plain they did not want to be watched while they undressed, or to be seen nude. The men were to turn their backs, and hide their eyes. As soon as the girls were established in the bed under the sheet, the men could come on.

Of course, both men peeked, and there was a good deal of squealing and giggling and scolding over this. What the men saw for their trouble were two lovely, firm-breasted, young slender woman bodies. Only on the tanned hands and faces were there any signs of that swift aging process that was so noticeable out here among the hill farms. Then the two girls tumbled into the bed, and told the men to come on.

And that was the way they stayed, more or less, till after seven the next morning, when the girls said they must get home in order to wash and get ready to go to church. Sometimes, rarely, they had slept, while outside the hotel around them the little town rocked and rippled with its influx of last-gasp, end-of-the-world servicemen. The shouts and fights and breaking of glass and harmony singing did not bother the girls, and it certainly did not bother Strange and the cook. It was amazing, how two couples fucking in the same bed could spend so much time there, and still be so absolutely far away from each other.

Strange, who had developed a healthy hunger and was thinking of hotcakes, butter, syrup and sausage somewhere in the sunshine of the spring morning, wanted to buy them all a scrumptious breakfast, but the girls refused. Outside the hotel, without even a kiss (they had never been much for kissing, even when fucking in the old brass bed), they said good-by and went away along the now-quiet street in the sunny morning, then off down a path, back into the shrubbery out of which they had come.

So Strange was left with his fat first cook for a breakfast companion. It did not ruin the breakfast, but it came close to ruining nearly everything else. The cook would not stop talking about what a great night they two had had. Strange wanted only to savor it in silence. Strange felt he ought to owe the cook a favor. Instead, Strange was only angry. Finally he told the cook savagely to shut up.

"Oh, okay. Okay, John, okay."

It was the first time the fat cook had ever dared use Strange's first name. Strange raised his eyes and gave him a cold, murderous, fishy-eyed stare.

But the cook couldn't ruin everything. Strange had come away from the whole thing, the bizarre night, the two girls, the drunken revel outside the hotel, with a feeling that the girls were a mythical impersonation of the spring itself, and this feeling stayed with him even in spite of the cook. Strange felt that if the spring, which had told him so much in other voiceless ways, had not been there, the girls would not have existed, either.

Together, he and the first cook slowly rounded up the rest of his kitchen force, going from place to place and group to group until they found them all. In the hot spring sunshine they had to take off their field jackets and carry them. Then they began the three-mile ride back to bivouac in the overcrowded jeep, past woods and fields that had leafed out noticeably since yesterday. They had four more days of maneuvers ahead, before they went back to camp. Most of that time was spent talking about the Saturday.

Strange would not talk about it. But this did not stop the cook from bragging to everybody about what a luckout and great night the two of them had had together, with their two hot farm girls. But Strange refused to answer all questions, even the most rollicking.

Strange was not at all proud of having doubled up with his fat cook in the same bed with two country girls. But more than that, the truth was that Strange had begun to fantasize about it.

It all had to do with whether the two girls had had orgasms or not. As far as Strange could tell, neither of the girls had come, not even once, all during the all-night lovemaking session. But this had not seemed to bother them. Or frustrate them. They seemed perfectly happy and satisfied, to be fucked over and over by the men who came on top of them.

They could not help but make him think of Linda Sue, when she was younger.

Strange had badly wanted to go down on his girl, and make her come that way. Maybe for perhaps the first time in her life. Frances Highsmith had told him that a come that way was twice as intense as a come from masturbating. But of course it had been impossible with the male cook present in the bed. And Strange himself was not so sure the girl herself would have accepted it without being shocked and horrified. It made the difference between himself and them intensely apparent.

Was he a pervert?

The whole thing was terribly distressing. And the following weekend when the company was back in out of the field, and he had gotten an overnight pass for himself into Luxor and had made a date ahead of time with Frances, he asked her about it.

They were lying in the bed with their arms around each other like two old buddies, after their first sexual thunderstorm, her breasts pressed deliciously against his stomach. Strange carefully had not questioned her about what she had been up to, or who she had been out with since he had seen her last.

"I want to ask you something," he said, his chin on the top of her head. "Seriously. Am I a pervert?"

"Pervert why?" Her voice was muffled by his chest.

"Because I like going down on girls so much, damn it. Why else?"

Frances pushed away from him, to look into his eyes in silence. Then she smiled. "Well, are dogs perverts?" she said, finally.

"What the hell does that mean?"

"Dogs lick each other's genitals. Just about every animal does, as far as I know. And none of them seem to worry about being perverts."

"They're dogs. We're people."

"What I'm trying to say is I think it's a perfectly natural act.

I don't know who first made the rules that it wasn't, but I think they're full of shit. So: I think you're only a pervert if you think you're a pervert."

Strange did not answer for a long moment. "I guess I think I'm a pervert," he said in a low voice. "For liking it so much. So I guess I am a pervert, hunh?"

"Okay, you're a pervert," Frances said. "If you think you are, you are." She began to laugh, "Isn't it great?"

Strange found himself beginning to laugh. "As a matter of fact, it is. I like it."

Her sense of humor was contagious. And it wiped all the dark fog off all of the windows. She was so sensible, Frances, and so unguilty. On the other hand, he wasn't going to have her sense of humor with him all the time, to fall back on. Especially after he left O'Bruyerre.

"But there are a lot of people who don't think like you and me," Strange said.

"Yes," she said. "Well, I guess you'll just have to pick your shots. Like I do."

Strange nodded. He told her the story of the two girls, the fat first cook, and the one bed.

Frances was laughing through most of it. "Yes. I would say that was one of the times when it was better to keep it to yourself.

"Are you a Christian?"

Strange had to think about that one. "I don't know," he said finally. "Any more."

"But you were raised as a Christian. By religious people."
"Yes."

"Well, that's your problem. So was I. And Christianity's ideas about sex are as primitive as a bunch of witch doctors'. I don't know where it all started," Frances said, "I guess with those Puritans the damned English sent over here in 1620. The English were smart to get rid of them."

"I'll be going to England before long," Strange smiled. "Maybe it'll be a little different over there."

"It ought to be, after the way they got rid of those Puritans. On the other hand, the Victorians didn't do so good with it, either." She shook her head. "I learned in college that in thirty-six of the forty-eight states it's illegal for you and me to go down on each other. Actually against the law. All spelled out, in the particulars. I think it is, in this state. We could go to jail, if somebody caught us. All laws made by damned Christians."

"But you still don't think you're a pervert," Strange said.

"No. Absolutely not. I just like to suck cock."

Strange felt himself beginning to laugh again, and when he left her the next day on the Sunday to go back to camp, he was feeling considerably better about the whole business of perversion.

It may have been partly those high spirits that caused him to go see Winch at the main PX and ask for a transfer out of the Signal Corps unit.

Strange had thought about doing it a number of times before. But the business with the fat first cook and the farm girls on that Saturday night had pushed him over the edge. The cook was never going to let up on it. He still insisted on calling Strange by his first name. Strange did not feel he should ask him to stop it. If he did, it might be taken the wrong way by the others. Strange had tried every silent way that he knew to let the cook know that he did not like it. But the cook had a hide like a rhinoceros. Or else he just chose to ignore it. Strange suspected it was the latter.

But the cook wasn't the main factor. The cook was just the last straw. Strange never had liked the outfit. Two of the company commanders had moved away. Two other officers had moved off and been replaced. Two of the section sergeants had been transferred out, upward. Strange heard later that one of them was going to go to OCS. If there had ever been any esprit and unit loyalty, it had diminished visibly since Strange had come in.

He explained all this carefully to Winch, and a little apologetically, while Winch sat and grinned at him crazily.

"And just where would your fucking majesty like to go?" Winch said, when he had finished.

"I'd like to go back to the infantry."

"You sure are a glutton for punishment. Well, I'll see what I can do."

They were seated at a small table a few feet from Winch's big table, in the crowded roaring 6:00 P.M. interior of the huge beerhall. Both of the Wurlitzers were going full blast. Winch had brought him over to the small table, after Strange had said he wanted to talk to him. It was Winch's local private office, apparently. Even in the 6:00 P.M. jam-up it was kept vacant for Winch's use by the management.

"You know our old buddy Jack Alexander has a big piece of this place," Winch said, with his crazy-grinning eyes.

"Sure, it figures."

"There's nothing I can do for you right at this moment," Winch went on. "Both of these Divisions are moving out. One is leaving for England in a week, and the other not too long after. They both have had their final medical exams and there aren't any vacancies." He stopped to rub and pull at his ear, something Strange had never seen him do before. "But there will be two new Divisions moving right in on their heels as soon as they clear."

"Sure. That's fine. But what about my limited duty status?"

Winch grinned again. "Are you trying to put me on?"

Strange shook his head. "When is my outfit due to leave?"

"Not for a while. There've been no orders cut for it yet.

"But that doesn't matter, either," Winch said. "I can pull you out of it and hold you as a casual. If the orders are cut."

"Okay, then. That's fine." Strange made as if to get up, but Winch put out a hand and held him down by his wrist.

"What have you decided about Landers?" he said.

Strange ruminated. "I aint decided nothing," he said. "Being out there in the field on maneuvers, I guess, makes it all seem pretty far away."

"I guess," Winch said.

Strange looked over at him, awkwardly. "You know, the spring came on while we were out there. I aint seen a real spring in a long time. Six years."

"Yes?" Winch said. His eyes seemed to have lost their crazy energetic glint, and become more open.

"Everybody has to die sometime. In some particular way, or other."

"Yes," Winch said. "And generally, the later the better."

"Yes," Strange said. "Generally. But not always. I don't honestly think there was anything anybody could have done."

"That's your considered opinion." It was not a question, but more of a statement, made almost as if to Winch himself.

"It is," Strange said. Winch had let go of his arm. He stood up. "I guess I better ought to be getting on."

"No, no. No, no," Winch cried, and his eyes began to heat up again. "You have to come over and have a few beers with this gang of bums. I want you to meet some of them."

Strange went, but he didn't want to. He felt he owed at least this much to Winch, but he did not like the quality, or the steady, sharply grinning faces around the table. He had never liked that kind of old-timer noncoms.

When he left, after two or three beers with them, Strange was careful to shake hands with every man he had been introduced to.

"You got to come back. You got to come back, Johnny Stranger," Winch shouted after him, his face and hot eyes still twisted over some joke or other. "Any time. Any time. Tomorrow."

Strange did not think Winch looked good at all.

CHAPTER 31

Strange's disapproval was not lost on Winch, at the big round table. If Strange thought it was, or thought Winch was unable to sense it and appreciate it, he was dead wrong.

On the other hand Winch was not in agreement at all with the way Strange had chosen to run out his string. The $7000 loss blown on the Peabody and its suite and parties was a ridiculous gesture, to Winch. Strange's set determination to get himself to England and Europe, when he did not have to, was even crazier. But to come down here and ask to have himself transferred out of an outfit he now more or less dominated, back into the infantry, was a clear insanity.

There had to be something insanely self-destructive in it. Strange had to have gone off his rocker and a little crazy, over that dumb wife of his. Winch may have gone a little odd, a little peculiar, himself. But not so much that he could not notice and analyze something as flagrant as those choices.

Winch might be a little crazy. But he wasn't that crazy. Statistically, they both knew, the mess/sgt of an infantry company stood a better chance of getting himself knocked off in Europe than the mess/sgt of a Signal Corps unit. For a large variety of reasons.

As for Strange's opinion about Landers, Winch did not go along with that either. All that bullshit about the springtime. Landers was not the springtime, or anything near like it. Landers was a human man, with arms, and legs, and blood, and a kooky, kinked-up, little-bit-crazy brain. And as such he could have been saved. Winch just had not known the combination. And neither had Strange. To say anything else, like that guff about the springtime, was to lie to yourself.

You could go on and say Landers was crazy. But that was no excuse either. Everybody was crazy. Strange, and Prell, those two crazy chief surgeons at the hospital, Winch himself. Every first-three-grader who came to this big round table in the beer hall was a nut. If the war hadn't made them crazy, they had brought the craziness with them from before. Which was probably the most likely in any case.

Winch and Strange had fucked up on Landers. That was all there was to say. Just as Winch, right now, was also fucking up on Strange himself. Because there was nothing to do but go ahead and put through his request for transfer. As soon as the two new Divisions began to show up. Strange would fight anything else like a crazy man.

What could you do with a crazy man? The only real answer was to convince him not to do what he wanted to do, or thought he ought to do. And Winch was not crazy enough to think he could do that with anybody as stubborn as Strange.

Shit, he hadn't even been able to do it with Landers.

Three days before Strange had come down there to the PX to see him, Winch had gone wild-ass crazy in Jack Alexander's nonstop poker game at the Claridge, and had won $12,000. For no appreciable reason he had begun to hold cards, and seemed unable to draw a bad hand. Hidden full houses at seven card high. Concealed lows in seven high low. Wired pairs that filled to trips against two pair in five stud. Winch had bet them wildly, crazily, making the other players think he was bluffing (nobody could believe he could keep on drawing such hands), and finally had broken the game. Everybody had quit, and dropped out of the game over such high losses, or else had gone flat broke. Until the game had closed down for the night. An almost unheard of thing. Winch and Alexander had even had a fight, an argument, while the game was still on, over the way Winch was playing.

"You damn fool," Jack who never played had said heatedly in front of the other players, his innate conservatism incensed by such extravagance. "You're going to lose all your fucking damn players, all your competition, if you don't play like a fucking damn human being."

"I don't give a shit," Winch had bellowed, and made his crazy, green-eyed smile. "The fuck do I care?"

Alexander was right, of course. And afterward the two had an even bigger argument, while the other players drifted off.

Winch had decided he did not want to carry the money away with him. That was what the disagreement was over.

"I want you to keep it and invest it for me," Winch said.

"Look," Alexander said. "I'll take all or part of it and keep it in the safe for you. If you don't want to carry that much on you. You can pick it up in a couple of days. But I don't want to take charge of it for you."

The two of them were completely alone in the two-room suite by now. Winch checked the bedroom to be sure.

"No, that's not what I want," he said. "I want you to keep it. For me. When the first good deal turns up, buy me into it. I don't want the fucking money."

"I won't take care of your money. I'm not your investment broker."

"Sure you are," Winch said, and grinned his sly grin.

Alexander shook his massive head. "No. I'm fucking not. There aint any deals coming up right now as far as I know. Take the money and put it in a bank. A safe deposit box, is preferable. Soon as something comes up, you give me what it needs. That's sensible. There's a lot of money there."

That much was true. It was a not inconsiderable stack of greenbacks, although Alexander had changed all the small bills for Winch that he could manage. It made a thick, unfolded sheaf, bound in its rubber band. Winch took it and dropped it on the green felt playing surface under the white, green-shaded light hanging over the table.

"There. There it is. I don't want it. And I aint taking it." He turned and walked to the door. "You can give me an IOU, if you want."

"God damn you," Alexander said. But he got a slip of paper and commenced writing the IOU. "Now, here. I'm keeping it. But I'm not going to invest it. Not without I talk to you first.

If something shows up, I'll give you a call. And you can tell me to buy in, or not buy in." He tore the slip off the pad. "But that's the only way I'll do it."

"Okay. Fine." Winch accepted the slip and went back to the door, and then turned back to wink and make his grin.

The big, hard turtle's face stared back at him icily. "Damn you," Alexander said, "you're the biggest goddamned problem I ever got from old Hoggenbeck. I don't know why you don't act more sensible. Now get the fuck out of here. And don't come back and play in my game unless you can act like a human being."

Winch laughed, low in his throat. But outside in the dark street he took out the little IOU slip and burnt it with a match. When the last white corner withered into ash, he snapped it away off his fingers into the night's spring breeze. What did he need with an IOU from Alexander? As long as Alexander knew he had one, it was the same thing. And even if Alexander knew he didn't have one, he knew Alexander wouldn't crook him. Or what if he did? It would be interesting.

But it wasn't any kind of craziness like Strange had shown with his $7000. Winch wasn't crazily taking his $12,000 and blowing it, on a bunch of parties and a ritzy hangout for a bunch of fuckheads who would never appreciate it anyway.

Along Luxor Main Street, almost empty now at 3:00 A.M., compared to earlier in the night, the soft Southern spring breeze had taken over the city as well as the country and in the parks the buds were out on the trees and cracking into leaf. Winch walked along it, looking at his watch. There were still servicemen and their girls abroad, or lonely men in uniform alone, meandering along Main Street, or down the hill on Union where Main crossed it in a T. The influx of servicemen in the past weeks had been enormous. But everything was closed. Winch wished there was a joint open, or even a hashhouse, where he could waste an hour before going home to the apartment. Carol would be getting up at four, to go home. Winch had been doing this kind of thing more and more lately, to avoid having to go to sleep beside Carol in the apartment when she was there.

It was hard on him, physically. All the fatigue. But he could not stand having her wake and hear him talking through his nightmares. He didn't like her waking him out of them.

But all the after-hours joints were scattered, hidden away out in the lowlife residential areas of the town. There weren't any down in the downtown section. Mostly they were places that sold barbeque, which he could not eat any more, little joints, run by blacks, where you could get beer, and which sold pints and half pints of bootleg out in the back under the branching trunks of huge old elm trees.

Winch no longer had much drive to go to places like that. And Carol did not like them. Standing in front of the Peabody, he decided to walk home to the apartment. It was only ten blocks. If he took it easy and walked slowly, he could do it without much discomfort. And Carol would just about be getting up when he got there.

Winch had been getting more and more of this breathlessness lately, but had not told anyone about it yet. Carol was the hardest one to fool. Especially if they had sex together. Which was just about every day, if Winch got up to the apartment soon enough. The high, open, outside staircase up to the apartment was giving him more trouble now, too. He had to stop twice now, to breathe, when he climbed it. If Carol was with him, he pretended he was looking off at the scenery, which was certainly beautiful enough to stop for. Fortunately Carol hadn't been with him that night.

Sitting in the beer hall after Strange had left, with the Wurlitzers blaring out conflicting tunes, Winch had pushed back his chair and got to his feet.

He favored his assembled stripers with his grin. It was running through his mind that he would love to drop a couple of hand grenades into those screaming jukeboxes. They were really the world of the future, it suddenly occurred to him. Chrome, and pipe, and plastic, and whirling iridescent lights, and jarred, canned music. To soothe the souls of men as they went to fight and die against other men, equally rabid and intent on saving their own canned tunes. Pho-o-o-ey-y-y! He wanted to shout it aloud. But he made himself hold back.

He wanted to stay, too. But he had promised Carol he would take her out to a nice dinner tonight.

"Well, gentlemen. Much as I love your illustrious company. But, as usual, I've got a lot of heavy work to do tonight," he grinned down at them.

"What's up, Mart?" one of them bawled. "Got some heavy duty cunt lined up tonight?"

"Hell," Winch said slyly. "I haven't seen one of those in so long I don't remember whether you play them sideways like a harmonica, or straight in like a tuba mouthpiece."

It got a big laugh all around, and was a good point to leave on. Outside beside his car he stopped, standing straight up in the spring night for a couple of minutes, to get his breath. In a kind of desolate way he knew that soon he was going to have to go up and turn himself over to them again at the hospital, where they might decide to keep him awhile or not decide to, but he did not want to think about that at the moment.

Strange had been right about one thing, anyway. Winch was not in good shape. Strange had not said what he thought, but Winch had read it in his eyes. Landers' death had hit Winch worse than he would admit to anyone, even to Strange. Even to Carol.

One evening in town at the apartment he had broken down, and had tried to tell Carol about it. About all of Landers, and what had happened, and where he Winch had failed. She had simply stared at him. Then after a little while tears had come in her eyes. For him Winch. Not for Landers.

It had been a mistake. To talk to her. Perhaps he had not been able to communicate very well. But people like Carol didn't really want to know that the Winches of the world cared. They preferred them to be tough and funny.

Anyway, he had learned enough so that he would never try to do it again.

She was waiting for him at the apartment when he got in, and pulled the little car up, and climbed those stairs. He waited a couple of minutes on the high outdoor landing before opening the door, to get his breath. But for some unaccountable reason he was feeling in much better shape tonight than usual. Maybe it was the glasses of wine he'd had.

In the beginning dusk off through the tall trees the spring was coming on furiously, like a madly galloping horse. People were out working in their yards and Victory gardens.

"I thought maybe you weren't going to be able to come to-night," Carol said lightly, when he'd shut the door. She had gotten herself all dolled up for the evening in a new spring dress he hadn't seen before. Off behind her somewhere, in an unobtrusive corner, were sitting two lady's suitcases, side by side.

"Are you kidding?" Winch grinned. She came to him and put herself into his arms, her breasts pushing against his blouse, and Winch felt the youth of her again, as he kissed her.

The kiss went on, and then further on, and Winch felt the old familiar ache in the back of his throat. But there was no way to possess a woman, really. Skin. Skin was as close as you could really get. Even the inside of the vagina was still skin.

"What do you say we have a drink first?" he said, breaking away.

"Of course," she said. "Of course. No rush. There's no rush."

"Have we still got any of that sauterne for me?"

"It's in the icebox. I'll get it. I'll have a Scotch and soda, will you make it for me?" She went off in that long, willowy, youthful stride.

"I've got two bits of news to tell you," she said, when they had their drinks and were seated on the couch, and she had snuggled up to him.

Winch had his arm around her. He smiled. "Let's let it wait till later. What do you say?"

With their drinks they went over to the bed. On the bed Winch began slowly undressing her out of her new outfit, and himself out of his uniform. That was one of the great things about her, she didn't give a damn about mussing her clothes. There was very little of his breathlessness. But there almost never was, before, and during. It was always afterward.

This time there was no breathlessness in Winch afterward. When Carol rolled out from under him to go and wash herself, as she invariably did, patting him on the ear and neck, Winch lay in the bed lazily and enjoyed his not having to get up and walk around the room quietly, to get his breath.

He had no idea at all why it should happen like that. He felt almost good. The only thing that was bothering him, now, was the distention in his belly that he got, whenever he tried to eat a meal. Lying nude in the bed, watching the closed bathroom door, he let out a long, quiet, but enormous fart.

Carol hadn't come. Not at all. Hadn't had any orgasm. Winch hadn't gone down on her and she hadn't masturbated, and those were the only two ways she could make it. Winch did not mind. Winch had learned long ago that this stuff of women coming and coming over and over, multiple orgasms, was largely a lot of baloney out of men's imaginations more than it was the truth out of women themselves. Carol seemed to have had enough apparent satisfaction out of his penetration of her. His using her. His coming himself satisfied her and gave her all the pleasure she needed this time.

She was quite a girl, Carol. But he would rather have taken a beating, than to have to go out for dinner.

They had quite a discussion, finally, about where they were going to go to eat.

She came out of the bathroom, nude, and began collecting her strewn clothes and getting dressed. Putting on the dress she started to laugh in a sort of half giggle. "I'm going to look like just what I am, and just what I've been doing."

"Does that bother you?" Winch grinned from the bed. He got up himself, and began collecting his warrant officer's uniform.

"You haven't let me tell you my two pieces of news," Carol said while they were dressing.

"Won't they keep till later?" Winch said. "Till after we've had dinner, say?"

"Well won't you let me tell you the one?" Carol said. "Or didn't you notice the suitcases?"

"I noticed them. You planning on going on a trip someplace?"

"No. No, that's just it. Those suitcases are because I'm moving in here, with you."

Winch did not honestly know whether to be happy, or pissed off. He decided to grin, while playing for time. "You're moving in here with me? What about your parents?"

Carol was trying, without total success, to smooth the wrinkles out of her skirt in front of the mirror. She brought her eyes up to her face in the mirror and took a deep breath like someone about to begin a reading in front of a declamation class. "It just seemed to me to be silly to keep on getting up at four in the morning and getting all made up and all dressed up to go home and try to get an extra hour and a half of good sleep. Nobody was ever waiting up for me. Nobody ever asked me about when I got in."

"So?"

She turned away from the mirror. "So I had it out with them. I got them together and sat them down and told them I had a lover. And that it seemed dumb to me to lose all that good sleep."

"You tell them about me?"

*   *   *

Carol had told Winch that she was going to move in with him in his small apartment in Luxor. Having found it ridiculous, finally, that she should wake up every morning at 4:00 A.M., get dressed, and go home, she had informed her parents in a moment of defiance that she had a lover and intended to live with him. She told Winch she had lied to her parents that he was a commander in the Navy. Winch did not know whether he should have been happy or unhappy over this new state of things.

Winch and Carol were preparing to go out for dinner. He had noticed the two suitcases which she had brought with her. She had explained that they were part of her move into the apartment. It had been implied that Winch thought these suitcases meant she was ending their affair and leaving Luxor, which was why he had first told her he did not want to hear her "two bits of news" until later.

They left the apartment and decided to have dinner in the rather staid and chic family-type restaurant of the Peabody Hotel rather than one of the Army hangouts. Winch tipped the waiter for a good table, and they were seated among the quiet, respectable citizens of Luxor.

Winch had an acute stomach discomfort which accompanied his heart ailment. What ensued in the restaurant was both a sign of his suffering and of his increasing craziness.

While sitting in conversation at the dinner table with Carol, he leaned forward slightly and let loose this enormous loud rippling fart which reverberated from the walls of the restaurant. There was a pronounced though short silence all over the place, a discreet turning of heads, and then the people in the surrounding tables went back to their dinners. Carol did not know how to react since this was a social gaffe she was incapable of coping with. Winch continued talking as though nothing had happened, although he watched Carol's eyes—they did not widen, they might have narrowed just the slightest bit—but she gave no indication that she had heard this enormous fart, and she, too, continued talking. Later, back at the apartment, after a cab ride through the beautiful April night, Carol told Winch the other bit of news. She had decided to go to summer school. Her new boyfriend, whom she had already told Winch about, who suited her so much better than the proper Luxor boy whom she had inveigled into going up to Western Reserve with her, wanted her to come back up to Ohio to get married. Carol told Winch she was about ready to agree with this, and had in her mind already.

So in essence this was the beginning of their good-by—a good-by that would take place in late May. Winch had been anticipating something of this sort for quite a long time. He knew, in fact, that had he wanted to keep her he could have talked her at any time into marrying him. She was still in love with him in a special private way, and enjoyed and had learned from their sexual relationship, but like him, and because of his reticence, she realized that for them to marry would be catastrophic.

Winch handled this news well enough, and near the end of this chapter he saw himself facing up to a future without Carol, all of this augmented by his approaching insanity. As he thought it all over, he seemed more concerned with having Carol not wake him up at night during his nightmares than he did with the fact that soon he would lose her.

At the end of the chapter Winch's thoughts turned to Bobby Prell, who appeared now to Winch—after Johnny Strange had told Winch of the telephone conversation with Prell from Kansas City—to have been the only one of the four old-company men to have found "peace" for himself in the wartime noncombat areas.

CHAPTER 32

When we last left Prell in Chapter 29, he was on his bond-selling tour in Kansas City, Lincoln, and Denver. Strange had telephoned him from Luxor in the Muehlebach Hotel in Kansas City to tell him of Marion Landers' death. Prell was feeling guilty about his own lack of reaction, during his talk with Strange, to Landers' apparent suicide. As with the others, he was being beset with nightmares involving the squad again, the patrol on New Georgia, and in his dreams Landers was now one of the dead. He was guilty also about his own position, the Medal of Honor hero, which he did not believe he deserved. He felt he was making speeches for a living—that he had become an entertainer, part of a vaudeville team.

His reaction when he returned briefly to Luxor from this first bond-selling tour was to avoid getting in touch with either Strange or Winch. He did not want to see them; he did not want to expose himself to the ridicule he imagined he would provoke in them because of what he considered his false role as a public relations man.

All he had left now, Prell felt, was his son-and-father relationship with former colonel, now Brigadier General Stevens, the commander of the hospital, a kindly relationship which began with Stevens' first visit to Prell in the hospital when the doctors were threatening to amputate his leg, and deepened as the months passed.

But in a scene with Brigadier Stevens in his office in the hospital in Luxor, Prell found to his sorrow that Stevens did not truly understand his feelings of guilt and inadequacy, and that in fact Stevens never had understood him. Prell did not feel up to explaining to Stevens what he believed to be his hypocritical role as a salesman and a fake hero.

Prell left his session with Stevens more desolate than ever, realizing that perhaps Strange and Winch were the only two people who genuinely did sympathize with what was happening to him. But he was still unwilling to call either one of them.

Warrant Officer Jack Alexander informed Winch that Prell had returned to the Luxor hospital for a few days. As far as Alexander could see, in his uncomprehending attitude, Prell was all right. Winch had hoped that Prell would come and see him and Strange, but his talk with Alexander nonetheless reassured him.

Prell was then ordered more or less permanently to Los Angeles with Major Kurntz and the same public relations crew with which he had made his first bond-selling trip. Since he had had a highly unsatisfactory reunion with his pregnant wife, Della Mae, and his ambitious mother-in-law in Luxor, he took an apartment in Los Angeles and did not give them his telephone or address.

In Los Angeles Prell made a couple of appearances with several movie stars and starlets. But after his first speech there, which was a huge success, he got drunk and went out that night in the limousine which had been put at his disposal with its Army driver, a sergeant. He ran around down in the low-bar areas of Los Angeles and ended up in a seedy bar filled with drunk servicemen. The driver waited for him outside.

With all the accumulated rage burning in him, he tried to pick a fight. But with his bad legs he was practically incapable of self-defense. Just as the irate soldiers whom he had insulted and challenged were about to beat him up, perhaps even kill him, one of them suddenly recognized the Medal of Honor ribbon he was wearing on his blouse, and then remembered him from his pictures in the Los Angeles papers. The soldier said: "Good God, we're about to beat up on a Medal of Honor winner!" and stopped the fight.

The soldiers found out that there was a sergeant waiting for Prell in the limousine outside the bar. They went and got him. The soldier who had recognized Prell warned the sergeant, "He shouldn't be in a place like this." The sergeant took Prell home. He did not inform Major Kurntz of what had happened, thinking that he was protecting Prell, and doing so with his natural soldier's instinct not ever to tell the authorities anything they did not already know.

The next speech was in Bakersfield. The entire bond-selling group drove out in limousines for the evening "performance." After his speech, Prell repeated the same pattern with a different driver. He got very drunk and asked the driver to let him off at another tough bar.

He got out of the limousine and hobbled into the bar on his ruined legs. There was an expression on his face of hard desperate determination. He walked into the bar. It was a green place, smoke-filled, with the rattling of pool balls, and mean drunken soldiers at the tables and on the bar stools, and a couple of poker games in the corner. After two or three drinks he began to bait some of the servicemen around him, and picked another fight. This time he was not recognized by the soldiers. The result was a bloody brawl, with Prell at the center, in which he seriously hurt someone. In the smoky haze one of the soldiers picked up a pool cue. He hit Prell over the head with it and killed him.

The sergeant driver, having heard the noise, rushed into the bar and saw Prell bleeding on the floor. He felt his pulse. He told the men what they had done, told them whom they had killed. The soldiers were horrified, but left the impression that Prell had brought it all on himself, as in fact he had done, deliberately picking the fight with them.

CHAPTER 33

This brief chapter is from Winch's viewpoint after learning of the death of Prell. In this chapter we see the progressive deterioration of Winch. He goes crazy.

We have already seen the signs of Winch's imminent crack-up: the night he saw the image of one of the platoon's dead infantrymen on the windshield of his car and skidded off the road; his urge to pinch the Gray Lady at Prell's wedding; his wild poker game at the Claridge and later his burning Jack Alexander's IOU; his bad dreams of the Japanese charging with the bayonet during the mortar fire and of the soldier in no man's land being wounded over and over again with no hope of rescue; the fart in the Peabody restaurant; his hatred for the two Wurlitzer jukeboxes in the main PX, which he viewed as the world of the future—"chrome, and pipe, and plastic, and whirling iridescent lights, and jarred, canned music;" his pent-up grief over the death of Landers. All of this mental stress was compounded by the increasing symptoms of congestive heart failure. When Strange left Winch in the Camp O'Bruyerre PX at the end of Chapter 30, he "did not think Winch looked good at all."

"Prell and Landers and Strange were what was left to him of his real life," the author wrote in Chapter 22. And now Winch hears of the death of Prell.

Beginning with Winch's dwelling on the fate of Prell, the action in this chapter took place in May, 1944, not long before the D-Day invasion.

Winch was still seeing Carol, but they were beginning to make their farewells. He had not yet broken up with her—she was not leaving Luxor until June—but he had in fact pushed her toward leaving and encouraged her to marry her new boyfriend from Ohio. When she finally departed, it was the end of their affair.

During the time he was making his farewells to Carol, and advising her to marry the second lover rather than the boy from Luxor, Winch had been wandering down to the grenade range of Camp O'Bruyerre in the afternoons. Being a top sergeant and now a junior warrant officer, he was on friendly terms with the grenade officer and grenade warrant officer, and there was a lot of amiable banter among them as they watched the raw draftees learn about hand grenades. While he was there one afternoon, when no one was looking he casually picked up a couple of grenades and slipped one into each pocket of his coat, then walked away unnoticed. Later, in his room, he unscrewed them with a pair of pliers and poured the powder into a jar, which he hid. For two or three nights he slept with the defused grenades under his pillow.

Then late one night, after he had been in the main PX drinking wine against the contradictory blasts of the two Wurlitzer jukeboxes, he returned to his room and put the powder back in the grenades. He waited for the base to quieten down. At 3:00 A.M. he put the grenades into his pockets and snuck across the deserted grounds to the PX.

Winch broke the window of the PX with the butt of one of the grenades. Then, very slowly and deliberately, he pulled out the pins and tossed the grenades one at a time through the broken windows into the empty room, so that they rolled across the floor and landed under the Wurlitzer machines.

Winch moved away and ducked. A terrific explosion followed, blowing up not only the Wurlitzers but most of the PX as well. Smoke and debris were everywhere.

Winch allowed the wreckage to settle and then peered in through the broken window at the results of his raid. He began to laugh maniacally. In no time at all the MPs descended on the area in jeeps. They spotted Winch hiding in the shrubbery. He tried to run from them, still laughing wildly, but because of his heart condition he could not get away from them, he bent over with breathlessness, and the MPs captured him and took him away. He wound up in the hospital prison ward.

CHAPTER 34

In this, the final chapter of Book 5—"The End of It"—and the novel, the viewpoint is Johnny Strange's, the last one of the old company.

The time shift from Winch's incarceration in the mental ward to the concluding chapter is roughly a month and a half, late June after the D-Day invasion. Strange was now happily set in with the infantry Division to which he had persuaded Winch to transfer him. With the destruction of the old company, he had given all his loyalties, affections, and emotions to his new company and Division. But curiously enough, having left the communications outfit in exactly the way he wanted, he now found he was so attached to the new men in the infantry unit that it was almost impossible for him, with his foreknowledge of what they were about to go through (they did not have this foreknowledge, and would be going into combat innocently), to relive the whole experience. This was to be the climax of Strange's story and the book.

In this last chapter, Strange and his new outfit were en route to England and Europe in a large troop convoy. It was generally known among the men that they would be thrown into the fighting in western France as cannon fodder as soon as possible.

The troop convoy was several days out from New York in the Atlantic. It was late on a foggy night and Strange was wandering around the ship alone. A series of flashback scenes took place in Strange's mind as he moved about. He pondered the fate of the old company.

He thought first of Winch. He remembered the early morning at Camp O'Bruyerre when someone at headquarters told him about Winch's mad raid on the PX. There was very little he could do to help Winch that morning, although he got a pass and loitered around outside the hospital prison ward for a long time.

Then Strange remembered going to the hospital ward the next day to visit Winch. As he walked down the corridor, Strange heard Winch crying out from his room that same old phrase from the day on Hill 27 on Guadalcanal: *"Get them out! Get them out of there! Can't you see the mortars got them bracketed!"* Strange acknowledged then to his sorrow that there was no point in visiting Winch, and he went back to his new outfit, which was getting ready to ship out to dry dock in New York. Just before he left Camp O'Bruyerre, another soldier told him he had seen Winch looking out the barred window of the mental ward shouting the same words.

Now, as he was roaming about the troop ship in the North Atlantic, Strange's thoughts turned to his wife, Linda, whom he realized he still loved, although he knew she could not care less. Then he thought of Marion Landers, and finally of his terrible grief when he had learned of the death of Bobby Prell in the bar fight in California.

As Strange looked out on the ocean and on the other darkened ships in the convoy moving eastward to Europe, there was an echo in his memory of their hospital ship from the Pacific as it finally approached the American landfall, "the great blue continent," almost a year before. Just as with Landers when he was struck by the car at Camp O'Bruyerre, Strange remembered as in a dream the slow white ship with the huge red crosses on its sides, his visits to Prell in the old main lounge where the serious casualties were segregated—"the repository, the collection-place and bank, of all human evil," his gazing out the window port on the California shore in the calm moonless night.

From these thoughts of the hospital ship those months before, Strange returned to reality, to the troop convoy:

> At this point comes the final scene, the final climax, the final everything of the book . . .
>
> As Strange gets out of the crowded hold with all the stinks and smells of overcrowded men, he goes up on deck in the drizzly, foggy night—an unpleasant night, quite chilly, although it is June—and leans against the boat davit.
>
> He faces finally the fact that he simply cannot go through the whole process again. He simply can't go into England and into Europe with this new outfit knowing what he knows from the Pacific, and sit back in his relatively safe position as a mess sergeant and watch the young men be

killed and maimed and lost. He can't stand being a witness again to all the anguish and mayhem and blood and suffering.

And when he reaches this realization he sees what a trap he has placed himself in by insisting that he should go to Europe, and that he should go in an outfit, an infantry Division, that he likes rather than the old Signal Corps unit he had a great deal of power in and didn't really care that much about.

With all this in his head, somewhat on the spur of the moment, wearing his overcoat, his helmet, his boots, and in the chill night his woolen gloves, he grabs the railing by the boat davit and just slips over the side, quietly without anyone around. No one hears, no one notices.

As he hits the water he himself is shocked by what he has done. It was such a sudden thing that he didn't know he was going to do it.

He treads water in the sea as the ship moves away and out of sight in the fog and the night. He doesn't try to attract attention . . . As he watches the ship go away he's not distressed really. And in his full uniform he treads water alone, the ship slowly moving out of sight in the fog.

He thinks now that he is never going to know the answer to those peculiar dreams of Roman justice or injustice he had both times coming out of the anesthetic during his hand operations. All that Strange thinks with a certain regret is that he will never find out now.

And then as he's treading water with his woolen GI gloves, he can feel the cold beginning to swell his hands. And from this, in a sort of semihallucination, all of him begins to seem to swell and he gets bigger and bigger, until he can see the ship moving away or thinks he can. And then he goes on getting bigger and bigger and swelling and swelling until he's bigger than the ocean, bigger than the planet, bigger than the solar system, bigger than the galaxy out in the universe.

And as he swells and grows this picture of a fully clothed soldier with his helmet, his boots, and his GI woolen gloves seems to be taking into himself all of the pain and anguish and sorrow and misery that is the lot of all soldiers, taking it into himself and into the universe as well.

And then still in the hallucination he begins to shrink

back to normal, and shrinks down through the other stages —the galaxy, the solar system, the planet, the ocean—back to Strange in the water. And then continues shrinking until he seems to be only the size of a seahorse, and then an amoeba, then finally an atom.

He did not know whether he would drown first or freeze.